THE
SOURCE

Jim Winslett

 FriesenPress

Suite 300 - 990 Fort St
Victoria, BC, V8V 3K2
Canada

www.friesenpress.com

Copyright © 2017 by Jim Winslett
First Edition — 2017

ISBN
978-1-5255-1418-0 (Hardcover)
978-1-5255-1419-7 (Paperback)
978-1-5255-1420-3 (eBook)

1. FICTION, MYSTERY & DETECTIVE

Distributed to the trade by The Ingram Book Company

To John —

Thanks for
Proofreading and for
all the insights.
Hope you enjoy the
final version!

Jim Wurm

*Dedicated to my wonderful husband Rob,
whose unwavering support and enthusiasm
for this project made it all possible.*

CHAPTER ONE
Sunday

Thelo Brown awoke to the sound of his cell phone ringing. He cursed himself for forgetting to silence it before going to bed last night, or more accurately, this morning. He'd usually have just let it ring, but calls from his editor were assigned a unique ringtone, and even in his groggy state he recognized the tune. He fumbled around the nightstand until he found the phone and clumsily tapped the screen as he put it to his ear. He tried to sound as if he had been awake for a while. It didn't work.

"Hello?"

"Sorry to wake you on your day off." Ivan's voice sounded patient but urgent.

"You didn't wake me."

"Bullshit. I know it's Sunday, but can you come in today? There's a story I want you to cover, and I don't want to sit on it until tomorrow."

Thelo sat up on the bed, suddenly more alert. "Me?"

At thirty years old, Thelo was *already* well-respected at the office and had over a decade of journalism under his belt. Still, most of the reporters at the *Riverside Post* were older and more experienced. He wondered why Ivan Carter wanted him specifically, to the point that he'd bring him in on a Sunday.

"Is it a racial story?" Thelo tried to stop the words from coming out, even as he was speaking them. He winced.

"No." Ivan sounded disappointed in him. "Can you come in today?"

"Sure."

"I'll see you at noon in my office."

"Sure, boss." Thelo hung up the phone and set it back on the nightstand. He yawned, stretched, and swung his feet off the edge of the bed. He looked at the time. "Shit."

Even though he wasn't due at work until noon, he only had a half hour to get dressed and ready if he was going to make it on time. Thelo stumbled the few short steps to the bathroom and after answering nature's call, looked at himself in the mirror. Not too bad, considering the night he'd just had. Thirty had been something of a turning point for him, the imaginary line he'd crossed where his body began to complain the morning after he'd had a late night of clubbing and drinking. His brain still refused to believe that line had been crossed, however, so he still had a bit too much fun on his nights out, which inevitably led to mornings like these. He opened his eyes wide and checked them in the mirror. Not too red, that's good. His close-cropped hair didn't require any maintenance, so no delay there.

As he finished brushing his teeth, he did another quick mirror check, grabbed a pair of jeans and a short-sleeved dress shirt from the closet, and tossed them onto the bed. He opened the drawer on his old dresser and discovered that there was only one pair of clean socks and no clean underwear.

"Guess I'm going commando today," he said aloud to himself.

Thelo put on his clothes and looked for his shoes. He found one under the bed, but the other wasn't with it. Shit. It didn't take long to find the other shoe, alone in the hallway, looking as if it had tried to make an escape. Thelo briefly wondered why he'd taken it off there, then decided that it wasn't important. Chalk it up to the G&T's.

He made his way to the front door and looked into the large bowl on the small table there. In it were his wallet, keys, and some change. He stuffed the contents of the bowl into his pockets, glad that he'd adopted this routine, so that he wouldn't forget anything. Even so, he habitually slapped his jeans pockets to check their contents one last time. Satisfied that he had everything, he turned the deadbolt on the door, stepped out onto the breezeway of his apartment complex, then closed and locked the door behind him.

Christine Marshall sat in Ivan's office sipping her coffee. Her shoulder-length auburn hair was styled in a simple cut, easy to maintain but classy enough for a night out. She was wearing a nice pantsuit, tan, with a pair of loafers that her mother would've referred to as "sensible shoes." She tapped her fingers on her coffee cup in the silence.

"Nervous?"

Ivan sat behind his desk with a coffee of his own, tapping on his laptop keyboard. He looked as if he might've just come from church, with a nice suit and tie, impeccably shined shoes, and neatly trimmed gray beard. He always looked sharp, and Christine knew Ivan didn't go to church. As a person of faith herself, it bothered her to know that someone she admired didn't have a place of worship, but she did appreciate the freedom he gave her as editor of the *Post's* religion section. She supposed that she was lucky to have an editor who didn't filter her content through his beliefs or lack thereof.

"No, just thinking. I'm still not sure what to make of it, honestly."

Ivan was a somewhat imposing figure at more than six feet tall with broad shoulders, but his tailored suit and killer smile took some of the intimidating edge off his appearance. Christine found him quite handsome even though he was almost old enough to be her grandfather. He'd been a wonderful mentor to her over the years.

She looked around the room at his framed accolades on the walls. Ivan had a long history in the newspaper business, but other than the awards for excellence and an occasional photo of him with a politician or business leader, his office seemed oddly impersonal. His desk was tidy to a fault, especially for an editor of a major newspaper, and completely devoid of family photos. The man was pushing sixty pretty hard, and you'd think there would be personal photos somewhere. She had asked him once about his family and got a stern but polite lecture on the dangers of mixing one's personal and professional lives. She didn't ask again. A knock at the door jarred her from the memory.

"Come in," Ivan called, and Thelo entered.

"Sorry I'm late."

Ivan glanced at his watch. "You're right on time."

"My mum always told me, if you're not five minutes early, you're late."

Ivan motioned him to sit down, then turned to Christine. "Christine Marshall, meet Thelonius Brown."

Christine gave the man a quick once-over. Thirtyish, rich mocha complexion, big brown eyes, maybe 5'10" or so, very short hair. Christine wondered if he'd shaved his head recently.

"Thelonius," Christine said as she stuck out her hand.

"My parents are big into jazz. You can call me Thelo."

"Oh, so you're Thelo Brown," she said. "Nice to meet you, finally. I've read some of your stuff. Investigative journalism." She gave him another once-over. "I figured you were older."

"Thanks, I think."

"It was a compliment. You write well and with a mature voice."

"Christine is the editor of the religion page," Ivan interrupted, saving Thelo from having to admit that he didn't know her work. "She has an interesting story to tell you."

Christine looked at Ivan, puzzled. "An investigative reporter? For this?"

Ivan nodded.

Thelo looked at Ivan, then at Christine. She wasn't as frumpy as he thought the editor of the religion page would be, although the tan pantsuit was certainly not going to ruffle many feathers. She was pretty, but she didn't go out of her way to showcase it. More Maryann than Ginger, as his dad might say. She had ridiculously blue eyes, and Thelo wondered if she might be wearing contacts.

"Can someone clue me in here?" he asked.

Christine sat at the edge of her chair. "I was at the Temple Beth Shalom this morning to interview Rabbi Jacob for a piece I'm writing about his work with the Children's Cancer Center. They're doing a huge fundraising campaign to help the CCC raise enough to build another wing onto the hospital. During the invocation, right in the middle of reading the Torah, his voice changed. It was almost like he had gone into a trance or something and he said some things that weren't in the reading. My Hebrew is rusty, but it got a strong reaction from the people there who understood what he said. Rabbi Jacob snapped out of it and he seemed surprised that people were upset. The whole thing came to a screeching halt, and the people were demanding to know why he would say what he said. I asked around until I found someone who could give me the gist of it, and it was 'the Torah is fiction, you're doing everything wrong, and I'm not happy' or something like that."

"Interesting," Thelo said. "Did he have an explanation?"

"I don't know. I tried to talk to him afterward, but he canceled the interview we had set up. He seemed genuinely surprised at what had happened, though. I'm not even sure he knew what he said."

Thelo turned to Ivan with a puzzled look. "What's this got to do with me? You said you wanted me on it, but this is clearly Christine's story."

Ivan turned his laptop around so they could see the screen. It was a video clip, and in the initial image, Christine recognized Joel Wood, pastor of Gloria Deo megachurch. Ivan tapped a key, and the video began.

Joel Wood addressed his congregation in the giant arena known as Gloria Deo. He was dressed in a suit with no tie, classy yet casual. His hair was a dark chestnut color and cascaded in waves almost to his shoulders. The style was meant to invoke the classic image of Jesus, obviously, although Jesus likely didn't have perfect teeth and he never wore a Hugo Boss jacket. A pair of Cole Hahn shoes and a Rolex watch completed the image. If Joel was familiar with the scripture that reads, "it is easier for a camel to pass through the eye of a needle than for a rich man to enter into the kingdom of heaven," then he clearly didn't buy into it.

Joel was delivering a message that was equal parts religious dogma and self-help seminar, effortlessly merging the two into a well-rehearsed pep talk, guaranteed to inspire the listener to feel good about themselves and about the role in the world that God had planned for them. He looked at least a decade younger than his forty-five years, thanks to the wonders of theatrical makeup and plastic surgery. Even his critics had to admit that the camera loved him. His congregation apparently loved him even more, judging from the 'amens' and 'hallelujahs' that rose from the crowd of ten thousand believers in the arena.

He told them that God wants them to be happy, that God has a plan for them, that everyone can…

His voice suddenly changed, his outstretched arms fell to his sides, and he spoke in a monotone as if in a trance:

"Your holy books are fiction. The rules you follow are not Mine. I am not pleased."

There was an audible gasp from the congregation, then murmurs, then shouts. The camera zoomed in on Joel's face, showing his apparent confusion at the crowd's reaction. A woman's voice cut in. The camera switched to Joel's wife, Holly, who was on the right side of the stage, trying to make herself heard over the crowd.

"Please, everyone, quiet down. Please."

The crowd eventually settled down enough for Holly to continue.

"While I'm sure that we're all wondering what we've just witnessed, we need to be silent for now in case there's more to hear."

She turned to her husband, still center stage. "Joel? Has God just spoken through you?"

The camera switched back to Joel, who stared at Holly, not fully comprehending what she's just asked him.

"What did I say? What happened?"

The crowd erupted again. The camera left Joel for a wide pan across the arena. Most people were on their feet, and their faces showed confusion and shock. Holly quieted them down once more.

"Brothers and sisters, it seems that we've been witness to a miracle this morning. Please, return to your homes and pray. Our Prayer Warriors Ministry will be at the front of the stage to sit with you if you want to pray with them before you go. Let us all reflect on the word of God that we received this day."

Holly stepped out of camera range, and a quick cut to a wide shot showed her cross the stage to her husband. She took him by the arm, and they walked off stage together.

Ivan stopped the video. Christine and Thelo continued to stare at the screen, unsure of what to say. A chill ran down Christine's spine.

Thelo looked at her and noticed that her eyes were glistening, and a tear had made its way down her cheek. "Are you okay?"

She nodded, and fought back another tear. "I'm just a bit overwhelmed. I guess I didn't expect to hear directly from God this morning."

Ivan got up from his desk and walked over to Christine. He put his hand on her shoulder.

"So you think that Joel's words might've been the same ones that Rabbi Jacob spoke?"

Christine thought for a moment. "Well, I didn't get a direct translation, but it seems to be pretty similar."

"I want you to find out. Also, get some reactions from both congregations, see how this news might change their beliefs."

"Boss?" Thelo interrupted. "I'm still not sure why you called me in for this. It's a bit out of my wheelhouse."

"I want you to find out if it was faked. If so, then how, why, who was behind it, what was their motive, what do they gain from it? The usual investigative stuff that you're good at. I also want you on the story because you won't let your own beliefs get in the way of finding out the truth."

"I don't have any beliefs," Thelo started to say, then realized that was what Ivan meant. He nodded.

Christine realized something suddenly. "Wait, Joel Wood broadcasts his services a week after he preaches them. Was that his service from last week? Why didn't we hear about it before now?"

Ivan shook his head. "That was from this morning. I've got a friend who edits their recordings for television. He sent it to me right after it happened. YouTube is already starting to get cluttered with phone cam videos from this morning. At first, I thought maybe my friend was pranking me with the video, but it matches the three or four I've seen from the congregation. It really happened."

"At around the same time that it happened to Rabbi Jacob," Christine realized.

"So the first step," Thelo said, "is to interview Joel and the rabbi, see if they know each other, and if so, ask them why they'd choose that particular message to fake out the people. Shouldn't be that hard."

"I tried to interview Rabbi Jacob already," Christine reminded him. "He wouldn't talk to me, and Joel Wood's not likely to give you an interview, either. He and his wife always tightly control his media presence, and he doesn't give interviews to anyone who might ask him a question that he didn't prepare for in advance."

Ivan's desk phone rang. He picked it up, knowing his assistant would be on the line. Everyone else called his cell phone.

"What is it, Claire?"

He listened for a moment, and then his eyes widened a bit. A few seconds later, he thanked Claire and hung up the phone.

"There's some kind of disturbance at Our Lady of Mt Carmel. Seems the priest over there said some stuff during Mass that nearly caused a riot."

"Father Matthew?" Christine asked with surprise.

"Not sure if he was giving Mass today, but he was almost certainly there to see it."

"If he's someone you know," Thelo told Christine, "then he's our best chance at an interview."

"We aren't close friends or anything, but I've interviewed him several times. He was a big player in the pedophile priest scandal."

Thelo looked at her and raised an eyebrow.

"No, no," Christine quickly added. "He wasn't a pedophile. He was helping the victims get counseling, and helping the diocese clean house. He was responsible for rooting out a few of the guilty priests and sending them to jail."

"I want you two to work independently, but compare notes from time to time," Ivan said. He turned to Thelo. "Christine will cover the impact on the faithful. You find out if it's a hoax."

Thelo and Christine stood up to leave, and Ivan returned to his desk.

"Be careful."

CHAPTER TWO

Joel Wood paced in his study. The marble floor echoed his footsteps, creating a cadence to accompany his thoughts. Holly entered unannounced, startling him. She had changed out of her church clothes and was now wearing a pair of navy slacks and a plain white t-shirt. She had an uncanny ability to make even a casual outfit look stylish, and Joel always enjoyed how that style came across on television. She upped the class quotient of their broadcasts considerably, he thought. She had washed off the TV makeup, but she looked just as good without any. He liked her new, shorter haircut better than the longer style she'd worn in her younger years. It suited her better as she got older and made her look more independent, even though her public role at Gloria Deo was to be his somewhat-submissive wife.

Holly spoke as she entered the room. Her voice was exasperated, firm, and had a slight edge of annoyance. "I've got everyone I can find answering phones, and it's not enough. There are a couple thousand people still at the church, saying they aren't going to leave until you talk to them. Apparently, there are a handful of videos of your little sermon floating around YouTube, and they've already gone viral. I think every reporter on earth has called wanting an interview. Some of them have even gotten my cell number."

"I turned my cell phone off an hour ago," Joel said, the shakiness of his voice exposing the lack of his usual confidence. "I wouldn't even know what to say."

"Were you serious when you asked me what had happened? You really don't remember saying that stuff?"

"I don't, Holly. I don't know where it came from or what it means."

"Well, wherever it came from, what it means is that you've singlehandedly destroyed everything we took so long to build. If the people stop believing what you tell them, they'll turn somewhere else for guidance, and then where will we be?"

"I know, I know."

Holly sat down in a large leather wingback chair beside floor-to-ceiling mahogany bookcases. She looked around the room and sighed. "I've gotten accustomed to having nice things, Joel. You've said all along that God wants us to have nice things and people believe that you know what God wants. How are they going to believe you now?"

"But nothing I said today changes that message. It was about the holy books and the laws of the church. If I have to start leaving Scripture out of my sermons because the Bible is fiction, I've still got a lot to work with. My sermons are mostly motivational speeches with some 'praise God' thrown in. You know that. Gloria Deo doesn't have a lot of rules that we expect people to follow, either, so if those rules have to go away, it's fine."

"Well, there's that one rule that says they're supposed to give ten percent of their income to the church, don't forget that one."

Joel stopped pacing and looked at his wife. They met eyes for several seconds before Joel finally blinked.

"If we don't find a way to spin this, we're doomed," Holly stated flatly, rising from her chair. "You start working on that. I'm going to get on social media and see how much damage has been done already."

She left him to his pacing and went upstairs to her study. She felt her mood improve a bit upon entering her domain. The decor in her study was more industrial than elegant, and the show of wealth presented itself in high-end electronics rather than in plush furnishings. Her desk, a chrome-and-glass monster that dominated the room, was covered with tech: three large monitors, a keyboard, two printers, a rack of backup storage drives, a pair of redundant servers, and a hardware-based encryption device that prevented any hacked data from being read by the thief. She had taught herself how to use all of this stuff and the more wealth that she and Joel accumulated, the more paranoid she became about keeping her data secure. She sat at the desk, took a deep breath, then brought the computer out of sleep mode. She sighed. All the money spent on technology to safeguard their business might be for naught because of just three sentences uttered by her husband that morning. It didn't seem fair.

Joel feared what Holly might find online. He expected the kind of vitriolic comments that often accompany stories of the "high and mighty knocked off their lofty perches." Their perches were particularly lofty, balanced on a combination of religion and wealth.

The two of them had built a media empire with his good looks and upbeat sermons, plus her media savvy and her careful control of their public image. Joel knew that Holly deserved as much credit for their success as he did, which made him doubly upset that he might've brought them down all by himself. It wasn't just his work in jeopardy; it was her life's work as well. What the hell had happened this morning, anyway? He had rehearsed his sermon for hours, as he always had, making sure that each word was the best choice and that his delivery would achieve the maximum impact. It was a craft that had served him well, despite what his father thought when he announced that he was going to a theater arts school rather than seminary. That day was almost as bleak as this one. Joel's father expected him to carry on as pastor of Gloria Deo, and the news that Joel would rather be an actor did not go over well at all.

Faith in God had always been front and center in their family, and Joel had gotten his fill of it by the time he hit his 'rebellious teen' phase. He stopped going to church, except to be seen sitting next to his mother on Sundays, which his father demanded. He got involved in the drama club in high school, where he found that he had a natural talent for acting. After landing the lead roles in both a drama and a musical comedy in his senior year, his mind was made up. He applied to the theater arts program at Berkeley and got in on the merits of some brilliant auditions and a recommendation letter from his drama teacher. His father scoffed at his "waste of time," but Joel was hooked on the thrill of performing and the adoration of the audience.

He applied to Juilliard after just two years at Berkeley, but that dream was cut short by news that his parents were both killed, innocent bystanders during a bank robbery gone bad. Joel was devastated, not just by the loss of his parents, but also for the loss of Juilliard. He didn't have the money to move to New York, and the church was the only source of income for the family. His father had become somewhat successful, building the church to a congregation of nearly five hundred worshippers, but there wasn't enough saved to finance Joel's dream, and neither of his parents had carried life insurance. Joel flew back home and began arrangements for the funeral services.

Every attempt at writing the eulogy was disastrous. He couldn't write about his loss without seeming selfish. Every mention of their lives being cut short and their dreams being unfulfilled rang hollow. Even a casual listener would hear those words and realize that it wasn't his father's unfulfilled dreams he was mourning; it was his own.

Eventually, Joel decided to treat the whole thing as a play, and he wrote the eulogy as a script. When it came time to deliver the words, Joel became "Joel," a character that he'd created. "Joel" was a young man who wanted to follow in his father's footsteps someday, but God took his father from him before enough knowledge had been passed down. He spoke for nearly a half-hour, a soliloquy that brought tears to the eyes of most who were there, including local news reporter Holly James.

Joel had intended to let Gloria Deo close, hoping the money from the sale of the church property would be enough to finance his Juilliard dream, but the response that he got from his eulogy performance was as good or better than any he'd experienced on stage. He decided to take over the pulpit for a few weeks while the lawyers finished their paperwork. That raised a few eyebrows, since Joel hadn't been to seminary. However, his first sermon, titled 'Grief Can Make You Stronger,' was so well-received that nobody much cared where he had gone to school. The congregation was larger than usual on that first Sunday, too, since people who had heard his touching eulogy had invited their friends to hear the young man speak again. The following Sunday was even better attended, and Joel was beginning to thrive on the attention. Holly James continued to cover his success as Gloria Deo increased its membership and Joel became famous.

Joel and Holly eventually began dating and were married two years later. By then, Joel was something of a celebrity, and the media had a field day with the fact that Holly James had become Holly Wood. That spawned dozens of articles with the obvious title, 'A Holly Wood Wedding for Joel.'

After the wedding, Holly's careful financial planning and media savvy matched Joel's showmanship and charisma. They quickly amassed enough money to move Gloria Deo into a larger building, and they began to televise the services. Joel then hired a biographer to pen his life story. He was careful to keep the events of his biography factual enough so as not to raise eyebrows, but he embellished the emotional aspects to a level just short of melodrama. It sold hundreds of thousands of copies, allowing the couple to buy a bigger house. The money also permitted Holly to dive into her love of technology, as she was finally able to afford the latest gadgets and hardware. She established an early presence for Gloria Deo on the internet, sharing videos and transcripts of Joel's sermons when many people still thought this 'internet' thing was just a fad. By the time other churches caught up to the online revolution, Gloria Deo was a media powerhouse with hours of content, an interactive prayer ministry, and an easy one-click method of sending the church a tax-deductible donation. Money poured in, and the church grew rapidly, forcing them to rent space in the city's convention center for four years while they raised funds and built a massive new campus.

All of this made the Woods wealthy and famous. They built a mansion in the ritzy part of town, and they became the kind of people that others like to see knocked down and humiliated. *Schadenfreude* is an unfortunate facet of human nature, and the anonymity of electronic communication allows people to wallow in it without fear of retribution.

Holly took a deep breath, launched an app she'd written to track every mention of their names on social media, and then steeled her nerves for an afternoon of reading what the world had to say.

"Do you mind if we take your car?" Christine asked Thelo on the way down to the parking lot. "I rode the bus this morning."

"No problem. Is your car in the shop?"

"No, I just like to take mass transit when I can. We need to keep the greenhouse gasses in check, so we don't wreck the climate any more than we already have."

"You know that buses emit more pollution than cars, yeah?"

"Yes, but they hold more people."

"And how many people were on your bus today?" Thelo asked with a smirk.

Christine blushed. "Three. No, four."

"Including the driver?"

"Yeah. 'A' for effort?"

They reached the parking lot, and Thelo tapped his remote key. A short pair of chirps from two rows over alerted them to the car's location, and they made their way to a metallic gray BMW 5-series.

"Wow, nice car," Christine marveled. "Your salary must be quite a bit more than mine."

"No, I just live in a shit studio apartment, and I eat a lot of ramen noodles. I saved up for years to get this car, even though I bought it used."

"We have different priorities." Christine opened the car door. "I take the bus most everywhere or ride my bicycle, but I have a two-bedroom house with a pool. To each his own, I guess."

They got in and buckled their seat belts. Christine ran her fingers across the leather seats and dash, enjoying the aroma and the feel of it.

Thelo backed out of the parking space and headed out of the lot. "Which way is Mt Carmel?"

"Take a left here, then get on the freeway and go south," Christine said, settling back into the comfort of the seat. She smiled. "Maybe I should've prioritized my ride over my house, too."

"You wouldn't say that if you saw my apartment. Or what's in my pantry."

They got on the freeway, and Thelo expertly made his way across traffic to the fast lane.

"Which exit do I take?"

"Exit 42A, then turn right."

"That far? I know you don't take the bus or your bicycle down there."

"Actually, I do. Or I walk. It's not that far from my house, maybe a mile or so." She admired the electronic display on the dash. She sighed. "My car is crap. Walking, biking, or taking the bus is not only good for the environment, but it's good for my ego not to be seen driving that thing."

Thelo laughed, then looked at Christine. He thought for a minute. "Hey, I'll need to apologize in advance for my language and anything I might say that you find offensive."

Christine turned to him, surprised. "What? What do you mean, where did that come from?"

"Well, you're a woman and a religious writer, and you're a church-goer and stuff. I'm not used to being paired up with anyone on a story, and so I don't usually filter my language or my thoughts when I'm working. I just wanted to get that out in the open before we get too far down the road."

Christine laughed. "Hey, just because I believe in God and go to church doesn't make me a saint," she said. "It just makes me more aware of what a fucking sinner I am sometimes."

Thelo laughed long and loud. "I think we'll get along pretty well."

Christine smiled. "As long as we've broached the subject, though," she said, turning in her seat to get a better look at him, "I assume by your remarks in Ivan's office that you're unchurched?"

"Unchurched? Is that what it's called now? I still refer to myself as an atheist."

"Ah. No, 'unchurched' is just someone who doesn't belong to any sort of organized religion. You can be a believer and still be unchurched."

"Well, I'm not a believer. My parents are, but I didn't buy into it. I had too many questions that I never got a satisfactory answer to."

"Like what?"

"Like why... um..."

Thelo fought for words as he maneuvered through traffic.

"Okay," he said finally. "You know the belief that God is all-knowing, all-powerful, and God can do absolutely anything?"

"Right." Christine anticipated where this was leading.

"If God can do anything, then God can cure cancer. Better yet, God can just remove the existence of cancer from the earth altogether."

"Theoretically, yes."

"Then why doesn't He?"

Christine had heard questions like this many times before. "We can't know for sure, of course, but I believe that God allows hardships into our lives to test us, to make us stronger, to show us that we can overcome obstacles."

"What about the people that die from it, though? They didn't overcome the obstacle, they died."

"I hate to sound cliché, but God works..."

"...In mysterious ways," Thelo interrupted. "That's bullshit."

"We can't possibly understand God's plan and how it all works. That's why He's God, and we're just people. We can't always see the big picture. You don't expect the lab rats who get injected with some virus to be able to understand that the information obtained from their death helped create a vaccine that saved thousands of lives."

"So we're just lab rats for God, then?"

"No, it's just an analogy. My point is that just because we don't understand God's plan and maybe we don't approve of it, that doesn't mean that there isn't a greater good behind our suffering. Just because we can't see the big picture doesn't mean that there isn't one. Here's your exit."

Thelo grunted, then checked his mirrors and moved over to the exit. "So I turn right, then what?" He slowed down onto the service road.

"It's about a mile down on the right side of the road."

Thelo made the turn, then checked his mirrors again. "Shit."

"What?" Christine quickly looked around. "Shit what?"

"The cop that was behind us on the freeway took our exit and made the turn. He's still back there."

"Were you speeding?"

"No, I was doing three under, just in case."

"Then what's..."

She was interrupted by a short blast from the police car's siren. Flashing red and blue lights danced into the car, illuminating it with an ironically festive atmosphere as Thelo pulled over and stopped. He shut off the engine.

"Get my info out of the glove compartment. I don't want him to think I'm going in there for a gun or something." A slight quiver in Thelo's voice exposed his nervousness.

"Okay, but if you weren't speeding, I don't know why you're so worried."

"I'm a black man in a nice car. That's enough to get me stopped. Having a white woman in the passenger seat only makes it worse."

Christine realized that he was serious and she began to feel uneasy as well. She had seen too many news reports of so-called routine traffic stops that had gone very badly. Her palms began to sweat as she fished through the glove compartment for his paperwork.

"Everything's in a blue plastic envelope," Thelo told her as he tapped the button on his door to lower the driver's side window.

"Got it." She handed the envelope to him.

Thelo glanced into the rearview mirror and saw the police car's door swing open. He switched his eyes to the side mirror and used the small joystick on the armrest to adjust the mirror upward so he could see the officer approach. He took a deep breath and lowered his voice to a whisper. "I'm going to sound different when I talk to him, so don't look surprised, okay?"

Christine looked at him, puzzled, but nodded.

Thelo looked back at the side mirror, which revealed a tall man in blue serge with mirrored sunglasses and a thick moustache. He fumbled to get his wallet out of his back pocket, then turned to see that his window was full of uniform. His eyes found the nameplate, "Mike Scott," then the shield with the officer's badge number. He quickly committed both to memory, just in case, then shifted his eyes to find the revolver, which was thankfully still in its holster. He eyed the pistol longest of all, swallowed what little spit he had left, and tried to relax. He exhaled slowly.

"License and registration, please."

The voice didn't convey aggression, at least. There wasn't an angry edge to it as far as Thelo could tell. So far, so good. He handed over the blue plastic envelope, then took his license out of his wallet and handed that over as well.

"Is there something wrong, officer?"

Christine had promised not to act surprised, but her head turned quickly toward Thelo as he spoke. He had asked the question in a perfect British accent, which she hadn't heard him use before.

The cop looked at Thelo's license, then bent down to look into the car.

"How long have you lived in the States?"

"All me life," Thelo answered, sounding as if he'd just stepped out of a pub somewhere near the river Thames. "My parents are from York, then moved to London. My father got a job with the government, then got transferred to a position at the British consulate here. They moved just before I was born."

The cop looked across at Christine, then back at Thelo.

"Friend of yours?"

"Coworker." Thelo tried to sound calm. His heart was pounding. He was sure that everyone could hear it.

"I'll need you to step out of the car."

The officer stepped back, and Thelo opened the car door. He got out, closed the door, and looked up at the officer. The cop was at least four inches taller than Thelo, with a solid, stocky frame made stockier by the bullet-proof vest under his uniform. Thelo tried to read the expression on the cop's face, but it was all mirrored shades and moustache.

"Wait here, please," the officer said, stepping around Thelo and heading back to his patrol car. When the officer got in and began feeding the information into his car's computer, Thelo turned and bent down to look at Christine through the car window.

"You okay?"

She nodded, then opened her mouth to say something, but the look on Thelo's face said, "not now," so she saved it. Thelo stood back up and leaned against the car.

In a few minutes, Officer Scott returned with Thelo's license and blue envelope in hand. He bent down and called to Christine through the window. "Ma'am, would you mind switching on the ignition?"

Christine unbuckled her seat belt and leaned over, looking for the key. She couldn't find a key nor even a place to put one. She heard Thelo's newly-British voice tell her that there was a start button on the dash. She pushed it.

"Now signal for a left turn," the cop instructed. Christine found the stalk next to the steering wheel and pulled it down.

"Let's go look." The officer led Thelo around to the back of the car. The yellow turn signal light was flashing, adding its color to the red and blue lights from the patrol car.

"Now signal a right turn," the officer called out. Christine moved the lever up. Thelo and the officer looked at the right signal lamp, which remained dark.

"Looks like you have a turn signal out."

"Those are LEDs," Thelo said. "Even if one was dead, the rest should still work."

"Might be a fuse or a loose wire somewhere. You need to get that checked out and fixed as soon as possible. I figured it must be a faulty signal since you'd used your signals to change lanes to the left, but not to the right. Then you made the turn without signaling, and I knew you'd seen me behind you, so I was sure it wasn't working properly. It's a safety issue; you should get it fixed as soon as you can."

"Yes, sir. You're right, of course."

The cop handed Thelo the blue envelope and driver's license. "Have a nice day and drive safely. Get that signal fixed."

"Yes, sir. Thank you."

The cop returned to his car, and Thelo let out a sigh of relief as he walked back to his BMW, opened the door, and sat down. His hands trembled as he handed Christine the blue envelope to put back into the glove compartment. Christine took the envelope, then took his hand in hers. She gave it a light squeeze.

"Everything okay?"

"Turn signal's out." His accent was gone. "That was it."

Thelo put his license into his wallet, then shimmied up off the seat enough to put the wallet in his back pocket.

"British consulate?" Christine looked at him. "That was a nice story, but I don't get the reason for it. What's up with the accent?"

"The story was true," Thelo said, as the patrol car pulled out around them and disappeared down the street. "I had the accent until grade six, when my mother stopped homeschooling me. The kids in public school teased me about it, so I learned to speak like the news anchors on television. Now, that Middle American accent is the one that feels the most natural to me, but the Yorkshire one is what I still use at home with my folks."

"But why use it at all?" Christine still didn't understand.

"Because cops see black men as thugs. As threats. But when you open your mouth and you sound like one of the cast of Downton Abbey, it instantly erases the stereotype. Hopefully, it also reduces the danger."

Christine shook her head in disgust. "Sorry."

"Not your fault," he said.

They buckled their seat belts. Thelo started the car, readjusted his side mirror, then pulled back onto the road.

CHAPTER THREE

Ivan Carter sat in his office, fielding calls from reporters and trying to keep up with the news. The incidents at Temple Beth Shalom, Gloria Deo, and Our Lady of Mt Carmel were apparently just a tiny piece of a much bigger picture. Reports were coming in from all over the country, from every faith he'd ever heard of and some he'd never knew existed. The television news was all over it, and YouTube's servers had already crashed twice from the excessive load. Videos were showing up from mosques, churches, synagogues, temples, all with the same message, all in the same trance-like delivery, all with the same voice.

It made his head spin. Ivan had grown up in an evangelical household and had been taught from an early age that God was very real and that there was a divine plan for his life. Ivan had loved going to church, and he loved the music. His parents gave him a toy piano for Christmas when he was four, and the first thing he learned to play was, "Jesus Loves Me." They couldn't have been more proud.

All of that changed somewhere around the age of sixteen, though, when his mother casually used the phrase, "God don't make mistakes." The grammatical inaccuracy of that had always irked him. It made the speaker seem uneducated and ignorant, but now, for the first time in his life, Ivan was upset with the idea behind the statement rather than the grammar. No mistakes? You could look around at the world and point out errors in the design. Why does the weather kill people sometimes? Why do people's bodies deteriorate in their later years, making old age so difficult? Those sorts of questions had always been in the back of his mind, but as Ivan matured, made it through puberty, and began the process of self-discovery, fresh doubts began to form. He learned early on that asking his parents about God's perceived mistakes only led to an argument and a repetition of that grammatically offensive phrase. Asking the church leaders didn't bring results, either. Their answers were basically a variation of the same expression, just camouflaged with flowery language and Scripture passages. "God don't make mistakes."

Bullshit. God had made some pretty damn big mistakes, and one of those mistakes was Ivan himself. Of course, nearly everyone assumed that his bitterness and questioning was just a phase, a part of growing up. He was doing and thinking the kinds of things that teenagers do and think. It would pass.

It didn't.

Ivan spent his adult years with a healthy skepticism. He didn't abandon his belief in the existence of God; he just rejected the trappings of organized religion. This is why he found today's news reports so overwhelming. Had God actually spoken directly through multiple people simultaneously? Did He really proclaim the Bible and other scripture as works of fiction? Did He discredit the rules and regulations of religion? If all this turned out to be a legitimate miracle, it could not only prove to everyone that God exists, but it could also show that organized religions, apparently all of them, had gotten it wrong. Ivan felt strangely vindicated by this idea and his first instinct was to call his parents, his former church leaders, his childhood friends, and everyone else from his past and say, "I fucking told you so!"

But of course, he couldn't do that. Not now. *Just move on*, he thought to himself.

Easier said than done.

Ivan was surprised to find that he was crying. The tears got his beard wet, something that drove him crazy, but he couldn't stop himself. He wasn't sure if the tears were brought on by the sad memories of his childhood or from the joy of vindication. Maybe both. He hadn't cried in ages, and it felt good to get it out.

A knock on his office door startled him from his thoughts. He grabbed a handful of tissues from the box in his desk drawer, patted his beard as dry as he could, then cleared his throat.

"Yes?"

Claire, Ivan's long-time assistant, poked her head in. "You okay?" She noticed his glistening eyes and the tissue in his hand.

"I'm fine, Claire, what is it?"

"Time zones, sir. We've been seeing reports from Sunday morning services here in central time."

"Right. So?"

Claire stared at him, holding eye contact. She raised an eyebrow as if to say, 'think!'

Ivan sat up in his chair, suddenly getting it. "So the west coast would be starting their Sunday services right about now. And Europe and Africa should've already had theirs and Australia's Sunday morning would've been several hours ago. There should be reports from overseas already and the west coast should have theirs any minute now. If this thing is legit, there would've already been lots of reports from overseas."

Claire smiled.

"That's why I keep you around, Claire. Leave it to you to jolt me out of my little bubble and make me think globally."

Ivan jumped online as Claire shut the door and went back to her desk. He scoured every news site and social media site he could think of, but found nothing of The Sermon (people were already beginning to capitalize it) in any place overseas, at least not at any regular church services. Suddenly, the odds that it could be a hoax were far greater. The reporter and newspaper editor in him was excited, but the rest of him was disappointed. He wanted to believe. He needed it to be true. He flipped on his television to see if he could find any live broadcasts from churches on the west coast, then picked up his phone.

Christine's phone rang as they were pulling into the parking lot. Our Lady of Mt Carmel was a large campus with a church, a private school, an activities building, and a rectory for the priest. Thelo parked in a spot near the back of the crowded lot. Dozens of people were milling around outside the church, talking. Christine dug her phone out of her purse, looked at the screen to see who was calling, and glanced at Thelo as she answered.

"Hello, Ivan. No, we haven't found Father Matthew yet, but it took a bit longer to get here than we anticipated. Long story. We're just now getting out of the car."

Thelo killed the engine. They both unbuckled their seatbelts and opened their doors. Christine swung her legs out of the car and stood up as she listened.

"Yes, he's right here, you want to talk to him? Speaker? Sure, hang on."

She pulled the phone away from her ear and tapped some icons on the screen as Thelo closed his car door and came around to the passenger's side. Christine made one more tap on the display, and the speaker came on.

"Thelo, I've got an angle for you."

"What's that, boss?"

"Claire just reminded me that all of the reports so far have been coming from the States. Europe and everyone else on that side of the world are several hours ahead of us, but apparently nobody preached The Sermon over there in their Sunday morning services."

"Interesting. So a hoax is definitely plausible."

"Exactly," Ivan said. "You've got some contacts in the UK. Find out if there were some churches over there who were involved and the word just hasn't gotten over here yet."

"I'm way ahead of you, boss," Thelo said as he took his phone out of his pocket. "I'm already on it."

"Good man. Christine, let me know how it goes with Father Matthew. As soon as you leave there, shoot me a text with a short synopsis. I'll save you some column space on the front page tomorrow if he was the one who preached it this morning."

"Front page?" Christine's eyes widened. "Holy shit."

"Christine," Ivan said, lowering his voice a bit, "don't say 'holy shit' when you're interviewing Father Matthew, okay?"

Christine and Thelo both laughed.

"You know me better than that," she said, still chuckling. "I'll text you later."

She hung up and looked over at Thelo, whose thumbs were flying across the screen on his phone. He texted faster than anyone she'd ever seen. She thought about how long it would take her to text a short message to Ivan later. Probably longer than it would take Thelo to text everyone he knew.

Thelo stopped typing and a few seconds later, his phone signaled a reply.

"Hey, can you do this interview solo?" he asked Christine. "I've got a couple of people I want to contact, but I don't want to do it from my phone."

"What's wrong with your phone?"

"I don't have a secure enough connection on a mobile. I need to use my computer at home."

"Wow." She felt a bit envious of him. As a religion page editor, she rarely dealt with any contacts that required such caution or generated that level of intrigue. "That sounds ominous. Well, um… sure, I got this. We're supposed to compare notes, though. You want to meet up somewhere later?"

"Sure. Pick you up here around six?"

"No, I doubt I'll be that long. I'll walk home when I'm done here. I'll need some time to type out my notes and stuff, anyway. Maybe pizza somewhere?"

"How about Sharkey's? That is, if you don't mind coming back into town."

"I love Sharkey's. See you at six." She turned to leave, then turned back again. "Promise not to laugh at my car."

Thelo chuckled. "Promise. Gotta run."

He walked around to the driver's side and got into the car. Christine was already walking toward the church as Thelo backed out and drove away.

The grounds around the church were full of people, and according to the snippets of conversations Christine heard as she walked through the crowd, everyone was talking about The Sermon that morning. She entered the church through the large wooden double doors and discovered that there were almost as many people inside as outside, but the people inside were mostly silent. Most everyone was kneeling in prayer at their pews, some were at the front of the church, praying near the large crucifix, and others were gathered in front of the statue of the Virgin Mary. A few were crying.

Christine felt like an intruder. These people had witnessed what appeared to be a genuine miracle, but she was just here to get a story. She wished she'd been more affected by Rabbi Jacob's bombshell, but because of the language barrier, she got the news second-hand. It was still a watershed moment for her, but it obviously hadn't had the impact that it had on these people.

She noticed a pair of nuns whispering to each other near the side entrance, and she made her way over to them.

"Excuse me, sisters, I don't mean to interrupt."

The nuns stopped talking, and one turned to her. "How can we help you?"

"I was wondering if you could tell me where Father Matthew is."

The nuns looked at each other, then back at Christine. "Are you a parishioner here?"

"No, but I've been to services here before. I'm a friend of his, and I thought he might like to talk to a friend now. He doesn't have a cell phone, and the line to the rectory is jammed."

Christine mentally crossed her fingers. Calling Father Matthew a 'friend' was a bit of a stretch, that was certain. She had interviewed him many times, and they had a good rapport, but that was the extent of it. Still, you could call it a friendship if you adopted a fast and loose definition of the word. She also knew that he didn't own a cell phone. The part about the rectory line being jammed was just a shot in the dark. She didn't even have that number, and she hoped that making up lies in a church wasn't going to send her to hell.

"He's in the rectory," the other nun replied. "You can buzz the door if you like, but he hasn't been speaking to anyone since this morning."

"Thanks."

Christine left the church through the side doors. She walked along the sidewalk that connected the church to the school and noticed that there was a campus expansion underway. They were adding another wing to the school, probably for classroom space or faculty offices, she couldn't tell. Whatever it was, it was a substantial addition, three stories high, maybe ten or twelve thousand square feet of space in total. She took a left where the sidewalk forked and walked to the rectory. Unlike the church grounds, the rectory grounds were eerily silent, nobody in sight. She climbed the few steps to the front door and rang the buzzer.

No answer. She rang again. Still no answer.

She turned to leave, then caught herself. She grinned, then turned back around.

She took a deep breath, then tapped the buzzer nine times: three short, three long, three short taps. Morse code for SOS.

The speaker by the door crackled alive, and a familiar voice came through.

"Christine?"

"You remembered! Yes, it's me. Can we talk?"

A long pause.

"Yes, that will be fine. Can you come around to the back door? I don't want anyone to see you come in."

"Sure."

Christine made her way around to the back of the rectory to a nondescript door in the rear. There was no sidewalk here, and this entrance apparently rarely got used. It likely existed to meet fire codes, Christine figured, but that was all. She heard the door unlock.

Joel knocked on the door to Holly's study. "Hey, how bad is it?"

Holly leaned over sideways to look at him around the three computer monitors that dominated her desk. "It's bad, but not as bad as I expected. We're getting off a lot easier than those churches that have a lot of restrictive rules. It seems the more rules people thought they had to follow to remain faithful, the more pissed off they are when God tells them they didn't have to be following them after all. We're pretty lenient in that regard."

"Yeah, I suppose so. What's the worst of it?"

"Well, we haven't gotten any death threats yet, so I guess that's a plus."

"You sound pretty upbeat for someone who's been reading internet comments for the last hour or so. That stuff usually makes me depressed about the state of humanity, even if it's just comments on a cat video or something."

"I'm pretty jaded. Besides, the comments on our sites aren't half as bad as some of the Catholic or Muslim sites."

"This is fairly widespread, then?"

"All over the US, apparently. Maybe elsewhere as well. At any rate, there were several more than just you and that priest we heard about. That certainly takes a lot of the focus off us. Hey, have you come up with a spin job yet?"

"Maybe. It's a bit shaky."

"Lemme hear it."

Joel thought for a moment, then took a deep breath. "Okay, so according to 'God,'" Joel began, holding up two crooked fingers on each hand to indicate quotation marks around 'God,' "the Bible and the other holy books can be tossed out because they're fiction, yes?"

"Apparently, yes."

"And the rules we follow, I'm assuming He means the rules that religions have put into place, are not legit, either."

"Right. Go on."

"And He's pissed."

"Well, that's a bit stronger than 'not pleased,' but yeah."

"So… if we can't rely on the Bible or the other books to know what God wants, and following the rules of the church doesn't get us closer to God either, what are we left with?"

"This is the part you were supposed to be working on."

Joel threw her a sly grin. "You can only rely on the people that God speaks through."

Holly pondered that, then grinned. "And one of those people is…"

"Is me!" Joel opened his arms wide and took a bow as if on stage. "This might be the biggest thing ever to happen to us, but not in the way we first thought. This could be a windfall. God chose Joel Wood as His mouthpiece."

"Well, God chose quite a few others as well, apparently."

"Doesn't matter. There are probably all kinds of places who don't have a single pastor who preached The Sermon today. Those people are going to want to hear the word of God from someone who did.

I'm already on TV every Sunday. I bet they start tuning in. Did God speak through any of the other biggies?"

"You mean other televangelists?"

Joel winced. "Oh, no, no, no… you know how much I hate that label."

"Sorry. You prefer 'TV preacher?'"

Joel chuckled. She was teasing him. "You know I prefer 'media minister.'"

Holly did a quick check of her notes. "It looks like you're the only 'media minister' who was affected."

They were both startled by the sound of a phone ringing downstairs.

"I thought you turned your phone off," Holly said.

"I've got my phone right here." Joel pulled his cell phone out of his pocket and checked it. "It's off."

"The landline in your study? Did some reporter get that number?"

Joel suddenly remembered.

"Dammit, I've got a poker game tonight. I completely forgot. That's gotta be one of the boys."

"Surely you're going to cancel. I mean… You aren't going to play tonight, are you?"

The ringing ceased. A short silence was followed by a click, then a recorded greeting from an answering machine.

Holly shook her head in mock disgust. "Couple hundred thousand dollars worth of tech in my study and you've still got a tape-based answering machine attached to a landline in yours."

"It works, doesn't it?" Joel winked at her, then headed downstairs to his study.

Thelo got on the freeway and headed back into town. He maneuvered his way across traffic into the fast lane, then tapped a button on the steering wheel. An electronic chime sounded.

"Call Zara," he said, slightly louder than his normal speaking voice.

A few seconds later, the sound of a telephone came through the car's stereo speakers. Thelo smiled. He always liked the "boop-boop" sound of phones in the UK better than the "brrrrring" of US phones. After three rings, Thelo heard the lilting Liverpudlian tones of Zara Davies.

"Bloody hell, what's going on over there, love?"

Zara rarely just said 'hello' when answering the phone. Right down to business, that was her style. Thelo liked it.

"Hello, love," Thelo said, again using his British accent. "I'm trying to figure that out me-self."

"You know I like your American accent better, dear. Have you given it up?"

"No, but when I'm talking to a Brit, it's hard to hear the Queen's English and then respond back in midwestern American. That takes more concentration than I can give you right now since I'm on the freeway."

"Queen's English?" Zara was amused. "Christ, you think the Queen ever sounded like a Scouser? No Queen ever came outta Liverpool, love. And you shouldn't be on the phone when you're driving! Are you on hands-free at least?"

"Yes, dear, don't worry. Anyway, I was wondering if you heard any reports of pastors preaching the trance sermon on your side of the pond."

"No, nothing I'm aware of." Zara thought for a moment. "That's a bit strange, innit? I mean, you'd think that if God was gonna start choosing people to be His microphone, He'd have picked a few blokes over here. Most of our churches are older than your country. Why would He leave them out?"

"My editor thinks the whole thing might be a hoax."

"Funny, that. My editor thinks the same thing. A lot of folks here are thinking that. I mean, what with it just being in the States and all. How do you think they pulled it off?"

"Who? Who pulled it off?"

"Whoever was behind it, of course. They must've gotten with all those preachers and talked them into it, yeah? That's the only thing I can figure."

"That's a lot of people that had to be in on it. At least twenty or thirty, maybe more. Plus, they're spread out all over the country, and some of these religions don't particularly like each other. How could they get everyone on board?"

"I didn't say I had any answers, did I?" Zara said.

"Well, if you think of any, let me know. And if you hear of any trance sermons over there, will you give me a ring?"

"Sure thing, love," she said, then thought of something else. "Hold on, how did an atheist get assigned to this story, anyway?"

"Ivan thinks my lack of faith is an asset in this case. He thinks it lets me look for a hoax more objectively without my beliefs getting in the way."

"And how is that silver fox doing? He still single?"

"Still? I didn't know he was single. I have no clue about any part of his personal life, actually."

"Well, in the picture I've seen of him, he's not wearing a ring, so I made an assumption. The way you talk about him, I think he'd be a nice catch. Promise to introduce us when I come visit someday."

"Yeah, sure. Just don't get your hopes up. He's probably got fifteen wives hidden away in a harem or something."

Zara laughed. "I can be number sixteen for that hottie, no worries. In the meantime, I've got to get back to the story I'm working on now. I've got a deadline coming up, and my editor isn't nearly as nice as your Ivan the Not-so-terrible."

"What's the story?"

"Oh, the usual. Some tart is claiming she sucked off half of Parliament. I've got to somehow write it in a way that won't make people throw up in their breakfast tomorrow morning. Filthy old codgers, nobody wants that picture in their heads while they're looking at bangers on their plate."

Thelo laughed. "Dammit, Zara, I knew I should've signed on at a tabloid. It's so much more fun."

"Don't patronize me, sweetie. Just hang up and concentrate on your driving."

"Bye, love."

Thelo hoped to meet Zara in person someday. They had met each other online three years ago in a discussion board for journalists, and became fast friends. A week or so after that, they did a Skype session, and they were both surprised by the other's appearance. Zara was surprised that Thelo was black. Thelo was surprised that Zara was over fifty years old and had bright blue hair.

"You don't write like you look," was the consensus. That led to a lengthy discussion about stereotypes that became filthier and more irreverent as the night went on. By the end of the call, they ached from laughing, and both felt they had found a confidant in the other. So far, every plan to meet in person had been unsuccessful, much to their disappointment.

"Life happens sometimes, and it fucks shit up," was how Zara put it.

Thelo understood.

CHAPTER FOUR

The back door to the rectory swung open just enough to allow Christine entry.

"Come in, come in!" Father Matthew urged.

She slipped inside, and the priest quickly closed the door behind her and turned the lock. He motioned for her to follow him.

"Sorry about the secrecy, but I don't want to see anyone else right now."

The rectory had been built to house the parish priest many years ago, and it looked as though the decor hadn't changed since the first day. The furnishings were comfortable but minimal. A small kitchen and study lay on one side of the short hallway, the bedroom and tiny bathroom on the other. The hallway ended at the living room, which was furnished with a sofa, coffee table, and a recliner. Two bookcases housed various trinkets the priest had been given over the years, as well as a small collection of books. Nothing, aside from the laptop she noticed on the desk in the study, was less than ten years old. The priest had no television. Apparently, Father Matthew Vergara took his vows of poverty seriously.

"Please, Christine, sit down," he said, motioning to the sofa. "Would you like some tea?"

"That would be lovely, thanks."

He disappeared into the kitchen, and Christine could hear water running into a kettle. He returned, looking a bit frazzled.

"It's been an interesting day," he said as he sat down in the recliner.

"It has. Thank you for letting me come in."

"I don't usually take visitors here in the rectory," he admitted. "I'm afraid I didn't have time to tidy up."

Christine started to laugh, then caught herself. "It looks better than my place even after I've tidied up."

Father Matthew smiled, almost. He was fifty years old, stocky with a little bit of a belly, and he kept his salt-and-pepper hair in a neat business-appropriate cut. His bright green eyes usually sparkled with the joy of life, but Christine saw only confusion and concern in them today.

"I assume that you're here to ask me about what happened this morning."

"Well, yes. It's quite something, isn't it?"

"I haven't talked to anyone. I'm not sure that I should. I'm not sure about any of this, to be honest."

"If you don't want to do an interview, that's fine. I'd really like to know what happened, though. We can talk about it off the record." Christine felt her first front page story slide into the trash bin.

Father Matthew sat for a moment, sighed, said nothing. Christine fidgeted in her seat, not sure what to do.

"I was at Temple Beth Shalom this morning," she finally said, breaking the awkward silence. "The same thing happened to Rabbi Jacob, only in Hebrew."

Father Matthew showed no reaction to the news. He looked at the floor and said nothing.

"We've heard that there were others, too," she continued. "I know that Joel Wood was one. I saw a video of his sermon this morning."

Father Matthew looked up with a start. His face indicated genuine surprise, and he stuttered to get the words out. "Wha… What? At Gloria Deo?"

"Yes. I don't speak enough Hebrew to know exactly what Rabbi Jacob said, but Joel Wood's trance sermon was word-for-word the same as the others given in English today. Do you remember what you said, exactly?"

From the kitchen, the kettle screamed at them.

"Excuse me." Father Matthew stood up. "I'll be right back."

Christine fished in her purse for her pocket recorder and placed it on the coffee table. She could hear pouring water and the clinking of teaspoons.

"Would you like English tea or herbal?" came the priest's voice from the kitchen. "Oh, I've got chai as well."

"Chai would be great, thanks."

Father Matthew returned a few minutes later with a ceramic teapot on a plastic tray. Two teacups, teaspoons, a small sugar bowl, and a tiny pitcher of milk accompanied them. He set them on the table.

"It's not fancy, save for the teapot. That was a gift. Like I said, I don't usually have visitors here."

"It's wonderful, thank you. I love the aroma."

"We should let it steep for a minute or two." He noticed the recorder. "Are you recording us? I thought we were off the record."

"We're off the record," Christine assured him. "I have it out in case you change your mind."

"I haven't talked to anyone. Not at all. I've been in here praying ever since..." He couldn't think of a word for his experience. "Ever since it happened."

"Well, I'm honored that you are willing to talk to me. I'll be honest, though, I'm surprised that your first contact is a reporter."

He looked at her, then looked at the floor, then back at her. Christine met his gaze.

"A few years ago," he said, "when that scandal was going on, we had to deal with reporters nearly every day. They wanted all the filthy details; they wanted to make their stories as graphic as possible. Shock sells, or so I'm told. Sex sells. Scandal sells. None of them ever stopped to think how it would affect the victims when their family or their friends read it or saw it on television. They didn't care about that, they only cared about the sensationalism and the ratings and how many copies they could sell."

He shifted in his seat.

"But you didn't write about those awful things the priests did. You wrote about what we were doing to help the victims, what we were doing to try to keep it from ever happening again. I read the things you wrote, and I appreciated your sensitivity to the kids who had to live with those memories. You got it right when very few others did. I should've thanked you properly for that."

"You just did." Christine reached out for his hand and gave it a squeeze. "I remember those days. I was the only reporter you'd talk to. We'd even worked out that 'SOS' knock as a code for you to let me into your office at the school when you were pretending to be out. I'm glad you remembered it."

He sat forward in his chair, let go of her hand, and picked up the teapot. He poured them both a cup of tea.

"Milk and sugar?"

"Just a touch of milk, thanks."

He poured some from the pitcher into her cup. She picked up a spoon and swirled it around until the tea was a rich golden color. Father Matthew dropped two sugar cubes into his cup, followed by a bit of milk. He sat back in his chair, and held the mug with both hands, enjoying the warmth.

"This is one of my favorite smells," he said as he held the cup under his nose. "Right up there with baking bread and a freshly-cut lawn.

"And bacon," Christine added.

"And bacon."

They both sat and sipped their tea without saying anything. Father Matthew seemed lost in thought. His expression changed from time to time as things crossed his mind.

Christine was patient. She knew the priest well enough to know that if she didn't push him for information, he would eventually relax and share.

"Can I trust you, Christine?" he finally asked.

She looked up from her teacup. "Of course you can." Her tone of her voice indicated a twinge of disappointment. Father Matthew noticed.

"I'm sorry, Christine. I know I can trust you. I'm just a bit shaken."

"No problem, Father. Yes, of course you can trust me."

"Go ahead and turn on your recorder, then. You can record our conversation, but I want it to remain off the record until I feel comfortable enough to let you use it. If that happens at all."

"I understand, Father." Christine leaned forward to pick up the recorder. "That will be fine."

"Besides," he said, "if another divine message comes out of my mouth, I want a recording of it so know what I said. I don't remember saying any of the last one."

Joel Wood hung up the phone in his study and went upstairs. He knocked on the door frame to Holly's study, and she peered out at him from around her monitors.

"I figured as much. It was Mark, wondering if the poker game was still on for tonight."

"And is it?" Holly raised an eyebrow.

"Of course it is! And we're going to meet a bit early tonight to discuss today's events."

"Is Mark one of the affected?"

Joel smiled. "Apparently not, but I really like the sound of that. 'The Affected.' Maybe we'll form a club or something, get some custom vestments made."

Joel was clearly in a better mood than before.

"Vestments make you look old-fashioned and fat," Holly said. "That's not your style."

"Maybe I need a change of style to mark the change in my ministry after I became one of The Affected."

"Sure, just don't change into a style that makes you look old-fashioned and fat."

Joel laughed. "I called the other two guys. They're both on board for tonight."

"Were either of them affected?"

"No." Joel grinned. "But they're dying to hear about it."

"Just be careful. They're going to have fallout over this with their congregations, too. If you're the only one in that group who can claim to have a direct line to God after this, well…"

Joel waited for her to finish, not fully understanding her point. "Well, what?"

"If they start to lose their power, their money, their status… and you're the only one who's figured out how to profit from it…", she fought for the words, couldn't find any that suited her. Joel finished for her.

"You're saying that they'll get jealous and resort to, what? Blackmail or something?"

"Or something. Just be careful. You don't want them getting jealous and spilling secrets."

"They'd have as much to lose as I do."

"As *we* do," she corrected him. "And they don't have a tenth of our wealth, so we'll fall a lot harder than they will if things go south."

"I'm not talking about the money. I'm talking about the status, the power, their reputation in the community. All of that is more important to them than the money."

"And they'll have already lost all of those things before the money runs out, and they will be able to point their fingers at you and say 'You preached the sermon that ruined me.'"

"I know these guys. Even if they lost everything else, they wouldn't jeopardize their marriages or break up their families by letting things get out in the open."

"You think not, but money or the lack of it can do strange things to people. Just don't be an arrogant jerk about being the only one with a direct line to God, okay?"

"Gotcha. Point made. I'm gonna go down and make myself a sandwich. You want one?"

"No, thanks. After reading some of these online comments, I don't have much of an appetite."

Thelo arrived back at his apartment complex, parked the car, and walked through the breezeway to his front door. For something called a 'breezeway,' he thought, there was almost never any breeze. He attempted to coin another word for it as he put the key into the lock, but couldn't think of anything.

Inside the door, he emptied his pockets into the bowl on the table. His entire apartment was only about the size of a hotel room, barely three hundred square feet. The bedroom was just big enough for a queen bed and a nightstand, but he put a twin bed in there to make room for the old dresser from the house where he grew up. He wasn't going to bring a date here anyway, so a larger bed wasn't needed.

The bathroom was cramped but functional. It had a corner shower, pedestal sink, a toilet, and medicine cabinet over the sink which doubled as a mirror.

The other room, which the apartment manager laughingly called a 'great room' when he was first shown the place, was barely larger than the bedroom. A stove, mini-fridge, and sink sat in one corner, and a tiny round table with a single chair sat next to the stove. An 'eat-in kitchen' is what the manager called that setup. Across from that on the other wall was a well-worn love seat with a narrow coffee table in front, a small table and lamp at one end, and a cheap area rug to tie it all together as a 'group setting.' In the opposite corner was a small desk with a laptop, a couple of external hard drives, a modem, and a printer. Thelo opened the laptop, then took his cell phone out of his pocket while the computer booted up.

He tapped the phone a few times, then put it to his ear.

"Hey, boss. I talked to Zara over in London. She hasn't heard of anyone there giving The Sermon, at least not yet. I think she'd know about it by now if it had happened. She's pretty connected over there."

"What about Europe?" Ivan asked. "Has she heard whether anything happened outside the UK?"

"When I said 'over there,' I meant that side of the world. She hadn't heard that anyone outside the US gave The Sermon this morning."

"Well, if YouTube is any indicator, it's mostly an American thing. There are five or six videos with local pastors, and maybe ten or twelve total from elsewhere around the country, but that's it. Oh, I think there was a Canadian one, too. I've got a couple of people looking for occurrences in Mexico and South America. My Spanish isn't good enough to search for it myself."

"Weird. So we're talking about, what, twenty or so pastors total?"

Ivan counted his list of names. "Twenty-two so far that I know of."

"And how many are local?"

"Six."

"Six out of twenty-two? We're pretty much ground zero, then. What about the west coast?"

"Not much from there. The one I did find did his thing at an early service, which puts it at the same time as our people here."

Thelo moved over to his laptop, which had booted up and was displaying a photo that he'd taken of his car the day he first drove it home.

"Sure sounds like a small enough number of people for a scam," he said.

"Yes, it does. You just need to find out how they're all connected. See if they've been in contact with each other."

"I'm on it. I figured we'd be looking at a lot more than twenty-two people, so this is good news."

"Go get 'em. I'm here if you need me."

Thelo hung up the phone and sat down at his desk. He launched his browser, which briefly showed an image of an onion, then loaded the home page. An alert box demanded a password, which he entered. A pop-up window warned him that he should use encryption from this point forward. Two more password prompts finally got him into a secure chat room. He scanned the list of users in the room. Nope. Not there. He tried another room, then another. Not in those, either.

He closed the forum window, typed in another address, and got a login screen featuring cartoon speech bubbles. He entered his username and password. At the 'who are you messaging' prompt, he typed: ADMIN

The screen replied, 'ADMIN not available.'

Thelo typed, 'summon ADMIN.'

The screen replied, 'ADMIN not available.'

Thelo sighed and tapped his fingers impatiently on the desk. He didn't have time for this.

He typed, 'force alert: ADMIN.' He took a deep breath, then tapped the ENTER key.

A few seconds later, a chime indicated that the alert had been sent. Thelo waited. He hoped he hadn't just ruined his sometimes-shaky relationship with his source.

Another sound, this time a bell, indicated a reply. Thelo anxiously looked at the screen. A small window had opened up, which read:

DUDE. WTF?

At The Bunker, a cinder-block storage building across town from his mansion, Joel Wood and two other men sat at a crude wooden table. Each side of the table had a number written in black marker, one through four. Joel sat on the side labeled 'one,' and one of the other two men sat to his left at the side marked 'two.' Two was forty-something, clean-shaven, with horn-rimmed glasses adorning his boyish face. His sandy blonde hair, even uncombed as it was, was stylishly cut to make him appear younger than his age. The seat at the side of the table marked 'four,' to Joel's right, was taken up by a fat man with a reddish beard and a baseball cap covering his short red hair. His hips splayed out over both sides of the folding chair he sat in, and his large gut made it difficult for him to reach the bowl of potato chips in the middle of the table. He was not slobbish, however. His beard and hair were impeccably trimmed, his clothes fit him well, and the whiteness of his teeth could practically blind a person when he smiled. All three men wore running shorts, sneakers, and t-shirts as if they'd dressed for a workout rather than a poker game.

The fat man looked at the empty chair on the side marked 'three,' then turned to the man across from him.

"I guess you've seen the video from Joel's service today."

Joel and the other man both shushed him.

"Numbers only in this room, Four. You know the rules."

"Yeah, I know," the fat man replied. "But Three isn't here with the prize yet, and we all know each other. What's the big deal?"

"We keep up the anonymity whenever we're in The Bunker. It needs to be a habit, even when it's just us. That reduces the chances of slip-ups when the prize is here. You know that."

"Yeah, yeah. I get it. Feels silly, though." He cleared his throat and addressed the man again. "So, 'Two,'" he began, with mockery in his voice, "did you happen to see any videos of One's service today?"

"Why yes, Four, I did," the man replied in the same tone. "But we might want to wait until Three gets here, so we can all discuss it."

"If we're going to keep our anonymity, Two, then that's a topic we'll need to steer clear of later, isn't it? One is the only guy who participated in that shit show today, and it would be pretty easy for the prize to figure things out if we mention it. It's bad enough that his voice is so recognizable."

"You're right," Two admitted. "We should go ahead and discuss the elephant in the room now."

Four then turned to Joel. "Well, One, perhaps you can tell us what the ever-loving fuck that was all about this morning?"

"You tell me," Joel said. "I don't even remember it. I was right in the middle of my sermon, and then it was like there was a gap in time, like a record skipping a groove. When the needle came back down, everyone was staring at me, and a few people started crying. I looked over at Holly like, 'what's going on?' and she was looking at me like I'd just sprouted horns or something."

"So you don't remember going into a trance like some second-rate fortune teller, and throwing the Bible and the Church under the bus?" Four asked, with an accusatory tone that barely hid his skepticism.

"That's what I'm saying."

Two shook his head.

"Well I'm glad that I was done with my sermon this morning before any of that hit the news," Four said. "Can you imagine how sixteen hundred Southern Baptists would react if I'd told them that the Bible wasn't the infallible Word of God?"

Two nodded. "How are you gonna explain this to them next Sunday?"

"I don't know yet," Four admitted. "Hell, I've been avoiding phone calls all day. I figured it was some kinda prank when I first heard about it on the news, but then they said that it happened to a lot of people. Then they showed ol' One here, and I figured, 'That's not his style, not that guy. He isn't gonna risk his money over some prank.' Then I got worried. I was holding out hope that he'd tell us tonight that it was all staged and he'd let us in on it. I honestly don't know what to think right now."

Joel turned to his left. "Two, what about you? How are you going to handle it?"

Two took a deep breath, then exhaled slowly. He shook his head slightly. "Well, it won't be very pretty, that's for sure. We've been using Scripture to justify our anti-gay rhetoric for so long that my congregation is going to be in a pickle if those Bible passages aren't legit. What can we use now to prove that God thinks queers are unholy?"

Four chuckled. "Well, there's always the 'eww, gross' angle."

The three men laughed. Two and Four both turned to Joel.

"What about you?" Two asked. "How are you going to spin this? I know you were avoiding calls, too. I had to call your private line just to see if the game was still on tonight."

Joel sat back in his chair and smiled. "Gentlemen, behold: If the holy books are fiction, and I mean all of them, since every major religion was apparently involved in this, then the only way to know what God wants from us is to listen to those people God has spoken through."

He paused to let that sink in. The other two men looked across the table at each other, and their eyes flashed with recognition of the gravity of what Joel had just said.

Four clenched his fists and slammed the table. "You fucking bastard," he seethed, "You've already figured out a way to line your pockets and undercut everyone else at the same time! You're the Voice of God now, I presume, or at least that's what you'll tell everyone."

Joel diffused the tension quickly. "It's true that I'm likely going to make a tidy profit from this, but that doesn't mean that I'm going to do it at the expense of everyone else," he assured them. "You both know far too much about me for me to screw you over. If we work together, we can all benefit from this, not to worry."

The other two men relaxed a little.

"Good. Glad to hear it," Two said.

The sound of tires crunching on the gravel driveway outside the door drew their attention.

"Finally," Joel said. "I was beginning to think there wouldn't be a prize for the game tonight."

The three men got up from the table. As they approached the door, they heard four short knocks, a pause, then one more. Joel unlocked it and swung it open.

In the doorway was a tall black man with graying hair and a big smile.

"Who am I tonight?" He had a thundering bass voice that seemed to reverberate off the walls.

"You're Three," Joel answered. His voice sounded like a whisper compared to the newcomer's.

"Three is the magic number, then!" The man laughed a hearty 'heh-heh-heh' as if he'd made a joke. Three's jovial mood brightened up the room and removed the remnants of the tension still lingering in the air. The other men smiled, then laughed along with him.

"Where's the prize?" Two asked, trying to look past him through the doorway.

"In the car," Three said. He turned around and walked outside to a large luxury sedan.

"Nice ride, Three," Joel said. "Rental?"

"Damn straight. Ain't nobody gonna see my car here."

The other men gathered around as Three opened the door. The interior light switched on automatically, revealing a very young blindfolded prostitute in a short black skirt, black hose, and red heels. The men smiled their approval.

CHAPTER FIVE

Christine picked up the recorder. Father Matthew nodded his approval, and she switched it on.

"Tell me about Mass this morning," she said.

Father Matthew thought for a minute, looked at the recorder that Christine had placed back on the coffee table, then took a sip of tea from the cup he still held with both hands. "It was all so odd," he began. "I was preparing the Eucharist, about to give the blessing. Then I wasn't."

"How do you mean?"

"Well, I was standing there with my arms outstretched, about to bless the bread and wine and then in an instant, I was standing back away from the table with my arms at my sides. I have no recollection of moving. I was simply in this place one moment and in that place the next. I was confused, and almost lost my balance. The expressions on the faces in the congregation showed that they were as startled as I was. They were talking under their breath. Some had knelt and were praying. Some just sat there and gaped at me."

"What did you think about what you'd said?"

"I didn't know what I'd said," he explained. "I thought their reaction was from seeing me teleport from one place to another." He chuckled slightly as he realized how crazy that sounded. "That's the only part I remember, being here one minute and there the next.

Deacon Hernandez came up to me and asked me what I'd meant. That was the first moment I was even aware I'd said anything at all."

"Do you know now what you said? Has someone told you?"

"Yes. Honestly, I might not have believed it if someone had just told me about it, but we make an audio recording of all our services. We include a copy of it with the Meals on Wheels lunches for folks who can't make it to church. I listened to the recording. It was quite disturbing, as you can imagine. It wasn't my voice that said those things." His hands trembled, sloshing the tea in the cup.

Christine fished a small spiral notepad out of her pocket, and flipped to a page she had marked. "Your holy books are fiction," she read. "The rules you follow are not Mine. I am not pleased."

Father Matthew was astonished. "That's what I said. It puts the Church in an awkward position, that's for sure."

Christine nodded. "That was from Joel Wood's service this morning. I'm sure he's as upset as you are."

Father Matthew stared at the floor, apparently deep in thought. When he looked up again, his eyes were moist.

"I've wanted to be a priest since I was six years old." His voice quivered. "I just want to help people. This is all too much."

"Since you were six? That's pretty young to be deciding to live such a dedicated life. I think at six years old, I still wanted to be a fairy princess."

Father Matthew chuckled, then managed a smile. Christine loved his smile. It was one of the things that endeared him to her right from the start, all those years ago. She smiled back.

"When I was six years old, my father became very ill. We had a very traditional family, as most did back then, and my father was the sole breadwinner. Mother was beside herself with worry, especially after they told us that father probably wouldn't make it. She sat beside his bed all day, held his hand, only left his side to make my sister and me a sandwich or open a can of soup. We ran out of money pretty quickly, and our parish priest, Father Grant, brought us a care package every week. Groceries, paper goods, and that sort of thing. He'd sit next to the bed with mother, and they'd pray that my father would get better. Then he'd spend time with me and my sister and play a game or toss a ball. He tried to make things as normal as possible for us. My dad eventually got better and went back to work, even though the doctor had said he was going to die. We all figured that Father Grant had a big part in that."

"So you wanted to do the same sort of thing for others."

"I didn't expect I'd be able to heal the sick or anything, but I knew that I could just be there for people when they need someone. Everyone felt more at ease when Father Grant was there at our house. All the rest of the time it was just worrying and sadness. Having that few minutes of distraction every time he came to visit was the best thing he could've done for my sister and me. I knew that I could someday be that person. Someone who could just be there when needed."

"That's a sweet story," Christine said, "and from what I know of you, not surprising at all. I can see that side of you quite easily."

Father Matthew blushed. "Thank you."

"During your blackout moment," Christine began, then immediately regretted the words she'd chosen, "err, I mean…. Well, you know."

He nodded.

"During that moment, you said, 'the rules you follow are not Mine.' What do you suppose that means?"

"The rules of the Church, I'm guessing."

"Like the Ten Commandments, those rules?"

"I hadn't considered those, but that's a good question. I was thinking of the rules instigated by the Church. If the Church says those rules are necessary, but God says they don't please Him, then things need to change."

"Like what, for example?"

"Well, in the Catholic Church, we have rules about when you should kneel and stand during Mass, or how to hold your hands when you receive the Eucharist wafer. Those are easy ones, just traditions that can be changed pretty easily. It's the priestly vows that are coming to my mind now, the vow of poverty, the vow of obedience."

"The vow of celibacy."

Father Matthew blushed. "Yes, that one as well. But it's not just Catholics. Other faiths have much more strict rules to follow. You mentioned Rabbi Jacob earlier. The Jews have more rules to follow than we do," he said. "Rabbi Jacob must be reeling right now."

"I wouldn't know. He wouldn't speak to me."

"That soon after it happened, I wouldn't have, either." The priest shifted in his chair, lost in thought.

"How's your tea?" He indicated her cup. "Would you like some more?"

"No, I've still got some, thanks."

Father Matthew sat his cup on the table and poured himself another serving. "It's too bad I don't have something stronger to drink," he sighed as he set the teapot back down. "It might help me sort things out."

Christine laughed suddenly, almost spilling her tea. "You aren't allowed to drink?"

"Yes, but we aren't allowed to get drunk." Father Matthew settled back in his chair with his fresh cup of tea. "My parents never had alcohol in the house, and my desire to enter the priesthood kept me away from it in my teenage years, even when my friends found a way to get some."

"So why don't you have a little stash somewhere, then? You don't have to get drunk every time you take a drink."

Father Matthew smiled as his face registered a fond remembrance. "I'll tell you a story. Many years ago, very early in my ministry, I was at St Francis of Assisi on the north side of town."

"Beautiful campus."

"Yes, and I was very lucky to be in that position at that age. It was a wonderful learning experience. Anyway, this is sometime in the late 80s, maybe '88 or '89. The AIDS epidemic was going full-tilt, and people suffering from it were being treated like outcasts, like modern-day lepers. A lot of churches were turning their backs on these people when they needed the Church the most."

"I've heard stories from that time," Christine said. "I don't remember any of it, though, obviously."

Father Matthew became suddenly aware of the difference in their ages. "Of course not. You were just a baby."

"Actually, I wasn't born yet."

Father Matthew cleared his throat. "Nevertheless, I kept thinking back to Father Grant and the way he cared for us when my father was ill, and it just made me angry that so many of the faith leaders couldn't get past their prejudice to help comfort these poor souls."

Christine nodded. She was unsure how this story related to drinking, but she let him continue.

"Sometime around then, the Fairmont United Church of Christ held a service to mourn those who had passed and to offer prayers of healing for those still living with AIDS. They wanted clergy from many different faiths to participate as a show of unity and solidarity. It was a wonderful idea, and I told the priest at St Francis, Father Brogan, that I wanted to represent our church. He said that I could do it, as long as I never said anything that made it appear that the Catholic Church approved of homosexuality in any way."

"Wow," said Christine with some disgust. "That's kinda harsh."

"Actually, that's pretty mild for those days. I was surprised he let me go at all."

"But, what does this have to do with getting drunk?"

Father Matthew cast her a sideways glance as he took a sip of his tea. "Patience is a virtue, Christine."

"Sorry, Father. Please continue." She settled back on the sofa.

"We had a worship service, which was quite lovely. There was a choir composed of members from several of the churches represented, maybe a hundred voices strong. It was quite an emotional thing to see all those people of different faiths coming together to sing. It was enough to bring tears, I'm telling you."

Christine nodded in agreement. She'd been to similar blended services in the past, usually revolving around a memorial of some kind, and the camaraderie and goodwill were always inspirational.

"Near the end of the service, we served the Eucharist, or as they put it, we 'took communion.'"

"And they had wine! Now we're getting there." She smiled and raised her cup of tea in a toast.

"Yes, they did. The pastor at Fairmont UCC explained that the clergy would stand at the altar, where the bread and cups would already be set up. People in the congregation would be directed by the ushers to come to the altar, select a host wafer from a plate, dip the wafer into one of the chalices, then consume the host and return to their seats. Afterward, we clergy would consume what wafers were left, then drink what was left in the cups. Because the elements have been blessed and are considered by some to be the literal body and blood of Christ, you never leave hosts or wine unconsumed."

"Okay. So you drank part of a glass of wine. That wouldn't get you drunk, I don't think."

"Keep in mind that all of this was being done by people from different faiths. I had a Baptist on my left. They used plain grape juice at his church since Baptists aren't supposed to drink. There was a Mormon on my right who also wasn't supposed to have alcohol, and his church used water in their services. Well, the man who prepared the altar table wasn't from either of those churches. He was from a tiny little independent church that only had twenty or so members, and they used wine in their services. They also used a loaf of bread instead of wafers and people would break off a piece and dip it in the cup. He was used to those pieces of bread soaking up quite a bit of wine, so he figured with such a large congregation, he'd better make sure to fill the cups up good."

"Uh oh, I think I see where this is going. You said 'wafers' earlier."

"Yes!" Father Matthew grinned. "Those wafers don't soak up much wine. And they're hard to hold onto. People usually just dip them into the wine a tiny bit, because nobody wants to accidentally drop their wafer into the cup. The chalices were still more than half full at the end, and they were big chalices. They were maybe twice the size of a regular wine glass."

"What about the two clergy on either side of you? What did they do?"

"When we went up to the altar and looked at the chalices, it was obvious that they were full of wine and not juice or water. The Baptist, his name was Joseph. Nice man. He and I had talked a bit before the service, and he told me he was a recovering alcoholic. His experience in AA was what led him into ministry. Anyway, he whispers to me that he can't drink from the cup. I told him that it wasn't a problem, he could just pour his cup into mine after we lifted them and gave thanks. Then the Mormon, I don't remember his name, heard me say that to Joseph, and he asked if he could do the same."

"He knew you were getting two helpings already. He couldn't ask the guy on his right?"

"He was on the end!" Father Matthew said, half-laughing. "So I told him that he could pour his cup into mine as well."

"So you all hoist your cups and…"

"…And I take a big sip from mine to make some room in it. John quickly poured his wine into my cup, and I gulped a bit more down, and then the Mormon poured his in. I looked at this thing, which was almost full to the brim now, and I figured that there was probably more wine in that cup than I'd had in my lifetime, all combined."

"It must've taken you a while to finish all that."

"That's the other thing. Everyone else had finished, and they were all waiting for me. The congregation must've wondered what was taking so long. I doubt they've have noticed the other two empty their cups into mine. All I could think about was how I was there to represent St Francis Church, and I didn't want to make a bad impression."

"So what did you do?"

"I gulped it."

Christine's mouth fell open. "The whole thing?"

"The whole thing."

Christine laughed. "Then what happened?" She sat up on the sofa and leaned toward him.

"It's a good thing that it was the last thing in the service. As soon as we said, 'amen,' I headed out the door and found a nice bench under a tree away from everyone. The world seemed a little unstable after a minute or two, and I got pretty lightheaded. It didn't take long at all to kick in. I was a total novice when it came to alcohol."

"Was it a bad experience for you?"

Father Matthew grinned and lowered his voice to a whisper. He leaned forward so she could hear. "I hate to admit it, but it was *fun*."

Christine giggled. She imagined a young Father Matthew clinging to a bench under a tree, waiting for the world to stop spinning.

"One of the other clergy who saw what happened noticed that I had disappeared and he found me and sat down next to me. He figured that I'd never been tipsy before, and the rascal took full advantage of it."

"What do you mean?"

"He spent the next half hour telling me all his terrible jokes, which caused me to laugh until my sides ached. He had great fun, since nobody ever laughed at his jokes, and I laughed harder than I had in ages."

Christine tried to picture the scene in her head. "I wish I'd have been there to see that. Maybe you'd have even laughed at my bad jokes. I've got some doozies."

Father Matthew sat back in his chair, thinking. He started to say something, then stopped.

"What?" Christine asked, noticing his hesitation.

"Nothing. It's a bad idea, and it's silly."

"We're still officially off the record. Silly is allowed."

He looked at the floor again for a moment, then back up at her. "Well, now that we know that God is unhappy with all those man-made rules…"

"Yes, go on."

"Then I don't suppose they hold much weight anymore."

"What are you planning?"

Father Matthew leaned forward and whispered again. "I'd love to get tipsy again, just once."

Christine laughed and clapped her hands. "You're serious?"

He could see that she wasn't judgmental about his admission and he relaxed. "Yes, I think so." He laughed. "No, I know so. I've thought about it lots of times before today, actually, but those pesky rules have always been in the way."

"I'd love to meet the Father Matthew that laughs at bad jokes!" Christine gave him a big smile. "Should I go buy a bottle of wine or something?"

"Oh no, we can't do it here." He shook his head, suddenly serious. "No, that still feels wrong to me."

Christine thought for a moment. "There's a nice little pub a few blocks from my house."

"I'm not sure I should be seen in a bar, either."

"It's not a bar, it's a pub. People go there to eat. I'll pop my head in on the way home and tell them to save me a booth in the back corner. Nobody will see us."

"Is it far from here?"

"Not at all. I'm going to pass right by it when I walk home. I live in the Briarwood subdivision, and the pub is on the corner right by the entrance. The Briar and Thistle."

"I think I've seen the place. What's the address?"

"It's at the intersection of Briar and Thistle."

"Ah. I should've guessed from the name. What time can I meet you there?"

Christine looked at her watch. "I'm supposed to meet my coworker for pizza at six, near downtown. I figure a couple hours or so for that, then drive home and walk to the pub.... How about nine-thirty? Is that too late?"

"That's fine." He was nervous but excited. "I'll meet you there."

"Fantastic." Christine set down her tea, picked up her recorder, and stood up to leave.

"I'm afraid that it's unlikely that much of what you recorded today is going to be allowed into your story," he said. "Sorry about that. I'm not even sure I told you anything you came to hear."

"We can pick it up later. Things will have settled down some by then, and you'll have had more time to sort it all out."

"Sure. If you don't mind leaving by the back door? I'm still not ready to talk to anyone else, and I don't want someone to see you leave and assume I'm taking visitors."

"No problem at all."

They walked down the short hallway to the back door. Father Matthew unlocked the door and opened it just enough to peer out.

"The coast is clear." He felt a bit silly for saying it.

Christine slipped through the door and onto the grass.

"Christine?"

She stopped and turned around.

"Thanks. I needed to talk. I feel much better."

She smiled, waved goodbye, then turned and headed home.

CHAPTER SIX

Thelo was thrilled that Admin had responded, but he feared that sending a forced alert might've been too much. Hackers don't like to be interrupted, and a forced alert is usually reserved for dire emergencies, like 'the FBI is on the way to your house.' This hardly qualified as that sort of urgent situation, and Thelo knew it. Still, he got a response, so that was something. He typed a reply.

Maybe we shouldn't text. VOIP?

A few seconds later, his speakers produced a robotic sound that was Admin's voice filtered through a vocoder. Anyone listening in wouldn't be able to discover the identity of the caller, even with vocal matching software. Also, the call itself was run through a Voice Over Internet Protocol system routed through multiple random nodes. The call was virtually impossible to trace.

"This better be good," the voice stated. It sounded more machine than human.

"Sorry to bother you, but I need to get someone started on this quickly, and I wanted to give you first dibs on it." Thelo's computer mic relayed the words through the same secure system back to Admin's computer.

"Go on," the voice said. "You got my attention."

"I've been assigned to cover the story today about The Sermon." Thelo hoped that Admin wouldn't just hang up on him after realizing that it wasn't an emergency.

"Good for you. Why did you call me?"

"My editor thinks it's a hoax."

"Half the world thinks it's a hoax. Why did you call me?"

"I need to find out if any of the people who preached The Sermon knew each other. If they did, I need to know how they planned it, why they planned it, and what they expected to get out of it."

There was a long pause, and Thelo thought Admin had just cut him off. Then the voice came through his speakers again.

"Email server hacks are easy but risky. What's in it for me?"

Thelo scrambled to think of something. Apparently, a thirst for the truth, which had served him well as a reporter, wasn't the sort of motivation that was good enough to convince a hacker to risk going to jail.

"Um... well, you'd be instrumental in debunking the biggest hoax in several lifetimes, which could land you book deals, speaking tours, tons of fame and fortune on the lecture circuit..."

"Money won't do me any good from jail. Even if I don't get caught, I can't do fame and fortune and keep my anonymity."

Thelo took a chance.

"If it's proven to be a hoax, it could mean the end of the careers of everyone who took part in it. They'd be labeled as frauds."

"So some holier-than-thou types get jacked. Okay, that's tasty. Look, I can probably get the emails, but I'm not going to have time to read them myself. Set up a secure file vault and I'll dump what I can get into it. You'll have to go through it on your own to see if any of it is useful."

"Fair enough. Thanks."

"Make sure that shit is absolutely untraceable, got it?"

"I'll use the same platform as last time. Is that okay?"

"That will work. Send me the link when you've got it set up. Gotta run."

Thelo sat back in his desk chair, exhaled a sigh of relief, and smiled. He was glad he hadn't pissed off his favorite source. He created an encrypted digital file vault on a remote server, then sent a link and the encryption key to Admin in separate messages from different accounts, using a VPN to hide his IP address.

Thelo looked at the time. He was supposed to meet Christine at six to compare notes. He didn't want her to know that he had a notorious hacker in his list of sources, so for the next hour or so, he dug up everything Google could find on The Sermon. He hoped that he'd have something to share with Christine over pizza.

The poker game was well underway at The Bunker, and so far, the winnings were pretty evenly divided between One, Two, and Three. Four, as usual, hadn't won a single hand all night and his stack of chips was nearly depleted. This hand would be different, he thought. He held a full house, kings and jacks, and it was the best chance he'd had of winning a hand all afternoon. The pot was piled high with chips. All four of the men apparently believed they had the winning hand and the pot had been raised three rounds straight. If someone raised again, Four realized, he wouldn't have enough left to cover it. They didn't allow all-in at their games, so if you couldn't cover the bet, you had to fold.

"Call." Four tossed the last of his chips onto the pile. He held his breath.

"Fat Four thinks he's going to have his first winning hand!" Joel smirked. "I should raise you to knock you out of the game, but I'm dying to see what you've got. Besides, I think the prize is probably wanting some variety by now. I'll call." Joel threw in a stack of chips.

Two looked across at Four and bit his lip. He had won the previous hand and the young prostitute they called 'the prize' was under the table providing her services to him. He hadn't expected this hand to last as long as it had and if he won another hand, she'd just keep going down on him, and he'd definitely climax before that hand was over. He looked at his cards, shook his head, and bit his lip again.

"I fold."

Three and Four both looked puzzled.

"You're folding after you raised three times?" Joel asked him.

Two bit his lip harder and gripped the edge of the table with both hands. "Yes, I fold. Get on with it!"

Three shot a quick glance at Joel and Four. He gave them a slight nod and a broad smile. "Fine then." His deep voice rumbled. "Let me see what I'm going to do."

Two looked at Three menacingly. "You know what you're going to do. We've gone three times around. Call, raise, or fold!" He gritted his teeth and tried to think about sports.

"I don't know. I thought I had it all figured out, but then you folded, and I wasn't expecting that, so I'm all confused," Three said. He drew out his words and stretched out the sentence as long as he could. "How much is it to call?"

"You damn well know how much!" Two yelled. The point of no return was nearly there for him, and he knew it.

"It's fifty dollars to you," Four said, winking at him.

Two tried to pull away from the table.

"Not allowed!" Joel said quickly. "You know the rules."

"They're stalling!" Two pleaded.

"I don't remember having a time limit," Joel said. "Fellas, did we ever make a rule about time limits?"

"No, I don't believe we did," Three laughed.

"I don't remember any rule, either," Four added.

"Fuck you bastards! Fuck all of you. You can… goddammit!"

Two beat his fists on the table as he climaxed, and the large pile of poker chips bounced and spread out on the table. Two pushed his chair back, away from the prize underneath. He stood and pulled his gym shorts back up to his waist, then sat down again. The other three men laughed at him.

"You know the rules," Three said, grinning. "If you 'finish,' you're finished. You can put all your chips into the pot now."

Two moved his chair back up to the table and angrily pushed all his chips to the pile in the center.

Three added two twenty-five-dollar chips to the pile. "I call." He turned to Four. "Whatcha got there, dough boy?"

Four grinned and laid down his full house triumphantly.

"Well, fuck," Joel said. "I just had a flush."

"A full house?" asked Three. "I've got one of those."

Four's face went pale.

Three laid down his full house. Eights and fours. "Not as good as yours, though."

Four let out a whoop and stood up. He leaned over the table and dragged the pile of chips to his side, then pushed his gym shorts to his ankles. He sat back down and spread his knees apart.

"It's about fucking time," he said. "It's been a long dry spell for me. Papa Bear's not getting any at home."

The other three men laughed. Two even joined in.

Three reached over, turned Two's cards up, and gawked at the hand. "You folded with four queens?"

"If I had won two hands in a row with that bitch under the table, then it was guaranteed I would have to forfeit. Either way, I lose my money. She's too good."

The other men laughed.

"There's no way you'll last for long," Two said to Four. "All that money you just won is going right back into the pot before this hand is up, mark my words."

"We'll see about that. C'mere, sweet thing." Four patted his big thighs under the table and spread his legs. "Daddy's got a present for ya."

Sharkey's Pizza was a remnant of the themed-restaurant fad from a few of decades back. The entrance was shaped like a giant set of shark jaws, the tables were made from surfboards with large 'bite marks' on the end, and the drink menu was full of cocktails with names like 'Terror From Below' and 'Bloody Water.' The place had gone from trendy to tacky to retro-campy over the years, even though it hadn't changed anything.

Thelo and Christine sat on bar chairs at a surfboard table near the jukebox.

"Good call, choosing this place," Christine said. "Best pizza in town."

"I don't usually eat here. I just have them deliver."

"You live close enough to get delivery?"

"Yes, in Eastmont."

"Ooh, that's trendy."

"Well, it's not trendy in my neighborhood, which is fine by me," Thelo said. "I don't want my rent going up."

"If I lived close enough to get delivery, I'd be twice this size. I don't have that much willpower."

"What's your favorite?"

Christine thought for a moment. "Depends on my mood. Sometimes I like the exotic ones, like calamari and scallop, and sometimes I just want comfort food, and get pepperoni."

"And what's your mood tonight?"

"Everything is so crazy right now, I don't know what I want. What do you like?"

"I usually get bacon, garlic, and banana."

Christine scrunched up her face. "What do they call that one?"

"It's my own creation. It's not on the menu."

"Sounds… um…"

"Gross?"

"No, just unusual. This whole day has been unusual, though, so I'm game. Split a large?"

"Sure. I'll go over and order it. Thin or thick crust?"

"Thin, if that's okay with you."

"Thin it is. Be right back."

Thelo slid down off his chair and went to the bar to order the pizza. Christine fished her phone from her purse and checked it. There was a text from Ivan. She read it, then sent a quick reply. Thelo came back to the table and climbed onto the bar chair.

"Ivan texted, wanting an update. I already told him that Father Matthew would only be interviewed off the record and so I wouldn't have a story for him tomorrow."

"I got one from him earlier, telling me to send him a Joe Friday ASAP."

"A what?"

"A story with just the facts. Basically, a 'here's what happened' and nothing else."

"Oh, gotcha."

"I told him to piss off, I was busy."

Christine giggled. "You did not!"

"I did," Thelo said. "I was already typing up my article from the notes I've been making all afternoon. I told him to wait until he read my article, and then he could whittle it down into a Joe Friday if that's what he wanted."

"You've got a piece written already? Can I read it?"

"I'll email it to you." He took out his phone and sent her the file. "You're lucky that the religion page only runs on Sunday. I'm envious of your deadline."

"I'm envious of you being able to tell Ivan to piss off."

"We have a very casual working relationship. If there isn't some level of irreverence between us, I know he's upset."

"I was sorta afraid of him at first," Christine admitted. "He looks like an angry Russian bear, but he's a sweetheart once you get to know him."

"My contact in the UK wants to marry him," Thelo chuckled. "She only knows what I've told her about him. She googled him once and turned up that picture of him with Senator What's-his-name, the one that hangs on the wall in his office. She's been drooling over it ever since."

"Is Ivan married? I asked him about his family once, but he didn't answer me."

"I have no idea," Thelo admitted. "We're pretty easy-going and informal around each other, but his personal life never comes up at all."

"Speaking of your contact in the UK, what did you find out?"

"Well, she says that as far as she knows, nobody outside the US gave The Sermon today."

"Really?" Christine was surprised. "I knew we hadn't heard of anything from Europe or Asia or Africa, but I figured there would be some stuff coming out of Mexico or Canada. They're in the same time zones as us."

"You think time zones have something to do with it?"

"Not exactly, but if God chose to do this Sunday morning, our time, then Europe and Asia and those others were already done with their Sunday services. Maybe they'll get The Sermon next Sunday."

"That seems like a stretch, Christine. And we don't know for sure about the rest of North America. Ivan has some Spanish speakers looking into anything south of the border right now. Oh, I think he said he did find one in Canada."

"Do we know how many total?"

"Ivan's found just twenty-two people so far, all but one in the US, and six of those were local."

"Wow," Christine said. "I thought it would be more. It's still creating a lot of news, though. Did you see any of the network stuff?"

"No, just online."

"People are really upset."

"They're upset that they've been following these religious rules all this time and they didn't have to?"

"Some of them," Christine said. "Some of them are disillusioned because they believed that the Bible was the literal Word of God and now apparently God has said that it's not."

"That's gotta sting. I expected people to be happy just to hear from God, no matter what He said. It's been a long time since we humans got a direct talking-to, yeah?"

"Yeah. No burning bushes this time, though, just preachers."

"How did it go with Father Matthew? I know you didn't get an on-the-record, but were you able to talk to him?"

"Yes, but I've got some more questions to ask him later. What I did find out was that he has no recollection of any of it. He said it was like a few seconds of time just got skipped. He thought he had teleported since he moved around during his trance and when he snapped out of it, he was in a different place."

"That's gotta be a wild experience," Thelo said, almost envious. "How is he handling it?"

"He seemed pretty good, considering. I didn't get a lot of information about the actual event because he doesn't remember it. He thinks some of those rules he has to follow as a priest are unnecessary, though. I think he's kinda relieved that they've been deemed bogus."

"He said that?"

"Not in those words, but he admitted that he's thought about breaking a couple of them, now that he has divine permission."

Thelo laughed. "Yeah, I'll bet he has. He an old guy?"

"Not really. Maybe fifty?"

"And never been laid. He's probably googling whorehouses right now."

Christine gasped and dropped her jaw in surprise. "Oh, I doubt it!" She gaped at Thelo. "I don't think he's the type. Anyway, I got a couple of things I can use, but I'm going to talk to him again in a day or two after he's had a chance to sort things out. What about you? What else have you found out?"

Thelo checked the notes he had put in his phone. "Um… in spite of it being just a couple dozen people, there's a pretty good range of religions covered. We've got Catholic, Jewish, Mormon, Muslim, most of the Protestant flavors of Christianity, Hindu, Buddhist, and even one from the Church of Scientology."

"That seems to cover all the bases."

"I listed Joel Wood under 'Protestant Christian,' is that accurate?"

"Yeah, that's pretty close. Gloria Deo is non-denominational but still Protestant."

"I tried to get an interview with him," Thelo said. "Twenty minutes of 'all lines are busy, would you like to leave a message?' When I finally got through, it was just another recording saying, 'Reverend Wood is not accepting requests for interviews at the moment.'"

"Reverend Wood?" Christine smirked. "I don't think he's ever called himself 'reverend' before."

"Probably worried about being struck by lightning if he does," Thelo scoffed. Christine cocked her head.

"You haven't heard the rumors?" he asked her.

"I don't like to wallow in gossip," she said in a tone that indicated the topic had reached its end.

Thelo dropped it.

"So apparently, just about every religion in the US had a representative this morning," Thelo said, scrolling through his notes. "Except I couldn't find any pastors from the Amish community, or any of the traditional Native American religions."

"Interesting." She thought for a moment. "I think that even if an Amish pastor had preached The Sermon, it wouldn't be out there in the media, certainly not on YouTube. They don't use technology. They don't even use electricity. I don't see that news getting out in the mainstream for awhile."

"Good point. But what about the Natives? There aren't many of those traditional services going on anymore, but if God were going to hit all the bases, you'd think that someone from at least one tribe would've preached it."

"What if they didn't need to get scolded by God because they're doing it right?"

"Or maybe whoever organized this prank forgot to include them," Thelo countered. "Or maybe they wanted to include them, but none of the tribes wanted to play along."

"You really think this is all a prank?" Christine asked. She shook her head.

"A prank, a hoax, something like that," Thelo said. "If it really was God, wouldn't it have been all over the world? Besides, I'd have to start believing that there's a God in the first place before I can even begin to believe that He's channeling His words through a bunch of American preachers."

Their pizza arrived courtesy of a waitress in a sea-green swimsuit emblazoned with a cartoon shark chomping a slice of pizza. She asked if they needed anything else, then turned and went back to the bar. Thelo slid a slice of the pie onto his plate.

"The theming in this place is really tacky," Christine said as she pulled off a slice for herself. "But the pizza's so good you don't care."

CHAPTER SEVEN

Joel returned home to find Holly still in her study. He called out an 'I'm home' as he approached, so as not to startle her. He couldn't see her behind the three computer monitors, but he could hear the clicking of the keyboard as she typed. Her face appeared around the side of one of the monitors, her eyes red from hours of reading the screens.

"Any more news?" He hoped there wasn't any.

"Just more of the same," she said. "It gets repetitive after a while. Every original thought gets posted in the first couple of hours, and then after that, people just repost or retweet what's already out there."

"I suppose that's a good thing. Have you had dinner?"

"No, I've been right here since you left. How'd you make out at the game?"

He hung his head in mock shame. "I'm broke."

"Lost all of it?"

He nodded.

"Did you have bad cards, did you play poorly, or did you shoot your wad too soon and have to forfeit?"

"All of the above."

Holly shook her head as she began shutting down all her equipment. She stood up and walked around the desk, then looked her husband in the eyes, shook her head again and sighed. She put one hand on his shoulder and used the other to lift his chin to look at her.

"We're going to have to make it a habit for you to take care of yourself with a porno or something before you go off to play cards," she said. "Then you won't be so quick on the draw when you win a hand. That's no guarantee you'll win big, but at least you won't be giving all your money to Cletus every time you have to forfeit."

"How did you know that Cletus got all the money?"

"Cletus made up the rule about 'finish, and you're finished,' didn't he?"

"Yes."

"And Cletus always brings the prize?"

"Yes. He's got a source that he trusts."

"Don't you think that he tells those girls to go easy on him if he wins a hand? They're probably not even doing anything with him under the table. He promises them some extra cash if they play along, then he doesn't even have to win to get all the money every week because the rest of you always have to forfeit."

Joel's eyes widened. "That sorry fucker. I should've known. I'm going to have to figure out a way to get a prize from somewhere else and take Cletus out of the equation."

"No, you won't. It's risky enough what you're doing, so don't go trying to line up another prize source whose silence might not be as easily bought as Cletus's. You keep letting Cletus bring the prizes, and you keep coming home spent and broke. We can afford you losing the money, but we can't afford your little escapades going public."

She playfully slapped his cheek, then walked out of the study.

"What about dinner?" Joel asked as she passed him.

"Call for some take-out. I'm going to go shower. I need to wash off all the filth I've been reading today."

Christine walked at a brisk pace. She feared that if she showed up late to the pub, Father Matthew might get cold feet and change his mind. After she met Thelo at Sharkey's, she drove home and called Ivan to update him on their progress. Then she typed a transcript of her conversation with Father Matthew. When she'd finished with that, she realized that she was due at the pub in just eight minutes.

She arrived two minutes late, a bit out of breath, and almost didn't recognize Father Matthew standing at the edge of the parking lot in his jeans, polo shirt, and a baseball cap. He got her attention with a short wave, then ducked his head down. The brim of his cap hid his face.

"Sorry, Father, I didn't recognize you in that outfit."

"I'm actually glad you didn't recognize me, that puts me a little more at ease. And call me 'Matthew.' I don't want anyone in there to hear you call me 'Father.'"

"Right. If I slip up, just kick me under the table. It'll take a bit of getting used to."

"There's a lot of 'getting used to' today," he said. They walked to the door, and Matthew opened it for her.

The place was crowded for a Sunday evening, but people were focused on their own conversations, and nobody noticed who came and went. Laughter and boisterous voices filled every corner of the room, and the background music had a hard time keeping up with the din. Christine looked around for the manager, a woman she'd come to know over the years, and caught her eye from across the room. The manager waved back and pointed to an empty booth in the back corner.

"Good," Christine said. "She saved our spot."

Christine led Matthew through the place. They skirted around tables and dodged a waiter carrying a tray of empty dishes. When they reached their booth, Christine sat facing the room, and Matthew took the seat facing the wall.

"I figured you'd want your back to everyone if you're going incognito."

"Yes, thank you."

"It's noisy enough in here that we won't have to whisper or anything. Nobody is going to recognize you, don't worry. I barely recognized you outside."

"It's perfect. Thanks again." Matthew relaxed a little.

"How was the rest of your day?" Christine asked.

"We can talk about it later. I don't want any shop talk this evening. I'm here to have fun, and I'm not sure I can do that if we mix the other stuff into it."

"I understand completely," Christine said as the manager came up to the table. She was forty-five or so and in great shape. Her long dark hair showed a few strands of gray as it tumbled down her back. She wore knee-length black shorts, an apron at the waist, and a man's white dress shirt, unbuttoned far enough to show some cleavage. No bra.

"Is this table kinda what you wanted?"

"Yes, Margaret, it's perfect."

"I wondered why you wouldn't just sit at the bar like usual," Margaret said, then looked at Matthew, "but it makes sense to me now." She winked at him.

"Don't jump to conclusions," Christine insisted. "We just wanted to be able to have a conversation without having to shout at each other."

"Right. What are we having tonight?"

Matthew shot Christine a quizzical look, and she interpreted it instantly.

"Give us a few minutes on that, okay?" Christine said. "I want to try something different tonight."

"You got it. I'll come back in a couple of minutes with some water. You need menus?"

Christine looked across at Matthew, who shook his head.

"No, but maybe a cocktail list?"

"Can do," Margaret said. She produced a small booklet from a pocket in her apron. "Be back in a bit."

"You must be a regular here," Matthew said after Margaret left them for another table.

"At least once or twice a week. I like to sit at the bar and strike up a conversation with anyone sitting next to me. It's better than eating in front of the TV by myself at home. Besides, the food's really good here."

"You had pizza with your coworker already, though," Matthew said.

"Yes. Did you eat something before you came?"

"Not really," Matthew said. "I was too nervous. I had a couple of crackers and some cheese, that was it."

"You should eat something. Especially if you're going to be drinking."

"The whole idea was to get tipsy, though, wasn't it?" he reminded her.

"Yes, you're right. But it's going to be a short night if you don't have some food in you."

"I'll be fine."

Christine looked through the booklet of cocktails.

"What would you like, Fa…," she quickly caught herself. "Matthew?"

He shrugged his shoulders. "I only know cocktails by their names. I have no idea what any of them taste like or which ones I might like to try."

"Well, have a look at the bottles behind the bar over there and see if one of them catches your eye."

Matthew leaned forward and craned his head around the edge of the booth to get a look. Rows of bottles adorned shelves in front of a large mirror behind the bar. Matthew ran his gaze from left to right and noticed a table full of twenty-somethings watching water drip into stemmed glasses from a contraption in the center of their table.

"What's that group over there having?" he asked. "The one with that glass tower in the middle."

Christine leaned out and looked.

"No idea. I've never seen one of those."

"It looks like they're having fun," he said. "I'm here to have fun."

"Then we'll ask."

"Ask what?" Margaret had returned with two glasses of water.

"What are those people having?" Christine said, pointing toward the table.

Margaret turned her head to see. "Absinthe. We just started carrying it a couple of weeks ago. It's starting to attract some younger folks in here, which is good."

"I've heard of that," Matthew said. "I thought it was banned."

"It was," Margaret said, "but not anymore. It's an interesting story. You should look it up."

"What does it taste like?" Christine asked.

"Every brand tastes different, but the main flavor is licorice."

"I love licorice," Matthew said.

"We'll have some of that, then," Christine decided.

"Which brand would you like to try? We have three." Margaret pointed to the page in the cocktail menu.

"Can we get a flight?" Christine asked. She saw the confused look on Matthew's face. "It's a smaller-sized sampling of all of them," she explained.

"Yeah, we can do that."

"Perfect. Thanks, Margaret."

Margaret left for the bar, and Christine studied Matthew's face.

"You still okay?" she asked.

"I think so. I'm nervous, but I'm excited. I haven't been tipsy since that day I told you about, and that was a long time ago." He winked at her. "Before you were born, as you pointed out."

She felt that she should apologize for that, but his smile assured her that no harm was done.

They sat in silence for a minute or two. Matthew listened to the happy chatter in the room at his back, and Christine attempted to find a conversation topic that wouldn't bring up Matthew's priesthood or The Sermon. Eventually, Margaret returned with a glass tank on a pedestal. It had tiny spigots protruding from opposite sides, and it was filled with ice water. She sat the thing in the center of their table.

"Be right back."

Matthew and Christine both stared at the contraption for a moment, and then Matthew leaned over to one side so he could see around it. Christine leaned at the same time, and their eyes met. Both of them laughed at the expression on the other's face.

"What have we gotten ourselves into?" Matthew asked.

"Are you sure you're up for this?"

"As ready as I'll ever be."

Margaret returned with a tray of six glasses, two slotted spoons, a small bowl of sugar cubes, and napkins. She unloaded the tray, placing three glasses each in front of them. Christine looked at all of the equipment on the table, then over at a bewildered Matthew, then back up at Margaret.

"Did you bring the instruction manual?"

Margaret laughed. "Everyone needs a walk-through the first time. No worries." She pointed at the slotted spoons. "Put the spoon on top of the glass, put a sugar cube on the spoon, then turn on the spigot, so water drips onto the sugar. When it's all dissolved, turn off the water, give it a stir, and drink up. I'll call you a cab when you're done."

"We walked here, no need for that," Christine said.

"Tell me that again after the third one," Margaret said, and went to attend to other tables.

"There's a green one, a clear one, and a greenish-brown one," Christine noticed. "Which one should we start with?"

"Lightest to darkest seems appropriate," Matthew said. "Clear one first?"

Christine and Matthew followed Margaret's instructions, and soon, ice water was dripping onto the sugar and then into the glasses.

Matthew was fascinated by the ritual. He watched each drop of water as it made contact with the absinthe and sank to the bottom of the glass with a cloudy trail behind it. Soon, the aroma of anise filled the air. Matthew looked away from his glass long enough to see that Christine was just as mesmerized by the show as he. She caught his glance.

"How fun is this?" she said. "It comes with its own entertainment!"

"It's a first for both of us, then." Matthew looked back at his glass. "I think mine's done."

"Same here."

They turned off the little spigots on the tank, took the spoons from the glasses, and stirred the cloudy elixir. Christine held hers up in a toast.

"To new adventures." She clinked her glass against Matthew's.

"To new adventures."

Christine brought her glass up to her nose and enjoyed the aroma. She took a sip as Matthew watched.

"Oh, it's good," she said. "Go ahead."

Matthew looked at his glass as if to say, 'here goes,' then took a sip. Christine waited for a reaction.

"Well?"

"I like it," he said. "I was afraid I wouldn't." He took another sip.

"This was a good choice. You can't taste much alcohol in it, and it's very smooth."

"If there's not much alcohol in it, will this be enough to do the job?"

"If not, we'll order more," Christine assured him, and they each took another sip.

Margaret returned to the table. "What do you think?"

"It's delicious," Christine told her, "but we'll probably want to order another round. Can you go ahead and set us up?"

"That shit is a hundred-and-sixty proof! What are you trying to do?"

"A hundred-and-sixty?" Christine gasped. "Are you serious? You can hardly taste any alcohol."

"Drink what you have," Margaret said. "If you're still sober enough to walk after that, we'll talk about another round."

Margaret left them to it. Christine shook her head in amazement.

"A hundred-and-sixty proof?" Matthew asked. "Is that bad?"

"It's around six or seven times more potent than that wine you drank." She hoisted her glass with a sly grin. "Cheers!"

Matthew flashed a hint of worry across his face, then a big smile. "All in," he said. "Cheers."

Thelo checked his computer to see if he'd gotten anything from Admin. Nothing yet, but that didn't surprise him. It was likely going to take some time, even if email hacking was as easy as Admin claimed. In the game of illegal computing, getting into the data you want is less important than erasing your digital footprints, so nobody knows you were there at all.

Even after a few high-profile hacks of financial systems, Admin's identity had remained secret. "Admin" showed up on the FBI's most-wanted list shortly afterward, but with no physical description, hometown, real name, or other information. Stealing emails from a bunch of pastors and priests wasn't as difficult as breaking into a big bank's files, but the potential for having it make the news was just as great, if not greater. The whole world was talking about The Sermon, and anything related to that would be big news.

Thelo spent some time chasing leads, making lists of potential contacts, and dictating some notes into his phone. It was too late to call any of these people tonight, but he had gotten the contact information for eighteen of the twenty-two pastors. That left only four to track down tomorrow, and he had their names, just not their numbers. Yet.

He made a quick call to Ivan.

"Where's my story?" Ivan asked. "I thought you'd have this cracked by now and I'd be able to run it on page fourteen tomorrow. I've saved space for it and everything!"

"It's a front page story, or I'm selling it to the tabloids, old man," Thelo shot back.

"All right, all right. Below the fold."

"Above the fold!" Thelo laughed. "Seriously, though, I've got some things in motion already, and I'm going to make a lot of calls tomorrow. If there's a connection between these people, I'm going to find it."

"What things have you got in motion?" Ivan asked, then thought better of it. "Wait. Never mind, don't tell me. I don't want to know about your secret sources."

"Smart man. I'll update you tomorrow. You need me to come into the office?"

"No, just don't make yourself unavailable. I'll keep you fed with the latest info if I get anything new. Keep your phone handy."

"Gotcha, boss. Later."

Thelo set his phone on the desk, stretched, and looked at the time. It was just before ten. There might still be a decent crowd at The Roadhouse tonight if he hurried, and he could use a drink and a diversion from the day's stress. Thelo picked up his phone again, tapped the icon for the taxi app, and arranged for a cab to come by in twenty minutes. He quickly shucked off his clothes, brushed his teeth, and hopped in the shower.

He'd barely dried off and gotten into his clean clothes when the phone beeped an alert that the cab was outside. Thelo grabbed the phone from the desk, filled his pockets with the contents of the glass bowl on the table by the door, and then slapped his pockets to double-check. He left the apartment and met the cab at the end of the sidewalk.

Thelo opened the back door and sat down on the faux leather seat. The cab smelled of curry and french fries. The driver wore a red cloth turban, and Thelo could see the profile of a bushy beard. He told the man to take him to The Roadhouse, then fished his phone out of his pants pocket, and buckled his seatbelt.

As soon as the driver had entered the address into his GPS and gotten underway, Thelo introduced himself.

"Excuse me if I'm being a pest," Thelo began. "But you're a Sikh, yeah?"

"I am."

"I'm Thelo Brown, a reporter at the *Post*. Do you mind if I ask your thoughts about what happened today? The Sermon?"

"Everyone wants to talk about that," the man said. "But you are a reporter, and I am not allowed to speak to the media while I am on the job. I don't mind if you ask questions, but it has to be off the record, just as a passenger, not as a reporter."

"I understand. That's not a problem."

Thelo checked his phone for the list of people who had preached The Sermon. There was one Sikh on the list, from Los Angeles.

"Are you familiar with Guru Anjab in California?"

"Only today," he answered. "He was a hot topic at the driver pool this afternoon before my shift began."

"What did you think of what he said? What did the other drivers say about it?"

"We are confused. Sikhs understand that the Guru Granth Sahib, our holy book, was written over time by ten human Gurus. Humans can make mistakes, so to say that the book is fiction is not as upsetting as it might have been for other religions."

"Okay," Thelo said.

"But the next part where he said that the rules we follow are displeasing..." the driver paused, then his voice became agitated.

"The rules we follow are to treat others with respect, to strive for justice, to avoid attachment to worldly things, and to be truthful in all areas of our lives. What could God find displeasing about that?" the driver asked.

"You're asking the wrong guy about what God finds pleasing or displeasing," Thelo said as they arrived at The Roadhouse. "Thanks for sharing your thoughts, though. I hope you find some answers."

Thelo paid the driver the fare plus a generous tip.

"Would you like me to come back for your ride home?" the driver asked as he took the money.

"Maybe, but I don't know when." Thelo looked at the driver's ID on the dash. "But I'll ask for Bishan if I need a ride."

"Thank you, sir. Enjoy your night."

Thelo got out of the cab and shot the driver a quick wave as he closed the door, then turned and entered The Roadhouse.

The crowd was a bit thinner than Thelo had hoped, but there were still thirty or forty guys here, most of them in jeans and cowboy hats. Several watched a football game on a large flat screen television that hung on the back wall. They occasionally cheered and clinked their beer mugs together in celebration. A pool table in the corner commanded the attention of a small group of guys who watched a game between a man barely old enough to drink and a gray-haired man probably three times his age. Judging by the balls left on the table, the younger guy was getting his ass handed to him by the older one. The onlookers were enjoying this fact immensely, and Thelo guessed that the kid had probably tried to hustle the older man, then got hustled himself. He smiled. He'd seen the old man do that before, as had many of the onlookers. The kid must be new.

Thelo took a seat at the bar.

"Evenin', T," the bartender said as Thelo took his stool. "The usual?"

"Hi, Ben. Yes, that would be great."

A short time later he was facing a gin and tonic, no lime.

"You're not usually this late on a Sunday," Ben said. "You don't have to work tomorrow?"

"Hell, I had to work today!"

"Really? You closed the place down last night," Ben recalled. "You usually head home early on work nights."

"I hadn't planned to go to work today, but it seems that God had other plans, and made a story big enough to get my ass into the office on my day off."

Ben laughed. "Yeah, that's a doozy. What do you think happened?"

"That's what I'm trying to find out. I think it might be a hoax. I've got some leads to follow tomorrow."

"A hoax? Well ain't that some shit."

Thelo felt the presence of someone coming up behind him. Ben glanced up over Thelo's shoulder, and Thelo heard a vaguely familiar voice.

"What happened to that accent you had before?"

Thelo turned around and looked up at the source of the question, but the lights above the barstools backlit the man. He could barely make out more than a silhouette.

"I'm sorry, I don't know what you mean. Have we met?"

"Earlier today, you had a malfunctioning turn signal and a British accent," the man said.

Thelo remembered where he had heard the voice.

"Aw, shit."

CHAPTER EIGHT

Ivan Carter had been on the phone all day. The story had legs, as the saying went, and he began to wonder if two reporters were enough to cover it. He liked the article that Thelo had sent, but it just covered the tip of the iceberg. Thelo was careful not to lean either way in regards to the miracle-versus-hoax possibility, leaving the readers to make up their own minds. When Ivan needed a reporter who could tackle a volatile story without a hint of bias, Thelo was his first choice. Ivan saw some prestigious journalism awards in Thelo's future if he kept up this level of integrity. The Associated Press had already chosen the article to go out on their wire, and they hadn't even edited it. It went out as-is, something that would make Thelo very happy in the morning. He hated when they rewrote his stuff.

Ivan checked the time. Well past the quitting hour, he thought. He tidied up a few loose ends, gathered his things, then left the office and made the half-hour drive home.

He parked his Mercedes in the garage, then closed the garage door behind him. He entered the house through the kitchen, where he was greeted enthusiastically by Bosco, his chocolate lab. He squatted down to the dog's level and allowed Bosco to lick his face for a few seconds while he stroked the dog's soft brown fur and said 'good boy.'

After licking Ivan's beard thoroughly wet, the dog barked once, which Ivan had long ago translated to mean, 'welcome home, where's my dinner?'

"Okay, Bosco," Ivan told him, "I'll get it, hang on."

Ivan picked up Bosco's food and water dishes from the floor at the end of the kitchen island, rinsed and dried them out, then filled one with fresh water. He sat the dish on the floor, then got a large bag of food from the pantry and filled the other one with crunchy morsels that the television ads had promised would make any dog love you forever. Ivan figured that Bosco would love him forever anyway, no matter what kind of food he served. Ivan put the bag of food back in the pantry, then sat the dish on the floor. Bosco's tail made a rhythmic thump-thump-thump against the wall as he ate.

Ivan left the kitchen and went out the back door to the fenced yard that Bosco had to himself. Ivan's long work hours necessitated installing a doggy door to the yard so Bosco could play and take care of his needs without Ivan being home. A dog walker comes by once per day as well to put down fresh food and take Bosco to the dog park down the street. Ivan did a quick check of the yard, picked up a few 'presents,' then went back inside to dispose of them in the waste bin.

He then headed to his bedroom, a thoroughly masculine retreat done up in dark browns and greens. A king-sized bed dominated one side of the room, a mahogany desk and chair, the other. Ivan removed his shoes, then his suit coat and slacks. He gave the suit a sniff test, wrinkled his nose, then set it and the slacks aside. They'd be going to the cleaners before he wore them again. He stripped out of his shirt and tie, took off his socks and briefs, then tossed everything into the clothes hamper in the large walk-in closet.

Ivan stepped into the master bathroom, reached into the large glass shower, and turned on the water. He hated that first cold blast of water, so he yanked his arm back before the water hit it. He brushed his teeth while the hot water in the shower warmed the tile floor. He hated cold tiles, too.

Ivan stepped into the shower and washed all the Bosco licks from his beard, then cleaned up the rest of his body. That slobbery beard felt nasty after Bosco kissed his face, and Ivan had occasionally considered shaving it off, but always changed his mind when he looked in the mirror. He loved the masculinity that the beard brought to his otherwise boyish face, something that Ivan wasn't ready to abandon. He'd just have to wash his face more often, that's all.

After he showered and dried himself off, Ivan returned to the bedroom and pulled back the covers. Usually, he'd watch an old movie or check a few emails to unwind after a long day at work, but today was too exhausting to even think about turning on the television or the computer. He slid under the covers, set the alarm clock on the nightstand, fluffed his pillow, and closed his eyes. Ivan sighed as his head sank into the pillow. He felt the tension of the day begin to leave his body.

A few moments later, the familiar bounce of the mattress signaled Bosco's arrival, fresh from dinner. Bosco bounded over to Ivan, licked his beard until it was wet again, then panted a happy, 'good night.' He circled in place three times, then laid down on the bed next to his master.

Christine and Matthew leaned on each other for stability as they staggered along the road leading away from the Briar and Thistle. They laughed and kidded each other and played a game that Christine came up with, where one would tell a story about something they'd done in the past, and the other would have to guess whether the story was true or made up. Christine was winning since Father Matthew was a terrible liar and even more so when tipsy. "Tipsy" wasn't exactly accurate, though. Matthew was beyond that, as was Christine.

They reached a crossroads, and Matthew stopped walking.

"I believe this is where we part," he said. "The church is that way." He pointed down the street to the right.

"What are you going to say," Christine giggled, "if someone sees you come back to the rectory like this?"

Matthew's grin vanished into worry. "Oh. That would be bad. Is there a hotel or something nearby?"

"No, but I've got a spare room. You can crash there until morning, no problem."

"Are you sure?"

"Yes, now come on. It's not far."

They reached Christine's house in no time, a two-bedroom brick house built in the 80's, when "master planned communities" were sprouting up like weeds all over suburbia. Careful observation would reveal that Christine's block had ten houses, but only two different floor plans. Slight variations in the front elevation, color, and window type were all that distinguished one from another. An attached garage could hold two cars, but Christine parked hers in the driveway, like nearly all her neighbors. The garage was being used as a storage room for winter clothes, holiday decorations, a bicycle, a lawn mower, and several boxes of stuff that she had been planning to go through, but hadn't.

"It's a nice house," Matthew said as they reached the front door.

"Nothing fancy," Christine said. "But it's home."

They entered the foyer, and Matthew took off his ball cap as he followed Christine into the living room.

The house had an open concept plan with the living area, kitchen, and dining room all combined into one large space. The rooms were visually divided by a long island with bar stools between the kitchen and dining area, and by a sofa between the dining table and the living space. A large sliding glass door led from the dining area to a small, fenced back yard which was dominated by a swimming pool and deck.

The furniture was clean and comfortable, most of it bought at thrift stores or discount furniture outlets, but Christine had a pretty good eye for choosing things that complemented the decor. The walls were adorned with framed movie posters, pop art prints, and one large photo of Christine in a graduation cap and gown, standing between her beaming parents. The latter hung over the gas fireplace.

"Your mom and dad?" Matthew asked, pointing to the photo as they entered the living area.

"Yes. Have a seat. Make yourself comfortable."

He sat down at one end of the sofa. Christine picked up a couple of magazines from the coffee table, then retrieved a throw pillow that had somehow made its way to the floor. She looked for someplace to stow the magazines, then decided just to put them back on the coffee table. She sighed.

"I wasn't expecting company," she said.

"I wasn't expecting to be company. Sorry for the trouble."

"No trouble whatsoever. Are you sleepy? I can go get your bed ready."

"I'm not sleepy at all, actually."

"How about some tea, then? Maybe some coffee to take the buzz off?"

"Actually, I'm enjoying the buzz," Matthew replied. "I'd like to ride the wave a bit longer if that's okay. I haven't had this much fun in ages."

"Good!" Christine said, pleased. "That was the whole idea."

"This is going to be bad tomorrow morning, isn't it?"

"Hangover, you mean?"

Matthew nodded.

"I don't know. I've never had absinthe before, so I'll find out when you do." She moved to sit down, then changed her mind. "I'll get us some water. That usually helps to reduce the effects in the morning."

She made her way to the kitchen. Matthew looked again at the photo above the fireplace.

"It's a nice photo. Did you get a journalism degree?"

"No," Christine said, her voice coming from behind him. "Sociology. I found it interesting, but by the time I graduated, I was tired of it and didn't really want to be in that field for the rest of my life. I had done some writing for the school newspaper in my junior and senior years, and that was what sparked the fire for me."

"How did you end up on the religion page?"

"I've always been a person of faith, but I never settled down into one denomination. I find all the flavors of worship really interesting, so my editor figured I'd be able to do a good job covering different faiths without bias. The editor of that section retired a couple years later, and I got the job."

She returned with two glasses of water, handed one to Matthew.

"Thank you," he said and took a sip.

Christine sat down in a chair that was complimentary to the style and color of the sofa.

"Do you still keep in touch with your parents?" Matthew asked.

"Yes, but not as much as they'd like. They retired early and moved to Florida. They keep complaining that I don't come see them enough, but I don't have that much time off from work nor the money for the airfare. I manage to get down there every couple of years, though."

Matthew looked at his watch. "It's nearly midnight," he said, surprised and a bit disappointed. "You should probably be getting to bed, as should I. We both are going to have busy days tomorrow, I'm sure."

"I hate to bring things to a close, but you're right. I've had so much fun this evening, Matthew. Thank you."

"No, I should thank you. This has been great."

"I'll go get your bed ready." Christine stood up. "Be right back."

She left, and Matthew could hear her scurry around the guest room. He looked around the living room at the posters and furnishings, then turned in his seat to get a look at the kitchen. It was much larger than the one in the rectory, but it looked like it didn't get used as often. Christine probably ate a lot of meals away from home, he decided.

She returned from the guest room and announced that his bed was ready. He stood up, wobbled, then fell back down to the sofa.

"Easy there, big fella!" Christine giggled. "You can't stand up too fast."

"So I've discovered. Help an old man up?"

He stuck out a hand, and she helped him to his feet. He thanked her, and then she led him to the guest bedroom. The covers were turned back on one side, and a teddy bear sat atop the pillow on the other side. She walked him to the edge of the bed, and in spite of his best efforts to be graceful, he sat down hard enough to bounce the bed. They both laughed.

Christine knelt down on the floor and took off his shoes and socks. She put his socks inside his shoes, then set the pair next to the nightstand. She stood up and looked him over, then smiled.

"That's the hard part done. You're good from here?"

"Yes, I believe so."

"I'll leave you to it, then. What time would you like to wake up in the morning?"

"What time are you getting up?" he asked.

"Seven-thirty, maybe. Is that okay, or do you need earlier?"

"That will be fine, I think. Thank you."

She left and shut the door behind her. She went to the kitchen and poured water into the coffee maker, then ground some beans and added them to the filter basket. She set the timer so that it would brew the coffee just before she woke. She loved this feature of her coffee maker most of all. Waking up to that aroma was often her favorite part of the day.

A loud *thud* sounded from the guest bedroom. She rushed to investigate, using furniture to steady herself along the way. She opened the door and found Matthew lying on his side on the floor, his cheek against the carpet. He was shirtless with his pants around his ankles. "Oh! Are you okay? Are you hurt?"

Matthew looked up at her from his awkward position, met her eyes, then burst into laughter. Christine laughed as well, mostly from relief that he wasn't hurt. She helped slide his pants off and then helped him up off the floor. He blushed.

"Sorry about the scare. My balance isn't so good right now."

"No problem. I should've helped you get undressed before I left." She gave him a once-over. "You're a lot hairier than I thought you'd be," she said, eyeing his bare chest.

"Sorry." He blushed again.

"Sorry for what? I love a man with a hairy chest." She placed her left hand into the forest of hair and ran her fingers through it. Matthew froze. She felt his sudden tension and quickly pulled her hand away.

"Oh," she said, embarrassed. "Oh, I'm sorry. That was really thoughtless of me. I'm so sorry."

"Don't be sorry," he said, taking her hand in his. "I just didn't know how to react. I wasn't expecting it."

"I wasn't thinking," she said. "I shouldn't have, I…"

He leaned in and kissed her, just for a second, then pulled away and grinned. "There! We're even. I shouldn't have done that, either."

Christine looked at him with wide eyes, then they both laughed out loud. They hugged each other as they laughed, then pulled away and locked eyes once more. Their laughter subsided.

Matthew took Christine's face in both his hands, and she put one hand behind his head, playfully tousling his hair. They kissed again. As the kiss became longer and more intense, Christine could feel the front of Matthew's boxers pressing against her thigh.

She pulled away from him, dropped her eyes toward his crotch, then back up to his face. She flashed a mischievous grin. "You wanna?"

Matthew gaped at her with surprise and disbelief. "Really?"

"Really!" She playfully ran her fingers through the hair on his chest again.

Matthew enjoyed the feeling of her hand, but he wrestled with conflicting thoughts as if he had the proverbial angel and devil giving advice from his shoulders. In spite of the little angel's best efforts, it was the little devil who won this round. "Okay, but only if you'll still respect me in the morning," he said. They both laughed, then she kissed him again as she slid her hand down into the front of his shorts.

"I've never been handcuffed before," Thelo said, rubbing his wrists.

"Sorry if they were too tight," the cop said as he rolled over on the bed and put the cuffs into a drawer in the nightstand.

"No, not too tight. It's just with all that moving around, they rubbed a bit."

Officer Mike Scott rolled over and put his arm around Thelo's bare chest. He traced a finger around one of Thelo's nipples, and then ran it down the center of his torso, past his waistline. "You didn't seem to mind at the time," he whispered into Thelo's ear, and then playfully nibbled the lobe.

Thelo giggled and pulled away.

"What?" Mike asked him, pretending to be upset. "I'm trying to be sexy and you're giggling like a girl."

"Your moustache tickled my ear."

Mike brushed his lips against Thelo's ear again and whispered, 'tickle tickle tickle.' Thelo laughed aloud and pushed away from the naked cop.

"Keep squirming away from me, and I'll have to put the cuffs back on."

"Absolutely, officer!" Thelo grinned at him. "But not tonight. I've really got to be a hundred percent tomorrow, and I need some sleep." Thelo could barely believe that he was turning down another hot session with this man in favor of sleep. The cop looked like a beefier version of Tom Selleck, for chrissakes, and not the older Tom, either. It was Thelo's ultimate fantasy man brought to life, and yet he was prioritizing sleep over sex.

"Yeah, I hear ya," Mike said. "I've gotta work tomorrow, too, but I don't go in until ten." He looked Thelo in the eyes for a moment. "Do you think you might want to go out for a bite tomorrow night? My treat."

"Sounds good, depending on how the workload is going." Thelo shot Mike a sly grin. "Which donut shop is your favorite?"

Mike grabbed the pillow from behind his head and swung it at Thelo, who laughed and blocked the blow. "You've gotta let go of those stereotypes," Mike said. "First you assume I'm pulling you over because of racial profiling and now you're stooping to the tired old cop-in-the-donut-shop bit."

Thelo's smile left him. "I'm sorry. You're right, that's way beneath me, I should know better."

"Apology accepted," Mike said. "Now about dinner. You want fried chicken or watermelon?"

"Oh, you asshole!" Thelo laughed, then grabbed his own pillow and swung it at Mike, who was already moving to counter the assault. The two men wrestled and fought with their pillows, each one trying to get the upper hand. They eventually collapsed onto the bed in a fit of laughter.

"I really do need to go home and get some sleep," Thelo said when he caught his breath. "I'm going to get out of bed now before this gets going again and I end up spending the night."

"Okay." Mike rolled away from Thelo and swung his legs over the edge of the bed. "But you're welcome to spend the night if you want." He sat up and stretched as Thelo got out of bed and looked around the floor for his clothes.

"I'd love to," Thelo said, "but I need sleep, and we both know that won't happen here."

Mike picked up a sock and shoe from the floor on his side of the bed and held them up for Thelo to see.

"These were over here," he said, "not sure how that happened." He tossed them to Thelo, who was already in his underwear and pulling on his pants. "Hey," Mike said as Thelo put his shirt on, "I had a great time."

"I did, too."

Thelo found his phone in his jeans pocket, pulled it out and launched the app for the taxi. He made sure to request Bishan, then asked Mike for the street address of his house.

"I can drive you home. You don't need to call a cab."

"I already promised the driver a return fare if he was available. It's not a problem."

Mike recited his address while Thelo typed the information into the app. Thelo tapped the screen one last time, then put the phone back in his pocket and finished dressing.

"I'll call you tomorrow about dinner," Mike said, "to make sure you're still available."

"I'll probably be able to come," Thelo said, "but if there are any big new developments in this sermon story, I might be too busy writing the article or chasing down a lead."

"Yeah, okay. Everyone was talking about it today. Some of the holy rollers at the precinct were freaking out."

Thelo stood up, then walked over and sat next to Mike on the bed. Mike put his arm around the Thelo's waist and gave him a squeeze. Thelo put his head on the cop's shoulder and rested his right hand on Mike's thigh. They sat for several minutes that way, each lost in his own train of thought. Thelo lightly ran his hand back and forth across the hair on Mike's leg.

"If I ask you something," Thelo said, "would you promise not to get upset?"

Mike pulled away to look at Thelo's face, and saw an expression on it that was more serious than he anticipated. He scrunched up his brow. "Sure, go ahead."

"The next time you want to use those handcuffs, do you think you could wear the uniform, too?"

Thelo flinched. He fully expected to get smacked with another pillow, but there was none. Mike looked at Thelo with a somber expression, and Thelo's smile vanished.

"I guess I could do that," Mike said. He looked Thelo in the eyes. "As long as you go back to that sexy British accent you had before."

Mike's face broke into a big smile, and Thelo laughed his relief. This guy knew how to push his buttons, for sure. Mike laughed, too.

Thelo's phone signaled that the cab had arrived. The two men got up from the bed and went to the front door. Mike opened it and stood behind the door to conceal his nakedness while Thelo stepped outside. Thelo gave Mike a short wave as he walked down the front steps toward the waiting taxi.

Mike blew him a kiss and closed the door.

CHAPTER NINE
Monday

Christine drove Matthew back to Our Lady of Mt Carmel. As she pulled into the parking lot, Matthew said his thanks to her and got out of the car.

The morning hadn't been nearly as awkward as she'd feared. They awoke snuggled up together, something that Matthew had found delightful. It was another first for him.

There had been no time for breakfast since neither had thought to set the alarm and they woke up later than either of them had planned. Christine offered to let Matthew shower with her, but he correctly suggested that it would be a bad idea, given the lateness of the hour. She was happy that he hadn't woken up full of regret and shame over the events of last night. She genuinely liked him and didn't want him to feel guilty.

"Catholics are better than just about anybody at booking guilt trips," he said with a laugh when she mentioned her concern. "But I'm not taking one. I had a wonderful time last night. No regrets. Please don't worry."

Matthew was happy to find that he could get into the rectory without being seen. There were a few cars parked in front of the church when they arrived, but apparently, everyone was inside. He unlocked the front door and entered, still thinking about the pub, getting tipsy, and the night with Christine. He certainly hadn't expected the last part. If he'd known that's where the night would lead, he'd have likely found an excuse not to go. Alcohol can make your inhibitions go away, he thought, just like everyone says. He felt like he should be ashamed of himself, not just for breaking his vow of celibacy, but for having sex outside of marriage with a woman young enough to be his daughter. Try as he might, however, the shame eluded him. He smiled with the remembrance of the evening as he took off his ball cap and unbuttoned his shirt. A shower was going to feel fantastic.

The phone rang as he made his way to the bathroom and he detoured into the small study to answer it.

"Hello?" His eyes widened when he heard the voice of Bishop Garza on the line. "Yes, Your Excellency, of course. An hour? That will be fine. I'll see you then."

Thelo's alarm went off at eight, considerably later than he'd normally set it on a work day, but yesterday's long hours at work followed by the late night with Officer Mike had exhausted him. He figured that an extra hour or two of sleep would be necessary if he was going to be worth a damn. He could make up for the lost time with stamina and clear thinking.

He padded to the kitchen, tried to pour himself a cup of coffee, then cursed himself when he realized he hadn't set up the coffee maker the night before. He sleepily put in the water and ground coffee, turned the machine on, then made his way to his desk.

There were dozens of emails in his inbox, most of them spam or advertisements, as usual. There was one email from Zara, though, which he opened and read:

By the time you read this, I'll be on my way to see you! I told my editor that he should send me over there to cover the story about all those preachers giving The Sermon. He said that it was a big news story, but we don't do real news, just gossip. He couldn't justify the cost to send me. That's when I told him that I had a contact who could get me an interview with Joel Wood. You should've seen the look on his face! He had me on the next plane!

I'm finally going to meet you in person. I'm so excited!

Please introduce me to Ivan. I promise not to swoon.

Zara.

PS: you can get me an interview with Joel Wood, right?

Thelo stared at the screen, unable to believe what he had just read. Why on earth would she think that he had any pull with Joel Wood? Was she crazy? He was thrilled to finally meet her, but the circumstances were sketchy at best. He wondered what her editor would say when she came back without an interview.

A beep-beep-beep from the kitchen indicated that coffee was ready. Thelo got up, crossed the room to the kitchen area and poured a cup, then sat back down at his computer. There was no need to reply to Zara's email right away, since she wouldn't be able to read it until the plane landed, anyway. He launched his browser, then dug through the multiple layers of logins and passwords until he got to the file vault he had set up for Admin. He opened it and found folders inside, each one named for one of the pastors who had preached The Sermon. He clicked the one labeled 'Rabbi Jacob,' and it unpacked into thousands of emails from the rabbi's work account and his two personal accounts. The most recent one was sent last night, and the earliest was sent nearly twenty years ago. Thelo sighed. No wonder Admin didn't want to dig through all of this.

He took a sip of coffee and looked through the folder names, checking them against the list of people who'd preached The Sermon. All twenty-two of the names matched his list. Perfect. There was a text file as well, which he opened and read. It was from Admin.

Easier than I expected. Preachers don't think anyone's going to hack them, I guess.

Thelo took another sip of coffee. He knew where he was going to be for the next several hours. He took a deep breath, stretched, and then got to work.

Ivan drove to work as he usually did, but the stop-and-go traffic didn't bother him much for a change. His mind was busy with the events of yesterday and the possible ramifications of it all, but mostly, it was replaying the dream he'd had just before waking up.

In it, he was back in his childhood, sitting in church between his parents. The preacher screamed about sin and the wrath of God and all of that noise. Ivan had never liked that man, but the music in the service made going to church bearable. Ivan loved to sing the hymns along with the congregation, and he always looked forward to the choir's anthem every week. Ivan hated the sermon, though.

The preacher made eye contact, and suddenly Ivan was a teenager.

"You are going to hell!" the preacher screamed as he pointed at Ivan.

Ivan rose from the pew and returned fire. "No, that's impossible!"

The preacher was shocked into silence, then regained his thoughts and lowered his voice to a growl. "Sure about that, are you?"

Ivan stared the preacher down while the congregation held its collective breath. "Yes, I am," Ivan said, "I can't go to hell because that's where you'll be and God promised me I'd never have to see you again if I left this church."

The congregation roared its disapproval as Ivan ran from the building. He stepped outside, and a woman blocked his path, but not in a threatening manner.

"Hello, Ivan," she said.

Ivan stopped and looked at her, puzzled. "Who are you?"

"I am The One."

That's when Ivan woke up. He had no idea what to make of the dream, at least not the last part. The part inside the church was nothing new to him. It was just memories he had from his childhood and teenage years, compressed into a single event. Ivan dreamed about that stuff from time to time, especially when there was some religious story in the news. What he hadn't dreamt before was the episode with the young woman outside the church, the woman who called herself 'The One.' He wasn't sure what that meant, and it wasn't any memory he had from his past.

'Ivan.' That's what she called him. She was young, maybe twenty, with a blonde pixie cut and big green eyes. She obviously knew him, but he didn't recall ever seeing her before. It was a puzzle.

Luckily, the puzzle kept his mind off the traffic. He tapped a button on the steering wheel to activate his hands-free phone and then told Claire he'd be a few minutes late.

Christine interviewed Rabbi Jacob in the morning, then spent some time afterward talking to people on the street and in a few other churches as well. She also interviewed members of churches whose pastor hadn't preached The Sermon, to see if their reactions differed from those who had heard it first-hand.

She got home late that afternoon and transcribed all the recordings she'd made that day. Afterward, she noticed that she had a missed call from Father Matthew. She called him back, figuring he'd be busy counseling parishioners who were upset by his words at Mass on Sunday. The church switchboard patched her through and he picked up on the first ring.

"Father Matthew, I'm surprised to find you available."

"Please, Christine. You can just call me Matthew. I've got some news."

"Good news, I hope."

"Not really. I had a visit from Bishop Garza. Someone saw me at the pub last night, and they saw us leave together in a 'state of intoxication' as he put it."

Christine recoiled in her chair at the news. "Oh, I'm so sorry," she said. Guilt began to wash over her. "We should've gone somewhere farther away from the church, or just not gone at all. I feel terrible."

"No, no," Matthew said, "I have no regrets about last night. Bishop Garza was already planning to talk to me about the events on Sunday, anyway. That was the main reason for his visit, not this."

Christine wasn't put much at ease. "Are you in trouble?"

"We had a bit of a disagreement, you might say. About The Sermon, I mean." Matthew tried to make his words sound nonchalant, but Christine wasn't convinced.

"Oh, dear. Should I ask?"

"He was upset that my words were contrary to the history and teachings of the Church. He said that they could cause the parishioners to question the Church and it's authority."

"He's right, of course. What did you say?"

"I agreed with him! I told him that I have those same questions myself and that's why I was in the pub."

"I hope you explained it better than that."

"I did, of course. We had a long talk about the rules of the Church and the vows I took when I became a priest and the expectations the Church has for the clergy."

"And?" Christine began to relax a bit, but she still felt a little guilty.

"He thinks that I might've been speaking my own mind that day, rather than speaking words from God."

"He thinks you did it on purpose?"

"I don't think that would matter to him whether it was intentional or just my subconscious speaking," he said. He took a deep breath before continuing. "I've been suspended pending an investigation."

Christine gasped and nearly dropped her phone.

"Oh no! Oh, Fath… Oh, Matthew, that's terrible. Please tell me it's just temporary." Her guilt returned with a vengeance.

"We'll know that later. Bishop Garza doesn't want me to talk with the parishioners about any of this until he's had a chance to discuss things with the Cardinal."

"That sounds serious. I hope they don't do anything rash. You've been a wonderful servant of God for all these years."

"Thank you. That's very nice of you to say."

"I'm so sorry about all of this. Please let me know if I can help in any way."

Matthew took a moment, then got up his nerve. "Christine, would you like to have dinner with me tonight? Nothing fancy, just someplace casual with good food."

"I'm supposed to meet up with my coworker to compare notes again, but if you don't mind eating a bit late, I can swing it."

"Wonderful!" he said, with equal parts excitement and relief. "I, uh…" He paused while he chose his words. "I won't presume to expect anything other than dinner, if you're worried about that."

Christine blushed. "A gentleman, as always."

"How about Zorba's?" he asked. "Do you like Greek food?"

"I haven't been there in ages, that's a great idea. Let me check with my coworker. I'll call you back when I have a time."

"Perfect. Thank you, Christine. I really appreciate your friendship right now."

Thelo's phone rang. He fished around for it on his desk amidst the Chinese take-out containers and soft drink cans.

"Hi, Christine. Anything new?"

"Father Matthew is being investigated by the Church. He's on suspension."

"Whoa! That's a pretty harsh for a few words, don't you think?"

"The bishop is upset that people might begin to question the authority of the Church. He isn't sure that Father Matthew is being completely honest about the way it all happened."

"I guess I can see that, but still… wow."

"Yeah. Apparently, the Bishop is going to discuss it all with the Cardinal, but he doesn't want Father Matthew dealing with parishioners until then."

"So it's just temporary."

"Hope so. He's a good man and a good priest. The people love him there."

"Who else have you talked to?"

"I've been interviewing people all day, mostly laity. But I did get to interview Rabbi Jacob finally."

"Good! What did he say?"

"Pretty much the same thing as Father Matthew. He was just doing the regular thing, then there was a gap in time, and then everyone was looking at him like he was an alien or something."

"Right. They've collaborated their stories, at least. Anyone else?"

"I talked to some people from a couple of congregations that didn't get The Sermon. They're quite a bit more skeptical about it being a genuine message from God, as you can imagine. I asked the ones who thought it might be faked if they had any idea how it could've been done and they said they didn't know. But they were sure that God wouldn't have just spoken through just a few pastors. They say He'd have spoken through all of them."

"It's funny how people are so sure that they know what God would or wouldn't do," Thelo said.

"A couple of people said that they were happy that their pastor didn't preach The Sermon because that meant that God must be pleased with them. They're doing everything right, or so they think."

"I guess you could see it that way if you were supremely arrogant. I assume they don't think that part about the Bible being fiction applies to their church, either?"

"I didn't wax philosophical with them," Christine said. "I just let them talk, and I recorded what they said."

"That's why you're doing the human interest part, and I'm doing the investigative part. I'd have called them out on that bullshit and made them explain it to me."

Christine thought about that for a moment, then brushed it from her mind. Badgering the person being interviewed wasn't her style. She preferred a more conversational approach. "Speaking of the investigative story, have you got anything new?"

Thelo hesitated. "Christine, I'm going to need you to assure me absolute confidentiality," he said. "You cannot discuss any of this with anyone, not even Ivan. Not yet."

Christine was suddenly intrigued. "Wow. Um, yeah, okay."

"I'm serious, Christine. Nobody."

"I promise. What have you found out?"

"I've been searching through and cross-referencing a shitload of emails from the pastors that…"

"Hold on," Christine interrupted. "How are you reading their emails?"

"I'm not going to tell you."

"But isn't it illegal to read someone's private email?"

"It's illegal to hack in and get the emails, yeah," Thelo said. "But I don't think it's illegal to read them if someone else did that and then gave them to you."

"I think that's a gray area, especially if you asked that person to get them. Did you?"

"That's why I need your confidentiality," Thelo said. "Anyway, I ran the emails through some filters and cross-referenced everything from a few of these people, and there are some interesting developments."

"Like?"

"Well, it took a while to set up all my parameters, so there's still a ton of data to sift through, but I found out that Rabbi Jacob and three of the other local pastors definitely know each other, at least well enough to have sent emails back and forth."

"Well, that's not much of a bombshell." Christine sounded a bit disappointed. "Lots of the church leaders do things together. You see them at charity functions and stuff like that all the time. I'm not surprised they know each other."

"I figured as much. So I branched out, and the next two names I put into the filters were the Buddhist in San Francisco and the Muslim in New Orleans. Surely, they wouldn't be connected to the rest."

"And?"

"Well, one of the local pastors had emailed the Buddhist a few times, but not the Muslim. However, the Buddhist and the Muslim had both emailed a third party who isn't on our list of names. I don't know if that person is a pastor or not, but it is just super weird that those two guys would both email the same person."

"Maybe that 'person' is a business email or something," Christine said, almost annoyed that the news wasn't juicier. At least, she thought, the less Thelo finds, the more likely that The Sermon was a genuine miracle. "It's all fascinating, and there might be something there, but it's circumstantial at best."

"Yeah, I know. I'm still looking for connections and flagging those emails to read later. Hopefully, I'll find something worth reading."

"I don't want to hear that you're reading people's emails," Christine said. "It seems unethical."

"Yeah, I feel a bit dirty when I actually get to that stage," Thelo admitted. "But if you think that any email you send to someone only gets read by the person you send it to, you're pretty naive."

Christine shuddered. She wondered how many of her emails had been read by someone else. Suddenly, she remembered her dinner date with Matthew.

"Hey," she said, glad to get her mind out of the paranoia gutter, "what's a good time for you to meet up to compare notes today?"

"Do we need to meet up in person?"

Christine thought for a minute. "No, I don't guess so. I can send you the transcripts of my interviews today once I type them up, and you send me a synopsis of whatever you find."

"Great," Thelo said. "I want to keep plugging away at this, and I've got someplace to be this evening anyway."

"Me, too," Christine said. "Talk to you later."

Christine hung up and then called Matthew.

"We're on for dinner."

"Wonderful!" Matthew's joy was apparent. "What's a good time?"

"How about seven?"

"Perfect. My treat."

"Only if you let me pay for the cab."

"Deal. I'll walk to your place, and the cab can pick us up there at seven."

Thelo texted Mike that he'd be free for dinner. Mike called him back, and they set up a time and place, talked for a few minutes, and then hung up.

Thelo got back to work.

Zara Davies walked down the long corridor between the airport gate and the luggage carousel. She silently cursed the people who designed these long walks into the airport layout. Not only do you have to endure hours of cramped, uncomfortable seating, she thought, but then you have to walk a mile to get your bags. Going through the long queues in customs just added salt to the wound.

She dug her phone out of her purse and called Thelo.

"'Ello, love," he said when he picked up. "You on the ground already?"

"Yes, and I'm a tad disappointed." She rounded a corner and sighed as another long stretch of corridor presented itself.

"About what?"

"I got off the plane expecting a giant welcome party with balloons and streamers and half-naked dancing boys, but I saw none of that. Did you send them to the wrong terminal?"

Thelo laughed. "It's not like you gave me much notice that you were coming. I'd have been there myself, but I'm swamped with work, and you didn't even tell me which flight you'd be on."

"An investigative reporter can't find that out?"

"Not today, he can't. Too busy. I'm glad you're here, anyway. I can't wait to meet you."

"Likewise. Dinner later?"

"Sorry, I can't. You've got to give me more notice, love. I'm booked solid the rest of the day. How about breakfast tomorrow?"

Zara sighed. "That's probably better, anyway. I'm absolutely knackered, and I haven't even got my bags yet. I'd likely fall asleep at dinner, anyway."

Thelo laughed. "Text me the address of your hotel, and I'll pick you up in front at seven-thirty tomorrow morning."

"Seven-thirty? Bloody hell! You don't give a girl much time to shake off the jet lag, do you?"

"If you're a good girl, I'll take you to the office after breakfast and introduce you to Ivan."

Suddenly, the early hour didn't seem so bad. "I'll be a good girl," she promised. "At least until I meet him."

CHAPTER TEN

Joel Wood and Holly spent the day answering calls from friends and avoiding calls from the media. Holly was insistent, and Joel agreed, that they would get their story out there on their own terms, to their own hand-picked journalists. It was a system that had worked well for them in the past, and as their wealth and fame grew, so did the need to control their image. It seemed that the more money you made, the more people wanted to bring you down.

"Okay," said Holly as she sipped a glass of wine in their living room, "we're clear on the spin." She picked up a page of notes she'd written and read. "'The Bible is not something we need to focus on anymore, since it's not the Word of God. The real Word of God came directly from God, through you. Therefore, if people want to know how best to follow God's will in their lives, they need to come to church at Gloria Deo, or they need to tune into your telecasts.'"

"After all," Joel added, "you never know when God will speak through me again. You don't want to miss it!" He raised his own glass to her as an exclamation point.

"Have you thought about which media outlets you'll grace with an interview?"

"I have a couple of the usuals in mind, but I'm still a bit skittish about what they might ask me. I think I should set up a list of questions and just have them select from those, as usual."

"That has worked in the past, but you were only doing an interview every few months. You can't do multiple interviews in a couple of days and have everyone ask the same questions. It would be too obvious."

"You're right," Joel said. "Maybe just one interview, then."

"Or we just put out a press release. You say whatever you want, we'll video it and do a transcript. Then we just send it out to anyone and everyone who will run it. That way we control the entire thing, and there won't be a Q & A at all."

"Perfect. I should get to work on that right away, while the iron is still hot."

"Yes, go do that," Holly said. "I'll get everything ready to send it out once you're done. Don't make it too long, though. You know people tune out after the first minute or two. Less is more."

"And less is easier to write." He stood up, drank the last of his wine, then set the glass down and left for his study.

Holly finished her glass and left for her study as well. She sat down at her computer and powered up all the components, enjoying the familiar and comforting beeps and tones that signaled her escape into her realm. Once everything was ready, she launched her browser, her email, and the app she developed to track any mention of Joel's name on social media. A quick glance at the results showed that while they were apparently a hot topic shortly after the YouTube videos went viral, mentions of Joel and Gloria Deo had decreased dramatically in the hours since then. Since twenty or more other people had given The Sermon, people were more interested in the diversity of the religions that were affected than they were about Joel specifically. That was bad. If they didn't get his press release out as soon as possible, his ability to spin this into a 'look at me' event would be lost. Their hits had decreased by thousands with every passing hour. She sent out a few tweets with the hashtag #GodChoseJoel, but it was likely too late to get that noticed. The top trending hashtags at the moment were, '#WhatDoWeDoNow' and '#FalseProphets.' They were nearly equal in hits, showing that the world seemed to be evenly split between the believers who felt the Church had led them astray, and the others who felt that it was either a hoax or a conspiracy to undermine the Church.

She waded into the fray for a few minutes and immediately got disgusted at the stupidity and vitriol in the comments sections of the sites she visited. She closed down her browser and got to work getting all their media sites ready for Joel's press release.

Even though she knew that Joel was a fraud as far as his faith was concerned, she admired the showman in him. She treated his on-stage persona as a character, just as he did. When she disconnected husband-Joel from preacher-Joel, she could easily stand by his side on stage and support him. Once the cameras were turned off, and the crowds went back to their homes, it was just Joel and Holly, husband and wife, business partners, and media moguls. She was seen on Sunday mornings at the church supporting him from the stage, but other than that, Holly preferred to be behind the scenes, working in the background. She maintained the church's website, Joel's Facebook and Twitter accounts, and Gloria Deo's YouTube channel.

It was a busy life, but a good one. She even learned to tolerate the society functions, the fundraisers, the costume galas, the opening night banquets, and all those other things that a woman of a certain wealth is supposed to attend. If that was the price she had to pay to live in a mansion, fly on a private jet, and have paid staff to do her chores for her, then so be it. Still, she preferred the shadows to the spotlight.

The cab showed up at Christine's house right on time, and Matthew was waiting next to it with the back door open for her when she came out of the house. She smiled, got in, and he closed the door, then walked around to the other side.

"Such a gentleman," she said. "I can't remember the last time a date opened the car door for me."

"Is this a date?"

"Technically, yes. It's a dinner date."

Matthew smiled. "That gives me a bit of a thrill, actually. Another first."

"It's good to see you smile. I was prepared to spend the evening trying to cheer you up."

"I've spent a lot of time in prayer today," he said. "I'm not sure I got any definitive answers, but I'm at peace with things at the moment."

"That's good."

The cab arrived at Zorba's, a long-standing casual Greek restaurant in a part of the city known as Little Santorini.

Matthew opened the door for Christine, then she paid the cab fare, as they had agreed. They entered the restaurant and found the decor delightfully tacky. The walls were adorned with amateurish murals depicting ancient Greek ruins, and tiny Greek flags hung from the ceiling on strings like pennants at a used car lot. The tables sported blue-and-white checkered tablecloths and miniature Greek sculpture replicas as centerpieces.

Zorba's was filled with happy, noisy people. Greek music played over speakers at each corner of the room, and occasionally, people would break into song. Christine had taken a bit of Greek in college, but she didn't understand a word of it anymore, especially when it was sung by a bunch of off-key diners.

They chose a table along the wall away from some of the rowdier patrons in hopes that it would be easier to hear each other. A waitress came by in a blue and white uniform and took their drink orders, which were non-alcoholic this time. Both of them thought it wise to get a good night's sleep for a change.

"Cheers." Christine raised her glass of diet cola.

"Cheers."

They tapped their glasses together, which made a dull clack as plastic met plastic.

"I was thinking," Matthew began, after a sip of his iced tea, "that I might as well give you a proper interview."

"Here? I didn't bring my recorder."

"Oh, no, not here. I meant tomorrow, perhaps. On the record this time."

"That would be great," she said. "We'll set up a time once you know what your day looks like."

"My days are mostly free now, aside from prayer. The bishop cleared my calendar for me."

Christine winced. "Sorry. I wasn't thinking."

"No offense taken. Perhaps in the morning?"

"I'm going to be at Muhammadi Majid in the morning," she said. "I've heard that there might be a demonstration tomorrow. One of their imams said The Sermon on Sunday."

Matthew looked surprised. "He gave it on Sunday? Muslim prayer service is usually on Friday afternoons."

"That's one of the things I want to find out about."

"It must be quite a shock for them," Matthew said. "They have so many rituals and rules to follow. To have them proclaimed displeasing to Allah must be devastating."

"As it was for you and your fellow Catholics, I'm sure."

"Many of us, yes," Matthew admitted. "There are those who worship the ritual and the lifestyle as much they worship God, I'm afraid."

"Maybe that was the problem."

Matthew pondered that for a moment. "Maybe it was. There are numerous passages in Scripture that tell of Jesus scolding religious leaders for doing that."

"Yes, there are." She took another sip of her cola. "But, I'm not familiar enough with the Qur'an to know if similar passages are in it, too."

The waitress arrived back at the table. Both Matthew and Christine hurriedly chose something from the menu, embarrassed that they hadn't even looked at it until that moment. The waitress took their order and their menus and headed for the kitchen.

"Call me when you know what time you'd like to do the interview," Matthew said. "I'll make sure I'm available."

"Will do."

"Do you have a pen?"

Christine opened her purse and rummaged through it briefly. "Here ya go."

Matthew took the pen and scratched out a phone number on a paper napkin, then handed it to her. "That's the landline number in the rectory. You can reach me directly there without going through the church office."

Christine put the napkin and the pen in her purse. "I feel like an insider now." She grinned. "Thanks."

They spent the rest of the evening talking about anything but The Sermon, his release from duties, or her work on the story. Even without alcohol, they found that they enjoyed each other's company a great deal. Matthew was delighted to find that despite her young age, Christine was a fan of the Beatles, old black-and-white movies, and *I Love Lucy* reruns. Christine was equally surprised that Matthew had not only heard of N'Sync, but he even knew a couple of their songs. Well, at least the choruses.

The food arrived and they continued their conversation as they ate. Afterward, they each ordered a baklava for dessert, as much to stretch out the evening as to enjoy the sweetness and delicacy of the dish.

The conversation continued on the ride home, until the cab stopped in front of Christine's house. They were both surprised when they realized they had been holding hands. Matthew blushed, let go of Christine's hand, and she paid the fare as Matthew got out of the cab. He walked around and opened her door, then took her hand again and helped her out of the cab.

"Thank you for a wonderful evening," she said after the cab had driven away.

"The pleasure was all mine."

She kissed him on the cheek. "I'll call you tomorrow."

Matthew watched as she walked across her front yard, then waited until she had opened the door to her house and stepped inside. She turned and blew him another kiss, which he pretended to catch, then felt silly for doing so. He covered his eyes in mock embarrassment and shook his head. Christine giggled as she closed the door.

Matthew stood there for a minute, basking in the warmth of the evening, then turned and whistled a happy tune as he walked home.

Thelo met Mike at Chubby's Diner, a throwback to the diners of the 1950's. Thankfully, the waitresses weren't required to wear poodle skirts, and the decor wasn't much reminiscent of that bygone age, either. The only retro vibe to the place was the menu, filled with classic American diner fare like cheeseburgers, meat loaf, and old-fashioned milkshakes. There was a jukebox in the corner filled with Elvis and Motown records, but it rarely got played.

"How was your day at work?" Thelo asked.

"Not too bad. I'm supposed to monitor a couple of demonstrations tomorrow to make sure they don't get rowdy. How about your day?"

"I'm still looking for connections that link all those pastors. I've actually found a few more outside the States who preached The Sermon. They didn't get much attention since Europe and Asia and Australia are too far ahead of us in the day."

"I don't follow."

"Well, it happened to all of them simultaneously. Most of the pastors here were either in the middle of their services or at least still at their churches where there would be witnesses. But because of time zones, it was mid-to-late afternoon overseas already and they were all somewhere other than church. Like the others, they don't recall any of it. It was just a gap in time to them, so unless someone was there to tell them it happened, they wouldn't even be aware. I'm guessing there were lots more people who were affected, but they were alone at the time and simply had no idea it even took place."

"So everything happened simultaneously? I didn't know that."

"Apparently so. That makes it a little harder for me to work the hoax angle, that's for sure. The more occurrences I find, the harder it would've been to fake it. Plus, if you're going to go to all that trouble to pull off a hoax, it makes doesn't make sense to have everyone do the trance act at the same time. You'd have them all do it during their sermons so it would have the most impact, wouldn't you? Unless they did that to make it more believable as a genuine miracle."

"So you still think it might be a hoax?"

"I haven't ruled it out."

"I wonder how bad it will be if it does turn out to be fake?" Mike pondered, shaking his head. "All these people who are angry with their churches and stuff because they've felt lied to will have to figure out how to reconcile with them. I'm afraid it won't ease the tension much, if at all."

"What tension?"

"Everywhere I go, people are split down the middle between the those who believe that God is unhappy with them and the others who believe that whatever happened on Sunday was either faked, or it came from someplace other than God."

"Other than God? You mean they think it was satanic?"

"Some do. They think their church leader was possessed by a demon or something." He chuckled. "Or aliens. No matter what happens, there's always somebody who thinks it's aliens."

Thelo nodded.

They were silent for a few minutes while they ate their meals.

"This cheeseburger is amazing," Mike finally said. "I think I can feel my arteries hardening as I eat it."

Thelo laughed. "This chicken pot pie is loads better than those kidney pies my mum makes."

Mike wrinkled his nose at the thought of kidney pie.

"What about you?" Thelo asked.

"What about me?" Mike finished the last of his burger and reached for a napkin.

"Do you think it was a hoax?"

"I hope not," Mike said. He poured some ketchup next to the pile of fries on his plate. "I've thought for a long time that churches had lost sight of the important stuff, that they're basically in it for their own survival. This would be kind of a validation for me."

"The opposite for me," Thelo said. "I've gone for years believing that God doesn't exist. If this is real, then it shifts my whole perception of how the universe works. I'm not quite ready for that kind of shakeup in my life right now."

"Doesn't your life seem a little empty without a belief in some kind of god? I mean, it's comforting to think that there's some divine structure holding all this together."

"Considering all the terrible things in the world, I actually find it more comforting to believe that there's not anything overseeing it. If there is a god, He's doing a shitty job of it."

"I believe in a Supreme Being," Mike said. "But I don't think of God as some old white guy with a beard sitting on a golden throne in the clouds wearing a toga."

Thelo laughed at that, nearly choking on his root beer float. "So if you reject that image, what does your Supreme Being look like?"

"I have no idea." Mike swirled a fry in the pool of ketchup. "And I think I prefer it that way. Maybe He or She or It is just an energy field or other kind of invisible thing, like gravity."

"Gravity." Thelo waited for an explanation, but got none. "You're gonna have to elaborate on that, I'm afraid."

Mike ate a fry, then took a sip of his root beer. "It's like…" He looked for the right words. "Well, gravity affects us, all day, every day. But we don't have to think about it. It's just there. We don't worship it, we don't sing songs about it or pray to it, but it's always there, and it has an effect on everything we do."

"I see," Thelo said. "I might be able to get on board with that as long as this whatever-it-is doesn't plan our decisions in advance. That's one part of some religions I just can't handle."

"You don't like the idea that your fate is predetermined."

"No, I don't. If everything that's going to happen is already laid out, why make decisions? In the end, I'm just going to end up doing what was already planned for me, right?"

"Yeah, I don't buy into that either," Mike agreed. "Takes all the fun out of it."

Thelo pondered Mike's analogy as he ate his fries. "Are you still going to a church?"

Mike shook his head. "Not since I came out. Shit was pretty awkward after that, so I stopped going." He paused. "I was Southern Baptist."

"Ouch." Thelo winced.

"I shopped around for a while, tried out some other churches, other denominations, but after growing up in a church that was sure they knew exactly what God wanted, it was hard to go to a different church and hear them claim the same thing."

"You still believed that the Baptists were right?"

"Oh, no. I just figured that maybe nobody was."

Thelo nodded, understanding. "I almost joined the Jedi Church once."

"You did not!" Mike laughed, then stopped abruptly when Thelo shot him a serious look. "Did you?"

"No." He gave Mike a big grin.

"Okay, you got me."

Thelo took a long sip of his float. "I did look into it, though," he said. "It's not as crazy as it sounds."

"Not any crazier than a talking snake with a magic apple or a five-hundred-year-old man building a boat big enough to hold all the animals."

"Preach it!" Thelo raised his arms in false praise. He leaned forward as if he had juicy gossip to tell. "I know otherwise intelligent people who literally believe that shit."

"Next time you see those folks," Mike winked at him, "ask them how the kangaroos got from Australia to the ark in the Middle East."

"That's easy," Thelo said. "Qantas."

Mike laughed.

Joel sat in front of a green backdrop in the small studio in the east wing of his mansion. This section of the house was intentionally built away from the main living areas and had separate entrances for workers and guests who could come in and be part of his broadcasts without venturing into the other areas of the house. Holly had insisted on such a design when they were working with the architect. She didn't want their private residence to be "Grand Central Station," as she had put it. Two of Joel's media staff had come in on short notice to help him record his press release. He had typed it up on his laptop, which he then fed into a teleprompter just out of camera range. Holly had gone over the text as well, suggesting a few minor changes, but not many.

He sat in a leather wingback chair in front of some plastic ferns that didn't look nearly as fake on television as they did in the studio. He cleared his throat, adjusted his tie, and tried to look relaxed. Holly had applied some stage makeup to his face to reduce the glare from the lights and to hide the bags that were beginning to show under his eyes. Joel asked the young man behind the camera if he was ready to start. He was, as was the woman behind the soundboard.

He looked into the camera and began.

Brothers and sisters, I know that by now most of you have heard about the extraordinary event that took place at Gloria Deo on Sunday. Many of you have seen videos online or on the news of my words that day. Many of you are upset by those words, unsure of how they apply to your beliefs. They might even challenge your faith. Many of you are wondering if it was real.

I feel your concerns, and I understand them.

I assure you that those words did not come from Joel Wood. They came directly from God, and God is not pleased with His people or His churches. Let's revisit those words now.

"Your holy books are fiction."

The Bible, just like all other holy books, was written by people. Centuries of translation and changing meanings have made the Bible unusable as a history book. Clearly, the inaccuracies and contradictions contained in it should've made us aware of that fact, but we continued to worship those words as if they came from God Himself. Is it any wonder that God is upset by this?

"The rules you follow are not Mine. I am not pleased."

Every religion has a set of rules that you're supposed to follow. There are rules about how you should behave, what you should or should not eat, what you should wear, or even how to cut your hair. Like Jesus told the religious leaders of his day, these laws can get in the way of God's love for us. We become focused on them instead of on Him. This is also why God is not pleased.

So what do we do now?

We listen. We have heard God speak to us, something that hasn't happened in two millennia. A direct message from

God through me, Joel Wood. God, for reasons that only He can know, has chosen me to be an instrument of His Word. I am humbled at being chosen for this incredible honor, and I will do my best to remain open to any further messages that God has in store for us.

I won't pretend to know what God wants. If we can't look to the Bible for guidance, and we can't rely on religion's rules to bring us closer to God, then the only thing we can do is wait for God to speak again and give us direction. Since I have been chosen as a vessel of God's Word, as a microphone for God's voice, then I pray that you'll join me at Gloria Deo church every Sunday to hear what God wants for us. If you live too far away, or can't make it to our church for another reason, then you can tune into my broadcast every Sunday from your own homes.

God is making Himself known to us for the first time in many lifetimes, and He is doing it through Joel Wood, His humble servant.

These are exciting times, brothers and sisters.

Let us share them.

Together.

Joel smiled for a few seconds, then made a slicing motion with his finger in front of his neck.

"Cut." He was quite happy with himself.

CHAPTER ELEVEN
Tuesday

Thelo picked up Zara at the hotel right on time. He tooted the horn in greeting as he approached, and she gave him a big wave.

"You look great!" Thelo said when she got into the car. She was dressed in a smart gray suit top and jeans, both of which complimented and contrasted her wild shock of royal blue hair. Zara stood about five-foot-nine, with a slender frame and narrow shoulders. Her hair was done in one of those styles that take quite some time to fix, but looks no time had been spent on it at all. Thelo might've guessed that she just woke up and let her hair do whatever it did, but he knew her better than that. She likely spent an hour or more to make it look perfectly unkempt. At any rate, it suited her personality very well. She had enough class in her appearance to pull off walking into a reputable establishment without being scoffed at, but enough wildness to hang with folks on the fringes of society without being seen as a sell-out.

"You do, too." She closed the door. "It's about time we finally met."

"How was the flight?"

"It was fairly smooth, but there was one family on there with about twelve kids. None of them behaved very well, and the youngest ones took turns screaming and crying."

"So you didn't sleep much on the plane, I presume."

"I didn't sleep at all. I had half a mind to go to the parents and ask them why the rest of the plane should suffer just because they can't figure out how a condom works."

Thelo laughed. "But you didn't do that."

"I had a window seat. I didn't want to climb over."

They arrived at the coffee shop in no time. After they found a table and took a seat, the talk inevitably turned to work.

"So please tell me that you don't really believe I can get you an interview with Joel Wood," Thelo said.

"I was hoping you could. But I figured it was a long shot."

"How are you going to explain it to your editor if he flew you over here and you come back with nothing?"

"If I can't get a proper interview," Zara said, "I'll go to Joel Wood's next service on Sunday and pretend to be a visitor interested in joining the church. Then maybe I can get to talk to him that way, or at least get some dirt from other people who work with him."

"From what I've heard in the rumor mill, there's plenty of dirt."

"And if I can get some of that, it might be enough," Zara said, smiling. "My editor hates Joel Wood with a passion. Anything I can bring back that makes the guy look bad is going to justify the trip."

"Well… you know I told you that I had a source that can get me stuff," Thelo half-whispered.

"Yeah?" Zara sat up a little straighter and leaned forward.

"I've got about ten thousand emails of his. Maybe you can find something in there. Off the record, of course." Thelo winked.

Zara's eyes became saucers. She leaned even closer and talked in an excited whisper.

"Holy shit, are you serious?"

Thelo nodded.

She eased back in the booth with a grin. "There has to be something in there that I could use. You're a dear!"

"You can't directly quote any of them, though. Nothing that will make it obvious you've seen his email. I can't risk exposing myself or my source, you understand."

"Yeah, yeah, love. No worries. But I'll bet I can find some other people in his church who'll talk about whatever I find. If Joel's up to something he shouldn't be, then somebody is bound to know about it."

"Yes, but he has deep pockets when it comes to keeping his confidants loyal to him."

"When can I see these emails?" Zara whispered.

"I'm going to be working from home most of the day. I'll set up a file vault for you and move copies of Joel's stuff to it. I should be able to have that done sometime after lunch."

After breakfast, they got in Thelo's car and buckled in. Thelo started the engine and backed out of his spot. "Do you have plans today?"

"I'm wide open, love," she replied. "I figured that today would be mostly getting over jet lag and finding my way around."

"I was going to head to the office for a few minutes. I can drop you back at the hotel if you like, or you can come with."

"You'll introduce me to Ivan?" Zara asked excitedly.

"On the condition that you don't say anything out of line. He's my boss, remember? Don't get me fired."

"I'll behave myself," Zara promised. She wished she had worn something less corporate.

Ivan wasn't in his office, much to Zara's disappointment, but Thelo said he'd wait as long as he could before heading home. He sat down at his desk and caught up on some email and inter-office memos. A couple of hours had gone by when Zara saw Ivan across the room above the cubicle walls. Thelo stood up and got Ivan's attention with a wave.

"Remember: behave!" Thelo warned as they sat back down.

Ivan appeared a few seconds later, and noticed Zara in the chair across from Thelo's desk.

"Hello." He extended a hand. "I'm Ivan Carter, editor of the *Riverside Post*."

She blushed. "Hi," she said, unable to hide her excitement. "It's nice to meet you. I'm Zara."

"That's a lovely name to go with your lovely accent," Ivan said. "You must be Thelo's contact person from the UK. I didn't realize you were coming to visit."

"Last minute thing," she said. "Thelo speaks very highly of you. It's nice to meet you in person."

Ivan smiled, then turned to Thelo. "How is the research going? Have you found anything significant?"

"I've got a lot of stuff cross-indexed and categorized. I'm going to get into the meat of it today. Hopefully, there will be something I can follow up on."

"Fingers crossed." Ivan turned back to Zara. "What brings you to this side of the pond, Zara?"

"My editor wants me to get an interview with Joel Wood."

"You may have wasted a flight, then. Joel rarely does interviews, and when he does, he previews the questions and only agrees to answer the ones he picks. Most of the time, he just sends out a press release like he did this morning."

"He sent out a press release?" Zara and Thelo asked in unison.

"Yeah, we got it an hour ago. Thelo can pull it up on his workstation." Thelo began tapping on his keyboard.

"My editor hates him," Zara said.

"Your editor is not alone," Ivan said. "He has as many detractors as he has followers, and that press release is likely to double the count of both."

Ivan turned to leave, and Zara quickly scanned her brain for anything to say that might keep him around.

"Say, love," she said, "is there a break room around here where a girl might get a cup of coffee?"

Thelo looked at her as if to say, 'you know where the break room is, I showed it to you already,' but Zara answered his look with one of her own that said, 'shut up, I'm working this.'

"Sure," Ivan said. "I was just about to head there myself. You can go with me if you like."

"I'd love to!" Zara stood up.

Claire appeared from around the corner and handed Ivan a printout. "There's been some kind of disturbance at Muhammadi Majid," she said. "Several people were injured. A few were sent to hospital. I sent Jack Crowther over there as soon as it came across the police scanner."

"Oh, shit," Thelo's voice came from inside the cubicle. "I think that's where Christine was going this morning."

Holly sat at her computer, reading her monitors. One was full of social media posts, the second was Gloria Deo's website, and the third showed a list of data files. Joel's voice sounded from the doorway and broke her concentration.

"How many hits do we have? Are we viral?"

She looked at the second screen. "Typical numbers for a press release, but it's still early. We got mentioned on a couple of local news programs this morning, and we'll probably pick up a few more once the west coast wakes up."

"I thought it might get a stronger reaction than that," he said, disappointed.

"They've got other things to cover. The whole country has gone nuts over this. Unfortunately, your press release is just a small part of a much bigger story. Even the two stations who mentioned it didn't play it, at least not all of it. They just said that you'd released a statement, but they didn't give any details. We got a couple of hits after those shows aired, but not many."

"What do you mean, 'the country has gone nuts?'"

"Everyone's on edge. There was a mosque here in town that had some kind of attack this morning. Four guys just rolled up and started beating on some women or something. There was a Catholic church in Texas that got looted, and they lost several pieces of priceless art. There's a bunch of Mormons arguing that the anti-polygamy laws should be null and void, since the Bible is fiction now, and the gays are demanding that all the 'religious freedom' laws be struck down for the same reason. Robert Patterson even released a statement last night telling his followers that he thinks that you were speaking the words of Satan, not God. Then there's..."

"Hold on," Joel interrupted. "Robert Patterson said I was speaking for Satan? Are you shitting me?"

"Well, he said that all of the pastors who gave The Sermon were speaking the words of Satan. But he did mention you by name, yes."

"He's just trying to save his own ass because God didn't speak through him and he's afraid that people will start watching someone else instead."

"Not too different than what we put out there this morning," Holly reminded him. "It's just the other side of the same coin,"

"No, it's not. I was touched by God. Those words I spoke were His, and I'm His messenger."

Holly laughed, then saw the look on his face. She gaped at him. "You're serious?"

"I am. When I wrote that press release, I meant those words. Holly, I've never felt like this before. I believe that God is using me for something bigger than myself, bigger than us."

"What brought this on?" Holly asked, barely masking her surprise. "I didn't even think you believed in God anymore."

"I feel it in my soul, Holly. Once I got past the shock, and things settled down, I really understood what happened. I'm one of God's chosen few."

"You're one of God's users," she scoffed. "God doesn't speak through you any more than He speaks through Robert Patterson or any of the other guys who beg the flock for money every Sunday."

Joel's gaze would've burned her to a crisp if that were possible. He took a deep breath and lowered his voice to a growl. "Don't be such a jealous bitch. I used God to get rich, that's true, just like you've been using me to get rich all these years. I didn't mind sharing it with you because you helped me get where I am today. But God has chosen me. Not you, Holly. Me. I am God's mouthpiece. If you can't believe that and support me, then maybe you should find another gravy train to ride."

Joel stormed out of the room and left Holly in stunned silence. His angry footsteps echoed off the marble floors.

Ivan had already dialed Christine before Thelo could even fish his phone from his pocket. After several rings, Ivan heard her voicemail cue, and he left a message asking her to call back ASAP.

Thelo sent her a text as well, then anxiously watched the screen for any reply. There was none.

Ivan called Jack Crowther, the reporter that Claire had sent to cover the story. He was still on the way to the mosque.

"Jack, do you know Christine Marshall, the religion page editor?"

"Not personally, but I've seen her around, yeah."

"She may have been there this morning, and she isn't answering her cell. Can you find out if she's there and if she's okay?"

"Sure, boss. Traffic is pretty heavy, but I should be there in fifteen minutes or so."

Ivan hung up and relayed the news to Thelo and Zara.

Thelo's phone indicated the arrival of a text message. Ivan watched his expression as he read it.

"Is she okay?" Ivan asked, urgently.

Thelo shook his head. "It's not from Christine, it's from a friend of mine," Thelo said when he saw Mike's name on the screen. "Unrelated."

Thelo sent Mike a reply saying that it wasn't a good time to talk.

The phone dinged again, and Thelo read the message. He sat up straight. "Oh, hang on. He's at the mosque! He thinks he saw Christine leave in an ambulance."

"Call him back!" Ivan said, but Thelo was already ahead of him.

Ivan and Zara impatiently waited through Thelo's call, not getting much information from his side of the conversation. Thelo hung up and sighed.

"He saw a woman that looked like Christine being put into an ambulance. He couldn't tell for sure if it was her. He said there was an argument that escalated into a fight and three women went to the hospital. One of them might've been Christine. That's all I know right now."

Ivan called Jack Crowther again and updated him, then called Christine's cell and got voicemail. He didn't leave a message this time.

"It's great that you care so much about your staff," Zara told him. "I wish I could say the same about my boss."

"My staff are my children," Ivan said. "I hired Christine right out of college. I've watched her grow into a fine young woman, and she's been a great part of my team. After I made her the head of her department, I stopped having to think about the religion page. I know that every Sunday, I'm going to have great content, on time and on subject. If I'm under the gun some weeks, I don't even proofread it first, I just put it in. Do you know how rare that is for an editor to be able to say that?"

Zara nodded. "My editor goes through everything with a microscope," she said. "Then he sends it to a gauntlet of lawyers to see if we could get sued for printing it. Then it comes back and we rewrite some parts, and the whole process starts over. It's a wonder anything makes it onto the page at all."

Ivan understood. They stood in silence for a moment.

"Well, standing here isn't going to make the update on Christine come any sooner," Ivan said with some resignation. "I could use a distraction." He turned to Zara. "I believe we were about to go get a coffee."

Zara nodded.

"Thelo," Ivan said, "if you get any news at all, forward it to me right away."

"Sure, boss. I'm sure she's fine. It probably wasn't even her who went to the hospital." He set his cell phone next to his keyboard and got to work.

Ivan and Zara left for the break room. Along the way, Ivan pointed out various things in the newsroom, and Zara tried not to swoon.

Father Matthew was praying when he was startled by a knock at the rectory door. He quickly finished his prayer, crossed himself, and answered the door. Bishop Garza stood on the stoop.

"Your Excellency, come in." Father Matthew moved aside so the bishop could enter.

Bishop Garza was short and stocky with a round face and ruddy cheeks. His salt-and-pepper hair was cut short and neat and his facial expression was stern, as it always was, so there was no way to tell if this was a friendly visit or a scolding.

Father Matthew offered him tea, which the bishop politely refused. Both men took a seat in the living room, and the bishop carefully adjusted his black cassock as he did so. His large pectoral cross rested against his chest and caught a shard of sunlight that broke through between the window and the shade. Father Matthew felt decidedly under-dressed without his clerical attire.

"I will make this brief," the bishop began. "I have been in contact with Rome."

Father Matthew was silent, but his face showed a nervous anticipation.

"I informed them," the bishop continued, "of your words at Mass on Sunday and of the unrest that they have caused the Church in the days following. They were, of course, already aware of it."

Father Matthew shifted uncomfortably in his chair.

"You have put the Church in an awkward position, as I explained to you at our last meeting." Bishop Garza looked at Father Matthew and indicated that he wanted a response.

Father Matthew cleared his throat and hoped that his voice would sound confident and assured. It did not. "I am truly sorry for that, Your Excellency," he said. "But please understand that I have not brought this about intentionally. I was unaware of the words I said during Mass until the recording was played back to me. Those words were not mine."

"I explained that to them, of course, just as you had told me. I told them that you consider it to be a miracle and a direct message from God Himself."

Father Matthew waited for him to continue. The bishop looked him in the eye and held his gaze until Father Matthew became uncomfortable.

"The Vatican is also aware that there are others who said the same words that day. Unlike you, however, the Cardinals do not believe that this fact supports your assumption that the message was divine."

"How can they presume to know what happened? They weren't here. They didn't feel what I felt. They don't know me." Father Matthew's frustration was obvious.

"They know about you." Bishop Garza's calm demeanor was a sharp contrast to Father Matthew's. "They are quite aware of you, in fact, since you were instrumental in the arrest and conviction of several priests in this diocese. You have a reputation in Rome of being something of a troublemaker, a priest who is willing to put his own agenda ahead of the well-being of the Church."

"Those priests were molesting children!" Father Matthew shook his head in amazement as tears of frustration welled up in his eyes.

"How can the Church condemn me for having them removed from the priesthood?"

"The Catholic Church is an important part of the lives of more than a billion people, Father. A billion people. If those people begin to doubt the sanctity of the Church or its leaders, then a billion people might lose their faith in the Church and may even lose their faith in God. Yes, what those priests did was wrong, and the Church would have taken action to prevent them from doing those things again. But by having them arrested, by bringing in the police rather than letting the Church handle it, you cast doubt upon the sanctity of the Church and its clergy. Can you understand this?"

"I cannot! I cannot understand how the reputation of the Church is more important than the well-being of those children!"

Bishop Garza waited for Father Matthew to calm down. He spoke with an even, steady tone. "Sometimes we must look beyond the immediate and focus on the greater good for the long term."

Father Matthew looked at the bishop with disgust. "I thought that's what I was doing." Tears rolled freely down his cheeks.

Bishop Garza shifted a bit in his seat as he continued. "Given your history, the Vatican doubts that God would choose you as the sole Catholic priest to deliver a divine message. Surely, if God had spoken, every priest would have also received that message. Surely, the Pope would've received the message as well. But the others who spoke those words were of different faiths, some of which are not even Christian. God would not speak through people who do not believe in the Messiah, in our Lord Jesus Christ. The only possibility is that it was not God who was speaking at all."

"I can't believe what I'm hearing," Father Matthew said. "So they think that I and all those others faked it?"

"That was a consideration. But it was quickly ruled out as implausible. They believe that this is a case of possession."

"*What?*" Father Matthew leaped from his chair. "Your Excellency, you can't believe that!"

"Calm down, Father, please."

Father Matthew fought to regain his composure, then sat back down. He shook his head in disbelief.

The bishop continued. "We cannot let this event bring down centuries of good works by the Catholic Church, nor can we allow the continued service of a priest who may be possessed by the forces of evil."

Father Matthew stared at the bishop through his tears in shocked silence. Try as he might, he was unable to find words.

The bishop wasn't finished. "The Cardinals have asked that you submit to an exorcism."

The bishop waited for a response, but was met with only silence. Father Matthew sat with his head down and his fists clenched.

Bishop Garza stood up to leave. "I understand that this is a shock," he said, "but we cannot allow this situation to fester. I will need an answer by the end of the day."

"I don't need that much time," Father Matthew said through clenched teeth, as he again rose from his chair. "I will not submit to an exorcism."

The bishop sighed. "Then you will be laicized. We feel that it is the only way."

Father Matthew gaped at him. "So now it's 'we,' and not 'they,'" he said, disgusted. He made his way to the front door and opened it. "You may leave now."

"Please pray about this, Father," the bishop pleaded as he stepped to the door. "We fear for your soul. Possession is not to be taken lightly."

Father Matthew fought to keep his voice calm. "You may leave now, Your Excellency."

The bishop stepped outside and heard the door slam behind him.

Father Matthew leaned against the door, put his head in his hands, and wept.

CHAPTER TWELVE

Holly felt as if she were walking a tightrope. Her world was hanging in a precipitous balance, and one wrong move could bring everything down into a bloody mess. She typed away feverishly at her keyboard, hidden behind her monitors, lost in a world of numbers, passwords, and account balances. Joel's newfound piety would be bad for business. It's one thing to play a role on stage, then come back to the real world when the show is over, but it's another thing to actually believe this shit. The role-playing Joel can think clearly, make rational decisions, and understand that what he says can either make money or cost money. But the Joel who believes that God has anointed him as some kind of modern-day messiah? That Joel is someone who can bet everything they have and lose. Even if God had actually spoken through him that one time, and Holly wasn't convinced of that, it might be another two thousand years before God speaks again. How long will Joel's followers wait?

The role-playing Joel would simply write the script, say some words while pretending to be in a trance, and then hundreds of thousands of people would tune in and send money. Everything would be fine. Pious Joel, however, would just sit and wait for another message to come from on high, people would get bored, and the money would stop coming in. Pious Joel needed a reality check.

Holly thought back to the early days. She had been impressed with Joel from the beginning. The day he delivered the ninety-minute eulogy for his father was a signature moment in her life. As a television journalist, she understood that both the choice of words and the delivery were important when you wanted the viewer to believe you. Joel's eulogy performance showed his talent for that as well as his natural charisma. She wept on camera as she delivered the coverage that day, a clip that was replayed across millions of screens after the national media picked it up. It helped make Joel a sympathetic superstar, and it also helped her get the best access whenever Joel did something newsworthy. They got to know each other, and when Holly broke through the professional barrier and asked him out to dinner, he was intrigued.

On that very first date, Holly was upfront about her motives. She wasn't one of those girls who was captivated by his good looks or his charm, she told him, but she was attracted to his talent and his potential. When she described her vision for them as a married couple, he was taken aback. He told her that he wasn't ready to settle down yet, certainly not after one date. She explained that he wouldn't have to settle down at all, that they would be business partners disguised as a married couple. If he could keep his promiscuity under the radar, then he could have a different woman every week. That was fine by her, just don't let anyone find out. Image is everything, she explained. Image and careful financial planning. She could give him both.

She wasn't successful in convincing him of her worth at first, but he was intrigued enough to give her a second date. More conversation, more visionary pitches about his potential fame and fortune, and a wild, uninhibited night of lovemaking got her a third date. When a photo of the up-and-coming boy preacher and his TV reporter girlfriend made the front page of a supermarket tabloid, Joel found himself getting recognized by strangers on the street. He loved the attention, he loved the women who wanted their photo taken with him, and he loved the extra money showing up in the collection plate every Sunday. When Holly let on that the tabloid thing had been her idea as a tiny example of her skills in marketing and image control, Joel was impressed rather than offended. Over the next two years, Holly had their courtship and 'romance' carefully documented by the tabloids, the celebrity magazines, and various newspapers. Joel Wood became a household name and a media darling.

Their wedding was covered extensively by the media, not only because they were the 'it couple' at the time, but also because Holly had sent invitations to celebrities, sports figures, politicians, high-profile CEOs, and anyone else she could think of who would draw attention. Most of the invitees declined since they didn't know the couple at all, but enough of them accepted out of curiosity that the wedding soon became a hot ticket. A few of those who initially declined even changed their minds and asked to be re-invited. Paparazzi showed up in droves to shoot the happy couple and all of their famous 'friends.'

In the years following, Joel polished his on-stage persona into a powerhouse of charisma. Holly quit her job as a television reporter to handle Joel's business affairs, but before she wrapped up her career as a journalist, she convinced the local TV station to begin airing Gloria Deo's Sunday service.

Joel's sermons made people feel good about themselves. There was no threat of eternal damnation, no need for repentance, just a message that God loves you and wants you to be happy. This was a far cry from the hellfire and brimstone message that the other tel-evangelists spewed each week, and those who liked to attend church via the magic box in the living room found Joel and his message irresistible. Ratings climbed, more stations picked up the program, and within a year, Gloria Deo was seen on television screens across the country.

Joel and Holly were perceived by many to be the perfect Christian couple. He was the head of the household, and she was the support-ive wife by his side. They were young, attractive, and successful.

When the media began to ask when they would have children, Holly came up with a story. She said they'd been trying to have a child and they were hoping that God would bless them with a child very soon. It kept them in the tabloids off and on for over a year, and when Holly invented and shared the 'heartbreaking news' that a fertility doctor said she couldn't conceive, the world wept with her. The donations to the church more than doubled for two months after that.

Joel asked her what they'd do if she accidentally got pregnant after telling everyone she couldn't have kids. Holly said that either she'd quietly have an abortion someplace, or they'd say it was a miracle from God, and then buy an island with all the money people would send. She hadn't seen Joel laugh like that in ages.

In spite of the business nature of their marriage, Joel and Holly were quite fond of each other. They both had 'friends with benefits' on the side, and Joel had his raunchy poker nights, but they still had the occasional romp in the sack with each other. It was an unusual relationship, but it worked for them.

Or at least it had. Now Joel had gone off his rocker, letting this God thing interfere with rational thinking. Holly wasn't about to let that sink them now, not after all they'd built together. She planned to get Joel to snap out of it by showing him the cold, hard financial future if he continued on this path, but she wasn't going to stick with just one plan. Holly never stuck with just one plan.

Ivan and Zara reached the employee break room, and he asked what she liked in her coffee. Ivan pushed the appropriate buttons on the automated coffee machine, a freestanding behemoth that could serve nearly limitless variations of tea and coffee beverages. Once Ivan had chosen Zara's preferred options, he pushed the button marked BREW and watched a cup drop into place behind a clear plastic shield. Then nothing. Ivan stared at it, shrugged, and pushed BREW again. A second cup dropped into place, neatly nested inside the first. Then nothing. The machine didn't even make its familiar grinding and hissing noises.

"Well, shit," Ivan said. "Looks like it's broken again."

He went across the room to a crowded countertop area that contained a small microwave, a sink, and a standard coffee maker that someone had labeled 'Plan B.' It was empty.

"I guess we're out of luck," Zara said.

Ivan checked the cabinets, but found no coffee to make a fresh pot. "This is not a 'do without coffee' kind of day," he said. "There's a coffee shop across the street, if you're up for a short walk."

"My jet lag thanks you for your ability to think of a Plan C."

They left the break room and made their way outside to the street, then walked to the corner to cross. On the opposite corner was a tiny building with a few tables and chairs outside. The sign above the building showed a pair of cartoon coffee beans wearing sunglasses. Under that, the name 'Beanz.'

Zara wrinkled up her nose. "I'll be so glad when the trend of ending plurals with a zed is over."

"Agreed," said Ivan, "but the coffee's good."

Zara took a seat at one of the tables outside while Ivan disappeared into the tiny shop. He returned a few minutes later, chuckling.

"The place is jammed in there, mostly with my employees. They all looked like scared rabbits when they saw me come in."

"Because they should be at work?"

"Yeah. I just raised my voice and announced that I was aware that there was no coffee in the break room, so nobody was getting fired for being there."

Zara laughed. "They're all afraid of you?"

"The rookies are. Maybe a few of the others, if they have a habit of missing deadlines. That's the one thing I can't tolerate. Reporters who don't understand the importance of deadlines probably think I'm the meanest boss ever."

Zara nodded, then sipped her coffee. "Thanks for the jet lag juice," she said. "It's perfect."

The two of them made small talk and Ivan periodically checked his phone for messages, hoping to hear some word about Christine. None came. Occasionally, some of Ivan's reporters would pass by their table on the way back to the office and introduce themselves to Zara, hear her accent, and welcome her to the US. That would be followed by a 'now get back to work,' from Ivan, delivered in a comically stern voice that Zara found sexy as hell.

"I couldn't work for you," she finally admitted.

"Why's that?"

"I have a personal rule about never sleeping with the boss."

Ivan nearly spit out his coffee at that, and he laughed. Zara was relieved that he wasn't offended by her remark and she laughed, too.

"I have the same rule," he said. "But it's never been one I've had to employ."

"But you're *gorgeous*. Surely some of them hit on you."

"Maybe they do," he said. "I'm just not in that zone when I'm at work. I wouldn't notice."

Zara shook her head and wondered how many of Ivan's employees were pining away in their cubicles for the handsome boss who never picked up on their flirting. She looked up at him over the brim of her cup. He was staring at something across the street, with his eyes wide and his mouth slightly open. She turned to see what had gotten his attention, but nothing struck her as out of the ordinary.

"What is it?" she asked him. "What's wrong?"

Ivan paused, not sure if he dared say anything. He was afraid that maybe what he saw wasn't there at all. "Do you see that group of people across the street, waiting for the light to change?"

"Yes. What about them?"

"Do you see a woman wearing a blue hoodie and green pants?"

Zara scanned the pedestrians as the light changed and the group crossed the street toward them. "Yes, I see her. Someone you know?"

Ivan was relieved that the woman wasn't just in his imagination, but that brought new questions to his mind. "Kind of," he said. "She showed up in a dream of mine the other night."

Thelo tried to keep his mind on his research, but there was only so much he could look up on the work computer. He didn't dare access his file vault from here. There just wasn't enough security on a network of interconnected machines like the one at the *Post*. His phone signaled an incoming text, and he rushed to pick it up.

I'm ok. No signal here. Just got wifi to work. Tell Ivan.

Thelo breathed a sigh of relief, then replied,

Where RU?

An eternity passed before her reply came.

St. Luke's. I'm fine, just bruises. No need to visit. Can't get a signal here, only wifi. Call a number for me and tell him I'm OK?

Thelo replied that he would do that, no problem, but he was going to visit anyway. She sent him the number.

He powered off his computer station and called Ivan's cell number. "Hello?"

"Christine is at St Luke's, she's bruised, but otherwise okay."

"Fantastic news, thanks."

"Is Zara still with you?" Thelo asked.

"Yes, she's here," he said. "Listen, why don't you go ahead and stop by to see Christine. Zara will be fine here awhile, and I can take her back to her hotel later."

"Err… okay," Thelo said. "What's going on?"

"We're busy. Call me back after you've seen Christine and give me an update."

"Will do," Thelo said.

Thelo hung up the phone, then called the number that Christine had given him.

"Hello?" came a man's voice on the other end.

"Um, hello, my name is Thelo Brown, I'm a coworker of Christine Marshall."

"She gave you this number? Is something wrong?"

"She was involved in a scuffle of some kind this morning. She's fine, but she wanted to let you know that she's at St Luke's hospital."

"Dear God," the man said. "Thank you for telling me, Thelo."

"You're welcome," Thelo said, realizing that he didn't even know the name of the person on the other end.

Father Matthew hung up the phone and dried the tears from his face. He was worried about Christine, even though Thelo said she was okay. Still, he would go to see her right away. Father Matthew felt a bit of relief to have his own sorrow pushed from the front of his mind, then felt guilty for it. He called for a taxi, paced the floor for a few minutes, then had an idea. He quickly undressed, then donned black slacks and a black shirt. He pulled out his priest's collar, which he affectionately called his 'dog collar,' and put it on. The taxi arrived, and he hurried out the door.

Christine ached. She had a couple of bruised ribs, but thankfully nothing had been broken. There were some ugly bruises on her arm where she'd tried to block the attacker's swings and a nasty scrape on her left knee where she had hit the pavement when she fell. Christine considered herself pretty lucky, all things considered. She hadn't even wanted to come to the hospital, but the paramedics told her that they needed to check for internal injuries, so she reluctantly agreed. After the adrenaline of the moment had subsided, she realized how much pain she was in, and was happy to be in a place that could prescribe pain meds.

A worried Father Matthew showed up in her room.

"Don't panic, I'm fine," she assured him.

"Thank God," he said. "I worried that maybe your coworker had just downplayed things on the phone."

"You're wearing your collar," she noticed. "So you've been rein-stated, then?" She managed a smile.

"No," he said, shaking his head sadly. "I didn't know if you were allowed visitors yet, and I've found that the collar can sometimes work as an all-access pass. I wore it just in case."

Matthew sat down beside her bed and took her hand in his. Christine turned to look at him and saw genuine concern for her on his face, even though his own life was in turmoil at the moment. The Church could use a lot more priests like him.

"Do you know when they'll come to their senses and let you go back to work?" she asked.

Matthew shushed her. "We can talk about it later. How are you? What happened?"

Christine took a deep breath, winced with pain, and reminded herself not to do that again. "I was at the mosque, Muhammadi Majid," she began. "Like you said, Muslims have a lot of rules they're supposed to follow. I wanted to find out if the people who worship there had stopped following any of them in light of the apparent message from Allah on Sunday. Plus, I'd heard there might be a dem-onstration there, so I wanted to be there to cover it."

"Right," Matthew said.

"There were some women outside the mosque when I got there," Christine continued. "They were having a rather heated discussion. Two of the women there were not wearing their hijabs and the other women, four or five maybe, were chastising them for it. I introduced myself and asked them if they would answer some questions. They were hesitant at first, but then one of the women with a hijab pointed to the pair of other women and said, 'Why don't you ask them why they want to disgrace themselves like that?'"

Christine took a sip of her water, then continued. "The pair of women didn't say anything, so I asked the group why they were upset, since I thought it was up to the individual woman whether or not she wore the head covering. One of the women said, 'the hijab is not required, but modest dress is. These harlots are dressed like whores.'"

Father Matthew whistled the sound of a bomb dropping. Christine nodded, then continued.

"They weren't dressed immodestly at all," she said. "They had on some bright colors, and one of them was wearing shorts, but they would've blended in most anywhere. That's when I heard a male voice behind me agree with the 'whores' comment. I turned around, and there were two men there. They joined in on the arguments and began calling the two women 'sluts' and 'tramps' and a number of other things. One of the men approached one of the two women like he was going to put a hand on her, but she got a clear shot and kicked him in the groin. The other man moved in and started swinging, and the other women joined in, too. I got caught in the ribs by a couple of the swings, and I bruised my arm blocking some others. I lost my balance and fell onto the sidewalk. Scraped my knee."

She pulled back the sheets and showed him her knee, which was covered in gauze and tape.

"What about the other women?" Matthew asked. "Are they okay?"

"I don't know," Christine said. "I think they ended up here as well, but I don't know how badly they were hurt. It was over pretty quickly because there happened to be a police officer driving by at the time. He hit the siren and ran over to us right after it got started."

"I'm guessing that the police are keeping a close eye on all of the houses of worship for a while," Matthew said. "I see a patrol car drive by Mt Carmel several times a day."

"So tell me what's the status with you," Christine asked him. "When do you get your job back?"

"We'll talk about it once you're out of here," he said. "You just focus on healing yourself and get some rest."

Christine nodded, even though she wanted the update. Matthew let go of her hand and stood up.

"You said the other women may have been brought here to this hospital. Do you know their names?"

"I hadn't gotten their names yet," Christine admitted.

"I'll see if I can find them, then. See if they're okay, let you know how they're doing."

"Thanks," Christine said. "You're an angel."

Matthew uttered a slight 'hmmph.' "Maybe you should tell that to the Vatican," he said.

Christine gave him a puzzled look, but he just bent down to kiss her cheek. She turned her head at the last second and planted her lips squarely on his. She put her hand on the back of his head and held him there, kissing him deeply. He pulled away quickly when he heard a man clear his throat to get their attention.

Thelo was standing at the doorway with a smirk on his face.

"I see you're feeling better," he said to Christine. He turned to the man beside her. "Father Matthew, I presume?"

CHAPTER THIRTEEN

"Can you see her?" Zara called.

"I lost her," Ivan yelled back. He scanned the people up and down the block.

Zara was having a hard time keeping up as she and Ivan maneuvered through the crowd on the sidewalk. He hadn't sufficiently explained what he meant when he said he had seen the woman in a dream, but Zara was certain that he meant it in a literal sense, as opposed to 'the woman of his dreams' sort of thing. Ivan had tried to brush it off. He told her it was crazy, that he had just imagined things. Zara finally convinced him that if he honestly thought this woman had shown up in his dream, he would forever regret not getting a better look at her, just to make sure. By the time she got him to agree, the woman had a two block head start on them.

Ivan reached the next intersection and had to wait at the corner for traffic to clear. Zara caught up with him, out of breath.

"Is that a metro station?" she asked, pointing to a set of descending stairs across the street. "Maybe she went down there."

The light changed, and the pair hurried across. Ivan gave one last look around, but he didn't see the woman anywhere.

"Come on," he said. "You're probably right about the metro."

They took the steps two at a time into a large underground room that glared with garish fluorescent lighting. Sounds echoed off the concrete walls and floor, turning the murmur of the crowd into a dull roar. A metro train sat at the platform and throngs of people navigated their way through the narrow doorways, some in, some out. Ivan caught sight of the woman as she made her way to the train.

"Hey!" he called out, but she didn't react.

Ivan tried to get closer, tried to get the woman's attention. He got as far as the turnstiles, but had to stop there because he didn't have a ticket. The metro train would be long gone by the time he could buy one. The woman in the hoodie was one of the last to board the train. The doors were still open, but she had her back to them. Ivan leaned as far as he could over the turnstiles and cupped his hands to his mouth for extra volume.

"Hey!" he called again. She did not turn, although a few other people on the train looked his way. "Are you The One?"

The woman turned around to face him. She was petite, slender, with green eyes and a blonde pixie cut under her hoodie. It was the girl he'd seen in his dream.

"I need to talk to you!" he pleaded.

The woman extended two fingers of each hand, crossed one set of fingers on top of the other, then moved her right hand back and forth twice. The doors closed and the train pulled away, leaving a bewildered Ivan and Zara behind.

"What was that?" Zara asked. "What was that thing she did with her hands?"

"Sign language. She said, 'soon.'"

Joel Wood sat in his study and prayed for the first time in a long time. Of course, he "prayed" during the services every Sunday at Gloria Deo, but those prayers were just a script, just words. This time he prayed with sincerity, alone in the quiet room. He knelt on the floor in front of his desk with his hands clasped together like his father had taught him at a very young age. He prayed for more guidance, for a better understanding of the words he'd said at the last service, and that people would come to a greater understanding of God through those words. Mostly, he prayed that God wouldn't wait too long before speaking to him again.

He was startled out of his meditation by a call on his landline. He picked it up and heard the booming bass voice of Cletus.

"I saw that press release you put out," he said. "What the fuck do you think you're doing?"

Joel was annoyed at the tone of Cletus' voice. "Good afternoon, Cletus. I told the other guys before you arrived at The Bunker that I wouldn't leave the three of you out of this."

"It sure as hell doesn't sound like anybody's included except for you. If people buy into your bullshit, my church will be empty next week."

"That may be true," Joel said. "But the important thing is that I've been contacted directly by God. I can't even explain how it feels."

"You didn't seem to be feeling it much at the game Sunday night."

"I was still in shock. I hadn't really thought it through then, other than how I could spin it. But then I realized the significance of the fact that the rest of the people who said the words were all from different faiths. God spoke to people from every religion, Cletus. All at once, all with the same message. Can't you see how that's obviously a miracle?"

"It's a miracle that God didn't lightning bolt your ass," Cletus said. "If God is gonna start talking through people, He sure as hell ain't gonna pick you. Or me. Or Mark or Jonas, either. We're not what you'd call model Christians, in case you've forgotten."

"That's the point." Joel was surprised that he'd need to explain. "If God is going to tell everyone that He's unhappy with us, who better to choose than a guy like me? A preacher with a huge audience who looks to him for guidance, but who is, in reality, a hypocritical sinner himself."

Cletus couldn't believe what he was hearing.

"I'm going to come clean, Cletus. I've been praying like crazy, but I haven't gotten much insight. I think my sins are blocking the reception."

"What to you mean, you're going to come clean?" There was twinge of fear in Cletus' voice.

"I'm going to confess my sins to the world. I need to be right with God if I'm going to be His spokesman. The people need to know that if God isn't pleased with us, it's our own fault. We've been fooling ourselves for too long, Cletus. We need to start making things right, and I need to lead by example."

"Surely, you're not going to tell everybody what you've been doing."

"I think I have to," Joel said. "It's the only way. God gave me a message, and that message was, 'I'm not pleased.' I need to make sure He sees that I have heeded that message before He speaks through me again."

"Well, you can leave me the fuck out of it," Cletus said. "Don't you dare mention me in your little confession."

"I'm sorry you feel that way, Cletus. I won't mention names, but I will confess my sinful ways. You should do the same."

"Fuck that. God knows what I do. I don't have to tell Him about it in front of the congregation. Do Mark and Jonas know about this?"

"Not yet. I've been too busy praying."

"I'll tell them," Cletus said. "They won't be any happier about it than I am, I can promise you that."

"Thank you, Cletus. I'll pray for all of you."

"Fuck off."

Cletus hung up.

Thelo grinned at Christine as Matthew left the room to check on the other women who had been attacked.

"Don't say it." She smiled weakly. "I've said it to myself a dozen times or more."

"He's old enough to be your father."

She made a face. "Bad pun."

Thelo caught the unintentional double entendre and chuckled.

"Sorry," he said. "How you doing?"

"Sore, but nothing's broken. What have I missed? Have you learned anything new?"

"Not really. I need to be on my home computer to dig through the data I have," Thelo said. "It's a more secure connection than the one at work."

"Gotcha. Did you tell Ivan that I'm okay?"

"Yeah, but just briefly. He said he was busy and we'd talk later."

"That's not like him," Christine said. "Is something wrong?"

"Last I know, he was going for coffee with Zara, my contact from the UK who arrived last night," Thelo explained. "She didn't answer her phone, either."

"Strange."

"She has a huge crush on him, and I wouldn't put it past her to put the moves on him as soon as they were alone. Now that I think about it, Ivan did seem to be a little out of breath when I called."

Christine's jaw dropped. "Holy shit, are you kidding me? Somebody finally broke through the ice? Do you think..." She shook her head as her voice trailed off. "No. No way. Ivan doesn't mix his personal life with his job. He's not gonna get a nooner on a work day."

They both laughed.

"I'll call him back." Thelo reached into his pocket for his phone.

"Not from here, you won't," Christine said. "No signal. I think they block it or something."

"I'll call him when I get back outside, then. Do you need anything?"

"No, thanks. I'm probably going to get released pretty soon. They aren't going to have me take up bed space just for bruised ribs."

"Send me a text if anything changes. I'm going back to the office for a bit. I can give you a ride to the mosque to get your car if you need me to."

"Thanks," she said. "I can get a cab. You get back to work."

Zara's phone rang inside her purse.

She fished it out and answered it. "It's bloody weird over here, where are you?"

"Nice to hear from you, finally. Is Ivan there?"

"No. I'm sitting in your cubicle and Ivan is in his office with the door closed. He's pretty freaked out right now."

"What happened? I tried to call you, but you didn't answer."

"We were running down the street chasing after some woman in a hoodie. I guess I didn't hear the phone."

"Why were you chasing a woman?"

"I'll explain it all when you get here, love. Did you get to see your friend? How is she?"

"She'll be fine. I'm on my way back to the office now, maybe half an hour."

"You want me to tell Ivan that your friend is okay, or are you gonna call him?"

"I already tried to call him," Thelo said. "His phone goes right to voicemail. He must've turned it off or something."

"I'll knock on his door, then. Tell me what you want me to say."

Thelo related the update on Christine's condition and her probable release from the hospital that day. He thanked Zara for relaying the message, told her he'd be there shortly, then pushed the button on the steering wheel to hang up the phone.

Holly was watching the progress bar on her download reach the 100% mark when her cell phone rang. She looked at the caller ID and raised an eyebrow.

"Cletus?" she asked, surprised. "Did you want to talk to Joel? I thought you had the number for his study."

"I do, and I've already talked to him today. Tell me, Holly, is your husband for real right now?"

"What do you mean?"

"About God talking through him and shit," Cletus said. "He actually believes that?"

"That's what he told me. I'm as shocked as you are."

"Do you believe him?"

"I don't know what to believe," she admitted. "But I'm preparing for the worst."

"So you know about his plan, then? He's really going to do it?"

"Wait," she said, suddenly nervous. "Do what? What plan?"

"He said that he's going to go out there on Sunday and tell everybody what he's been doing."

"What he's been doing? Surely you don't mean…"

"The girls, the poker games, the fucking around… all of it, I guess. He says he needs to confess his sins, so God will keep speaking to him."

Holly sat in shocked silence. She began plotting a new course in her mind.

"Is he going to drag you and the boys down with him?" she finally asked.

"I wouldn't put it past him. I called Mark and Jonas already, and they're scared shitless right now. They wanted me to call and check with you. Maybe you'd tell us he was joking or something."

"I don't think he's joking," Holly said, "but I didn't know he was planning to confess to everything on Sunday. Thanks for letting me know."

"You need to stop him, Holly."

Holly hung up the phone, and ran possible plans of action through her mind. She settled on one, took a deep breath, and went back to her computer.

"Here goes," she said to herself.

Zara knocked on Ivan's office door. There was no answer. She knocked again.

"Ivan, it's Zara. Thelo called about Christine."

Zara heard footsteps inside, then Ivan opened the door.

"Sorry," he said. "Come in. How is she?"

Zara came into the office and sat down in a chair while Ivan closed the door behind her.

Ivan returned to his desk and sat down. "How's Christine?" He silently scolded himself for letting his own drama push her from his mind.

"Thelo says that he saw Christine at the hospital, and she has some bruised ribs and a skinned knee, but she's going to be fine. He thinks she might even get released from hospital later today."

Ivan sighed in relief. "I should call her." He reached for his phone.

"Don't bother. Thelo said the reception there is shit, and that's why she didn't answer the calls before. You can text her, though. I think she has wifi."

Ivan sent Christine a short text saying he was glad to hear that she was okay and to call him whenever she could get a signal.

"So who was that woman on the metro?" Zara asked after he'd finished.

Ivan exhaled slowly. He started to say something, then changed his mind. After several false starts, he tried to explain.

"I had a dream the other night where I was a kid back in church. It was one of those hellfire and damnation churches where everyone is going to hell if they aren't perfect. And nobody's perfect, of course.

The preacher singled me out. He pointed at me and yelled 'You're going to hell.'"

"That's inexcusable," Zara scoffed. "You were just a kid. You weren't ready for that."

"Anyway, I ran out of the church after I told the preacher off."

"Well done you! I hope you let him have it."

"That part of the dream was just a replay of stuff that happened in real life, and yes, I did let him have it. I've dreamt that part before, nothing new. I guess all this talk of God lately brought it back up."

"Oy," Zara said with a tinge of sadness. "Sorry, love." She paused, then asked, "what's that got to do with the hoodie woman, though?"

"The part of the dream after I ran out of the church was all new. A woman was outside the church on the sidewalk. I ran out the door, and there she was. I'd never seen her before, but she called me 'Ivan.' I asked who she was and she said, 'I am The One.'"

"And that's the woman you saw outside the coffee shop?"

Ivan looked down at his desk, afraid to see the look on Zara's face. "I wasn't sure at first, but once she turned around on the metro train and looked at me, I was absolutely certain it was the same woman from my dream."

"Bloody hell," Zara said. "Not gonna lie, mate, that's spooky as shit."

"You'd think so, yeah." Ivan looked up at her. "But it isn't. I don't know why, but it doesn't feel spooky to me at all."

"Well, I'm spooked enough for both of us, then. What was the thing with the sign language?"

"I yelled that I needed to talk to her and she signed, 'soon.'"

"Yeah, I remember. I mean how did she know you'd understand it?"

"No idea," Ivan said. "I haven't signed in a long time. My little sister was deaf, so I learned it as a boy. I only use it occasionally when we need to interview someone who's deaf and our other interpreter is unavailable. I tag along with the reporter. I'm not very good anymore, but I can still understand what others sign."

"So this woman must've known you or your sister or something. Maybe?"

"This woman isn't old enough to have known me then. I haven't spoken to my family since I was in my late teens."

"Wow, that's rough," Zara said. "Sorry."

"It's okay. I don't usually think about it."

Zara stared and studied Ivan's face until he became uncomfortable.

"What?" he asked.

"I googled you a few years ago when Thelo and I first started talking. He kept going on about how awesome you are, so I got curious. I couldn't find much on you at all. For a guy in the media business, you certainly avoid being searchable online."

"I've met a lot of important and fascinating people, and maybe I'll write a bestselling memoir one day, but for now I'm content to print the news, not be the subject of it."

"Well, anyway, I thought it was strange. I hope you aren't freaked out by this, but I tried to find out more. It became kind of a quest. I wasn't stalking you or anything, but when I googled you the first time, all I found were your professional credentials and that one photo of you and some politician, the one hanging on the wall over there."

"Senator Lakey. That one shows up online because he put it on his Facebook. I didn't know it was online for quite a while since I'm not on Facebook myself. He took it down after I asked him to, but once something is online, it's never really gone, is it?"

"Well, it's a nice picture, and I'll just go ahead and say it, I thought you were bloody hot, so I started digging around looking for other pictures. The more I dug, the less I came up with. There's nothing about your early days anywhere. It's like you didn't even exist before age thirty or so."

"When I was thirty, nothing was online because there was no internet," Ivan reminded her.

"Yeah, but..." Zara fidgeted. She went for broke. "Look, my stellar opinion of you won't change one bit no matter how you answer my next question. I will totally keep it between us, and you don't even have to answer it because it's really none of my business, but..." Zara paused, wondering whether she should spit it out.

Ivan was sweating. He almost wanted her to ask, but he didn't know if he could answer. He dropped his gaze to his desk, afraid to look at her. After a long silence, he raised his head and his eyes met hers. There was no judgment in them. It would be a huge step for him to tell his secret to someone and even though he hadn't known her very long, he trusted her.

Zara held Ivan's gaze and took a deep breath.

"Did you used to be a woman?"

CHAPTER FOURTEEN

Thelo returned to the *Post* expecting to find Zara at his workstation, but she wasn't there. He made his way to Ivan's office and saw that the door was closed, and the blinds were drawn. Ivan hardly ever closed the door unless he was in a meeting, and the blinds were rarely ever drawn. Thelo knocked on the door.

"Can it wait?" from behind the door. Thelo figured he had interrupted something important. Perhaps someone was getting chewed out or fired.

"Sorry, boss," he said through the door. "I'm looking for Zara, have you seen her?"

He heard a bit of unintelligible conversation, then footsteps. The door opened just a crack, and Zara's face appeared in the narrow opening.

"Hey, love," she said. "Go on about your business, whatever you were going to do today. I'm going to be here awhile. I'll call you later, and we can get together then. All right?"

Thelo's eyes widened. "Are you… You and Ivan… um…" he couldn't stifle his grin. Zara caught on.

"Oh no, nothing like that! Look, we're having a bit of a chat, and we're not finished, that's all. Go on, get to work, I'll catch up with you later."

"Okay. Tell Ivan that I'll be working from my home the rest of the day. You can use my workstation here if you need to."

"Brilliant. Now go, get on with it." Zara smiled at him and closed the door.

Thelo shook his head, confused. He went back to his cubicle, made sure he had everything he'd need to work from home, then headed out to his car.

On the way home, he used his hands-free system to call Christine. It went right to voicemail, so Thelo assumed that she hadn't been released from the hospital yet and couldn't get a signal.

When he got to his apartment, he emptied his pockets into the glass bowl by the door, made some coffee, sorted his mail, and changed into shorts and a t-shirt. He poured himself a cup of coffee and sat down at his computer, ready for a long afternoon of reading the emails that Admin had sent him.

He decided to start with Father Matthew, since he seemed the most interesting at the moment. He chuckled to himself as he remembered the scene he'd walked in on at St Luke's. He had suspected that Christine was a little more open-minded about things than your stereotypical Christian girl, but seeing her locking lips with a priest twice her age was surprising. Even more surprising was the fact that the priest was someone connected with the story she was working on. That crossed the line of professional ethics. How can you remain unbiased and keep your journalistic integrity if you're snogging one of the people in your story? How close were they, anyway? She'd said that she knew him already, but that they weren't friends or anything. It sure as hell looked like they were friends.

Holy shit, are they fucking?

No, surely not.

Are they?

On the one hand, if Christine and the priest were getting it on, he would lose some respect for her on a professional level. On the other hand... Damn, girl, didn't know you had it in ya!

He finished logging in through the multiple layers of security and opened the file vault. He selected the folder of emails labeled 'Father Matthew Vergara,' opened it, and began reading.

Father Matthew had definitely been in contact with Rabbi Jacob. He also had contact with Imam Zahid at Muhammadi Majid. Thelo kept digging and found that Father Matthew knew five of the six local leaders who preached The Sermon. The only one he didn't know was Joel Wood, but he knew his father. He suspected that they had probably been communicating since before email was commonplace. Father Matthew also had an email trail to three of the out-of-town pastors who had given The Sermon.

Thelo started with those. Nothing much was interesting, just friendly chatter, small talk. People in the same profession often do that sort of thing, Thelo figured, and electronic communication had made it easy. Hell, he and Zara had become good friends across an ocean without even meeting in person. Thelo began to suspect that this might be a dead end.

He noticed that Father Matthew sent and received quite a few emails over the years from a Baptist minister named Joseph Singleton. There were quite a few in the earlier years, but as time went by, they became less frequent. One of the more recent ones said, 'hey, look what I found!' and it had an attachment. Thelo had a look.

The attached file was a scanned image of a program from a worship service that had taken place at Fairmont United Church of Christ in 1989. It was an interfaith service in support of people with AIDS and their families. There was a list on the back page of all the clergy who attended the service, and Thelo wasn't surprised to find that all five of the clergy that Father Matthew communicated with were at the service. Thelo looked down the list to see if any of the rest of the Sermon preachers were on it. Joel Wood wasn't there, but his father was. Joel would've been too young, Thelo figured. It made sense now how the local pastors knew each other, but Thelo didn't yet have a connection to the others. He also hadn't discovered a motive for faking a message from God, nor did he have any idea how these pastors could've convinced so many people of different faiths to go along with it. Probably another dead end, Thelo thought, but at least it's a starting point.

An alert in a small pop-up window at the corner of his screen let him know that Admin had dumped some more files into his vault. Thelo did a quick check and saw that all of them had gone into Joel Wood's folder. That reminded him that he'd promised to let Zara see Joel's emails. He made a copy of the folder, uploaded it to the file vault he had set up for her, and then went back to where he'd left off in 1989.

An hour or so later, Thelo struck gold. A time stamp from Sunday evening, just a few hours after The Sermon had happened, showed that Father Matthew received an email from a Methodist preacher who was at the interfaith service all those years ago. The preacher had apparently moved away to Virginia between then and now, but had kept in touch. The email was cc'd to the other local pastors who had preached The Sermon, save for Joel Wood. It read:

I can't believe you guys went through with it! I thought the idea died years ago.

Hope everything turns out, 'cause things are getting crazy here. What happens now?

Thelo looked for replies to the email, but there were none. Admin had apparently gotten into the servers before any of the pastors had sent a response. Dammit.

He called Christine and was surprised to hear the phone ring.

"Hey," she answered, "what's up?"

"You're out of the hospital, then?"

"Just a few minutes ago. I'm taking a cab back to Muhammadi Majid to get my car and maybe get some follow-up on the attack. I'll see if anyone knows anything about the two guys."

"Right back to it, huh?" Thelo said, impressed. "You might want to have a chat with the Friendly Father as well."

He read her the email from the pastor in Virginia.

"Maybe he's got an explanation for it," Thelo said, "but it sounds a lot like a smoking gun to me."

"It has to be something else," Christine said. "Matthew wouldn't…"

"First-name basis now? Look, Christine, what you do with your personal life is your business, but you can't let it get in the way of finding out the truth."

Zara and Ivan were in another world, secluded in Ivan's office. Claire had been told not to disturb them for any reason, and she had complied. Ivan's beard was soaking wet from tears, as was Zara's face and shirt. In the simple but enormous act of sharing his secret with her, Ivan felt decades of tension melt away from him in an instant. He had always hated the idiom about a weight being lifted from one's shoulders, but that's exactly how he felt.

Ivan told her about a rare condition called 5-ARD where an infant is born with a Y chromosome and is, therefore male, but doesn't produce enough dihydrotestosterone, called DHT, during development in the womb. Zara needed an explanation, of course, and Ivan went through the whole process of fetal development with her.

"Until the sixth week after conception," he said, "an embryo has the makings for both male and female reproductive organs. The Y chromosome then kicks in lots of DHT, and the female organs melt away as the male organs develop. Without enough DHT, the male organs don't take over, and the child is born with what appear to be female organs, just without all the internal 'plumbing.'"

Zara was fascinated. Her non-judgmental attitude encouraged Ivan to continue, and he felt more relaxed as he told his story.

"Since everything looked female at birth, they raised me as a girl."

"What was your name back then?" Zara asked.

"Emily."

"That's pretty."

"That's why I was so freaked out when the woman in my dream called me 'Ivan,' because in my dream, I was still a teenager."

"And you were still Emily then."

"Yes. Anyway, after I was a bit older, the doctors realized that my girl parts weren't fully formed and that I'd never bear children. But 5-ARD is so rare that they didn't understand why. They'd never even heard of it. So my parents went full-tilt on religion, figuring that God was the only one who could 'fix' me so I could have kids someday."

"Oh, boy," Zara said. "Not good."

"It was bad. Every time I got a checkup, nothing was different. The preacher told my parents that they had been given a deformed child because of their sinful ways and that I'd never be 'right' if they didn't repent."

"Holy shit. That's fucked up."

"It got worse when my sister Laura was born deaf. My parents were convinced that if they prayed hard enough, they could fix her, too. Obviously, that didn't work out."

Zara shook her head in sadness. She wished she could go back in time and smack some sense into his parents.

"Since they figured Laura's deafness was going to be cured any day through the miracle of prayer, my parents didn't even try to learn sign language. After some time, when Laura got older and still couldn't hear, they sent the two of us to a class where we learned to sign. So I ended up being her interpreter when she needed to talk to them or vice-versa. Just until God could make her speak normally, you understand. It turned out to be a good thing, since she and

I could have long conversations without being heard by them. We became very close."

"Are you still close?"

Ivan's eyes welled up again. He was amazed that he had any tears left. "No." He reached for a tissue, dried his face again, then continued.

"Fast forward to puberty. Hormones start kicking in hard and with that, my body is finally producing enough DHT to make things happen downstairs. You'd think that this would be a miracle, exactly what my parents had been dreaming of, except that DHT doesn't make girl parts, it makes boy parts."

"Oh, shit."

"Exactly. If you already believe that God is punishing you by giving you an Emily with undeveloped girl parts, imagine how you feel when your Emily starts to grow balls."

Zara laughed at that, then stopped herself. "Sorry," she said. "That just caught me off-guard."

"Well, it caught them off-guard, too. My voice changed, I started growing facial hair, my boobs never formed. I wasn't becoming the woman they were expecting me to be."

"Didn't it eventually become obvious that you were simply a guy? Downstairs, I mean."

Ivan paused for several moments, wondering how much he could tell her. The relief he'd felt divulging this much led him to continue. "Not entirely," he said, finally. "My testicles had descended, but most of the other stuff never fully formed. My parents were mortified. They saw me as their cross to bear, some kind of monster they were forced to raise."

Zara cried as much as Ivan did. She wanted nothing more than to erase all those years of anguish from his life and she felt helpless in her inability to do so.

"The final sword through my heart came from my sister." Ivan's voice quivered as tears began to flow again. "Laura had been so brainwashed by that church that she started to believe the bullshit that we were both God's punishment for our parents' sins. She believed that she would eventually be cured of her deafness if she prayed as hard as my parents did. The more she fell into that way of thinking, the less close we became."

Zara didn't know if she could bear to hear the rest of it. She closed her eyes and gripped the arms of her chair. She wanted to hit something.

"When I started sprouting up into a boy, she blamed me. She said that if I had been praying like I was supposed to, then I'd have become a girl like God wanted me to be. She tried to make me go to church every day and pray for forgiveness."

"For forgiveness?" Zara's voice came out louder than she had planned. "For what?"

"For whatever sins I must've committed to cause my body to go against the will of God."

Zara was furious. She gripped the chair so tightly her fingers ached. Ivan continued.

"I told her that if anyone needed forgiving, it was our parents, for the way they had treated us. She completely lost it, said I was hopeless, and that I would be damning the whole family to hell if I didn't change. That was the last time she had anything to do with me."

Zara was speechless. She shook her head and cried angry tears.

"It wasn't long after that," Ivan said, "that we had the little incident at the church where the pastor singled me out, and I told him off and ran out the door. I was nineteen then, and about as fully-formed a man as I would ever be and I was quite frankly not going to be a fucking 'Emily' anymore. I went home, crammed as much as I could in a couple of suitcases, and went to a friend's house for a few days while I figured out what to do with my life. My family never even tried to find me."

The two of them sat in silence for awhile. Ivan felt angry and hurt as he relived his painful past, but he felt free in having gotten it out of his system after all this time.

"Eventually, I scraped up enough for a bus ticket to the big city and hooked up with a support group for runaways and outcasts. They helped me get on my feet, find a job, even donated some money to file the paperwork to change my name from Emily to Ivan. I didn't want any ties to my past life."

"And look at you now," Zara said. "Successful, charming, and totally hot."

They laughed. It was a welcome break in the mood for both of them.

"Ivan?" Zara asked him after a moment. "Can I give you a hug?"

Ivan stood up and moved from behind his desk. Zara stood up and opened her arms wide. Their embrace was long and genuine.

Holly finished up at her computer, shut everything down, and made her way to Joel's study. He was sitting at his computer, typing an outline for his upcoming sermon.

"Is that the big confession you're working on?" she asked.

"Who have you been talking to?" He didn't look up from his keyboard.

"Cletus," she said. "He says you're going to be an idiot on Sunday."

"Did he?" Joel asked, obviously not interested in the answer.

"Not in those words, but if you do what he said you're planning to do, then those words would be appropriate. What the hell are you thinking?"

Joel stopped typing and looked up at her. "Holly, I cannot expect God to continue to use me as a vessel for His Holy Word if that vessel is broken."

"Joel, you cannot expect me to believe that God would use you as a vessel for His Word at all. Look, I don't know what happened last Sunday, but I seriously doubt that it's anything like you believe it is."

Joel glared at her. "Well, what do you think I should believe? How do you explain that I said the exact same words as all those other people without even knowing I said them? I'll bet that if you check with them, they didn't know what they had said, either. I'll bet we all have the same story."

"And you think that makes it look like a miracle, but in my eyes, all of you having the same story looks fishy. It looks planned. It looks like you cooked it up as a way to justify your lack of religious training and your ignorance of Scripture. How you talked the other ones into going along with it is the only part that's a miracle as far as I'm concerned."

Joel's stare burned into her. He spoke softly, but with palpable rage just under the surface. "Get out of my sight," he said, "or it won't just be *my* sins I confess on Sunday."

Holly laughed at his attempt to intimidate her. "If you think I'm going to go down on this ship with you, then you don't know me at all."

She turned and left. He clenched both fists and slammed them on the desk.

"Hello?" Matthew said as he picked up the phone in the rectory.

"Hello, handsome."

Matthew was happy to hear Christine's voice on the other end. "You're out of the hospital, then? Everything's fine?"

"Yes, just sore is all. I'm in a cab, heading to the mosque to get my car. Did you find the other women?"

"Yes, I did. They're both going to be fine as well. One just had some bruises, but the other's jaw was broken."

"That's terrible," Christine said, "but I suppose it could've been a lot worse."

"Yes, it could have. You were all very lucky."

"Do you have some time this evening to talk?"

"Of course," he said, his mood suddenly better. "Dinner?"

"How about after? I've been away from work all day, and I really need to catch up on things first. Besides, I'm not sure I want to have the conversation in a public place."

"Uh oh, that sounds ominous. But sure, that's fine. I'd offer to have you over to the rectory, but I can't guarantee we won't be interrupted. Bishop Garza said he wanted an answer by tonight and even though I gave him one already, he might show up to try to change my mind."

"Change your mind about what?"

"Long story. I'll fill you in tonight."

"We can talk at my place," Christine said. "How's eight o'clock sound?"

Christine drove to the *Post* and spoke to Ivan in his office. She met Zara there, and Zara introduced herself as Thelo's contact from the UK.

"I noticed Thelo's cubicle was empty," Christine said. "I assume he's working from home?" She turned to Zara. "Do you need a ride to your hotel? I'll drive right by it on the way home after I check a few things here."

"No, dear, but that's very sweet of you." Zara looked at Ivan, winked at him, then turned back to Christine. "I've got an invitation to dinner from this lovely gentleman behind the desk."

"Well, then," Christine said, surprised. "Ivan has a social life after all. How did you break through that wall?"

Ivan showed a flash of concern, but Zara smiled a 'don't worry' at him, and he relaxed.

"It's the accent, love," Zara said. "American blokes can't resist a girl with an accent, even if she's just a Scouser from Liverpool."

Christine chuckled, genuinely happy to find that Ivan had a personal life outside the office. It made him seem more human, somehow.

She left Ivan's office, checked her work email at her cubicle, tidied up her desk, then started home. She grabbed a combo meal from a drive-thru on the way, which she ate while she drove. She mentally practiced her upcoming conversation with Matthew, but couldn't find a suitable way to bring up what she knew without letting on that she'd been privy to his private email. She couldn't just let it go without finding out some answers, though. That wasn't an option since Thelo was absolutely right about not allowing her relationship with Matthew to get in the way of the truth. Could she even call it a relationship? They had certainly developed a friendship, and they had slept together once in a drunken stupor, but whether that qualified as a relationship, she didn't know. She wondered how Matthew saw it.

When she arrived home, she carefully undressed and stood in front of the mirror to examine her wounds. There were some angry bruises on her left arm and left side, and she didn't want to remove the gauze from her knee just yet. Luckily, her face hadn't been hit, and she could simply wear long pants and long sleeves tomorrow to cover up the evidence. She'd be just like new in a few days. She turned on the shower and stepped in after the water had warmed up. She realized too late that she was still wearing the gauze on her knee. She'd be replacing that tonight after all. Shit.

What was she going to say to Matthew?

CHAPTER FIFTEEN

"You look different," Zara told Ivan as she twirled the spaghetti around on her fork.

"I feel different. Is it a good different or a bad different?"

"Good different," she assured him. "Seems like you've got an inner glow you didn't have before."

"Thanks. It sorta feels that way, too, but it's all so new. I never thought I'd ever tell anyone."

"Surely you don't think your friends are going to turn away if they find out. Your coworkers all love you, and I'm sure your friends do, too. Look how good it felt to tell me, then imagine that multiplied by however many people."

"I'm not ready to take that step yet," he warned her. "You gotta promise not to tell anyone."

"It's not my secret to tell. Mum's the word."

"Thank you," he said. "It's a minefield. Some people would definitely have an adverse reaction like my parents had. They'd see me as a freak, a mistake. I don't want those people to know, obviously, but you can't always predict which people will have that reaction. Even if I carefully choose the people I tell, I'm not naive enough to think that my secret would stay with just them. Not only that, but if I tell friends who've known me for a long time, they'll be upset that I didn't trust them enough to confide in them a long time ago."

"Thank you for trusting me."

"Well, you pretty much forced my hand with the question. It's not my fault you had it figured out. How did you manage that, when nobody else had?"

Zara shifted in her seat uncomfortably. "Since we're being honest with each other, I hadn't really figured it out."

It was Ivan's turn to squirm. "But…"

"I figured you had some big secret in your past," she said, "since you're all but invisible online. But I assumed you wouldn't tell me, so I came up with this bollocks idea that you'd had a sex change, figuring that if you thought I'd be fine with that, then whatever your secret really was would be no biggie, and you'd just spill it."

Ivan just stared at her, incredulous. "So you didn't know."

"I didn't know. And I deserve a bloody Oscar for not looking surprised as fuck when you told me."

They both had a laugh at that, and Ivan raised his glass of wine to her. "To the truth," he said.

"To the truth."

They spent the rest of their mealtime getting to know each other better. They talked about everything and nothing, but they didn't bring up Ivan's secret again.

Ivan couldn't remember the last time he had been this happy.

Matthew knocked on Christine's door at precisely eight o'clock, dressed smartly in a new shirt and slacks that he'd bought on the way home from St Luke's. He smiled his greeting when Christine opened the door and held up a bottle of red wine for her to see. "I promise to sip it slowly," he said, and she chuckled.

Christine invited him in and offered him a seat while she opened the wine. She sat down next to him on the sofa, poured them both a glass of wine, and they toasted to a speedy recovery for her.

After a bit of small talk and Christine's assurance to him that she hadn't discovered any more injuries from the attack, Matthew related the developments between his priesthood and the Vatican.

"An exorcism?" She was stunned with equal parts shock and disgust. "Who do they think they are?"

"I know." He absentmindedly swirled the wine around in his glass. "I'm absolutely not going to be doing it, don't worry."

"But if you don't, they'll remove you from the priesthood."

"Yes, it seems that way," he sighed. "But I have to have faith that God has a plan for me in all of this. I just need to figure out what it is."

"So you obviously don't believe that Satan or some demon possessed you to say those things."

"Of course not," he said. "And I know that it wasn't something I said on my own, so that only leaves God. Why would God have me say something that would get me removed from the priesthood if He didn't have a place for me to serve in the future? I don't believe He would do that."

"You're sure it was divine intervention, then."

"Yes." He became a bit frustrated. "I thought we had agreed on that already."

Christine fidgeted, unsure how to begin. "You met my coworker Thelo at the hospital today."

Matthew blushed. "Yes. Sorry about the awkward introduction."

"My fault," Christine assured him. "I caused it."

Matthew smiled.

"Anyway," she continued, "he's an investigative reporter, and he's good at snooping around and finding stuff."

"Okay." Matthew wondered where this was headed.

"He found an old worship bulletin from that interfaith service a long time ago, the one where you got drunk."

"You're kidding," Matthew said, impressed. "He really does his homework."

"He noticed that all of the local pastors who preached The Sermon last Sunday were at that service."

"Yes, I believe they were," Matthew said after some thought, "except for Joel Wood. His father was there, though."

"Right. So Thelo started looking for the possibility that all of you knew each other, or at least got to know each other after that day."

"Most of us kept in touch afterward. We were all involved in helping the AIDS patients back then, and we did several more inter-faith services and fundraisers, that kind of thing. So what?"

Christine sighed. "Thelo is pretty convinced that he's found some stuff that makes it look like some of you had planned to do something. Something that might be like what happened on Sunday."

"What kind of evidence is that?" Matthew wanted to know. "What has he been poking around in?"

"I don't know," Christine lied. "He just sounded pretty convinced that there was something there, something maybe you and the others had been planning to do. I told him I'd ask you about it."

"So he thinks I and the others conjured up the whole thing, that I put my priesthood on the line for some prank?" Matthew's voice was edged with anger and disbelief.

"Matthew, please," Christine said. "I'm not saying he believes that. He doesn't believe anything until he's got solid proof. Hell, that's probably why he's an atheist." She took a sip of her wine. "I just told him that I'd ask you about it, so that's what I'm doing. Was there any sort of thing that you and the others had been planning?"

Matthew looked into her eyes for a moment. "I've always been truthful with you, Christine," he said. "And I'll be truthful with you now. It's accurate to say that a group of us were questioning some of the rules and restrictions of our particular religions. We all followed different rules and customs, but we could see that we were equally faithful to God. Did God see our devotion to Him differently, based on which rules we followed? We didn't think so. We didn't believe, for example, that God would think more highly of a priest for being celibate than He would of a Baptist minister who married and raised a loving Christian family. It didn't make sense to us, but we were all expected to follow our church's rules anyway. We were looking for a way to treat those tenets as traditions rather than rules, so if they became a barrier to our faith rather than an enhancement of it, they could be broken or discarded without much consequence."

"Ok, go on."

"We had many discussions about how to start that process. One of those ideas was just to go to the heads of our respective churches and plead our case. That got shot down pretty quickly. None of us could think of a way to do it without risking our jobs. Then one of the evangelical pastors said that we could just all start speaking in tongues one day and claim that God had told us to change the rules."

"And?"

Matthew took a sip of his wine. "Oh, it got a big laugh." He smiled. "It became a running joke. Whenever we'd run across a problem, no matter what it was, if nobody had a solution right away then someone would inevitably suggest that we all just start speaking in tongues and say that God wanted it that way. It was our go-to solution for everything."

"So it was all just in fun?" Christine tried to hide her relief.

"Of course. The best part, though," Matthew said, "is one of our group had moved to the east coast, and I hardly ever heard from him anymore." He began to giggle. "Well, Sunday afternoon, after he'd seen the news reports, he sent an email to a bunch of us that basically said, "Holy cow, you guys, I can't believe you actually did it!""

Matthew let out a hearty laugh, and Christine joined him. She was glad to find out that he hadn't been lying to her, but that left them back at square one on their investigation.

After a moment, she stopped laughing and took on a more somber tone. She caught Matthew's gaze.

"I hope you're right about God having a plan for you after this," she said. "I know how much you loved the priesthood and how much you'll miss it if you have to give it up."

"Yes, but I had many wonderful years. Perhaps it's time to move onto other things."

"Like what? Have you given it any thought?"

"One thing at a time. At the moment, I'm enjoying a glass of wine with a good friend."

Zara made her way to her hotel room after Ivan dropped her off. She had offered him a nightcap, but he politely refused. That was okay, she thought, he's got a lot on his mind.

She opened the door to her room and tossed her handbag onto the bed. A quick shower felt fantastic after the long day, and the fluffy robe that came with the room was warm and luxurious. She usually skimped on accommodations when she traveled, but it was her first trip to America, so she splurged. Adding a bit of money to the stipend her editor gave her for lodging was worth it for the comfortable room.

She opened her laptop and checked her email. Some spam, some ads, a quick note from her editor asking if she'd gotten an interview with Joel Wood yet, and a 'call me' note from Thelo. He'd have to wait a minute.

She typed a quick thank you email to Ivan, told him that she was very proud of his bravery, promised again that she'd keep his secret, and offered her support anytime he wanted to talk. She hit 'send' then grabbed her phone from her handbag on the bed and called Thelo.

He walked her through the multiple layers of security necessary to get to the encrypted file vault he'd set up for her. It took longer than Thelo had expected, she was sure, but she eventually got access to it. She thanked Thelo for his trouble, then got to work.

In the vault was a folder labeled 'Joel Wood' and inside that folder were two subfolders. One had been uploaded late Sunday night, and the other, just this evening. She chose the one from Sunday night.

Most of Joel's emails were business stuff, boring crap involving the placement of cameras on stage, the theme of the upcoming services, how much money had been collected in the offering plate, that kind of thing. Zara began to doubt that she'd find anything of much interest.

She opened the newer folder and saw that the emails in it weren't just from the last few days. Odd. There were a few recent ones, yes, but mostly they were older, going back more than ten years. The date stamps were unusual as well. In the first folder, it was evident that Joel sent several emails per day. The emails in this new folder, however, appeared to have been purposely selected. There would often be days or even weeks between date stamps. If these had been specifically chosen, they must be important. She was about to start reading, then had a thought. She brought up the other folder and began to cross-reference the date stamps. Just as she suspected, none of the emails in the new folder were duplicated in the folder that had been uploaded Sunday. These new emails had been intentionally left out of the previous batch. There were also quite a few sent from an email address that was different than the one Joel used in the other folder. Zara sat up in her chair, suddenly excited.

She grabbed the hotel's complimentary notepad and pen, made some coffee in the tiny little pot on the desk, and braced herself for a long night of reading. From the very first email, she knew she'd hit pay dirt.

"You're a cheeky little bugger, aren't you?" she said aloud and smiled.

Ivan pulled into the garage at his home, tapped the remote to close the door, then entered through the door to the kitchen. Bosco was just on the other side, tail wagging. Ivan bent down so Bosco could lick his face, then fed the grateful dog.

"You're a happy boy," Ivan said. "It was a beautiful day. Did you play out in the back yard? I hope my flower beds are still in one piece."

Bosco wagged his tail feverishly and barked once.

Ivan was happy, too, although still a bit in disbelief that he'd actually shared his story. He hoped that Zara would keep her word about not telling anyone, even though the feeling of freedom was intoxicating. He almost hoped that she didn't keep the secret, that she'd shout it from the rooftops to anyone who'd listen. He could do that himself, of course, but he didn't have the guts. Not yet.

He undressed, brushed his teeth, turned on the water in the shower, then got a clean towel from the linen closet. He was about to step into the shower, then had a better idea. He turned off the shower and turned on the water in the large soaker tub in the corner of the room. Ivan had spent quite a lot of money on this *tub* when he had the house built, but his busy life rarely afforded the opportunity to use it, other than for bathing the dog. Today was a special day, he reasoned, so he'd indulge himself. Bosco heard the water running and ran into the room. Ivan laughed, tousled the dog's hair, and scratched him behind the ears.

"Sorry, buddy," Ivan told him, "this bath is for me. Shocker, right? I'll give you a bath soon, I promise."

Bosco uses this tub twice as much as I do, Ivan mused as he added some bath salts to the water. The subtle aroma of eucalyptus and spearmint began to fill the room. Ivan took a deep breath, enjoying the scent. The label on the salts promised that the benefits of aromatherapy would help him relax and unwind after a hard day. Whatever. Ivan just liked the way they smelled. Bosco finally understood that he wasn't getting a bath tonight, and left the room to finish his dinner.

Ivan stepped back into the bedroom, grabbed his tablet computer, and did a quick scan of his email while he waited for the large tub to fill. His face lit up when he saw the thank you email from Zara, and he read it several times before moving on to the rest of the list. He took the tablet into the bathroom with him and set it down on the tile platform that surrounded the tub, then turned off the water. He stepped into the foamy bath with one foot, sucked in some air as the heat of the water met his skin, then added his other foot. He stood there for a moment, letting his legs adjust to the hot water, then slowly lowered himself down. God, it felt good. Ivan relaxed and felt the tension in his muscles melt away. He enjoyed the heat, the aroma, and the sound of the bubbles as they crackled and hissed around him.

After several minutes, he sat up and turned the tap to add more hot water, then turned it off and picked up his tablet computer. Bosco had returned to the room and was looking at him with envy.

"Oh, okay," Ivan promised, "You can get in when I'm done, after the water cools down some."

Bosco seemed to understand, barked a single 'thank you,' and curled up on the bathmat to wait his turn. Ivan launched the browser on his tablet to check the news sites. The stock market was down again, and everyone was blaming it on the uncertainty created by The Sermon. No surprise. Some places of worship had protests, some were denouncing The Sermon as a hoax, and others claimed it was the work of the devil. More of the same from the day before, Ivan thought.

He switched over to YouTube, and a newly-uploaded video caught his eye. He played it and saw a concert at Riverside City Park. Some woman was talking to the folks around her, and people began paying attention to her instead of to the music. The band took notice from the stage, and they had security escort her away. She was young, petite, with a blonde pixie cut. She was wearing a blue hoodie and green pants. Ivan nearly dropped the tablet into the tub.

CHAPTER SIXTEEN

The alarm hadn't yet gone off when Matthew woke. Christine was still asleep next to him in her bed, snoring. He found it rather endearing, then wondered if he also snored when he slept. He brushed the hair from her cheek. Last night had been incredible. Lovemaking was even better when you're sober, he realized. He allowed himself to drift off into fantasies of them spending their futures together, maybe getting married, maybe... kids? That could be an issue, considering his age. Did he want to start a family in his fifties? Would Christine insist on having children? Surely she would want kids. That's going to be a hurdle they'll have to cross at some point. What if it becomes a wedge between them? What if...

The alarm sprang to life with a cacophony of irritation. Christine moaned, rolled over toward the nightstand, and flailed her arm around until she knocked the alarm clock to the floor. The sudden silence was almost as jarring as the alarm. Matthew chuckled.

"Good morning, sunshine," he said.

"Really?"

"Of course it's a good morning," he teased her. "I woke up next to you."

She turned to look at him, rubbed the sleep from her eyes, and looked at him again. She made a face. "Oh, God, you're serious. How many romantic comedies have you seen, anyway?"

"Don't be cynical," he said as he kissed her cheek.

"I'm always cynical before coffee. You'll learn that eventually."

"Eventually? So there will be more of these mornings, then?"

She realized the implication of what she'd said. "Maybe," she stammered. "Probably. Hell, I don't know. I haven't planned anything beyond the point where I have some coffee."

"Fair enough," Matthew said and gave her another quick kiss on the cheek. "I'll get you some."

He pulled on his boxers and undershirt and headed for the kitchen. Christine headed for the bathroom to answer nature's call and to check on her bruises. She could hear Matthew opening cabinets and drawers looking for coffee mugs, sugar, and spoons. Christine had thankfully remembered to set the timer on the coffee maker, so the coffee was ready to pour. She could smell the aroma.

Her bruises didn't look any worse than yesterday, but they didn't look any better, either. She figured she'd give them a week to go away, then… then what, exactly? You can't just will them away. She needed coffee.

Matthew was a sweet man. He genuinely cared for her, but that was no surprise, given his profession. She wondered if his was just a case of puppy love, his first crush, riding the wave of new emotions. Those relationships never end well, she thought. When the new wears off and the person realizes that there are others out there who might be interested, then someone is bound to get hurt. She remembered her first boyfriend. Billy Newman, a freckle-faced redhead in fourth grade who stood up for her that day when a sixth grader pulled her hair. It lasted nearly three weeks, an eternity for grade-school crushes, but her heart was still broken the day he announced that Julie Dunbar wanted to be his girlfriend now, sorry. Christine wondered how long it would be before Matthew's Julie Dunbar came along.

She put her bathrobe on and plodded to the kitchen, still half asleep. Matthew was sitting in the breakfast nook with her cup of coffee already prepared to her liking. She sat down without a word, grabbed the cup in both hands, and took a sip. Matthew smiled at Christine, then opened his mouth to say something. Christine noticed and placed her finger to her lips, indicating that she wanted silence, then she pointed to an imaginary line on her coffee mug, very near the bottom.

"When it gets down to here," she said, "then you can talk."

Matthew chuckled, amused at her morning crankiness. This was heaven.

Joel Wood sat down to toast and a bowl of oatmeal to go with his morning paper. The headlines still involved The Sermon and the unrest it had caused at some churches and other houses of worship. Gloria Deo had been spared much of that drama, thankfully. He wondered how his followers would react to his upcoming confession, though. Last night, he made a list of all the things he was going to confess, and today he would work on how best to word it so that his followers would empathize with him rather than chastise him for his sins. He would admit to the infidelity, the prostitutes, the gambling, even that he had stopped believing in God. He knew that his followers could identify with one or more of those things, and they would appreciate his bravery in coming clean, perhaps even begin their own journey of repentance. It felt good to confess, Joel thought, and he hadn't even done it yet. Joel did have limits on what he would admit to, however. Other than the prostitutes, which he never hired himself, nothing he planned to confess could land him in jail. Joel was repentant, but he wasn't stupid.

He scanned the articles for his name, but didn't see any mentions. Once he made his confession, of course, he would be the headline, but in the interim he wanted to prime the pump, to have the largest audience possible for Sunday. Having no mentions in the local newspaper was not a good start. He considered asking Holly to put out notices on social media that Sunday's service would be special, but thought better of it. She wasn't going to go along with that plan since she was likely building up her argument for him to forego the confession and stick with business as usual. That would be playing it safe, Joel thought, and this was no time for that. God had spoken through him, and that changed everything.

Joel finished his breakfast, then checked his email. Nothing of much interest. A few emails from his poker buddies, probably begging him not to come clean. Joel might read those later, might not. They wouldn't change his mind, anyway.

Another email was sent from a name he didn't recognize. He figured it was spam, but the subject line gave him pause: 'I know what you did. We should talk.' Who the hell was this? He opened the email and read that someone, apparently the person who sent the email, had found out multiple things about him that 'would be detrimental to his ministry' if they were published. It went on to say that he was being given an opportunity to answer questions relating to the findings so that he could explain any or all of the accusations. Joel smiled. This might be just what he needed to stoke the fires of interest before his big day on Sunday. God had everything all planned out for him, he thought. He said a prayer of thanks, then began typing his reply.

Officer Mike Scott swung by the Muhammadi Majid mosque where Christine had been attacked the day before. There were other officers investigating that case, but the mosque was part of his beat, so he kept an eye on it anyway. When he turned the corner, Mike could see a group of thirty or so people gathered around someone. He swung his patrol car into the parking lot and killed the engine. If this turned into another fight, he thought, he'd need backup. He radioed in and gave his location, then got out of the car and approached the group.

The people were peaceful, which was good, and they were all gathered around in a circle, listening to someone Mike couldn't see in the middle of the group. A woman's voice. He eavesdropped for a bit to make sure that she wasn't trying to incite violence. These days, he thought, you can't be too careful.

The woman was talking about balance and harmony and all kinds of hippie stuff. It sounded like a church service more than a pep talk for a riot, so Mike turned to leave.

The woman's voice cut through the crowd. "Don't leave yet. There's much more to hear."

Mike turned around. The crowd parted so he could see the source of the voice. A young woman looked back at him with bright green eyes and a killer smile. She was maybe twenty or so, if that. She had blonde hair formed into a pixie cut, a pair of faded jeans, and a Sex Pistols t-shirt. She didn't look like the kind of girl who'd be holding court in front of a mosque, Mike thought.

"We aren't planning a revolt or anything, if that's what you're worried about," she said.

"I was just checking up. After the incident yesterday, I just wanted to make sure everything was okay."

"That's very good of you, officer. Please stay and listen for a while. You might learn something."

"Thank you, but I need to get on with my rounds. Have a good day, folks." Mike turned to go back to his car.

"We'll meet again," she called to him. "Thank you, officer."

Mike got back to the car and radioed in. He gave a brief report, said there was no need for backup, then drove off to continue his rounds.

Zara sat at her laptop and dug through more of Joel's emails. She made notes and occasionally shook her head in disbelief. This guy was a real piece of work, she thought, and all those people follow him like he's their messiah. He was an adulterer, a con artist, a manipulator, and depending on how young some of these poker 'prizes' were, possibly even a child molester. She imagined that he had gotten her email by now and was already phoning a gaggle of lawyers. She checked the temporary email account she'd set up last night and found a reply. She took a deep breath and clicked the message, expecting to read a cease-and-desist order from an attorney. Instead, she saw a reply from Joel Wood himself, inviting her to speak with him.

"Holy shit." Zara stared at the screen in disbelief. "Holy shit!" She called Thelo as soon as she could fumble her phone out of her handbag.

"Hello, love," Thelo said. "How was your dinner with Ivan?"

"Look, mate, I've got in over me head, bloody hell."

"What do you mean?"

"I was reading those emails from Joel Wood, and he's a right proper git."

"No surprise," Thelo said. "What did you find?"

"All kinds of shit."

"And?"

"He's granted me an interview." Zara's disbelief was apparent.

"Whaaaaat?" Thelo was as shocked as she was. "How did you manage that?"

"I hinted at what I'd found and offered to give him a chance to deny everything before it went to print."

"No shit?" Thelo shook his head. "That's all it took?"

"Yeah."

"So what was it you found? Is he cheating on his wife?"

"Oh, not just that. He's having his mates hire whores, maybe under-age ones, and they get together and use them for some kind of prize."

"Prize for what?"

"Poker, maybe? I dunno. Anyway, that's not all. I think the fellas he's doing it with are preachers, too."

"No way! Who?"

"No idea, it's just first names, probably nicknames. I did a reverse lookup on their email addresses but got nothing."

"They probably use a different email address than their regular ones when they're talking about these things," Thelo said. "They'd be stupid if they didn't."

"Yeah, I did that when I sent him the email last night," she said.

"Wait," Thelo said with a sudden change in tone. He thought for a moment. "When you sent him the email last night, did you send it to his regular email address? The one that's listed on the church's website? Or did you send it to the address he was using in those emails you read?"

Zara's breath caught in her throat. "Oh, fuck me! He will know I've been reading those emails, won't he?"

"Pretty much. How else would you have known about that address? Not good, Zara."

"Shit! Shit! Shit!" She beat her fist on her head. "It was late, I was tired, and I wasn't thinking properly. Bloody hell!"

"You can't tell him how you got those emails."

"Of course not! I won't divulge my source."

"He'll probably assume that one of his buddies ratted him out. That's the best case scenario, anyway."

"I hope you're right. I'm interviewing him at noon."

"Good luck."

"Thanks, mate. I'll need it."

Ivan spent the morning in his office trying to track down information on the woman at the concert yesterday. He called the police precinct, but since the woman had only been escorted out of the park, but not arrested, they had no information to give him. He sent a message to the man who had posted the video, but he didn't know who she was, either. Dead end after dead end. Ivan sighed.

He took a break from his search to catch up on some email, attend to some items on his desk, and return some phone calls. He checked again for any news about the woman in the blue hoodie. Nothing.

He got up and went to the break room for a cup of coffee, but the machine was in pieces, under repair by a burly man in a blue mechanic's shirt.

"Hi, Fred," Ivan said to the man.

"Oh, hey, long time no see." He grinned.

"Yeah, almost ten days since the last call. I think that's a new record."

The man chuckled. "I think you've got a lemon," he said. "If it's still under warranty, I'll be happy to give you documentation of all the times I've been out to repair it, so you can request a new one."

"It worked fine until the warranty ran out. Maybe we should just hire you on full time."

Ivan left the break room and swung by Claire's desk.

"I'm going to Beanz for a coffee. Can I bring you one?"

"That would be lovely." She reached under her desk to get her purse.

"No, no," he insisted. "My treat."

He left the *Post* building and walked to the corner, scanning the pedestrians as he went. No sign of her. After he had picked up the coffee, Ivan looked across the street at the corner where he had seen the woman before, but she wasn't there. He briefly considered checking the metro station, but told himself he was crazy and headed back to the office.

"Here's your coffee," he said as he got to Claire's desk.

"You're a dear." She winked at him. "No matter what people say about you."

Ivan chuckled.

"There was a woman here to see you," she said. "I told her you'd be right back, but she said she couldn't stay."

Ivan took a sip of his coffee. "Did she leave a name? Say what she wanted?"

"She said her name was Lisa, didn't give a last name."

"I don't think I know a Lisa. What did she look like?"

"Early twenties, maybe. Petite. Short blonde hair, faded jeans, pretty green eyes."

Ivan's breath caught in his throat. "Where is she now?"

"She said she couldn't stick around, but she would meet you at this address at one o'clock. She said it was important."

Claire handed him a scrap of paper. Ivan looked at it in disbelief.

"Clear my calendar for the afternoon."

"What is it?" Claire asked. "Do you know the place?"

"Yeah. I live there."

Mike's cell phone rang with the tone that he'd assigned to Thelo's number. He smiled as he pulled the patrol car over to the curb and answered it. "Hey there, Pookie," he said.

"Aw, geez, are we at the pet names stage already?"

"Would you prefer a different one? I've got at least a hundred or so I can pass by you, to see which one you like best."

"You mean to see which one makes me gag the least," Thelo corrected him. "Listen, you have an early shift today, yeah?"

"Yeah, I'm off at eleven. We still on for lunch?"

"That's why I'm calling. I'm hoping you can do me a favor."

"Anything for you, Pumpkin," Mike said, clearly enjoying himself as he heard Thelo cringe on the other end.

"My reporter friend Zara is over from the UK, and she's landed an interview with Joel Wood."

"Okay, so?"

"She's found some shit on him that could end his career, and she's going to confront him with it. You know how people can get when there's a ton of money at stake. Could you go with her to the interview? You don't have to do anything, but I think he might behave better if you're there."

"You think he'd try to hurt her?"

"Probably not, but he might try to threaten her in some way. If you're there, he likely won't say anything too intimidating."

"Yeah, I can do that. I guess our lunch is canceled, then?"

"I'll make it up to you, promise."

They worked out the logistics, then Thelo called Zara with the news.

"I don't need an escort," she said. "I'm a big girl."

"Just humor me. Mike is a nice guy, but he's big and imposing. He'll be in uniform, so Joel won't dare get out of hand."

"What if he won't do the interview with Mike there?"

"Then Mike can wait outside. Just knowing he's there should be enough of a deterrent."

"I still don't know what you're afraid of. He's not a psycho or anything. He's just a preacher."

"He's just a preacher worth millions of dollars," Thelo reminded her, "and you're walking in there with the means to take it all away from him. I wouldn't put anything past him."

"Yeah, all right. Better safe than sorry," Zara admitted. "Where do I meet up with Mike?"

"He's going to stop by your hotel right after his shift ends at eleven. You should still make it to Gloria Deo by noon, no problem."

"Thanks, love," Zara said.

"Be careful."

CHAPTER SEVENTEEN

Matthew arrived back at Our Lady of Mt Carmel after a brisk walk from Christine's house. He whistled a selection of his favorite hymns along the way, ending his trip with "Here I Am, Lord" as he reached the steps of the rectory.

"Good afternoon, Father."

Father Matthew flinched and spun around, nearly dropped his keys.

"Sorry, Father," Bishop Garza said. "I didn't mean to startle you."

"It's all right, Your Excellency. May I help you?"

"We need to talk. May I come in?"

Matthew hesitated, then decided to take the high road. "Yes, of course."

The two men entered, and Father Matthew offered the bishop a cup of tea. Bishop Garza declined.

"Father, I realize that our last meeting left you in a bit of a daze and for that, I must apologize," he began. "You must understand that your actions have sent shockwaves through the Church. You have committed an act that is quite simply unprecedented and sometimes people, even well-meaning people, can and do overreact to such things."

"I can understand that, Your Excellency, but to accuse me of being possessed is…"

"Yes, yes, I know. That's why I'm here," Bishop Garza interrupted. "Please, let's not bring it up again. It was a mistake."

"Thank you, Your Excellency."

"Archbishop Bolado and I have spoken to the Cardinals who suggested the exorcism…"

"It didn't sound like a suggestion."

Bishop Garza shot him a look that showed he was not accustomed to being interrupted. He continued.

"We spoke to them and explained that you have been a true and faithful servant of God for many years and that you are beloved by your parishioners, many of whom have come to your defense in these last few days."

Father Matthew's mood improved greatly on those words. He had missed being able to meet his parishioners and to care for their needs. He felt cut off. It was encouraging to know that they were fighting for him.

"Upon this evidence," Bishop Garza said, "and with much prayer, the Vatican has withdrawn its suggestion of exorcism." He looked at Father Matthew for a reaction. He got none. "They have also suggested that you be reinstated into service, with two conditions."

Father Matthew was guardedly hopeful. While his heart sang at the prospect of being able to return to his ministry, he was wary of any conditions that the Church had imposed on it.

"The first condition is that you must confess your sins against God and the Church. It won't be a public confession, but it is still one that you must take seriously. You have done real damage to the Church with your words, damage that may be irreparable. We pray that this is not the case, but it is a sin that must be acknowledged and forgiven."

"You are saying that I need to be forgiven for speaking words that were not even mine?" Father Matthew asked, making sure that his voice was calm in spite of his rising resentment of this man and the system he represented. "I told you that I spoke those words with no forethought, with no malice. I didn't even know I had said them until they were played back to me. How can I ask to be forgiven for something I did not do?"

"Father Matthew, I understand your position. Please understand mine. You are a good man and a good priest. Archbishop Bolado and I value your service, as do the people of this parish. We are trying to keep you in the priesthood. Please, hear me out."

"I will hear you out, Your Excellency, but I must tell you that I believe giving a false confession is worse than what you accuse me of."

"Is it?" Bishop Garza steeled his gaze. "Is it worse than public intoxication? Two people saw you drunk on Sunday night. They saw you leave with a woman half your age, and you followed her to her house. You did not return to the rectory that night. Father, the speculations are already spreading through the parish. Even those parishioners who supported you after your blasphemy at Mass are less forgiving of these latest accusations."

Father Matthew could not deny his actions. He put his head down and spoke quietly. "So I confess my sins. What is the other condition?"

Bishop Garza waited until Father Matthew finally looked up at him. "You will be relocated to another parish, far enough away that your tarnished reputation won't follow you."

Tears welled up in Father Matthew's eyes as he considered the ramifications of a move. It would be a fresh start, yes, but it was the severing of the relationships he'd spent years building in this parish that was hard to take. It would also mean moving away from Christine. He knew he wouldn't be able to have a physical relationship with her if he remained a priest, but the loss of her friendship and companionship seemed the greater blow.

"I will need some time," Father Matthew said, finally. "I need to pray about it. You understand."

"Of course." Bishop Garza stood up to leave. "We will all pray. The sooner you make a decision, however, the better. For you and for the parish."

Father Matthew rose from his chair and saw the bishop out.

Zara and Mike showed up at Gloria Deo just in time for the twelve o'clock interview. On the way, Zara told Mike that she had evidence that seemed to indicate that Joel was cheating on his wife, messing around with prostitutes, and a host of other things. Mike said he was disgusted, but not surprised. He had heard the rumors for years, but as far as he knew, nobody ever had proof.

"I can't wait to see the look on his face when he denies everything, and then I hit him with the evidence," Zara grinned.

"I suppose it would be rude to take a picture of that moment."

Zara laughed. "Yeah, probably. Too bad, though."

Mike parked the car, and they walked up a short flight of steps to the church offices adjacent to the massive sanctuary. Zara pressed the buzzer next to the double glass doors. Mike looked over at the huge sanctuary building.

"It looks more like a theater than a church," he said.

"It's both at once."

The doors clicked as they unlocked.

They entered the building and found themselves in a wide hallway with glass walls on both sides. Behind the glass, they could see large offices with multiple desks, each staffed with a person sitting behind a computer screen, talking on a headset, or both at the same time. Joel Wood appeared at the end of the hall and flashed his famous television-friendly smile as he approached them.

"Good afternoon," he said, and extended his hand. "I'm Joel Wood. Welcome to Gloria Deo."

"Zara Davies." She shook his hand.

Joel looked at the uniformed police officer standing next to Zara. "You brought a friend."

"Officer Mike Scott," Mike said, extending his hand. "Chauffeur."

"You're here from overseas," Joel said to Zara. "Liverpool?"

"Yes! You've a good ear if you picked that up just from me saying my name."

"I've seen lots of documentaries on the Beatles," he said. "It's a lovely accent."

"To me, you're the one with the accent."

Joel laughed slightly. "Will Officer Scott be joining us? It's fine if he does. If he doesn't hear it first-hand today, he'll just read it later anyway, correct?"

"I suppose so," she said.

Joel led them down the hallway to his office. Zara and Mike both took a seat in comfortable leather chairs facing Joel's large mahogany desk. Bookcases lined the walls, most of the shelves filled with books on public speaking, dramatic arts, film, and television. Zara scanned the shelves for any sort of religious book. She eventually spotted one NIV Bible on the bottom shelf of one of the cases. Joel sat down behind the desk in a high-backed burgundy leather chair. Zara figured that his desk and chair probably cost more than the entire contents of her apartment.

"Nice office," she said.

"Thank you. It's quite comfortable, I think."

"Where's Jesus?" Mike interrupted.

"Sorry?"

"I don't see any pictures of Jesus. There's not even a crucifix or anything."

Zara shot him a look that said, 'shut up.' Mike back-pedaled quickly.

"Sorry," he said. "Don't mind me."

"No, it's fine," Joel said. "I don't have a crucifix in my office because we celebrate the risen Christ at Gloria Deo. Jesus is no longer on that cross. We have a large cross behind the altar in the sanctuary, of course, but it's just a cross, not a crucifix. Also, I don't have any artwork depicting Jesus because we have no idea what he looked like. All the usual art shows him as a white man, long hair, beard, white robes. It's his generally-accepted look, even though there's no real basis for it. It's like how Saint Nicholas had dozens of different interpretations until 'The Night Before Christmas' was published. Based on that description, Coke started putting a fat Santa in a red suit on their Christmas advertising, and now everyone's depiction of Santa looks like that."

Mike and Zara just stared at him, unsure of what to make of that analogy.

"I'm just saying that the traditional image of Jesus in paintings probably isn't accurate, so we don't put them up," Joel explained. "But you aren't here to talk about art."

Zara got right to it. "I've come across some information that paints you in a less-than-favorable light. I'd like to give you a chance to explain or deny some of the things that I've found."

"Of course," he said, his famous smile returning. "I'm sure that I can help clear things up for you. But just so I'm absolutely certain of things before we begin, you're a reporter from the UK, is that correct?"

"Yes, with the *London Daily News*. Sorry, I should've mentioned that at the start."

"Isn't that a gossip tabloid?"

Zara hesitated, hoping that her interview wasn't over before it had begun. "Partially," she fudged. "We cover celebrities and political sex scandals and that sort of thing, but we also carry real news as well."

"I see."

"This interview fits our format either way, what with you being a celebrity and all."

"Yes, I understand. I was just hoping for a more local audience, that's all. And no offense, but a lot of people don't believe what they read in the tabloids. If I'm going to bare my soul here, I want people to take it seriously. Again, no offense."

"None taken." Zara thought quickly. "What if I could get the interview into the *Riverside Post* as well? London is several hours ahead of us here, so the piece could run the same day in both papers and the *Daily News* could still claim they had it first. That's good enough for my editor. Besides, it gives us some credibility if a major newspaper in the States also runs one of our stories."

"You can promise that it will run here as well as London?"

"Almost," she said. "Give me a second." She took her phone from her handbag and called Ivan. "Hello, gorgeous. I'm at Gloria Deo about to interview Joel Wood about The Sermon and some other things. He says that he'd like the interview to run in the *Post* as well, would that be all right? Brilliant. Thanks, love."

She hung up the phone.

"Yes," she said. "I can promise."

"Then let's begin," Joel said.

Zara took out a small digital recorder from her bag and turned it on. She had Joel state his name, and then she stated her name as well.

"Ok, let's begin."

"Where did you get the email address you used when you contacted me?" Joel interrupted.

Zara was ready for it. "I won't divulge my sources. They wish to remain anonymous, and I can't break that trust."

"Did you hack into my email?" he asked, all traces of the smile gone from his face.

"I did not," Zara said, truthfully.

"But you read them."

Zara took a deep breath. "I did. But I didn't hack your email, nor did I ask anyone to do it for me. They had already been hacked before I even knew they existed. I only read what was given to me by sources I will not name."

"Fair enough," Joel said. "Thank you for being honest with me."

The tension in the room lessened, but just a bit.

"Now that you know where I got my information, then," Zara began, "my first question should be no surprise."

Joel sat back in his chair, apparently unconcerned.

Zara cleared her throat. "Have you ever cheated on your wife?"

Joel met Zara's gaze. "Yes," he said. "Many times."

Zara nearly dropped her recorder.

Ivan rushed home to a confused Bosco after finishing up as much business as he could. Ivan had to convince the dog that he didn't get more food every time Ivan came home, something the dog still hadn't grasped after all these years. Ivan eventually gave into Bosco's pitiful looks and gave him a treat which seemed to satisfy the dog, at least temporarily. 'That dog has me figured out,' he thought. 'He knows just which look will get him what he wants.'

Check the time. Twelve forty-five. Ivan made a few short business calls and picked up a dog toy that Bosco had left in the living room. He adjusted the throw pillows on the sofa and paced back and forth. Would Lisa expect him to be out front? He looked out the window, saw no-one, checked the time. Twelve fifty-eight. He looked around the room for something to straighten or tidy up, but found nothing. Check the time. Still twelve fifty-eight. Dammit.

He went into the guest bath, checked himself in the mirror, used his hand to straighten his hair. Check the time. One o'clock. The doorbell rang.

Ivan rushed to the door and looked through the peephole. It was the woman from his dream, from the news story, the woman who was outside the coffee shop yesterday. He opened the door and tried to appear casual. His heart was racing.

"Hello, Ivan," she said. The words sounded exactly as they had in his dream.

"Hello, Lisa. Do I know you?"

"Not yet. We have things to talk about."

"Please, come in."

She entered Ivan's home and was shown to the living room. Bosco eyed the woman quizzically. His master rarely had guests. His tail quickly showed his approval, however.

"Can I offer you a beverage?" Ivan asked. "Coffee? Tea? Something else?"

"Coffee would be good," she said as she made her acquaintance with Bosco.

Ivan retreated to the kitchen and made them both a cup from his single-serving coffee maker. He returned with the coffee and two spoons, then left and returned again with a box of sugar cubes and a pint carton of milk.

Bosco was enjoying having his ears scratched by his new friend. Ivan smiled.

"Bosco likes you," he said. "That puts me at ease a bit."

"Dogs are wonderful. They know and understand a lot more than most humans."

Ivan started to ask what she meant by that, then changed his mind.

Lisa patted the dog on the head, then reached over him to attend to her coffee. She poured a bit of milk into the cup from the carton, then picked up a spoon and stirred. She set the spoon down, sipped from the cup, and smiled.

"Very nice," she said. "Thank you."

"I don't entertain many visitors here. I never bought a proper serving set." Ivan seemed embarrassed.

"It's the coffee that matters, though, isn't it?" she said as she took another sip. "It's delicious."

Ivan fixed his own coffee, then looked at the woman on his sofa. Bosco had curled up next to her feet.

"Why did you come looking for me at the office today?" he asked.

"Why did you chase me down yesterday?"

Ivan didn't have an answer for that, at least not one that wouldn't make him sound crazy. Lisa sipped her coffee and watched Ivan search for words.

"We have a lot to talk about," she said, finally taking him off the hook. "I need your help."

Ivan was confused. "Help with what? Who are you?"

"I am The One," she said, as if that were enough explanation. "But you may call me Lisa, if that's easier for you."

Ivan stared at her, unsure of what to think. Was this another dream, perhaps?

"What do you mean, you are The One? The one what?"

"I am the one who will fix things."

"Fix what things?"

"Life," she said. "Life is broken. All the things that make up life need fixing, and I need your help to start that process."

Ivan might've tossed her out and called her a crackpot, were it not for the fact that he needed her to answer one nagging question.

"How did you get into my dream the other night?" Ivan suddenly realized that his question sounded as bonkers as anything she'd just said.

Lisa met his eyes and smiled. Ivan was immediately calmed by her gaze and she waited a moment for his anxiousness to subside.

"You wouldn't understand, even if I tried to explain, because I don't understand it myself. But I did it because I knew that your curiosity about how I got into your dream is the only reason you let me into your home. Every action sets off a chain of events, which lead to an inevitable conclusion. I could see that the only way I could get to talk to you would be to make you so intrigued that you would let down your guard and invite me into your home for a chat."

Ivan took a moment to process that. "Then why wouldn't you talk to me yesterday outside the coffee shop? Why did you tell me 'soon' instead of talking to me then?"

"It wasn't the right time or place. You weren't ready yet." She smiled and sipped her coffee as if her answer was self-explanatory.

"I don't understand," Ivan said. "Not ready for what?" He felt as though he had entered into an alternate universe where these kinds of conversations were commonplace.

She set her cup down and looked into his eyes. "I need you to tell my story. And I knew you wouldn't have the courage to tell my story until you had the courage to tell your own."

Thelo's phone rang. It was Zara.

"Hello, love, how did it go?" he asked.

"Not how I expected, that's for sure." Thelo could hear Mike say 'no shit.'

"You're on your way back to the hotel, then?"

"Yeah, we just left the church. I need to go get this typed up and then fire it off to my editor. I texted him to stay in the office, and if he gets this tonight, it could run in tomorrow's edition."

"Did you ask him the juicy stuff? What did he say?"

"That's what I meant when I said it didn't go like I expected," she said. "He admitted to all of it. Fucking all of it!"

Thelo was speechless.

"I know the look on my face must've been like the look on yours right now," she said.

"I can't believe that he wouldn't deny that stuff. What the hell is he thinking? It will ruin him."

"That's the other bit," Zara explained. "He says that 'since God chose Joel Wood to be His messenger,' he needs to 'confess all his sins' so he will be 'more open to receive the Holy Word' or some shit like that. I asked him why he needed to do that, since God apparently talked to him already. He said that he had stopped believing in God a while back, so last Sunday was just God's way of making him believe again. So God says 'here I am, I exist after all,' and now Joel wants to be a good boy."

"Holy shit, he actually said on the record that he didn't believe in God?"

"I was as gobsmacked as you, love, believe me."

Thelo looked at his watch. "You weren't there very long. Did he cut the interview short?"

"No, I just wasn't prepared to have him be so cooperative. Half of the questions I'd written were geared to try to get him to slip up and admit to something without realizing it. I started off with the hammer blow, which was asking him if he had ever cheated on his wife and he just fucking went 'yeah, all the time' or some shit like that. Bloody well had to throw out half my interview at that point."

Thelo laughed. He could hear Mike laughing as well.

"Hey," he said, "can you put me on speaker? I want to talk to Mike for a second."

"Sure, love, hang on."

Thelo heard the phone switch to speaker. He spoke louder.

"Hey, Mike."

"Yeah, bud?" Mike's voice sounded distant even though he was sitting right beside Zara.

"You still wanna grab some lunch? I haven't eaten yet."

"Sure, that would be great." He turned to Zara. "You wanna come with?"

"No, I need to get back and start working."

"Lunch for two, then," Mike said.

"You're on. Sharkey's in a half hour?"

"Sure. I might be a minute or two late depending on traffic, but I'll be there."

"We're pulling up at the hotel now," Zara said. "Gotta run."

"Bye, love. Good luck."

Zara hung up the phone. Mike pulled the car up to the front door of the hotel.

"Thank you very much for the ride and the escort."

"No problem at all. It was an afternoon I won't soon forget, and it was very nice to meet you as well."

"Nice to meet you, too," she said. She opened the car door, then hesitated. She turned to Mike.

"Say, if you don't have plans, how about you come back tonight and I'll treat you to a nice dinner. The hotel restaurant looks pretty good. After that maybe we can go up to my room for a nightcap." She winked at him.

"Oh," Mike stammered, caught off-guard. "I guess Thelo didn't tell you."

"You're married." Zara threw up her hands. "I should've known. You weren't wearing a ring, so I took a shot."

Mike chuckled. "I'm not married. I'm gay. Thelo and I are dating."

"Oh, bloody hell! He should've told me, the cheeky bastard! I wouldn't have…"

"It's all right," Mike assured her with a big smile. "I'm flattered, honestly. I've gotta get going if I want to make lunch, though."

"Right." Zara got out of the car. "Tell Thelo that I'm jealous and that he has good taste."

She closed the car door.

CHAPTER EIGHTEEN

Holly Wood sat in her study, glued to her screens. She had been feverishly digging into their bank account sites, double and triple-checking that she had covered her digital tracks. She was glad that she had been planning her divorce from Joel for years now and had everything set up ages ago. She hadn't planned on him being the one to pull the plug, though, that much was a surprise. Holly had looked forward to the day when she could see the expression on Joel's face as she announced her departure, but now she was going to be denied that pleasure. No matter, she would still have plenty of bad news for him. She darted her eyes from one screen to another, double checking, making sure. Can't be too careful. Leave a digital fingerprint somewhere, and it all goes bad, and somebody ends up in jail.

"I just had an interview with a reporter from the UK," Joel said as he entered the room. Holly hadn't heard him coming, and he startled her.

"Yeah?" She tried to sound as if she wasn't recovering from a jolt. "How'd it go?"

"She knew all about the poker games, the prostitutes, everything."

"Did she know about Cletus and Mark and Jonas?" Holly was stalling, still feverishly typing, trying to log out of everything in case Joel came around to her side of the desk where he could see the screens.

"She knew there were others, but I don't think she knew their names. I didn't tell her."

"They'll appreciate that," she said. "No need to drown them when your ship sinks."

"My ship isn't sinking. In fact, I just got new sails."

"Oh?" Holly asked, finishing up. She closed the last window and looked at Joel from around her wall of screens.

"I confessed my sins to the press," he said. "People will be impressed. People will see how a man can change, become an instrument for God's will, a messenger for God's Word. They'll be inspired, and they will tune in by the millions."

"They'll be tuning in, but only to see if God smites you on live television."

"I need to know something, though," Joel said. "That reporter contacted me on my secret email account. There are maybe eight people who know that email address, maybe even fewer. I asked how she got it, and she said that she didn't hack my account, that someone else had given her my emails."

"And?"

"How did she get them?" Joel asked, with a tone that indicated he thought he already knew the answer.

"Didn't you ask her?"

"She wouldn't tell me. But I have a hunch."

Holly stared at him, daring him to make the accusation. "Go on, then," she said with an iciness in her voice. "Ask me."

"Did you give her those emails?"

"No. I don't even know her."

"You bitch," Joel seethed. "Don't lie to me." He moved toward her.

Holly stood up from behind the desk to face him. "I'm not lying to you," she said coldly. "And I'm not going down with your ship, either, new sails or not."

"You're right," Joel said. "I'm divorcing you."

"Then you'd better hope you're right about your ratings. Because you won't have anything after the divorce."

Joel laughed at her. "I guess you forgot about the prenuptial agreement, then? I get to keep my money."

Holly stared him down. "Yes, you keep your money. Too bad don't have much money to keep."

Joel blinked and gave her a puzzled look. She returned a wicked smile.

"You're broke," she said. "You might have enough money to keep up your lifestyle for a month or two. I guess you could sell the house. By then, I'll be living somewhere on a tropical island, or maybe I'll get a cottage in the Hamptons. Maybe I'll do both. I can afford it. "

"I can't be broke. We've got lots of money."

"Yes, we do," she said. "But when you take me out of that 'we,' then you're decidedly lower middle class, maybe not even that. Such a pity that you can't manage your money."

"You've always managed my money."

She grinned, and the realization hit him like a hammer.

Joel shook in anger. He lunged at her, but she stepped aside and dodged him.

"Careful," she warned. "If you lay one finger on me, I will have the police here so fast you won't even know what happened."

"Go ahead and call the police. They'll be happy to hear how you stole my money."

"That's the thing," Holly said. "If they go snooping, they'll see that you were ass deep into shady deals, money laundering, embezzlement, lots of terribly illegal activities."

"I haven't done any of that!"

"Oh, but you have!" She had a wicked grin on her face. "The digital paper trail will prove it. You've been doing it for years."

Joel couldn't contain his rage. He rushed Holly and grabbed her by the throat. He pushed her several steps backward and pinned her against the wall, then put his other hand over her mouth and nose. She could barely breathe.

"You think you have it all worked out, don't you?" he hissed, inches from her face. "The prenup might say that we split with our accounts separated, but your *will* leaves everything to me." He tightened his grip on her throat. Holly began to tremble as her lungs ached for air. "I don't know what you did to steal my money, but I want it all back in my accounts by tomorrow morning, and any hint of illegal activity goes away as well, do I make myself clear?"

Holly managed to nod her head a little, and he let go of her. Holly collapsed to the floor, gasping for breath. Joel swung his leg back to kick her, then caught himself at the last second. Can't leave a mark, he thought. He stormed out of the room.

Holly waited until he was out of earshot, then began to cry softly. She clenched her fists until her nails nearly broke the skin on her palms. She pulled herself up with the aid of an end table, then made her way to her desk, sat down, and fished a tissue out of a drawer. She dabbed her face dry. This hadn't gone at all like she'd expected. She should've just waited until he filed for divorce and let him find out then that he didn't have any money, but dammit, she wanted to see the look on his face when she told him. She sighed, dabbed her eyes again and launched the browser on her computer. Time for plan B.

Christine had been on the road ever since she left home this morning. She had done interviews with pastors, imams, rabbis, and members of congregations all over town. The people who believed that The Sermon was a miracle and those who thought it was faked still seemed to be roughly equal in number. Those on the side of the miraculous had various reactions ranging from 'I've had those same suspicions' to 'I'm disturbed by the words that God spoke to us.' A small handful thought the pastors who preached The Sermon were possessed by evil forces. A few of them were planning to protest outside the places where The Sermon was preached.

Christine's phone rang. She pulled over to answer.

"Hello, young lady."

"Matthew, good to hear your voice. How are things at Mt Carmel?"

"I'll tell you at dinner, if you're free." She could hear the hopefulness in his voice.

"Sounds good, but I've been on the road all day, and I'm exhausted. I don't think I'm up for dinner out tonight. How about we get a pizza or some takeout and have it at my place?"

"That's a great idea. I could pick up something from the Briar and Thistle on the way over."

"Are you sure you want to be seen there again?" she asked, half-joking.

"I will only be there long enough to pick up the food."

"Dress is casual," she said. "I might be in a bathrobe."

"How are you feeling today with your bruises?"

"I'm still sore and look like hell, but I'll be fine."

"Good. I'm looking forward to dinner. I have some news to share, and I'd like your thoughts on it."

"Is it good news or bad news?"

"It could be either, or both," he said. "I haven't got it all sorted out yet, and I'd like you to help me."

"I'll do what I can. See you tonight. How about six o'clock?"

"Perfect, I'll see you then."

Thelo sat at his desk, deep in the bowels of the Dark Web, searching for anything that would link together the people who had been at the interfaith so many years ago. If he could trace connections between those people and the rest of the list of Sermon preachers, he might be able to get beyond circumstantial evidence and find something he could use to prove it was a hoax.

Zara's interview with Joel Wood wouldn't help. Joel said that The Sermon changed his mind about the existence of God. Thelo wondered if it would change his mind at some point, too. Perhaps, but not until he'd ruled out every other explanation. If there was a God, then He had some serious explaining to do about a lot of shit.

He was surprised to hear the alert tone signaling new files in the encrypted vault. He moved his cursor over to check them out, but was interrupted by a message from Admin wanting to talk over VOIP. He accepted the link and heard the familiar robotic voice of Admin's vocal masking software.

"You have some new files," it said.

"I was just about to look at them."

"It doesn't shed much light on The Sermon, I'm sorry," Admin continued, "but at least one of those pompous pastors is going down."

"Joel Wood?"

"Yes. He's not as rich as everyone thinks."

"He could be only half as rich as everyone thinks and still have more than I'll make in my lifetime," Thelo said.

"Don't bet on it," the digitized voice told him.

"Seriously? So what's in the files you sent me just now?"

"Evidence. Joel Wood is a felon."

"White collar felon or serial killer felon?" Thelo joked.

"Embezzlement, insider trading, tax evasion, money laundering, charity fraud, all kinds of stuff. It's quite the list, actually. You'll have fun with it."

"Wow. You've been busy."

"It was all pretty easy to find if you know where to look. I suggest that you be careful when this gets out. No telling what he might do."

"I'll be careful."

"You have some time to dig through the information and check it for accuracy. When this gets leaked publicly, you'll already have your homework done, and you'll already have your article written and ready to publish. That's my gift to you for pointing me at these fakers and their hypocrisy."

"When it gets leaked?" Thelo asked. "You're going to put it out there?"

"If you're the only one with this information, the spotlight will be on you. You'll be asked a lot of questions about where you got it and I trust you not to tell, but I don't trust the feds to leave you alone. If they seize your equipment, it could eventually lead back to me, as careful as we've been. I don't want them making that link. I'll drop it onto an anonymous whistleblower site or two and let the world see it. Then your story will be based on the same information that everyone else has. You just get to look at it before they do and vet it beforehand."

"I'd love an exclusive, but I appreciate your concern. You're right, of course."

"Get to work." The connection ended.

Thelo felt like a kid on Christmas morning as he excitedly opened the latest folder in his file vault.

"How do you know my story?" Ivan asked his visitor. Everything about this woman was odd, yet he didn't find her intimidating. His question to her was pure curiosity with no animosity, even though he figured that he should be upset about the invasion of privacy. Maybe he would've thought differently yesterday, and she was right that he wasn't ready.

"I can't explain that," she said. "I can't explain how I can get into your head to find out things any more than I can explain how I can put myself into your dreams. I just can, that's all, and the important part isn't how I can get the information but what I do with it. That's where you come in."

"Why me?"

"You are the editor of the largest newspaper in the city. The Associated Press often picks up stories from your paper for their worldwide feed. I have been telling people my story for months, but nobody believed me until those people all preached that sermon the other day. Now people are paying attention, but time is running short, and I'm just one person. I can only talk to so many people at a time. People have got to hear me, and you've got a tool that I can use to get the word out."

"You could've gone to anyone. There are other papers, magazines, television, the internet… Why me?"

"I saw what happens with the other choices," she said. "It has to be you."

"What happened with the others?"

"Not what happened," she said. "What *happens*. I followed the chain of events from the beginning to their future conclusion. The only one that has a chance is the one that starts with you."

"Okay, you're going to have to tell me what you're talking about," Ivan said. "None of this makes any sense. You can see the future?"

"No, not *the* future. I see multiple futures. What happens in the future isn't set in stone. It can be changed by decisions that people make. I can only see the outcomes of those decisions, and then I use that knowledge to make the right choices."

"I'm not sure I understand the difference," Ivan said. "It's still seeing the future, isn't it?"

Lisa sighed. She didn't want to waste time on this, but she knew that Ivan would have to grasp a few basic ideas before he would trust her enough to carry out her plan.

"Let's say that there's a charity that needs to fill a vacancy for president. There are seven voting members on the board, including yourself, and there are six candidates who've applied for the president's position. Each of your six fellow board members casts their vote, and each one has voted for a different candidate. All six of the candidates now have one vote each, so whichever person you vote for will be the winner."

"Got it," Ivan said.

"If I could see the future in the way that you're thinking," Lisa explained, "then I would already know how you cast your vote, and I would already know who the president of the charity would be. Right?"

"Right. Go on."

"But I don't know how you will vote. I only know that if you vote for candidate one, then he will win. If you vote for candidate two, she will win. I don't see the outcome of your vote. I see all the outcomes of all the ways you could vote."

"Everyone can do that," Ivan said. "That's not special."

"Not everyone can see beyond the election results, though. I can see down the timeline created by each possible choice and I can see all the future outcomes for the charity based on which person won the election. I then use that information to try to help."

"So you're saying that you would be able to determine the future for the charity for each one of the candidates?" Ivan asked. "You'd be able to see which one of them would be the best choice?"

"Exactly," Lisa said. "Then I would try to influence you to make the right choice."

"You'd tell me how to vote?"

"Yes, if I knew you," she said. "But I could also get into your dreams and hopefully stick that person's name in your head, so you subconsciously favor that candidate. I can find out a lot of stuff about a person when I get in their head like that, and I use that information to figure out the best way to influence them. That's why all I did in your dream was call you by name and introduce myself. Your curiosity is very strong, Ivan, I knew that would be enough to get you to sit down and talk to me."

Ivan's head was spinning. "How can you possibly make sense of all that data? Even if each of those candidates only had to make three or four decisions as president, each one of those decisions would lead to a different timeline, and each of those timelines would have its own set of outcomes. It would be impossible to know all the millions of different variations. Impossible."

"I can sympathize with your skepticism," she said. "I don't understand it myself, but that isn't important. It's getting my message out there that's important."

Ivan's brain was reeling, but the reporter in him wanted to get past the exposition to the root of the story. "So what's your message, then?"

"Life is broken," she said flatly. "We need to fix it. I've seen the timelines if it stays broken and there are no good outcomes. If we want to survive as a species, we have to get the word out, and quickly."

Holly was nervous. The incident with Joel had left her shaken and afraid, two feelings that were mostly foreign to her. She prided herself on her ability to adapt to the unexpected, but Joel's newfound belief in God had blindsided her. She would soon have her exit, though, and she would be able to sit back and watch Joel squirm. All of the illegal dealings were done with Joel's accounts, in his name. Her accounts were all clean. She patted herself on the back for making that decision so long ago.

If… no, *when* the shit hit the fan, Joel would be the one in court trying to explain away the evidence. If Holly got asked to testify, she could plead ignorance. Their accounts were and had always been separate, so even though she managed his checkbook, he could've been doing those dealings on his own without her knowledge. That would be enough to provide reasonable doubt in court, at least. She had covered her tracks well, and once two or three more steps were finished, she'd be home free. They'd have to wait, though. She had an exit window coming up.

When she knew that Joel was out of the house and heading to the church for the Wednesday evening service, she made her move. She went to her study and unplugged the four external hard drives that housed her system backups and all her data files, then she logged into her computer and erased the internal hard drive. She put the external drives into a suitcase with a few changes of clothes and her laptop, then called her Aunt Millie and invited herself over for a visit. She would set up her laptop there and finish erasing any evidence that could link her to the fraud. She hoped that by the time she'd worn out her welcome with Aunt Millie, Joel would be in jail and she could come home without worrying about her own safety. She could only cross her fingers and hope that the information she planned to dump onto the Dark Web tomorrow would find its way into the right hands.

She threw the suitcase into the trunk of the car and had been on the road just half an hour when her cell phone rang. She recognized the ringtone as Joel's. She didn't answer. She had nothing to say to him right now. A short time later, she heard the tone indicating a text message. She fished into her purse with her right hand, trying to locate the phone. She found it and pulled it out, then fumbled and dropped it to the floor.

"Shit."

She stretched her arm to the floorboard to search for the phone. Nothing. It dinged with another text. The sound came from just under the seat. She bent down and fumbled around for it.

The noise was deafening and sudden. The blast of a truck horn, the squeal of tires on pavement, the crunch of crushed fiberglass, the crackle of the shattered windshield, the gunfire-like *pop* of the airbag.

It was over in an instant.

Officer Mike was driving home after his lunch with Thelo. He heard the eighteen-wheeler hit the brakes and saw the smoke of the trailer's wheels. Mike had his car off to the side of the road in no time and called 911 as he jumped out to see if he could be of any help. He hadn't seen a wreck this bad in a while, and it always shook him up. The woman in the Lexus had crossed the center line into an oncoming truck. She was apparently leaning over on the seat, which made the airbag utterly useless as a safety device, but Mike was fairly sure it wouldn't have saved her, anyway. The driver of the eighteen-wheeler was only slightly injured, but he would have nightmares for a long time, that much was sure.

Mike hated accident scenes. It unnerved him to see how quickly your world could get upended, and it made him uneasy. One life gone, another forever changed, just like that.

Just like that.

CHAPTER NINETEEN

Matthew rang the doorbell at precisely six o'clock. He wore a short-sleeved dress shirt and slacks, and in his hands were two bags of takeout from the Briar and Thistle. Christine answered the door in her bathrobe with a towel wrapped around her head.

"You're right on time," she said. "And way overdressed."

Matthew chuckled at her appearance in spite of himself. "You weren't kidding about the bathrobe."

"I've only been home a couple of minutes," she admitted. "Just got out of the shower. Come in. I need to tidy myself up a bit more. I was running a little late."

"I got two dozen wings and a side of grilled veggies," he said as he stepped into the house. "I hope that's okay."

"Sounds delicious, and I'm starving." She closed the door behind him. "Just put everything on the counter there, I'll be right back."

She retreated to the master bath, and Matthew put the food on the kitchen counter. Christine had put out a bottle of wine, two stemmed glasses, and a corkscrew. He smiled.

"Should I go ahead and plate the food?" he called out to her.

"Sure," came the reply from down the hall. "Plates are above the dishwasher."

He opened the cabinet, got out two large plates, then artfully arranged the wings on one and the grilled vegetables on the other. He placed them in the middle of the dining table, then got two smaller plates, found the silverware, and arranged those on the table as well. From down the hall, the sound of a hair dryer indicated that he had a few more minutes, so he opened the wine, poured two glasses, and set them on the table. Matthew considered stopping there, since he didn't know where to find napkins or placemats, but quickly decided that Christine wouldn't mind if he opened a drawer or two to search. Matthew felt comfortable in her home, which was entirely due to her easygoing nature and welcoming attitude. She was, he thought, the type of Christian that he wished more people would be. She wasn't one to throw phrases like "Praise God" or "Thank you, Jesus" into her speech, but she instead showed her faith through her actions.

He found the drawer he needed, and fished out two placemats and two cloth napkins. He added those to the table setting and stepped back to admire his handiwork. 'Not bad,' he thought. Christine emerged from the hallway with freshly dried hair. She had changed into yoga pants and a t-shirt.

"The bathrobe was fine," Matthew said. "You didn't need to change."

"I felt a bit underdressed, with you looking so nice. But I have my limits. This is as good as it gets for my dinner attire tonight, sorry."

"You look lovely." He blew her a kiss.

"So does the table," she admired. "Look at you with your fancy plating skills! I see you found the placemats, too."

"Yes. Hope you don't mind me opening a few drawers."

"Not at all. *Mi casa es su casa.*"

They sat down at the table, toasted their friendship, then they both loaded their plates with wings and vegetables. Matthew requested that they wait until after dinner to discuss his day, so Christine talked about all the interviews she had done and the differing factions of belief as to what The Sermon meant. Matthew was a good listener, and Christine enjoyed having someone to talk to after a long day at work. The strangers at the Briar and Thistle used to fill that need, but this was far better.

After they'd finished dinner, Matthew rose and collected the dishes. He took them to the kitchen and turned on the tap at the sink.

"Oh, just leave those for now," Christine suggested. "I can tidy up later."

"Not a chance. Pour yourself another glass of wine and relax. This won't take a minute."

"I'm at least going to help, then." She got up and fished a drying towel out of a drawer. The two of them finished up the dishes, poured some wine into their glasses, then sat down in the living room.

"So," Christine said as she settled back in her chair. "How was your day?"

"First of all, I'd like to apologize in advance for dragging this wonderful evening down into the depths of heavy topic discussion."

"Uh oh. It doesn't sound like we're celebrating your return to the priesthood."

"We could be," he said, without much enthusiasm. "But it doesn't feel like a celebration."

He told her about Bishop Garza's visit and the ultimatum he was given. She asked a question or two when she needed clarification, but mostly Christine just let Matthew talk, feeling sorry for him as he told the story, wishing she had an easy answer to give. When he'd finished, he heaved a heavy sigh and hung his head.

"I've been praying all afternoon, but I'm still no closer to making a decision than I was before," he said. "I used to be able to pray and receive guidance for my parishioners no matter how complex their situation, but now that I need help myself, I feel like the line has gone dead."

"We all feel like that sometimes. Once in a while, everyone will feel like God isn't listening. Just because you're a priest doesn't mean that you get a pass on that. I'm sure that God has a lot of calls to answer right now, so you might be on hold for awhile."

"Thanks," Matthew said. "But I need Him to answer pretty soon. I know they must be already looking for someone who can take over here, which they'll do no matter what I decide. Whether I remain a priest and move to another parish or whether I leave the priesthood and stay in Riverside, the fact is that there will be a new priest at Our Lady of Mt Carmel."

"The parishioners will be devastated. They all love you very much."

"Thank you for saying that," he said. "I love them, too."

They sat in silence for a few moments and sipped their wine. Christine topped off their glasses, saw that there was just a small amount left in the bottle, then divided the last of it between them.

Matthew watched Christine as she poured, and in spite of all the drama in his life at the moment, he was smitten. It was an old-fashioned word, one that she and others in her generation had probably never used, but it summed up his feelings pretty well. He wondered if she had any feelings for him aside from their friendship. For people in his generation, the fact that they'd slept together twice would be a good indication there was romance between them, but Matthew knew that people of Christine's age group were different. She likely viewed sex as something that could be done just for fun without the emotional trappings of a relationship. If he asked her how she felt about him, his heart could be broken by her reply and she would then forever be uncomfortable around him. It could ruin their friendship.

"Matthew?"

He looked up at her.

"What are you thinking? You've been staring at your glass for a while, are you okay?"

"I'm just new at this," he said. "I don't know how to handle what I'm feeling."

"That's understandable. It's a big decision, and it will determine the direction of your life. That's a lot to deal with. You're allowed to be overwhelmed."

"I left some things out," he said.

"Like what?"

Matthew couldn't answer. He stared at his glass and took another sip.

"You're wondering what happens to us if you move away," Christine guessed.

Matthew nodded, then looked up at her. "Christine, I don't even know how to describe us. You and I are from different generations, and we see life differently. I don't know if you feel the same way I do."

"I probably do. I think we're good together. I look forward to spending time with you."

"As do I," he said. "But if I stay in the priesthood, that would end. I'd be far away from here. Even if we could overcome the distance, I would still have to treat you as a parishioner, not as…" He fought for a word that wouldn't sound inappropriate given their short time together.

"As a girlfriend?"

Matthew was surprised to hear her say it. He nodded.

"I'd be lying if I said that I hadn't considered all of that," she said. "But I didn't want to get in the way of your decision. We've known each other for a long time, but we've only known each other intimately for a few days. I like you a lot, and I love our times together, but I wasn't about to expect you to base your decision about the rest of your life on a couple of sleepovers."

Matthew looked hurt. Christine saw it and quickly apologized.

"Oh, I'm sorry. I didn't mean for that to sound so impersonal. Although to be honest, the first time sorta was that. We were both drunk, and it was your first time, and everything was sorta crazy."

Matthew couldn't argue that.

"But the second time was because I liked you and wanted to be with you again when we were both sober. I don't see that one as a sleepover. That was me wanting you to spend the night." She took a sip of wine while she let Matthew process that. "It was wonderful, by the way, even though I was still sore from the attack."

"Thank you," he said. "I thought it was wonderful, too."

They both sat in silence for a while. Matthew hunted for a way to make sentences out of his feelings.

"I'm brand new to relationships," he finally said. "I don't know what to feel. I don't know what to call it, and I don't know if you feel the same way. I need some help sorting it all out. I know we've just been seeing each other a few days, but when I'm honest with myself, I know that ending our relationship is as upsetting to me as ending my career as a priest."

"New relationships are like that. When it's new, everything on earth revolves around that person, and you push aside anything that gets in the way. It's normal to feel like that. But what if you give up the priesthood and then we don't work out after all? Then what will you do? Have you considered that?"

"Yes, of course. I'm very aware that the odds are stacked against us becoming more than we are now. I'm nearly twice your age, you've got your career ahead of you, I would need to find a new career, and we haven't even discussed children."

Christine laughed suddenly, almost choking on her wine. "Easy, big fella! That's looking down the road a bit far, don't ya think?"

"Yes, I know. But I've counseled several couples who were on the verge of divorce because they had very different desires when it came to how many kids they wanted, or if they wanted any at all. It's something that people should discuss before things get too involved, I think."

"Well, do you want kids, then?" she asked.

"I love kids, but I think I'm too old to be starting a family. I don't want to show up at my child's high school graduation with a walker and a bad toupee."

"Well, I don't particularly like kids," Christine said. "And I can't imagine ever liking them enough to want to come home to one every night after work. So that's settled, then. No kids."

"One potential crisis averted." Matthew smiled and raised his glass.

"I do appreciate you considering what would happen to us if you moved away," Christine said. "That's very sweet. I'm just concerned that you'd give up the priesthood, something you'd wanted all your life, over a long shot of a relationship. Like you said, the odds aren't in our favor."

Matthew nodded his understanding. "So we're back to square one. I don't know what to do."

"Tell me this, then. Why did you want to be a priest?"

"I wanted to help people. Like I told you in that first interview at the rectory. I wanted to be able to help people like Father Grant helped me and my family."

"Could you still find a way to help people if you weren't a priest?"

Matthew looked at her and thought for a moment. "I suppose so."

"But you'd be doing it outside the Catholic Church. Would that bother you?"

"I loved the structure of the Church life," he said. "I loved the traditions, the rites, the music. All of that felt very secure, something I could hang onto. I would certainly miss that."

"Could you get all that as a parishioner? I mean, would you have to be a priest to feel that, or could you feel it from the pews rather than the altar?"

"Hadn't really thought about it," he admitted. "I suppose I could."

"And if you remained in the priesthood and moved far away, would that structure and those traditions be enough to keep you happy? What about all the parishioners here that you'd never see again?"

"Honestly, ever since the first meeting with Bishop Garza, the structure and traditions of the Church have begun to feel more like a barrier than a foundation. I was kept away from my parishioners because the Church wanted to protect the traditions. I can't see them the same way I used to. The people are more important than the traditions, at least that's how I feel about it."

"So let's say that you go ahead and confess your sins against the Church, which you told me would feel like lying," she said, "and you're sent to a new parish far from here. You get there, and you've got to start all over. The traditions and rites of the Church are your foundation, but they don't feel so secure anymore."

"That doesn't sound very appealing," Matthew admitted.

"Or you leave the priesthood and find another career that still lets you help people. You go to church as a parishioner, so you can still enjoy the mass, the music, all of that tradition that you love. You can even go to other churches if you like. There are lots of wonderful congregations in this city, and they all have different traditions and music and rituals, but there's enough commonality to really give you a sense of the universality of God. I find it quite uplifting."

"Go on," he said. "This is helpful."

"So you still get to help people, you still get to enjoy the traditions of the Church, you'll still be able to see the other parishioners that you've spent most of your life with, and they'll get to see you, too. They would miss you a lot if you left," she said. "And so would I."

Matthew beamed at her.

"And if it turns out that we don't beat the odds," she continued, "you still have all the other things. I would hope that we'd still remain friends and enjoy each other's company, even if we don't end up being a romantic couple."

"Christine, you might be the answer to my prayers. Thank you."

Thelo stared at his computer screen in amazement. He called Zara.

"I'm just about to send this article off to my editor, can you call back in a few?" She never just said, 'hello.' Thelo was used to it.

"You might not want to send it off just yet," Thelo warned. "That's why I called. I just copied a bunch of stuff over to your file vault that you might want to look at."

"Hang on." Zara began the security process to get to the file vault. "Can you give me the gist of it?"

"Joel Wood is apparently involved in all kinds of unscrupulous and illegal financial dealings. Most of it could lead to a felony conviction."

Zara got to the file vault and opened it. She began to sift through the data. "Who sent you this stuff, your hacker buddy?"

"Same as the emails, yes."

"And he can get into all these accounts?"

"Apparently so."

A few moments of silence passed as Zara looked at the files. "Something doesn't smell right," she said. "This isn't the kind of thing that you'd find by accident. This stuff was surgically removed. You'd have to know exactly what you were looking for and where to look if you were going to come up with all this in such a short time. You just put him on it Sunday, yeah?"

"Sunday night, yes."

"Three days ago. Did you specifically say to look at Joel Wood?"

"No, just to look for connections between the people who… I see your point, right. All I got on the others was an email dump. Maybe he has a personal beef with Joel."

"Well, it's a beef that's been around awhile, I'd think," Zara said as she looked through the files. "The emails from the other pastors was a ton of stuff. You had to look through it to get the good shit. But there's nothing extra in here. You know how long it takes to sift through that stuff, even with filters. This came too quickly. Either he knows Joel and his finances pretty well, or he's been digging around and saving up this stuff for a while."

"You're making this investigative reporter feel pretty stupid for not seeing that myself. But you're right. I'll ask him next time I'm in contact."

"I wouldn't. Anonymity is his greatest treasure. Don't let on that you've figured out a piece of who he might be."

"Right again," Thelo said. "I know you'll need to check that information before you can print it, but I wanted you to see it before you sent your article."

"I can't put any of this new information into my article until I have a chance to vet it. I'll send my article to my editor tonight as-is, but let him know that there might be more coming later."

"I think that's a good idea, yes."

"I think Joel Wood owes me another interview."

"Don't expect him to be so cooperative this time."

"No, of course not. But maybe this time I'll get to see the shocked look on his face that I was hoping to see last time."

"You realize, of course, that he's going to want to know where you got the information."

"Yeah, but I'm not going to tell him. Hell, we don't even know who sent it. What I am going to tell him is that after the interview, I'm going to the police with it."

"Zara, that evidence was obtained illegally. If you go to the police with it, they can follow the trail right back to me and my source."

"Do you know who your source is?" Zara asked.

"No. But I know that he's on the FBI Most Wanted list, and I don't want to be linked to him in any way. I don't think I could end up in jail, but I would certainly be under FBI surveillance after that, which gives me the creeps. Plus, I'd lose my source."

"Then we need to figure out how to get this information out there where anyone can see it, so there's no direct link."

"He said he was going to post the information on a couple of whistleblower sites on the Dark Web. As soon as it shows up there, we're free to use whatever we like."

"Do you know which sites, specifically?"

"No, he didn't say. I'll snoop around a bit. If I can't find it, I'll contact him again, and ask where he leaked it."

"Sounds like a plan," Zara said. She hung up the phone and dove back into the data.

Joel had just finished giving his Wednesday service at Gloria Deo. The crowd was nearly double what Wednesday evenings usually bring, a good indicator for a big crowd on Sunday, he thought. Everyone wanted to be there in person if God spoke through him again. It didn't happen tonight, but that was okay. His Sunday services were better attended, plus they went out on television. God must know this, of course, and Joel assured the congregation that God was simply waiting until the message could be heard by more people.

He hinted at his upcoming confessions, saying only that there were going to be stories about him in the newspapers, stories that would paint him as a terrible person. He teased them with a few weighted comments designed to keep them talking until Sunday, and then he promised them that it would be a can't-miss event.

When the service was over, he found a police officer waiting for him offstage. The officer told Joel about Holly's crash, and that he needed to make a positive ID of the body. Joel barely heard most of it through the shock. He had tried to call her before the service, but she didn't pick up. He had left a rather threatening message on her voicemail. He tried to remember whether he'd said anything bad enough to create suspicion against him. He couldn't remember.

Joel followed the officer to the county morgue and identified Holly's body.

"Where are her things?" Joel asked the officer as they left the examining room. "I'd like to take them home."

"I'm afraid that you won't be able to do that just yet, pastor," the officer told him. "We're currently holding them as evidence."

"Evidence of what? I don't understand."

"Your wife crossed the center line of the highway directly into an oncoming truck at full speed. That's an unusual situation, and we need to keep her belongings from the car until we rule out any foul play or other circumstances. Please understand, it's just a precaution. You'll be able to take the items home soon."

"Why would you suspect foul play in a car crash?" he asked.

The officer stopped walking and faced Joel.

"Pastor," he said. "I know this is difficult for you. I've watched you on TV for years, and I don't think you'd do anything wrong. You're a man of God. But one of our officers who happened to be at the scene of the accident says that he sat in on an interview you gave to a reporter this afternoon. He said that you confessed to some things during the interview that might have caused tension between you and your wife. Please understand that you are not a suspect, and we will probably discover that this was just a terrible accident. But we have to do our jobs, and that will involve keeping the items from the car as evidence until things are cleared up. I'm sorry."

Joel's mind was racing. What had he said in that voicemail? Surely they won't think that he tried to kill her, even if he might've threatened to. Would they? She drove into a truck. Not his fault, right? Unless they thought it was suicide. They couldn't pin that on him, could they? He needed to call his attorney. This was not how he'd planned for the evening to go.

"Hey, good looking!" Thelo answered his phone when he saw Mike's name on the screen.

"Hey." Mike sounded pretty down.

"Whoa, what's wrong?"

"Saw a bad accident on the way home. Head-on between a car and a semi."

"Damn." Thelo suddenly understood Mike's mood. "Anyone hurt?"

"The truck driver will be okay, at least physically. The driver of the car is dead."

"Sorry you had to see that. I know you hate working accidents."

"Yeah."

"Hey, I thought you were off duty before lunch today, what were you doing working a scene?"

"I was on my way home, and it happened right in front of me."

"Wow. I'm glad you weren't involved. You okay?"

"Yeah, but get this: the driver of the car was Joel Wood's wife."

Thelo sat up straight in his chair. "What? You're shitting me."

"No, it was her. I saw her license."

"Holy crap." Thelo's reporter instincts suddenly kicked in. "They're sure it was an accident?"

"Pretty sure, yeah. I told them about the bombshell interview your friend had just had with him, though, so they're holding all the stuff they found in the car as evidence, just in case."

"Do you think he might've done something to the car?"

"Don't know. I do know that it looked like she was bugging out for a while, though. She had a suitcase in the trunk."

"What was in it?"

"I don't know. I'm sure they'll go through it. She was probably just upset and getting out of the house for a while. Maybe she had her mind on stuff and wasn't paying attention."

"Maybe she did it on purpose."

"Suicide? I don't think so," Mike said. "But I've been wrong before. Maybe they'll find something in the suitcase. Anyway, I just thought I'd tell you since I know that you're kinda investigating Joel Wood at the moment."

"Thanks for the update," Thelo said. "Do you want to come over? You sound like you could use a drink or a hug or both."

"I appreciate that. But I'm at home already, and I'm about to have a long soak in the tub. Can I get a rain check?"

"Absolutely."

Thelo hung up the phone and went back to his computer. He searched all the whistleblower sites he could think of for the information that Admin was supposed to post, but he found nothing. He tried to contact Admin through the usual methods, but there was no answer. He hadn't known Admin to delay his actions like this before and wondered what was keeping him from getting the information uploaded. He tried contacting Admin again, even used a forced alert. Still nothing.

Thelo thought about what Zara had said regarding the nature of the information in the folder. It was all stuff that would be very tricky to dig up quickly unless you had a password to the accounts and prior knowledge of what was in the accounts. It looked like it had been cherry picked to incriminate Joel with numerous felonies. This data was very different than the stuff he'd gotten on the other pastors. Could Admin be trying to take Joel down? Maybe he had been gathering this stuff for years and was just waiting for a good time to leak it. Still, some of it was recent stuff, so Admin would've had to get into those accounts, all of them, in a short period of time. There had to be a connection of some kind between him and Joel Wood.

Or *her* and Joel Wood.

Thelo hadn't even considered that one of the world's best hackers might be a woman. He cursed himself for his sexism. It's a great cover, he thought, because when the feds try to find hackers, they hardly ever suspect women. They look for people who fit the profile: twenty-something guys, loners without much of a social life, that sort of thing. The last person they'd look at would be the millionaire wife of a TV preacher. Even Thelo had a hard time believing it, but it made sense.

He tried to contact Admin repeatedly for an hour afterward. The longer it went without an answer, the more Thelo was convinced he'd cracked the identity of the world's most elusive hacker.

Ivan's phone rang just as Lisa left his home. He watched her walk down the sidewalk toward the street, then picked up the call.

"Hey, boss," Thelo said, obviously excited.

"You sound like a man with a scoop. I've got one, too."

"Joel Wood's wife was killed in a car wreck today."

"Really? I hadn't heard about it. That's your big news? Does it have anything to do with your investigation into The Sermon?"

"It might," Thelo said. "You're familiar with the hacker called 'Admin?'"

"Yes, of course. FBI most wanted list for awhile now, what about him?"

"*Her*. I'm almost certain that Holly Wood is Admin."

"Holy shit! Really?"

"Yes! But I can't prove it, at least not yet. You know a couple of people at the FBI, don't you? Maybe you can toss them a bone, get them on it."

"Why do you care? What would it matter to you?"

"You didn't hear this from me," Thelo said. "You are going to forget everything you are about to hear, understand?"

"Um… Aw, geez. If you're going to tell me that Admin has been your secret source, I don't want to hear it."

"I got some information from Admin that could land Joel Wood in federal prison for a long time."

"I don't want to hear that you've got illegally hacked information," Ivan said.

"That's just it," Thelo explained. "If Holly Wood is Admin, then the information on Joel wasn't hacked at all. All of it would've been obtained through proper login with her own password, nothing illegal at all."

"Nice. How do we prove it was her?"

"Put the FBI on it. They'll search everything they can get their hands on. If there's a link, they'll find it."

"I'm not sure the FBI is going to launch an investigation into the rich wife of a celebrity preacher over a hunch. It's a long shot."

"Then tell them to look into it because her husband committed multiple acts of fraud, embezzlement, money laundering, and lots of other stuff. They can look into that, and if they happen to turn up evidence that his wife is Admin while they're at it, then it's a bonus."

"So this isn't about The Sermon at all."

"No," Thelo said. "This is about you being the editor of the newspaper that scoops the story on the identity of the world's most elusive hacker as well as exposing the world's most popular televangelist as a felon."

"I like the sound of that," Ivan admitted. "I'll call my buddy over at the FBI and see what he thinks."

"So what was your scoop?" Thelo asked.

"Well, unlike yours, my scoop deals directly with the story you're supposed to be working on. I was just about to text you and Christine to have you come into the office tomorrow morning at nine. There's someone I'd like you both to meet."

CHAPTER TWENTY
Thursday

"Christine," Thelo called from two rows over in the parking lot at the *Post*.

"Hey," she called back. They met up and entered the building together.

"Any idea what this is about?" Thelo asked her.

"Not a clue. I just got a text last night saying to make sure I was here."

"I talked to him on the phone last night, but he didn't say much, only that he wanted us to meet someone."

"Oh?"

"It has to do with The Sermon, apparently," Thelo said as they got to Ivan's office. "That's all I know."

Christine knocked on the door, and they heard Ivan's voice from the other side asking them in. A young woman sat in a chair across from Ivan. She had short spiked hair and bright green eyes. She was wearing a Morrissey concert t-shirt and leather shorts with black hose. Her leather boots came halfway to the knee and had silver studs on the heels. Christine and Thelo both looked at her, then each other. Christine turned to Ivan, who was smiling as if he'd won the lottery.

"Lisa, I'd like you to meet Christine Marshall and Thelonius Brown."

"Pleased to meet you both." She stood and shook both their hands, then sat down again. Christine and Thelo each took a chair.

"Lisa is a very special young woman," Ivan began. "She has quite a story to tell, and the *Post* is going to help her tell it."

"I'm on pins and needles," Christine said. "I haven't seen a grin that big on your face in a long time."

"You'll have to wait a moment. We've got one more coming."

As if on cue, there was a knock on the door.

"Come in," Ivan called out.

"Sorry I'm late," Zara said as she closed the door behind her. "I'm not used to driving on the wrong side of the road. Took it a bit slow in the traffic."

Ivan introduced Zara to Lisa and Christine.

"Who does your hair, love?" Zara admired as she shook Lisa's hand.

"You can discuss all that later," Ivan said. "Lisa has something to share."

Lisa let go of Zara's hand, and the two women took their seats. Lisa made eye contact with each of them, smiled, then began.

"I know you've all been following the events of the last few days after those preachers gave The Sermon. Things are in turmoil because people are unsure of their beliefs now. They are questioning the religion that they truly believed in just a few days before."

The group nodded.

"But if we're honest with each other, things were in turmoil long before Sunday, just the other way around."

"What do you mean by that?" Christine asked.

"People were sure of their religion then. They believed their religion's dogma and traditions, and they acted on those beliefs because they felt that it was what their Supreme Being wanted them to do. But those religions all believed something different, and everyone believed that their religion's version of God was correct and the others were wrong."

"That's been going on nearly forever," Thelo said.

"Yes, but as the religions evolved, they've strayed away from the core message of love and acceptance, and they've focused on evangelism, trying to convert everyone else to their way of thinking. They're doing it with their sermons, literature, television and radio programs. Governments, and not just the theocracies, are passing laws designed to force the population to adhere to their faith-based rules. Countries are going to war with each other based on different interpretations of what they think their god wants them to do. It has gotten worse as time has gone on."

"Pardon me, love," Zara broke in, "But this is a story we all know already."

"Give her a chance," Ivan scolded.

"Sorry. Go on."

"Everyone thinks they've got it right, but the truth is, nobody does. That's what The Sermon was about on Sunday. They've all got it wrong. Not one religion understands what The Source is."

"The Source?" Christine asked.

"That's just the name I invented for it. I didn't want to use a name that any of the existing religions use," Lisa explained. "Everyone needs to start fresh with a new idea, so we can't use any of the old names. It wouldn't be right."

"So you understand what God…" Christine quickly corrected herself, "what The Source is."

"Yes, I do. I think. Pretty sure."

"I don't mean to sound rude," Christine scoffed, "but if you chastise people for thinking they know what God is, then you claim that you're the only one who knows, doesn't that make you a hypocrite?"

"I know it sounds that way," Lisa replied, "but hear me out. I don't use the old names for God because it conjures up images of a sentient being who sits in judgment and answers prayers and all of that. That's not what The Source is, not even close."

"Fill us in, then," Thelo said.

"Have you ever heard of something called dark energy?"

"I've heard of dark matter. Same thing?"

"Not exactly," Lisa answered, "But you're in the right field. Dark energy is a form of energy that exists across all of the known universe. It's everywhere, and it's a part of everything."

"Sounds like God," Christine said.

"Sounds more like Star Wars," Thelo said. "You're thinking of The Force, not The Source."

Zara giggled at that, but Ivan shot her a look that stifled it.

"Don't be cynical, Thelo," Ivan said. "Hear her out."

"It does sound a bit like our perception of God," Lisa agreed, "But unlike God, dark energy doesn't answer prayers, it doesn't judge us, we weren't made in its image. Scientists have theorized its existence for quite some time, but it's only been in the last three decades or so that they've begun to understand it better. They know that dark energy and dark matter comprise around ninety-five percent of the universe. It's everywhere, and even though we can't see it, we can be sure of its existence because it affects things that we can see. Kinda like gravity. We can't see it, but we know it's there because we can see how it affects things in our world."

"Gravity," Thelo said to himself. "*Déjà vu.*"

"Well, if it doesn't act like God, what does it do?" Zara asked.

"It seeks balance. For every action, a reaction. Things must be balanced to be stable."

"How can an inanimate energy field seek anything?" Christine asked.

"You would agree that water is also inanimate, but if you pour it out of a container, it will seek the lowest point it can find before it comes to rest. The act of seeking in that case isn't about desire. It's about physics. The Source is much like that; only it seeks order. It seeks balance."

Ivan scanned their faces. They weren't yet comprehending, but they hadn't shut Lisa out, either.

"The religions of the world are throwing everything out of balance," Lisa continued. "It's a course that we can't continue to follow. I have seen where we are heading, and I know that if we continue down our present course, we will throw off the balance even more and The Source will correct it. It's not dogma or divine intervention. It's just how things work."

"What do you mean by, 'The Source will correct it?'" Christine asked.

"Every timeline I can see ends abruptly." She looked at them as if they should understand what she meant. She got blank stares. "The Source will remove the cause of the imbalance, and the cause is us."

Joel invited his attorney, Steve Purcell, into his study. Steve was very tall and thin, in his seventies but still fit and active. His gray hair had a fresh cut, and his steel-rimmed glasses shielded a pair of bright brown eyes. He wore a navy blue suit, a red silk tie, and polished leather shoes. Joel was more casual in slacks and a knit polo. He noticed the concerned look on Steve's face as they sat down.

"Thank you for coming on such short notice," Joel said.

"I will admit that I was quite shocked when you phoned me last night with the news," Steve replied. "I'm so sorry. I know you must be shouldering a lot of grief."

"Yes, thank you. I will miss her a great deal."

"I was able to contact Holly's attorney early this morning. He had heard the news on television, and he was already pulling her files when I called. He emailed them to me before I came over."

"Excellent, thank you."

"I haven't read it in detail yet, you understand, since I just got it, but everything seems fairly straightforward."

"I have my own copy of her will," Joel said. "We both had them done when we got married. I know what it says."

"This one is dated last year, though. She obviously updated hers since then."

Joel gaped at him. "She didn't tell me she'd updated her will. Don't we both have to agree on changes? Wouldn't I have to be notified that she'd done it?"

"Legally, you would only need to be notified if she made changes to joint property. But you apparently kept your finances separated."

Joel felt a sickness in the pit of his stomach. He dreaded the answer to his next question.

"What does it say?"

"Like I said, I haven't been over it in detail," Steve admitted. "But it looks like she left twenty percent to her sole remaining family, a Ms. Mildred James."

"Her Aunt Millie, yes. Holly was apparently off to visit her when she had the accident."

"I would imagine that Aunt Millie should be well taken care of with twenty percent," Steve said.

"And the other eighty percent goes to me."

"No. The other eighty percent is split among a handful of local charities."

"Charities?" Joel was incredulous. "She was a selfish bitch. That's going to look suspicious."

"Actually, she had been directly involved with them through volunteer work and had given them substantial donations in the past. Nothing about that will seem unusual, if you were thinking about contesting it. She even donated more than a million dollars of seed money last year to a grief counseling center startup, and the biggest chunk of her estate goes to keep it running."

"So she left me out of it entirely?" Joel asked. "I could contest it on the grounds that she forgot to include me."

"No. She left you one dollar."

Joel exploded. "That bitch! She can't do that, can she?"

"There's nothing illegal about that, Joel. Because you kept separate finances, the accounts were in her name only. She was free to bequeath the money however she saw fit. Your accounts are unaffected. Plus, the house is in your name, though, so you don't have to worry with that."

"Assuming I don't have to sell it," Joel said. "She told me I was broke."

"So what you're saying," Thelo said, even more skeptical than before, "is that The Source is going to destroy the world because we can't agree on the nature of God?"

"In a nutshell, yes," Lisa said, "but the world will likely remain. We just won't be on it."

"That's crazy." He turned to Ivan. "This is the story you're going to publish in the *Post*? Really?"

"I understand that it's hard to grasp at first," Ivan agreed. "I had difficulty wrapping my head around it at first, too."

"Think back through history," Lisa suggested. "This wouldn't be the first time that an imbalance has been corrected. Ice ages, a meteor that wiped out the dinosaurs, floods, earthquakes, hurricanes, that sort of thing. Not everything dies, of course, just enough to regain balance."

"That's nature," Thelo said. "Things just happen."

"Yes," Lisa said. "But The Source is *why* those things happen. It's not about an angry God punishing us for sins; it's about the universe correcting things we've done to upset the balance. We're on a course that is going to end in another cleansing, and this time humankind doesn't appear to be part of what's left afterward."

"Scientists have been talking about this kind of thing for a while now," Zara chimed in. "All you hear anymore is climate change this and greenhouse gasses that and melting ice caps and all that stuff. We're already aware, and people are working on it."

"It's not just climate change," Lisa said. "We could slow that down or even reverse it, and it wouldn't matter. The Source will find a way to achieve balance much sooner than that. We have to stop fighting each other over our beliefs. That's the key. I've seen it. It's the only way we survive."

"Okay," Thelo said, "let's just say that everything you just told us is true. Fine. Why do you know all this and nobody else does?"

Lisa hesitated. She looked at the floor. "I don't know how I know," she admitted. "I just do."

Thelo threw up his hands in resignation. "Oh come on!" He looked at Ivan with exasperation. "This is ridiculous. She is so sure of everything, but she can't even tell us how she knows."

"I've got to agree with Thelo," Christine added. "It's another case of 'I'm right about God, and everyone else is wrong.' Just because her version is more scientific than supernatural doesn't mean it's any more correct."

"Ivan," Zara asked, "are you sure that you don't believe her story just because she showed up in your dream the other day?"

Thelo and Christine both turned and gaped at Ivan.

"That was enough to get me to listen to her," Ivan admitted. "But it's not why I believe her. I think she's got a gift, the ability to see things that the rest of us can't see. It doesn't matter if she knows why or how she got this gift. It only matters that we help her use it to fix what's wrong with the world before it's too late."

"She got into your dreams?" Christine wasn't sure she'd heard it correctly.

"Into one dream, that's all," Ivan said. "Very briefly. She was just standing there, and she called me by name."

"I can do that sometimes," Lisa said. "And no, I don't know how. I just can. It doesn't always work."

"Hang on," Thelo interrupted, the wheels in his mind spinning like mad. "If you can stick yourself into his dream, can you also put yourself in people's heads and make them say things? Are you the one who caused those people to preach The Sermon on Sunday?"

"No. That wasn't me. I don't know how that happened. I do know that our timelines got extended a bit right after that, but still… They all end."

Thelo shook his head. "I'm not buying any of this. Sorry, Ivan, but I think it's all a load of crap."

"I'm afraid I have to agree," Christine said. "It's an interesting theory, but there's no evidence other than what Lisa is telling us."

Thelo and Christine looked at Zara for her opinion. Zara looked at Ivan, who was clearly frustrated.

"Well," she said, "I'm not going to rule it out just yet. It doesn't sound any more bollocks than worshipping a guy who came back from the dead, does it?"

"It's not about worship at all," Lisa corrected her. "The Source doesn't need worship or prayers or offerings or any of that. It only needs balance. I know that's not a good word to describe it, but we don't really have a good word. Balance, harmony, synergy, equilibrium, all of those words hint at what I mean, but none of them are completely accurate. I wish you could feel what I feel. Then you'd understand."

"The only thing I understand," Thelo said, "is that if the *Post* prints this as if it were fact, we will lose our credibility as a serious newspaper."

"Then it's a good thing you're not the editor," Ivan said. "We're printing it."

Christine looked directly into Ivan's eyes. "I think you should step back and look at this from an editor's viewpoint. Thelo's right, it's only a theory by one person. We can't print it as if it were anything more."

"I was going to ask you to write the piece," Ivan told her. "As a woman of faith, I expected you to be thrilled at having a better understanding of God. And you," Ivan said to Thelo, "as an atheist, I expected you to embrace a version of God that was based on science rather than superstition."

"Sorry, boss," Thelo said. "But I don't think you'd want me to write that piece, either."

"I'll write it," Zara interrupted. Thelo and Christine both turned to face her.

"You don't work here," Christine said.

"That's true," Ivan said. He turned to Zara. "How would you like a job?"

"You're serious?" Zara couldn't hide her surprise.

"If you want it," Ivan told her. "I've read your stuff. You're a good writer. Your article on Joel Wood was very well done. The job's yours if you want it. I've got some connections, and we can get you a temporary work visa in no time. You can apply for a green card after that, so you can move here."

Zara was speechless.

"Ivan, I think this is a mistake," Thelo said.

"What, you don't think I'm good enough to write for a real newspaper, is that it?" Zara accused him.

"That's not it at all," Thelo said. "The story is bullshit."

"We're going to run it," Ivan said. "I've made up my mind. Welcome aboard, Zara."

"Your Excellency, thank you for coming," Father Matthew said as he opened the door.

"I hope you have some good news for me, Father," the bishop said as he came into the rectory.

"Please sit down."

The bishop took a seat on the sofa, and Father Matthew sat down in the recliner across from it.

"I won't keep you longer than necessary," Father Matthew said, "so I'll get right to it." He took a deep breath, steeled his nerves, and spoke. "After much prayer, I have decided to decline your offer. I'll be leaving the priesthood."

"Father Matthew, I must say that I am shocked. I cannot believe that you would so easily leave behind a lifetime of ministry. The Church needs you, especially in times such as these."

"The Church asks me to lie. I could never confess to those sins, not truthfully. The confession would be a sham, as would be the rest of my days in the priesthood. How could I honestly hear anyone else's confession after I'd falsified one of my own?"

Bishop Garza opened his mouth to answer, but Father Matthew kept talking. He needed to get it out.

"I didn't join the priesthood because I needed to be part of this institution. I joined because a priest helped me through a very dark time in my life when I was just a boy. I wanted to be able to help others in the same way."

"And you have, Father. That's why you need to continue your ministry."

"I can help people without wearing the collar. I can help people without the rituals and the traditions. I can help people without the restrictions that the Church puts on me. I can serve God and His people more freely without those trappings. But I cannot serve God by giving a false confession. I cannot, and I will not."

Bishop Garza shook his head sadly. "Father Matthew, I am deeply sorry that you have come to this decision. I fear that your guidance is coming from the same source that gave you those words you spoke on Sunday. I am sorry that you have been corrupted in this way, and I will pray that God will rescue your soul before it's too late."

Father Matthew spoke through gritted teeth. "Thank you, Your Excellency. You have just solidified my belief that I've made the right choice."

The bishop stood to leave, and Father Matthew got up from his chair, went to the door, and opened it.

"You will need to vacate the rectory," Bishop Garza said. "The sooner, the better."

CHAPTER
TWENTY-ONE

Thelo and Christine left Ivan's office and agreed to have lunch so they could discuss the events of the morning. They met at Burger Biggie, a hamburger spot not far from their offices at the *Post*. They sat sipping glasses of water while they waited for their food.

"So, tell me," Thelo said, "what the hell is Ivan thinking, running that story?"

"I could see it as a human interest piece, maybe, but not as a news story."

"By the time we left there, it sounded like he was going to devote the whole religion section to Lisa."

"I hope not. There are plenty of religions to cover, and they all deserve their place. I'm the editor of that section, after all. I won't let the others get pushed out in favor of Lisa's Source thing."

"Careful," Thelo said. "I haven't seen Ivan like this before. He lets you have carte blanche over your section now, but he might start overruling you if you don't play nice. I'd walk on eggshells for a while if I were you."

"Do you think we can get him to see this from our perspective? Maybe he'll see how crazy it all sounds. Lisa's story is interesting. I'll give her that. But it's too ridiculous for many people to take seriously."

"Is it? I mean, I agree with you, but let's be honest here. Believing that stuff Lisa was talking about is no more crazy than believing the story of Noah's ark or Jonah and the whale."

"Most people understand those stories as parables or allegories. They don't believe that those stories are literally true."

"But some people do. And the farther back you go in time, the more people you'd find who believed those stories were factual."

"I can't argue that. But even now, some scientists still hang onto their belief in God for those things they can't yet explain with science. I've allowed science to replace a lot of my own religious beliefs over the years, but I'm not ready to give up all of them. I can't just toss my Bible into the trash and read a science book for inspiration. I need God to be there." She took a sip of water. "I do."

"Well, I don't. But I'm not on board with Lisa's ideas, either. If I believe her, then I have to believe that she's somehow knowledge-able than anyone else about dark energy at, what, twenty years old? Maybe? Scientists have been working on dark energy and dark matter for decades. I don't think Little Miss Pixie Cut has just suddenly figured it all out by herself."

"We can agree on that much," Christine said.

Their food arrived, and Thelo jumped right in. Christine took apart her grilled chicken sandwich, shook on some black pepper, removed the tomato slice, centered the lettuce leaf on the chicken breast, then reassembled it. By the time she finally picked up her sandwich and took a bite, Thelo was almost finished eating his burger.

"I read Zara's piece on Joel Wood," she said after she'd swallowed her first bite. "It was really good."

"I can't deny that she's a good writer. She was being wasted at *The London Times*. I can't blame Ivan for hiring her."

"How do you think Joel Wood is going to react to it?"

"Zara said he admitted to everything during her interview with him. We were both shocked. She said that he's all born-again now and wants to confess his sins to everyone."

Christine took another bite. "So I guess he really believes that God spoke to him. Some of the others aren't so sure."

"Like Father Matthew?"

"He thinks it was probably God, but I think he's open-minded to other explanations. The Vatican thinks he was possessed."

Thelo's eyes showed his surprise. "Holy shit, really?"

"I didn't tell you? They wanted him to submit to an exorcism."

"An exorcism, seriously?" Thelo shook his head in disgust. "I'll say it again. Compared to some of the bullshit that people believe now, Lisa's theory isn't all that weird."

Ivan led Zara and Lisa to a small meeting room around the corner from his office. It was sparsely furnished, save for a few simple chairs and a desk.

"You can use this room for the moment," Ivan said, "until I can get you set up with your own workstation and cubicle. I'll get started on your work visa tomorrow, and you'll have to fill out some forms with human resources before we can get you access to the network here, but it shouldn't be a problem. Of course, until the paperwork is done and filed, we can't officially put you on the payroll, so we'll be buying your stories as if you were a freelance writer until we're able to officially bring you on as an employee. We don't want to be accused of hiring undocumented aliens, after all." He smiled. "Welcome to the *Post*."

"Thank you, sir," Zara said.

He left and closed the door behind him.

Zara still couldn't believe that she was going to work for him. For a reputable newspaper. In America. It was all surreal. Almost as surreal as the story by this spiky-haired woman who sat across from her.

"All right, then," Zara said. "Don't want to waste your time, let's get on with it, shall we?"

"Thank you for believing me."

"Let's not jump to conclusions, love. I only said I'd write the story. That doesn't mean that I believe you, at least not fully. Not yet."

"Fair enough."

"Okay, so let's start with the obvious," Zara said, launching the word processor on her laptop. "Spell your name for me."

"L-I-S-A."

"And your surname?"

"I'd rather not, if you don't mind."

Zara looked up from her screen. "Why not?"

"It's not important."

"Of course it's important," Zara argued. "If you want to be credible, you can't just go with your given name and no surname."

"It worked for Cher."

"You aren't bloody Cher, are you?" The words came out with more frustration than she'd have liked. "Besides, she used her surname in the early days."

Lisa sighed. "Fine. Put 'Jones.'"

Zara shot her a look. "Why don't I put your real name instead?"

"Why were you so willing to believe that 'Lisa' was my real first name, but you can't accept 'Jones' as my last name?"

Zara had no answer. She stumbled over a response, then thought better of it. "Fine. 'Lisa Jones.' I'll say it's an alias to protect your privacy. Let's move on."

Lisa shifted in her chair.

"Where are you from?" Zara asked.

"Can we just get to the important part?"

"Look." Zara felt like she was going in circles. "Your story is way out there, I mean the kind of thing where the reader is going to think you're a lunatic. If I can't give them something right at the start that makes you sound like you're a normal person, then it's all rubbish. They'll think that the *Post* has gone full tabloid on them, especially if they look at the byline and google me. I write about sex scandals and celebrity gossip, and on a slow news day, I'll do a piece about some bloke or another who says he's the reincarnation of Napoleon. So if you want anyone to believe your story, you've got to give me a foundation I can work with, something to build on."

"Sorry," Lisa said. "You're probably right. You can say I'm Lisa Jones from Chicago."

Zara sighed. "I'm guessing that if I try to look you up, I won't find a Lisa Jones in Chicago."

"I'm guessing that if you look me up, there will be a lot of Lisa Joneses in Chicago. I want the message to get the attention, not the messenger."

Zara glared at her. She counted to ten in her head, trying to diffuse her frustration.

"Okay." She took a deep breath. "We'll move on for now. What is it you're trying to do by getting your story in the paper?"

"I want to save the world."

"That's a bit dramatic, innit?"

"It's the truth."

"How about you explain again about this Source thing and dark energy and all that, so I can get it down properly."

Lisa spent the next few minutes going back over the concept of The Source.

"And if we can't correct things fairly quickly, our timeline will simply end."

"How will it end?"

"I don't know. I can't see specifics like that. I can only follow timelines to their conclusion, and I can see whether that conclusion is good or bad."

"So you believe that if enough people are aware of this, then we can fix the problem before we're wiped out by this Source thing?"

"You say it like The Source makes decisions, like a god, but that's not how it is."

"How is it, then?"

"Think of Mother Nature," Lisa explained. "We give nature a human persona because it's easier for us to comprehend. Mother Nature grows a forest, which becomes lush and vibrant. Then the forest becomes overgrown, and some of the plants begin to be choked out because there are too many roots for the amount of nutrition in the soil. The forest is out of balance and so 'Mother Nature' sends a few bolts of lightning down to set the whole forest on fire. Everything is burned, but the ashes fertilize the ground, and the process begins again. That's just The Source working on a very small level, which we call 'Mother Nature.' When The Source adjusts things on a much larger scale, we call it an 'Act of God.' Hurricanes, tornadoes, earthquakes. It's all just The Source making corrections, but we call it 'God' because we don't understand dark energy well enough right now."

"So those people who say that catastrophes happen because we're acting against the will of God, they're not that far off?"

"No, this is different. Those people believe that disasters happen because of lapses in morality. We sin, God sees it, God punishes us for it. This isn't about morality or punishment. This is about balance. Morality is a human-created thing that changes and evolves over time. What is considered morally right or wrong depends on the culture and the point in time. The Source has nothing to do with morals, only about balance. When we live peacefully together, we are balanced. Morality, or at least the demand for it, rarely creates peace. Usually the opposite, in fact."

"So people attribute nature's attempts at balancing out the universe as acts of God. That makes sense, thank you," Zara said, furiously typing away on her laptop. "Like when the Greeks and Romans invented gods to explain lightning and thunder because they didn't have the science yet."

"Yes! That's exactly it. Although what you just called 'nature' is only part of The Source. Nature is Earth-centric, The Source is universal."

"So how is it that you understood all of this before the scientists figured it out?"

"I am The One."

Zara stopped typing and looked over her screen at Lisa. "I presume that I should capitalize that?"

"If you like," Lisa said.

"I'm going to need you to explain that, I think."

"Throughout history, there have been people like myself who have understood The Source on a subconscious level. We don't know why or how; it's just with us from birth. Perhaps we are just an element of how The Source seeks balance, or at least that's how I perceive it."

"There have been people like you in the past?"

"Yes, but they didn't have the benefit of living in a time when dark energy was a known concept. They relied on the spiritual language of their time because that's what people understood and believed."

"Hang on," Zara said, suddenly understanding. "Are you saying that Jesus was one of you?"

"Most likely, yes," Lisa answered. "The stories about him have been exaggerated over time, of course, but there is the basic truth that he was a man who understood that the people needed to move away from the religious laws of that day. That much is history. He could also probably do things that other people couldn't do, which they saw as miracles. We all get different abilities in that regard. I can't walk on water or multiply a food basket to feed thousands, but I can insert myself into peoples' dreams sometimes, and I can see patterns in future timelines."

"We've just gone back into tabloid territory now."

"Jesus wasn't the only one, of course. Most major religions were founded by people like me, all of them just trying to keep things in balance. The problem is that once The One was gone, the people needed someone to lead them. Those leaders couldn't understand what The One understood, but they were elevated to positions of power to lead the young religion into the future. Corruption gets woven into the fabric of the religion when those leaders make laws designed to keep them in power. Eventually, it's all out of balance again."

"I can run with that," Zara said as her fingers flew across her keyboard. "Keep talking."

"In those early days, people mostly kept to the same part of the world where they were born. Travel was slow and dangerous. Back then, you could have this religion here, that religion there, another religion somewhere else and it was all fine. The problem comes when people of different beliefs run into each other, and each one thinks the other should convert. It caused enough problems then, but now that our world has been made smaller by technology and the ease of travel, it is no longer feasible to have all these different religions, at least not as long as they keep trying to convert those who believe differently."

"So you're going to start a new religion to get everyone on the same page?"

"No," Lisa said. "I'm going to try to make people understand The Source as a matter of science, not religion. I want people to see that the gods they worship today can be explained in scientific terms and those gods need to be relegated to mythology, where they can join Zeus and Hera and Poseidon and all the other gods we've abandoned."

"Bloody hell," Zara said. "This article is going to get me killed."

Zara closed her eyes for a few seconds and concentrated. "No," she said. "But it does buy us some time."

Matthew picked up the phone on the second ring. "Hello?"

"How are you doing?" Christine's voice was a welcome sound in his ear.

"Better, now that I am talking to you. Reality is setting in, though."

"Did you have your meeting with the bishop?"

"Yes. He didn't like my decision."

"Was he rude?"

"No, of course not," Matthew assured her. "But he wasn't happy. He wants me to move out of the rectory as soon as I can."

"I can understand that. It must be awkward for everyone while you're staying there. They probably want to get it ready for the next priest."

The words stung more than Matthew would've liked. "Yes," he said. "I've been spending the afternoon looking for an apartment."

"Oh? Have you found one that you like?"

"I've been looking online, and I've found several that seem nice enough. You know me, I don't need anything fancy."

"Right."

"But the problem is that when I call them and they ask me the usual questions, I have to admit that I don't yet have a job. Nobody wants to rent to me if I'm unemployed."

"You can't really blame them."

"No, I understand it, of course," Matthew agreed. "One place offered to let me sign a lease if I could pay the rent in full upfront, but the shortest lease they offered was for one year. If I gave them that much now, I'd be up against it for living expenses while I look for work."

"And you'd need to buy furniture, too."

"Yes, just one more expense. I'm now looking for people who might have just a room to rent, or maybe a garage apartment. Perhaps they would be more willing to take in someone without a job or at least let me have a shorter upfront lease."

"Good idea." Christine thought for a moment. "But I've got an even better one."

"All ears."

"You can move into my spare bedroom. It's already furnished, you know the neighborhood, and if you pitch in for half the utilities, we'll call it even. I like your company, and I can always use some extra money."

"Are you sure about this?" The tone of his voice indicated cautious joy and relief. "Is that a good idea?"

"On one condition."

"Go on."

"We sleep in our own beds. I'm guessing that we'll share one sometimes, but that will be by invitation rather than assumption."

"Thank you," he said. "In fact, that makes me more comfortable about accepting your proposal. I agree completely."

"It's done, then." She sounded quite pleased. "I'll have a spare key made on the way home and drop it off tonight."

"Thank you so much, Christine. You've answered my prayers again."

Thelo was at his computer typing up the article about Admin's secret identity. A knock at the door pulled him out of his 'write brain,' as he called it, and startled him. He went to the front door and peered through the peephole. A black, middle-aged man in a dark colored suit waited on the other side. Thelo made sure the chain was latched, then opened the door a crack and looked through.

"May I help you?"

The man held up a leather wallet with an ID card so Thelo could see. "I'm Special Agent Kenneth Ward, FBI. I'd like to ask you a few questions."

"What's this about? Do you have a warrant?"

"I believe that you might be able to help us regarding a case that we are working on. You are not a suspect, and you're not in any trouble, but you may have some useful information."

"Hold on," Thelo said. "Give me a second to make a call." He closed the door and fished his cell phone out of his pocket. He stepped away from the door and called Ivan.

"Hello, Thelo."

"Hey, boss," Thelo said, trying to sound calm. "When you called your friend at the FBI, did you tell them that I had been dealing with Admin?"

"Yes," Ivan said, noticing the nervousness in Thelo's voice. "But don't panic, I told them that you were trying to discover his identity and were just sharing information with him hoping to gain his trust."

"And the person you told that to, what was his name?"

"Ken Ward."

"He's at my door right now. He wants to ask me questions. I'm really not okay with this."

"He's a good man," Ivan assured him. "It'll be fine."

Thelo hung up the phone, stepped over to his desk and closed his laptop, then went back to the door. He slid the chain off the catch and opened the door.

"I can try to answer your questions," Thelo told him. "But I'm not sure you'll learn much."

"Thank you," Ken said. He entered Thelo's apartment and began making mental notes of the surroundings, a habit he'd picked up from many years on the job.

Thelo led the man into the living area, which was just a few steps from the front door. Agent Ward appeared to be in his fifties, but Thelo guessed that he might be a few years younger. Stress can age you quickly, after all, and he assumed that an FBI agent must have plenty of stress.

"Have a seat." Thelo pulled up the chair from his desk and sat across from Special Agent Ward, who took the love seat and got right to business.

"Are you familiar with a hacker known as 'Admin,' currently on the FBI most-wanted list?"

"I am, yes," Thelo answered. "I've been working on trying to discover Admin's identity."

"Yes, so we were told," Ken said. "And have you discovered the identity?"

"I have a hunch, but I can't prove it yet."

"We may be able to help each other. We are investigating an individual who may be involved in some illegal financial activities. Information about our target's financial dealings may have been uncovered by Admin. We have some computer equipment that we obtained from this person, but we are finding it difficult to get the information off of them. We are making progress, but we believe that you might be able to speed up the process."

"I can see where that would help you," Thelo said. "But how does that help me?"

"You need information to prove that you are correct about the identity of Admin to back up your article. Those hard drives we obtained belonged to a person that we believe to be Admin. From what we can tell, the information on those drives is encrypted. It has also been backed up and uploaded to an encrypted file vault in the cloud. We haven't been able to crack the encryption on the drives themselves, so we can't yet read the files."

"So you think I might have a copy of the information on the hard drives."

"Actually," Agent Ward said, "we thought you might have the encryption key to the backup file vault. If you do, we can get our files. Then we will tell you the name of the person the hard drives belonged to. If it matches the name of the person you believe Admin to be, then you can write your article knowing that you have the right person. It seems like a fair trade."

"And that's it? That's all you want?"

"Not quite," Agent Ward said. "I'm going to assume that if you have the encryption key, then you've seen the files, and you're already writing your news story about the person we're investigating. I want you to sit on that story until we have been able to move forward. We don't want to alert the man at the center of our investigation that we're digging up evidence on him."

"But I can still run the story exposing the identity of Admin, as soon as you confirm I'm right?"

"Yes."

"Fair enough," Thelo said. "Let me get you that encryption key."

CHAPTER TWENTY-TWO
Friday

Ivan dropped in on Zara in the meeting room that was serving as her office. She was on her laptop, monitoring the comments section of the video she uploaded the night before.

"How many views now?" Ivan asked.

"About a hundred thousand," she said. "It's climbing pretty quickly, now that people are reading the article."

"Great idea, making a video to go with the article," Ivan said. "Brilliant! Well done, you!"

"I didn't know people used those expressions over here."

"They don't, really," Ivan admitted. "I was trying to make you feel at home."

"Thanks." She refreshed the page on her browser. "I think this is going viral. It's got another six hundred views since you walked in."

"Well, Lisa said that she wanted to get the word out. The video is going to get seen by a lot more people than will read the article."

"The unfortunate reality of printed news these days, I'm afraid," Zara sighed. "I wonder how long we'll all have jobs."

"Yes, but the article made people aware of the video, and now people are sharing it on their social media and emailing it to their friends. I think people are going to be really excited about her message."

"Excited, yes, but it's not all positive. The negative ones have stopped just short of death threats, but I fully expect a few of those before the day is done."

"If you see any death threats, tell me right away. I'll notify the police."

"Will do." She refreshed the page again. "Eight hundred more just now. It's snowballing."

"Fantastic news, Zara. Congratulations."

Zara's laptop dinged with incoming email. She checked it, and her mouth fell open. "Are you ready for this?"

"Ready for what?"

"Joel Wood read the article and watched the video. He wants to speak to Lisa in person."

"Fantastic! Set it up. You should be there, too."

Ivan turned to leave.

"Sir?" Zara called. "Thanks again for the job."

"Please, call me 'Ivan' like everyone else does." He smiled at her. "And you're welcome. Glad to have you here."

He left the meeting room and made his way to Christine's cubicle. He knocked lightly on top of her cubicle's wall.

"Busy?"

"Oh, hey," she said. "I didn't see you there. I'm just finishing up the last of the articles for Sunday's edition. I've got reactions from most of the major religions, both clergy and laity."

"Good," Ivan said. "That's going to be a pretty long article."

"I did separate articles, one for each faith. You know how people are nowadays… If they see an article that's too long, they won't even bother to read it."

"Sad but true. I'm looking forward to reading them."

Christine held up a finger, then tapped a few keys on her keyboard. "They're in your box now," she said. "Enjoy."

Ivan smiled and turned to leave.

"Can I have a word before you go?" she asked.

Ivan stopped and turned back around. "Of course."

"I know that you're really excited about Lisa and her beliefs," Christine acknowledged. "And I know that others will be, too."

"But?"

"But I hope you remember that hers is just one of many beliefs. If you put her beliefs in the news section and the rest stay on the religion page, then you jeopardize the *Post*'s neutrality. It looks as if we've chosen one set of beliefs as fact and the rest fiction."

"Thank you for your honesty," he said. "You're absolutely right, of course. Once the excitement died down yesterday, I considered what you and Thelo said in our meeting, and I agree with you. I should thank you for that, for keeping me in check."

Christine hadn't expected this response from him. Ivan was always open to alternate viewpoints, but he rarely changed his mind on something once it was made up. "Um, you're welcome," she stammered.

"I got with Zara shortly after that and asked her to make sure that her story treated Lisa as newsworthy person, but not make it sound as if we were endorsing her views. To that end, I thought she did a fantastic job of it."

"Yes, she did," Christine agreed. "I didn't know you had helped steer her in that direction. Good idea about the video, too."

"The decision to do the video was all hers. That was a genius move. It gave Lisa a way to explain her beliefs without the *Post* having to spell them out in the article, which might've looked like an endorsement."

"That was Zara's idea?" Christine was impressed.

Ivan nodded. "It's going viral. It had over a hundred thousand views as of a few minutes ago."

"Holy cow." She launched her browser and found the video. Her eyes widened. "A hundred thousand? It's pushing a quarter million now. This is going to be big."

Thelo was already sitting in a booth at the diner when Mike came in. He waved to Mike to get his attention and smiled as the cop sat across from him. Mike's smile vanished when he realized there were no mugs on the table.

"No coffee?"

"On the way," Thelo assured him. "I just got here. I ordered one for you, too."

"Thanks," Mike said with some relief. "I was barely awake enough to drive over here."

"You're not in uniform."

"Day off. I don't go back in until Monday morning. I can't remember the last time I had three days off in a row."

"Your schedule seems to be pretty erratic."

"They're phasing in a new system," Mike explained. "I used to work five eight-hour shifts with two days off; now it's four tens with three days off. They say it will save money and give the officers more relief from stress with the extra off-day. My schedule is all wonky while they change from the old system to the new one."

"Speaking of stress," Thelo said, "I got a visit from the FBI last night."

"Should I even be seen with you right now?" Mike joked, quickly looking around. "What did you do?"

"You know that suitcase in Holly Wood's car? Turns out she had some hard drives in it, and they were looking at those."

"What's that got to do with you?"

"Are you familiar with a hacker called 'Admin'?"

"Yeah, he's been on the FBI list for a long time."

"She."

Mike was surprised. "She?"

"I gave the FBI a key piece of evidence that proved that Admin was Holly Wood."

"Fuck me. You're kidding."

"I wrote the article last night, but it was too late to make this morning's edition. It will be in the afternoon edition, though, and it's already on the *Post's* website."

"You're going to be famous!" Mike said. "The next Woodward and Bernstein, right across the table from me."

"Thank you so much for your restraint," Thelo said, nearly laughing.

"Restraint?"

"For calling me 'Woodward and Bernstein' rather than 'Deep Throat.'"

"That would've been too easy, even before coffee."

The waitress arrived at the table with the coffee and took their orders. She double-checked what she'd written on her pad.

"A cheese omelet and wheat toast for you," she said to Thelo, "and a lumberjack breakfast for your handsome friend." She winked at Mike suggestively. "Is there anything else I can get you, darlin'?"

Mike smiled up at her. "No thanks, sweetie, my boyfriend here can take care of anything else I might need."

She blushed and quickly left to turn their orders into the kitchen.

"Am I your boyfriend?" Thelo asked in his British accent. He loved the way Mike swooned when he used it. "I thought we were just shagging."

"I'd like you to be," Mike said.

"Well, blimey, mate," Thelo was hamming it up. "I think I might have a go at it, yeah, that'd be bloody brilliant."

"Keep that up," Mike teased, "and I'll have a go at you right now, right here on the table."

"Down, boy," Thelo laughed, dropping his accent. "One of us still has to work today."

"That was a fascinating piece I read this morning on that Lisa woman. I saw her the other day talking to some people outside the mosque where Christine was attacked."

"Christine and I had a bit of a disagreement with our editor about that piece. We were afraid that putting it in the news section rather than on the religion page would make it seem like the *Post* considered it factual. I was pretty relieved when I read the article, though. Zara did a great job walking that tightrope."

"The video was helpful," Mike added. "She explained it pretty well. I could easily get on board with her ideas."

"Really? I'm not convinced by it at all. It's just another religion like all the others. She believes something that can't be proven, but she's presenting it like she's right and everyone else is wrong. The only difference is that she's got enough science in there to make it seem more plausible."

"I like that there are still some unknowns in it," Mike said. "I don't think I ever want to know exactly how the universe works. I want some mystery."

"That's not me at all," Thelo said. "My job is to erase the unknowns, to solve the mystery. Why wouldn't you want to find all the answers?"

"It's like that time I went to a nude beach."

Thelo stared at Mike, waiting for him to say more. Mike just sipped his coffee.

"I can't wait to see how you're going to connect those dots," Thelo said. "Hit me with it."

Mike set his cup down. "I had been looking forward to going to a nude beach for a long time. I'd never been to one before, and I was expecting it to be all erotic and sexy. I couldn't wait to stroll down the sand checking everybody out."

"And?"

"And it wasn't erotic at all. Everyone was having an ordinary day at the beach, just without clothes. I realized that swimsuits made it sexy by covering up just enough to make us fantasize about what's behind the cloth. It's the mystery that makes it exciting."

"Okay, I can understand that." He shook his head. "But I'm still not ready to believe her theory, no matter how much mystery she leaves in it. Especially the bit about the world ending if we don't get balanced, or however she put it."

"To be fair," Mike said, "she didn't say the world would end, just that humans wouldn't be around."

"To this human, that's the same thing."

Matthew spent the morning packing up his belongings and removing his personal information from the computer, so it would be ready for a new priest to take over.

Throughout the morning, he was interrupted by knocks at the door from parishioners who had heard he was leaving and had come to say goodbye. Matthew assured them that he would still see them from time to time. Many of the visitors shed tears. Matthew wept several times himself, as he realized the depth of love and respect these people had for him. He would miss ministering to them.

Another knock at the door interrupted him just after lunch. Simon Forrester, a long-time parishioner, was standing on the steps. Matthew opened the door.

"Simon, wonderful to see you, please come in."

"Thank you, Father," the man said as he entered. Simon was a fireplug of a man, short and stocky, but solidly built. He wore a military-style buzz cut and a full beard, carefully trimmed and combed. A few strands of gray interrupted the pelt of brown on his face. His dress shirt was starched and pressed, as were his slacks.

"You should probably get used to calling me 'Matthew.'"

"Yes, of course. That will be strange for awhile, I'm sure."

"I'm having to adjust to it myself," Matthew admitted. "Please, come sit down."

"I don't have much time, I'm afraid, but I couldn't let you leave without telling you goodbye and making sure that you understand how much you have meant to me."

"That means a great deal to me, Simon."

"I want to thank you in particular for your support several years ago when the whole sex abuse scandal was tearing our church apart. Lots of the parishioners were in denial that it even happened."

"I remember it all too well."

"Telling people what happened to me here as a boy was the hardest thing I'd ever done in my life. Then people accused me of making it up, saying that if it were true, I would've said something back when it happened. They didn't understand, and that hurt me almost as bad as what that priest did when I was seven."

"I'm sorry you went through that. I thought you were very brave to tell the truth, and it helped put him behind bars where he can't ever do that to another child."

"Your belief in me and the support you gave me was the only thing that kept me going during that whole ordeal, Father," he said. "Err, Matthew. Sorry."

"I did my best," Matthew replied. "I wish I could have done more."

"You can. That's the other reason I'm here."

"Oh?"

"I've done quite well for myself, as you know, and I try to give back where I can. I've given substantial sums of money to the Church and to other charities, but I'm working on a bigger project. I've got an idea I want to pass by you."

"I'm listening."

"I have created a charity organization that will offer counseling and temporary housing to people who are dealing with issues like I did. I don't mean sexual abuse specifically, but a place where adults can go when they find their lives still impacted by traumatic events from their childhood."

"That's very good of you, Simon."

"There are plenty of places to turn for help if something is happening to you in the present, but if the traumatic events were from years past, then you're told, 'that was a long time ago, just get over it.' I don't know how I could've made it if you hadn't believed me or if you hadn't been so supportive. It made all the difference."

"And you want to create a place where other people can find that kind of support."

"Yes," Simon said. "And I want you to help run it."

Matthew was stunned. "I'm flattered, but…"

"But what?"

Matthew knew that his lifetime of work experience didn't necessarily translate to marketable skills in the secular world. "I don't have any experience in running a charity, and I'm not a licensed counselor."

"I've already hired people to run it. They'll do the bookkeeping, and they'll make sure we follow all the rules for a non-profit organization. What I would like you to do is oversee the caretakers and counselors. They are all licensed, and they know the textbook techniques, but you have that special empathy, that ability to understand how best to comfort a person who is dealing with trauma. It's a gift that God has given you. Your job will be to lead and inspire the counselors and to make sure that clients are receiving the help and support they need. In time, you can get licensed as well and then you can offer some of that support to the clients yourself. You're very good at it, and I think that others would follow your lead and would be happy to work for you."

Matthew was speechless.

"We can discuss salary later," Simon continued, "but I'll make sure you're taken care of, I promise."

"I don't know what to say."

"Say you'll do it! I've been working on this for several years, and everything has fallen into place except for filling this position. I've been praying every day that God would help me find someone like you. And when I say 'like you,' I mean that I literally prayed for God to send me someone just like Father Matthew Vergara. Then this morning, I heard that you were leaving the priesthood, and I knew that this was God's answer to my prayers. I prayed for someone like you, and He sent me you. How much clearer could it be that this is God's plan?"

Matthew looked at the tears on Simon's face and was humbled. He felt the presence of God in a way he hadn't felt in some time. "I think God may have answered both our prayers at once."

"Welcome to Gloria Deo," Joel said as he opened the glass door. "You must be Lisa. It's nice to meet you." He shook her hand. "Nice to see you again, Zara. You handled the piece about me very well. I was afraid it would be mean-spirited, but it wasn't. Thank you."

"To be honest," Zara said, "you gave me enough dirt on your own, there was no need to spice it up beyond that."

"I suppose that's true," he admitted. "Come on, let's go to my office."

Zara and Lisa followed him down the hall to the room where Zara had interviewed him before. They all took their seats.

"I'm very sorry to hear about your wife," Zara began.

"Yes. I'm still in shock, as you can imagine."

"I've got some more questions I'd like to ask you about things we didn't cover in our last interview, if you're up to it."

"Actually, it's a bit too soon. You understand."

"Of course."

"I invited you both here so I could meet this remarkable young woman," he said, turning to Lisa. "You have some very interesting ideas."

"They aren't ideas, they're facts."

"They're theories," Joel corrected her. "They aren't facts until they're proven."

"General relativity is a theory, but scientists and engineers still use it every day. Just because we can't yet prove it, doesn't mean we can't act on it."

"Good point, yes. But when you use relativity in your calculations, you can see that it's working right away. We could act on your theories for several generations and never know if it's working or even if we're doing anything right."

"I can see if we're doing things right," Lisa said. "When our timelines all stop at the same point, I know we have to change what we're doing to save ourselves. We make those changes and I can see whether they extend our timelines. We need more people on board, though. You can help me spread the word."

"Why would I help spread your theory?" Joel asked, taken aback. "I invited you here to change your mind."

Zara suddenly realized that she hadn't turned on her recorder. She quickly reached into her pocket and pulled it out. She turned it on and cursed herself for not remembering it sooner.

"You won't change my mind," Lisa told him. "I am The One. It is my duty to educate the world about The Source and help the human race avoid extinction."

"And I serve the one true God," Joel said, "the God who spoke directly through me, the God who will speak through me again."

"The Source isn't a god," Lisa said. "It doesn't speak through anybody."

"Well, God spoke through me," Joel said. "I didn't see any explanation for that in your article or your video. How do you suppose that I and those others all got the same message delivered through us at the same time?"

"I don't know how," Lisa admitted.

"Then how can you be so sure it wasn't God?"

"Because there is no god," Lisa said. "There is only The Source."

"But you still can't explain how we all preached the same message."

"No, I can't."

Joel smiled as if he'd just won an argument. "Perhaps you need to be spreading my beliefs and not the other way around."

"That would be disastrous, actually," Lisa said. "I've seen those timelines. They all end quickly."

Joel and Lisa stared at each other in silence, each one measuring up the other. Zara tried to think of something to break the silence, but Joel beat her to it.

"We are done here," he said flatly. "I was hoping to convince you to stop your nonsensical preaching and help me spread the Word of God."

"I was hoping that you had invited me here to learn about The Source," Lisa said. "I'm sorry we wasted each others' time."

Lisa stood up to leave. Zara picked up her recorder and stood up as well.

"May I call you to set up an interview in a day or so?" Zara asked Joel.

"Perhaps. We'll see."

"We can show ourselves out," Zara said. "Thanks for your time."

As the women made their way down the hallway, Lisa shook her head sadly.

Zara noticed. "What?"

"If he becomes too popular, it's going to be very, very bad. All those timelines end sooner rather than later."

"How soon?"

"Couple days, maybe," Lisa said. "Four at the most."

Zara stopped in her tracks. "Bloody hell, are you serious?"

"We have to get people to our side. The more of us there are, the fewer people Joel will be able to convert. We can't let him get too popular."

"People are just now reading about all his affairs and prostitutes and stuff," Zara reminded her. "Once those stories get spread around, his popularity will suffer."

"No, it won't. Your article makes him more popular, not less."

CHAPTER
TWENTY-THREE

"I know a friend with an SUV, should I call him?" Christine asked Matthew as she arrived at the rectory.

"Oh, that won't be necessary," he assured her. "I've gotten everything into a few suitcases. Other than clothes and a few photos and small items, everything else belonged to the parish."

"This will be easy, then."

"Easy from a physical standpoint, yes," Matthew said. "Still hard on the emotional side."

"I'm sure it is." Christine felt sorry for him. She followed him into the rectory and found four suitcases and three small boxes packed and ready to go.

"I've got good news, though," he said as they each picked up two suitcases.

"Oh?"

"I've got a job."

"Already? That's fantastic! I hope it's something you'll enjoy. What will you be doing?"

Matthew explained the offer he'd accepted from Simon as they put the suitcases into Christine's car and made the short drive to her house.

"The job sounds perfect for you. I'm so glad you'll be doing something that makes use of your gifts."

"I'm glad to hear you say that. I've never had a job in the secular world. I'm grateful, but nervous."

They carried Matthew's things into the house. Christine had emptied the closet in the guest bedroom to make room for his clothes and had cleared some space for toiletries in the guest bathroom as well. Matthew gave her a hug.

"What should we do about dinner?" Christine asked. "I can run up to the Briar and Thistle for some takeout or maybe have a pizza delivered."

"Pizza sounds great." Matthew looked around his new bedroom. He would be very comfortable here.

"Any preference?"

"I've never met a pizza I didn't like."

Christine called for the pizza while Matthew unpacked his things. He heard her shower running and then her hair dryer, which he thought sounded more like a jet engine. She appeared in the doorway wearing workout shorts and a t-shirt.

"We aren't dressing for dinner, then?" Matthew teased her. "I'd usually just be in a bathrobe, but I don't want to give the pizza guy the wrong idea."

Matthew chuckled at that.

"You might wait about ten minutes before you shower," she suggested. "The hot water tank isn't very big, I'm afraid."

"Thanks for the warning."

She disappeared into the kitchen and got some plates and napkins out. After a few minutes, she heard the shower running in the guest bathroom and her mind pictured him undressing and stepping into the warm spray. She had always been quite fond of him, and in the last few days, she had grown to have genuine feelings for him. Not surprising, she thought. He is a kind and decent man. What did surprise her, though, was her sexual attraction to him. She had never dated anyone so much older than herself before, and had it not been for the booze, she wouldn't have made a pass at him that first night.

His lovemaking was a delightful combination of exploration, tenderness, and aggression, and she couldn't deny that his hairy chest was a big turn-on. She wondered how his bedroom techniques would evolve as he became more experienced.

The shower became silent, and Christine tried to force herself to think of other things. She had insisted that they have separate bedrooms and she intended to keep that stipulation. She would also sit him down and explain that since they aren't in a committed relationship, neither of them should be jealous if the other dated someone else. That sounded good and proper to her, although she had to admit that she loved the fact that she was the only woman he'd ever been with. She wondered how she would feel if that changed.

A knock on the door signaled the arrival of the pizza, and she grabbed her purse from the kitchen counter. Matthew appeared shortly afterward in jeans and a plain white undershirt.

"Smells good," he said. "How much do I owe you?"

"My treat tonight. You can get the next one."

They sat down at the table, and each took a slice of the pie.

"You're almost overdressed for dinner at this restaurant," she teased him. "But I like the look. Something about a man in an undershirt, I dunno. Very masculine."

"I'll keep that in mind," he winked. "I hope you can help me discover a few looks that might do me well as I dip a toe into the dating pool."

The statement took Christine by surprise and stung more than she wanted to admit.

"The prospect of having to start dating at my age is terrifying," he said. "I don't even know where to start."

"Maybe we'll go shopping tomorrow and find some clothes that look good on you. You'll need a new wardrobe anyway. You can't wear your cassocks at a secular job."

"I much appreciate the offer," Matthew said. "Thank you."

Christine's phone rang inside her purse on the counter. She recognized the ringtone she'd set for Ivan.

"Sorry," she said, as she pushed her chair back from the table. "I know it's rude, but that's the boss calling."

She got the phone and answered it.

"Hello?" She listened for a moment. "Ivan, let me put you on speaker. I've got Father Matthew here. He should hear this, too."

"Father Matthew from Mt Carmel?" Ivan's voice asked as the phone switched to speaker mode. "Sorry, I didn't mean to interrupt an interview. You can call me back later."

"No, it's not an interview, we're just..." Christine realized that Ivan was unaware of recent developments. "Nothing. What's your news?"

"Zara called me just now," Ivan said. "She and Lisa met with Joel Wood today. Joel didn't believe Lisa's theory. He basically blew her off, then he tried to get her to believe that he was a messenger of God."

"I can't say I'm surprised."

"After the interview, Lisa told Zara that if Joel gets too popular, if he gets too many followers, then we only have a few days."

"What do you mean?"

"That's when our time is up. She says all our timelines end in a few days. Lisa has got to start getting people to understand the truth before they get on board with Joel or anyone else."

"Ivan," Christine said, "do you have any idea how crazy that sounds to a rational person?"

"I am a rational person." Ivan's voice was stern. "And I'm still your boss."

"Sorry," Christine quickly added. "No disrespect intended."

"I suggested to Zara that we take a portable microphone and amp to City Park tomorrow. Lisa can broadcast her message there and get a head start on Joel, since he won't be doing his preaching until Sunday."

"What time tomorrow?"

"Lunch hour," Ivan said. "Noonish. The food trucks will all be there, so the park should be full of people having lunch on the grass. I want you to be there to talk to them, find out what they think about her message."

"Saturday is usually my off-day," Christine said.

"Working one Saturday afternoon is a small price to pay to help save the world, don't you think?"

Christine sighed. Ivan rarely asked any special favors of his employees. She whispered to Matthew.

"Shopping tomorrow evening okay?"

Matthew nodded.

"I'll be there."

"Thank you," Ivan said and hung up.

"Christine," Matthew said as she sat back down at the table, "I've been a bit preoccupied with my own drama this week. I'm afraid you'll have to fill me in on what that all meant."

Christine tried to explain, but found it difficult. She eventually remembered the video that Lisa had made, and she brought out the laptop from her bedroom. Matthew watched it.

"That's fascinating," he said. "There are some things about it that I could probably believe, but other parts I'm not so sure."

"That's kinda how I feel," Christine admitted. "I mean we know that dark energy exists, even if we don't really understand it. I learned about it in physics class."

"Well, I took physics far too long ago to remember whether I did or not. We tended to gloss over science that contradicted biblical beliefs."

"I'm not sure I can buy into her doomsday scenario," Christine said. "Why should we believe her any more than we believed the other crackpots who predicted the end of the world in the past? There was that one guy, I don't remember his name, and he even gave a specific date and everything. People cleaned out their bank accounts and spent all their money to make what they thought would be their last days on earth awesome, but the world didn't end, and those people were bankrupt fools."

"Harold Camping," Matthew reminded her. "Back in 2011, he said the rapture would happen in May. It didn't, so he changed it to October. Didn't happen then, either, obviously."

"That's the guy. Anyway, the point is that people did these rash things because they were convinced the world would end. If Lisa goes into City Park and gets people riled up about the end of the world, and it looks like the *Post* is sponsoring it, then our credibility as a reliable news source is history. Even more so once the doomsday date passes and nothing happens."

"It sounds like you need to be there," Matthew said.

Christine's phone rang again. She looked at the screen and saw Thelo's name, then answered.

"I assume you got the call, too?"

"Yeah." Thelo sounded angry. "What the fuck is Ivan thinking?"

Joel set the video camera on the tripod and aimed it at the desk in his office. He adjusted it until the view framed what he wanted, then pressed 'record,' and sat down at his desk. He wore a sports coat and dress shirt to look good for the video, but shorts and sneakers for comfort. Nobody would see those behind the desk anyway. He cleared his throat and began.

"Brothers and sisters, I am coming to you humbly, with a deep sense of humility and shame. By now, many of you have read the news story about me and my past transgressions. I wish I could tell you that the article is untrue, but it is not. I am guilty of those sins, just as everyone is guilty of sin. My sins are numerous; I will not lie. I freely agreed to give that interview because I heard the voice of God speak through me last Sunday and it shook me to my very core. I needed to cleanse myself of my sinful ways and begin again with a purity of heart so that God can speak through me again and again. It felt wonderful to confess my sins and to be forgiven by God. I hope and pray that you can find it in your hearts to forgive me as well."

Tears began to roll down Joel's cheeks as he spoke. He paused to keep his voice from cracking.

"As most of you have also heard, God chose to take Holly, my lovely wife, as punishment for my sins. I have been assured by the doctors that she died almost instantly in the crash. She didn't suffer. The suffering is for me to do, knowing that I must bear the burden of guilt. If I had not been such a sinner, she would not have left our home that day. I will miss her terribly."

He took a deep breath and exhaled slowly as he dropped his eyes. His lower lip quivered. He bit it, steeled himself, then looked directly into the camera.

"I come to you today, however, not just to ask your forgiveness, but to bring you a warning. Many of you have seen a video by a lovely young woman named Lisa. She talks about a dark energy that she calls The Source, and she claims that we all must abandon our belief in God. She says that the world will end if we continue to serve the Lord."

He shook his head in defiance.

"I met with Lisa this afternoon. She is a charming young woman and can be quite persuasive, but when I asked her to explain how more than two dozen people of God were all given the same message on the same day, she didn't have an answer. It clearly happened, you all saw it, yet she could not explain it."

He leaned toward the camera.

"I ask you, brothers and sisters, who do you believe? Do you believe Lisa, a woman barely twenty years old, who predicts the end of the world with certainty, yet can't even explain what happened a few days ago? Or do you put your faith and trust in Joel Wood, a man who was chosen to receive a direct message from God Himself?

"Brothers and sisters, I realize that you may feel that I've betrayed your trust in me. I realize that you may be angry with me because I am not the man you thought me to be. I understand that, and I can't blame you.

"But God didn't give up on me. God made Himself known to me in the most direct, most amazing way I can imagine. He spoke through me and in that instant, I was transformed from the sinful man of my past into a vessel of God's Word for the future.

"I invite you to join me this Sunday at Gloria Deo, either in person or via live television, to hear the Word of God spoken again. And Lisa, if you are listening, I invite you to share the stage with me. When God speaks through me again, I want you to be right there to share the amazing, powerful moment. See for yourself that no dark energy can compare to the glorious Light of God."

Joel smiled, waited a few moments, then got up and turned off the camera. He sent the video to his media staff, then called them to ask that they spread it far and wide. By the time he went to bed that evening, his video had almost as many views as Lisa's.

Lisa might think her world is ending, he thought. But mine's just getting started. God will prevail. Amen.

CHAPTER TWENTY-FOUR
Saturday

Ivan showed up at City Park around eleven that morning with a portable amplifier and a microphone. He selected a central area in the grass near where the food trucks were setting up, figuring that would be the best spot to draw a crowd. Ivan hated that he was enabling Lisa to ruin peoples' perfectly nice afternoon in the park with amplified preaching, a practice that he loathed, but Lisa's message was important. He hoped that people wouldn't tune her out or leave the park before they heard what she had to say.

Ivan knew that Christine and Thelo didn't understand why he was so taken with Lisa's theory. He initially chalked it up to her ability to infiltrate his dream, but there had to me more to it than that. In the years since his falling out with his church, he had felt a hole in his life, a void that hadn't been filled. Ivan needed to believe in something; he needed the knowledge that there was a being or a force out in the universe that was bigger than humanity. Lisa's theory was radical, yes, but it was based on science. That was something that Ivan could latch onto, something that he could believe. Science provided the truth while the rest of Lisa's theory provided the faith. Ivan's belief in The Source, even though it was still in its fledgling stages, had already given him a peace of mind that he hadn't felt since his childhood. He knew that others must also be searching to fill a void in their lives, and he wanted them to know this feeling. Ivan felt better than he had in ages.

Lisa arrived with Zara, and the three of them discussed their plan. Zara had brought some copies of her article, and planned to hand one to anyone who would take it.

Christine arrived a few minutes later and found the group. She said hello to Zara and Lisa, then pulled Ivan off to the side.

"We need to talk," she told him.

"Of course. What is it?"

"I want to apologize for my attitude on the phone last night. You're right. I was disrespectful and out of place."

"And your boss was calling you with business outside of your regular work hours, so we were both in error. My apologies as well."

"I need to help you understand how bad this can be for the *Post*," Christine warned. "Lisa is going to give her doomsday prediction. If she insinuates that she is here on behalf of the *Post*, then it looks like we are endorsing her prediction as fact."

"Go on."

"Do you remember Harold Camping?"

Ivan nodded.

"People believed him," Christine said, "and they did some pretty rash things in the days before his deadline, figuring they had nothing to lose. If the same thing happens here, if some people believe Lisa's story because the *Post* apparently endorsed it, then we could be liable for whatever idiotic things people do. We could be the cause of someone's death, albeit indirectly."

"You're overreacting," Ivan told her, "but I appreciate your concern. I'll ask Lisa not to mention the *Post* in her comments."

"Thank you."

"But I still want you to get some interviews and reactions from the crowd."

"The gang's all here," a voice said from behind her.

She turned around and saw Thelo with a ruggedly handsome man who looked vaguely familiar.

"You remember Mike," Thelo said as he introduced the man to her.

"Possibly," Christine admitted, "but I can't recall where we've met."

"He's a cop," Zara chimed in. "They're dating."

Christine's eyes widened. "From when we got pulled over the other day?" she said.

Mike grinned. "Nice to see you again."

"When did this happen?"

"Later that same night," Thelo said. "He saw me in the club, we talked, and the next thing I knew, I was handcuffed to his bed."

"I'm shocked!"

"I'm not shocked at all," Zara said with a grin.

"I don't think you're allowed to be shocked," Thelo told Christine. "Not after I saw you snogging that priest in the hospital."

"So that's why Father Matthew was at your house last night!" Ivan teased.

"Father kissy-face was at your house?" Thelo's eyes were wide.

"Okay, okay," Christine laughed. "Point made." She turned back to Mike. "Thelo's a keeper. You be good to him."

"Yes, ma'am," he said.

Christine pulled Thelo off to the side so she could talk to him privately.

"Ivan has promised that he'll keep Lisa from making it sound like the *Post* is endorsing her message."

"Good," Thelo said, relieved. "I was going to talk to him about that."

"Secondly," she said, turning back to look at Mike, "that guy is *hot*. Good for you!"

"So the priest was at your house last night, huh?"

"He lives there now."

"Holy shit, woman, you move fast!"

"No, no, it's not like that."

She filled Thelo in on Matthew's leaving the priesthood and needing a place to stay. She also told him about Matthew's potential new job running Simon's charity.

"Sounds like things will work out well for him, then," Thelo said. They rejoined the group.

"I have gotten a ton of feedback on your story about Admin," Ivan said to Thelo. "Everyone is jealous that we had such a scoop. When I told them that you had figured out her identity yourself, they were even more impressed. I had to turn down at least three job offers on your behalf already today. You can thank me later."

"I got more than that," Thelo said. "I just haven't turned them down yet." He winked at Ivan, who wasn't sure if he was kidding.

"There seems to be a pretty good crowd now," Lisa interrupted. "Maybe we should start."

Lisa turned on the amp and picked up the microphone. A loud squeal burst forth from the speaker, and she quickly moved the microphone away from the amp to cancel the feedback.

"Sorry," she said. "Good afternoon, everyone."

A few people turned to scowl at her. Many more turned their backs, hoping to ignore the intrusion into their day.

"Some of you may recognize me from the YouTube video that went viral yesterday," she said.

A few people looked to see who was speaking. Ivan noticed several who appeared to recognize Lisa now that she had made the connection to the video.

"I'm here to help us save the world."

She began to deliver her message. She spoke softly, letting the amplifier do the heavy lifting. Before long, a crowd had gathered, and some of them were captivated by her ideas. Ivan sent Christine and Thelo into the crowd to get reactions, then turned to Mike, who seemed to be quite interested in her speech.

"It's pretty compelling when you hear her in person, isn't it?" Ivan said to him.

"Yes," Mike replied. "I've had a similar idea about God being an energy field for a while now. It makes at least as much sense as the other concepts of God, I suppose."

A couple of people in the crowd began to heckle Lisa as she spoke.

"Joel Wood says you're a phony," one called out.

Lisa stopped her speech in mid-sentence.

"I'm sorry," she said to the crowd in the direction of the heckler, "what was that?"

"Joel Wood says you're a phony," the male voice repeated. "God spoke to him. Has God ever spoken to you?"

"God could not speak to Joel Wood nor anyone else," Lisa replied. "There is no God. There is only The Source."

A shocked gasp sounded from the crowd. Several more voices joined the heckler's after that. Lisa tried to remain calm and keep on with her message, but the group got louder, more voices joined them, and the crowd began to turn on her. The escalated volume of the shouts only worked to attract more people to the park.

"You can't tell me there's no God!" Ivan could hear someone yell through the din. The voices of dissent came from every part of the crowd, drowning out Lisa's voice, even with the amp's speaker turned up to maximum volume.

"We should leave," Mike said. "Now."

The comfortable circle of space they had made for themselves in the center of the park was closing in on them, and they had no escape route.

Someone began to chant, 'shut her up,' and it caught on. Someone else chanted, 'let her speak,' and that caught on as well.

The two groups got louder and more insistent, then some of them began to turn on each other.

Lisa continued on with her message, undaunted. Either she was oblivious to the increasing threat, or she didn't care. Their circle was almost gone, and the crowd pressed in on them.

"Get her out of here!" Ivan shouted to Mike above the noise. Mike took Lisa by the waist with one hand and pulled her alongside him as he shoved his way through the mass of people. A wall of shouts and chanting followed them. Fights had broken out. They pushed through the edge of the crowd, and Mike took Lisa around the corner, out of view.

"You stay out of sight, don't go back over there," he warned.

"Okay," Lisa said, rattled by the realization that her message of harmony had fueled exactly the opposite.

Mike ran back toward the action. The scene had become a full-blown brawl. Mike called 911 for police and ambulance as he searched for Thelo and the others. Eventually, he spotted Christine on the edge of the lawn. She looked shaken, but unhurt.

"You all right?"

"Yeah, I'm fine."

"I got Lisa out. She's around the corner by the deli. Go meet her there, and I'll send everyone else over when I find them."

Christine left in the direction of the deli and Mike pushed his way back into the crowd. He found Thelo about midway in, trying to get to the center of the brawl.

"Thelo!" Mike called to him.

Thelo turned around at the sound of his name.

"Go meet up by the corner deli," Mike yelled to him.

"What about Ivan?" Thelo was still trying to make his way to the area where Ivan and Lisa had been.

"He's fine," Mike lied. "Now go!"

Thelo reversed course and made his way out of the fracas as Mike pushed farther in. Near the center of the throng, the microphone caught the sounds of the brawl and blasted them through the speaker. Mike heard 'get off, get off,' and then the noise quickly subsided. People began to run away, trying to distance themselves from the center of the park where Lisa had been.

Mike could see Ivan and two other people on the ground. A space around them was rapidly growing as people fled the area. Mike knelt down by Ivan and slapped his face a couple of times, but he didn't get a response. He held the back of his hand near Ivan's face and felt a very slight breath. Good, he thought. He checked the second man, who was also breathing. The third man moaned and tried to sit up.

"Easy there, buddy," Mike told him. "Ambulance is on the way, just lie down."

"That guy," he pointed at the man next to Mike, "tripped over the amplifier. He went down, then me and the other guy went down with him." The man held his sides in pain. "Everyone was on top of us. We were getting trampled."

"Just relax," Mike told him. "Help will be here shortly."

The sound of approaching sirens scattered the rest of the crowd. Only a few people stayed behind as a police car and ambulance arrived on the scene. Mike stood and waved to get the paramedic's attention as she got out of the ambulance, and then motioned to the police officer as well.

"These three all have injuries," Mike told the paramedic as she got to him. "They were trampled beneath a bunch of people. Probably some broken bones or worse."

"Jesus, Mike," the police officer said as he approached. "What the hell happened?"

Mike filled the cop in on the events and mentioned that he had friends who were witnesses. The officer wanted to see them, so Mike phoned Thelo and told him to bring everyone back.

As the group walked back to the park, they saw a stretcher being loaded into an ambulance. It left before Thelo could see who had been put inside.

Thelo saw Mike talking to another cop. Two men were lying on the ground being attended to by a paramedic.

"Where's Ivan?" Thelo asked Mike.

"On his way to the hospital."

"Oh my God," Christine said. "Is he going to be all right?"

"He got trapped under a lot of people," Mike said. "He was still breathing, but unconscious. I don't know much beyond that."

"We'll go there now," Christine said.

"Hang on," Mike told her. "This is Officer Wilson. He'll need to take statements from everyone first."

Thelo spun around to Lisa. "This is on you," he snarled. "I don't know how you convinced Ivan to believe in your bullshit, but he did, and now he's hurt because you just had to go and broadcast it to the whole fucking world."

Lisa started to say something, but Thelo cut her off with a finger pointed at her face. "Don't you say another word!" he screamed. "You've done enough damage for one day. How is it you got out safe when Ivan was on the ground?"

"Thelo," Mike interrupted, "She didn't leave anyone behind. I grabbed her and pulled her through the crowd to safety."

Thelo gaped at Mike. "I can't believe it. You left a good man behind and saved this bitch instead?"

"It wasn't like that."

Thelo would hear no more about it. He gave his statement to Officer Wilson, then ran to his car and headed to the hospital. The rest of them gave their statements as well.

"Christine," Mike said after the officer had released them to go, "do you think I could get a lift home? Thelo was my ride."

"Sure. I'm going to the hospital to check on Ivan, do you want to stop there first?"

"I'd better not. I'm sure Thelo's there already. Let's not have another scene today."

They walked to Christine's car, then had a mostly silent drive, save for Mike giving her directions to his house. Christine pulled to the curb when they arrived.

"Thanks for the ride."

"No problem."

"Will you call or text me later and let me know how Ivan's doing? And Thelo?"

"Sure."

Mike got out, and Christine drove to the hospital.

Zara parked her rental car in the lot at Saint Luke's. She was thankful that Lisa knew how to get there.

"I probably shouldn't go in," Lisa said. "I don't want Thelo to have another blowup."

"Should I take you home, then?" Zara asked.

"No, I can walk from here. It's not far."

The two women got out of the car.

"I'd love to see your place," Zara said. "Also, the article I wrote was all about The Source. I'd like to do a follow-up article about you. I'm sure people are curious about who you are and what you're all about. Mind if I stop by after?"

"Another time, perhaps," Lisa answered. "You belong here right now."

Lisa closed the car door. "I'm going to be at Joel Wood's church tomorrow morning."

"After what happened today?" Zara asked in astonishment. "You got a death wish or something?"

"I told the officer at the park that Joel's service might get some of the same reactions that mine did today. He said he'd let his superiors know. They'll have plenty of security there, I'm sure."

"Still a bloody bad idea, I'd say. I sure as hell won't be there."

"I figured you would want that story," Lisa said.

"I'll watch it on the telly."

The two women parted ways, and Zara went into the hospital. Christine was there already.

"I don't know where to go," Zara told her. "Where did they take him?"

"Emergency is this way. I was just here a few days ago myself."

Zara followed Christine down a long hallway into the south wing and up to the emergency room admitting desk. The receptionist looked up from her computer at Christine.

"May I help you?"

"We're looking for Ivan Carter, he would've been brought here less than an hour ago."

The receptionist typed on her keyboard and checked the screen.

"Yes, he's here, but he's being treated at the moment. There's a waiting room down the hall to your right, or you can come back later after he's assigned a room."

"We'll wait, thanks."

The two women walked to the waiting room, where they found a dozen or so people waiting to hear news about loved ones. Thelo was already there.

"Any news?" Christine asked him.

Thelo shook his head, but said nothing. The three of them sat in silence. Minutes passed like hours. Doctors occasionally came in and gave news to other people, then left. The longer they waited without news, the worse they imagined Ivan's condition to be.

"Family of Ivan Carter?" a voice asked.

"Here," Christine answered quickly and stuck her hand up.

The doctor made his way over to them. "Are you his family?"

"As close to family as you'll get today," Christine said. "He's our boss."

"Mr. Carter's condition is stable but critical. He has multiple internal injuries and a concussion. I'm afraid I can't be more specific than that to non-family. Do any of you know how to contact them?"

"We don't even know if he still has a family," Christine said.

Zara said nothing.

"Can we see him?" Christine asked.

"No, I'm afraid that the ICU is limited to one visitor at a time, and only to immediate family. I'm sorry."

"We understand."

"We'll try to find his family," the doctor said. "Once he's out of ICU, he'll be allowed visitors, but that could be several days from now."

"Okay," Christine said. "Thank you, doctor."

The three of them left the waiting room.

"I'm sure he'll be all right," Zara said, trying to sound optimistic. "He's been through some shit before. He'll get through this."

"I hope so," Christine said.

Thelo said nothing.

CHAPTER
TWENTY-FIVE
Sunday

"Good morning," Matthew said as he made his way into the kitchen. Christine was already up and pouring her second cup of coffee.

"Oh, good morning. Coffee?"

"You read my mind."

Christine got a second mug from the cupboard and poured a cup for her new housemate. The two sat at the breakfast table and sipped their coffee.

"Did you sleep well?" she asked.

"Yes, once I finally drifted off," Matthew said. "The bed is really comfortable, but I couldn't get my brain to slow down for the longest time. Too many changes all at once, I suppose."

"Understandable."

"Have you gotten an update on your editor?"

"No. Thelo texted that he was going back to the hospital this morning. I said that I would come in later and take over. Someone needs to be there in case there's news, or if they let him have visitors."

"Thelo will send word if there's any change, I'm sure."

They were silent for a while.

"Zara told me that Lisa is going to be at Joel Wood's service this morning," Christine said.

"Is that really a good idea?"

"Joel made a video right after they met and he invited her to be on stage with him. I'm sure there will be security there, but I still wouldn't do it."

Thelo sat in the waiting room outside the intensive care unit. Ivan's condition had gotten worse overnight, but he was still hanging on. Rage had consumed Thelo since the rally yesterday, and he hadn't slept much. He was angry at Lisa for getting people riled up, he was furious at Mike for choosing to save her rather than Ivan, and he was disappointed in Ivan for being weak-minded enough to fall for Lisa's bullshit ideas. It was just another fucking religion, that's all. It was a mistake for Ivan to buy into that crap, and now he's paying for it.

Mike had never been inside the worship building Gloria Deo before. The arena-like sanctuary usually looked full on TV, but today he figured that the place would reach maximum capacity long before the last of the people arrived. Traffic was backed up for nearly a mile in every direction, and even more people poured out of the commuter trains that stopped at a station a half-block away.

Mike had volunteered to help out with the extra security even though it was his day off. He knew they would need the help, and he was curious to see what would happen when Lisa and Joel met on stage. Joel's video had eclipsed Lisa's in the number of views, and judging by the online comments, his was better received than hers as well.

Besides, Mike thought, being here got his mind off other things. He had planned to surprise Thelo with a nice dinner and a romantic evening tonight, but yesterday's events blew that out of the water. Thelo wouldn't even return his calls or texts.

Lisa took the commuter train to Gloria Deo. She wore sunglasses and a ball cap to keep from being recognized, and she kept her head down as well. Everyone on the train was talking about the videos that she and Joel had put out. From the sound of the conversations around her, everyone on the train was in support of Joel. She kept her mouth shut.

Lisa closed her eyes and tried to find the right set of events that would extend humanity's existence. If things continued along the current path, she knew, humans would be exterminated to achieve balance. She couldn't see specific times and days, but she knew that she could usually get a year or two into her scope and these timelines ended much, much sooner than that. When she told Zara they only had a few days, she might've been generous.

She searched her mind, but found no sequence of events that would extend the timelines more than a tiny bit. Could it be that nothing she could do would change things? That all of this had been for naught? She opened her eyes and took a deep breath. There were other timelines she hadn't considered, she knew. She intentionally blocked those out as unacceptable, but if humanity's days were numbered anyway, no harm done. She closed her eyes again and searched through the timelines that would only come into play if she or Joel were to die.

Zara found Thelo in the waiting room at Saint Luke's.

"Any news?"

"Not yet," he said. "But at least they'll update me now."

"Did they find his family?"

"No, but they looked at Ivan's phone and found his ICE number."

"Sorry, his what?"

"ICE. In Case of Emergency. You put an emergency contact number in your phone under 'ICE,' and if there's an emergency, they call that number."

"And Ivan had one of those?"

"Yeah," Thelo said, "and they called it several times but got no answer."

"Whose number were they calling?" she asked.

"Mine. But you can't get a damn signal in here, so it went to voicemail all morning. It wasn't until I stepped outside for some fresh air that I saw the missed calls."

"Ivan had you as his emergency contact?"

"Apparently so," Thelo said. "I don't even know if he still has any family."

Zara said nothing. She wondered if Ivan's family would even care.

Matthew and Christine were both finishing up their second cup of coffee, and Christine offered to start a fresh pot.

"Not for me, thanks," Matthew said. "Two cups is my limit."

"I'll finish off this pot, then," Christine said. "I want to be alert later, when I relieve Thelo at the hospital."

"I'll go with you if you like."

"That would be nice," she said. "But aren't you going to Mass at Mount Carmel today?"

"I think not today. The parish needs to move on and get used to the changes that are coming. My being there would only be a distraction."

"That's kind of you."

"I'll give it a few weeks," he said. "By then, there will be a new parish priest and things will be getting back to normal. Are you going to church somewhere this morning? I'd like to visit some of your favorite congregations."

"Actually, I thought I'd stay in and watch Joel Wood's service on television. It's going to be crazy with Lisa there, and I want to see it. Just not in person."

"Smart woman. But I thought Joel taped his services and televised them a week later."

"He did," Christine said as she turned on the TV, "but in that YouTube video he made, he said to join him on live television. Maybe they do it differently now, I dunno."

"Ah, right, I saw that video."

"I think everybody saw that video." Christine found the channel, and she watched as the camera panned across the crowd.

"That place is packed."

A few people in the crowd held signs saying, 'We forgive you,' and 'God is light, evil is dark' and 'if God is energy, is my electricity bill Scripture?' Christine chuckled at that last one.

"I should be there covering this," she said.

"You can cover it from here, since it's a live broadcast."

"Yeah, but I feel like I'm letting Ivan down by not being there in person."

"You're going to be able to report on it far better from here. You can record the broadcast and watch it as many times as you need to. If you were there in all that craziness, you'd be lucky to come out with anything useful. Besides, it's your day off."

"I hate it when you're right," she teased. "But thank you."

Christine used the remote to start recording the broadcast, then used her phone to send a text to Thelo. 'No news yet' was the reply.

Lisa closed her eyes and searched through timelines that began with her own death. She discovered that getting herself killed only made the timelines shorter. In some cases, humanity's timeline ended almost immediately after her death.

No, she thought, I can't die today. I have to keep bringing people to understand The Source. The longer I do that, the longer we live.

But what if Joel were the one to die? She closed her eyes again and concentrated. The timelines that began with Joel's death shifted into view, and she saw that the outlook for humanity was much better. Some of the timelines even extended beyond the reach of Lisa's ability to see. It was the first time she had seen any set of events that would keep The Source from doing a global reboot.

A tear rolled down Lisa's cheek. She knew what had to be done, but could she go through with it? If so, how? She knew that somehow, she had to live, and Joel Wood had to die. It was the only way. She was sure she would be arrested and charged with murder. Could she still educate people about The Source from prison? From death row? Too many questions and not enough answers. She wished that her visions were more specific.

The commuter train stopped, and the throng of people filed out onto the platform near Gloria Deo. Lisa kept her head down and made her way to the church. She was afraid.

CHAPTER TWENTY-SIX

Joel was thrilled with the size of the crowd at Gloria Deo. People were being turned away at the doors due to capacity, and a large group had gathered outside in the courtyard to watch the live stream on their phones.

Lisa made her way to the church and was stopped by security at the door. She told the police officer that she was an invited guest, but the officer stood fast. Lisa didn't want to make a scene for fear that if her identity were discovered in this crowd, yesterday's event might be tame by comparison. As she turned to go, she caught a glimpse of Mike just inside the glass entry door. She turned and tapped on the glass.

"I told you you're not going in," the officer at the door warned.

"That's Mike in there," she insisted, pointing through the glass. "He'll vouch for me."

Mike opened the door from the inside and motioned for Lisa to follow him. "It's okay, Steve," Mike told the officer. "She's supposed to be on stage with Pastor Wood today."

Lisa slipped through the door and followed Mike down a stair-stepped aisle between long rows of stadium seating. People were milling about, searching for empty seats. The pair got near the stage, and Mike got the attention of one of the media techs, who was putting cameras in place.

"This is Lisa," Mike told him. "Joel invited her to share the stage today."

"Aw, hell," the tech said. "We didn't think she was coming." He tapped a button near the earpiece of his headset. "Hey, that Lisa woman is here after all. We need to reset the position of cameras three and four and put the extra chair back on stage. Yeah, I know, but she just got here. I'll send her around."

The tech told Mike and Lisa how to get backstage and where to go from there.

"Thanks for your help," she told Mike. She eyed the gun on his belt. "I may need your help again."

Zara looked up as the door to the intensive care unit opened. A doctor in a white lab coat came through with a somber look on his face. She tapped Thelo on the arm, and when he raised his head and saw the doctor's expression, his mood sank.

"I'm sorry," the doctor said.

Zara began to cry, and Thelo's fists clenched in anger. He slammed them onto the arms of the chair repeatedly. Zara reached to put her arm around him, but he angrily pushed it away.

"No. Not now."

Thelo got up and stormed down the hall. He needed to be away from this place, away from these people, away from any reminder of yesterday.

Zara watched him through her tears. She needed someone familiar to hold onto. She felt isolated here, away from her home and her London friends. Thelo and Ivan were her lifelines to normality in this unfamiliar city, and they were both gone.

She wondered if Ivan had felt this kind of loneliness when he left his family behind. She wondered if his family had felt it, too.

"Doctor?" she said. "You should find his family. They didn't know about his life, about his success, about how his friends and coworkers loved him."

"We've tried," the doctor said. "We can't find any family."

"Don't look for Ivan's family," Zara said. "Look for Emily's."

"No way," Mike whispered sternly. "You've lost your mind if you think I'm going to do that."

"Mike, please," Lisa pleaded. "It's the only way that we're going to survive. I've looked for other alternatives, I promise. Taking Joel out of the picture is the only way to avoid all of humanity being wiped out."

"I know you believe that, but I can't. I'm not going to do it."

Lisa started to say something, but he interrupted her.

"And if you try to do it, I'll have no choice but to stop you."

Lisa sighed. It was a long shot, she knew, but Mike had seemed to be accepting of her ideas in the past. Besides, he had a gun. That would make it so much easier. She resigned herself to coming up with another plan.

A stagehand motioned for Lisa to come onto the stage and take a seat next to Joel. The show was about to begin.

"Do you need a pen and paper to take notes?" Matthew asked as they settled down on the sofa to watch the broadcast.

"I've got my laptop right here," Christine said. "I type much faster than I write."

"It's the opposite for me, I'm afraid. Although my typing is a lot more legible."

Lisa and Joel were in place on stage, the cameras were set up and ready, the website was streaming live, and the crowd was pumped up. Joel saw the director count down: three, two, one…

The stage was suddenly ablaze with lights. A drummer kick-started the praise band into Gloria Deo's unofficial theme song, 'It's a Brand New Day,' and the crowd sang along and swayed with the rhythms. Some even danced in the aisles. Lisa remained seated with her eyes closed. She needed to make sure about what she'd seen, what she would have to do. She was terrified that she might actually go through with it. She was equally terrified that she wouldn't.

When the song was over, Joel thanked the band and the choir for the music, thanked the crowd for joining him, thanked the people around the world who were watching the live stream, and thanked the television audience for tuning in.

He addressed the crowd and brought the joyous mood down quickly when he asked for a moment of silence for Holly. The people in the audience bowed their heads in prayer. The camera zoomed in on Joel's tear-streaked face as he ended the moment of silence and then recounted his sins. He asked for forgiveness from God and from the people in the arena. Shouts of 'we forgive you,' rained down on the stage from the audience. Joel was humbled.

Mike stood at his post just offstage in the wings. He had a good view of Lisa and Joel, as well as the first several rows of seats. If anyone tried to get onto the stage, Mike would see. He noticed a fellow officer, Stan Thompson, in the opposite wing across the stage. Mike was glad to see this event so well-guarded. The last thing anyone needed, he thought, was a repeat of yesterday.

"Now I would like you all to meet our very special guest today," Joel said to the crowd. "This is Lisa Jones, a bright young woman with some truly interesting ideas to share with us." The crowd erupted in boos, and several people began to chant, 'not my God.' Joel waved his hands until the crowd settled down.

"We do not treat our guests that way," Joel admonished them. He turned to Lisa. "I'm very sorry. It seems that I'm not the only one in the room who needs to be forgiven."

That shut the crowd down. The tension in the room was electric, but the shouts had subsided, at least.

"I'm afraid for Lisa," Matthew said to Christine as they watched from her living room. He prayed that Lisa would remain safe and unharmed. Christine joined him.

Lisa stood up next to Joel, and he handed her a microphone. Joel wore a dark gray suit and royal blue tie, with perfectly coiffed hair. Stage makeup hid the glare of the lights and enhanced his skin tone for the cameras. Lisa wore a black t-shirt, her nicest pair of jeans, and spiked hair that had become mussed by the ball cap she had worn earlier.

She took the mic and cleared her throat.

"Good morning," she said. Her voice was as shaky as the microphone she held in her trembling hands. Joel's years in television and his acting experience provided the most uneven playing field imaginable for a showdown on this stage. He was confident, talented, spoke with an air of authority, and the cameras loved him. She was none of those things. She cleared her throat again.

"Thank you, Pastor Wood, for inviting me here today."

"You're welcome, Lisa," he said with a smile. "Don't be afraid. You're doing fine." The crowd laughed at that.

Joel's patronizing tone angered her. She didn't stand a chance on his home turf, and he knew it. She could not allow him to get in any more jabs at her credibility. She didn't know how long Joel would let her speak, so she had to get right to the point.

"I am here to bring you a warning," she said, more forcefully than before. "I can see where things are headed. We are on the wrong path." She fought to keep her voice steady. "The Source will seek balance. If we don't change our path and quickly, we will be wiped off the earth."

"Hey, hang on," Joel interrupted. "That's a pretty big claim. Let's not get everyone into a panic here." He looked around the arena, then flashed a sly smile to the camera, then turned back to Lisa. "I think you should explain."

Lisa was flustered. She had written down everything she had planned to say and had rehearsed it in front of her mirror at home for hours. None of it was coming back to her now. He cursed herself for not bringing her speech with her, but she'd decided that people wouldn't listen if she just stood up there and read from a page. Even so, that would be preferable to the rambling mess in her head now.

Joel looked at her as if to say, 'well?'

"People have been fighting each other since the dawn of time," she began. "Religions were founded in order to bring peace, but over the centuries, those religions were changed by men who wanted more power and control for themselves. Power leads to corruption, mistrust, and then war. We've been at war with each other for so long that the imbalance has become critical. We are at a crossroads. We face extinction."

"Extinction?" Joel asked.

"The Source will remove the cause of the imbalance, which means us. People. Humankind."

"Is God going to send another flood to wipe out the sinners and start over, like He did before?"

There was a smattering of laughter from the crowd. They knew he was teasing her, but Lisa was too focused on getting her message out to notice.

"Maybe a flood. Maybe a meteor, like the one that wiped out the dinosaurs, or maybe some other thing. I don't know how it will happen."

"You don't know how," Joel repeated. "When I spoke with you the other day, I asked you how I and many others all spoke the same words at the same time. You gave me that answer then: 'I don't know how.'"

Lisa was silent. She knew that any chance she had of winning over the crowd was gone.

"So now you say that everyone will be wiped off the earth," Joel continued, "but you don't know how. Last week, I spoke a direct message from God right here in this room, but you don't know how. Others all over the world spoke that same message at the same time, but you don't know how."

The crowd began to stir excitedly. Joel was on a roll, and they loved it.

"But," he continued, "you say that you know the future. You say that unless we turn our backs on God, some kind of magical energy field is going to kill us all." He went for the killing blow. "We have proof that God is real." He waved his arm in a circle, indicating the people around the room. "We all heard that proof with our own ears."

There were several 'amens' from the crowd.

"You, however, have no proof of anything you've said, and I don't believe your words. I believe God's Word, which was spoken through me, right here on this stage in front of thousands of people. We all saw it. That's proof that God is real."

The crowd roared to life again with 'amens' and cheers. Lisa needed to get the upper hand, and fast. If she couldn't sway the crowd by getting them on her side, maybe she could turn the crowd against Joel.

Joel soaked up the applause for a moment, then quieted the crowd again. He indicated that Lisa could continue.

"You said that you confessed your sins to clean your soul so God could use you." Lisa's voice was still a bit shaky, but the prospect of having nothing else to lose steeled her nerves a little.

"I did," Joel said. "I told them to your reporter friend the other day, and you just heard me do it again, right here in front of everyone."

Lisa looked him in the eyes. "Only the sins you chose to confess, though. What about the rest of them that you didn't mention? The ones that would put you in prison? Why didn't you confess those?"

The crowd gasped and collectively leaned forward. Had Joel held something back?

"Are you referring to the financial trickery, the charity fraud, that sort of thing?"

Lisa felt the rug pulled from under her. This was her secret weapon, she thought, the thing that would catch him off-guard. She hadn't expected him to see it coming.

"All of that was done by my late wife, Holly," Joel told Lisa and the crowd. "She handled all of the financial dealings in my accounts as well as her own. She was the one who committed all those crimes, even though she did it with accounts under my name. The FBI has already spoken to me about this, and they have cleared me of suspicion. Apparently, Holly hadn't finished covering her tracks before the accident. I have nothing to confess regarding those matters. Holly was guilty of those sins, and she has already been judged by God for them."

"She wasn't judged by God."

"She obviously was, Lisa. She was taken right out of this world. I was judged by God as well, and God knew that I would repent after I spoke His words last Sunday."

"I don't know why you spoke those words," Lisa admitted. "But it wasn't a message from God, because there is no god."

The crowd erupted in anger, and Lisa knew she'd blown it. How could she have let those words come out of her mouth, especially after seeing the reaction they got at the park yesterday? She would never get the crowd on her side now. She feared that if she kept talking, her life might be in danger, and she knew that every timeline involving her death ended almost immediately. She handed the mic back to Joel, hung her head in resignation, and walked away toward the opposite side of the stage.

Mike watched her leave the pulpit, and he wished she had come his way instead. He scanned the crowd to make sure nobody rushed the stage.

Lisa looked around the stage for anything that she could use as a weapon. She shuffled with her head down in apparent defeat. That could help with the element of surprise, she thought. Nobody would be expecting her to attack. Lisa crossed in front of the band and noticed a mic stand with a heavy steel disc for a base. It wasn't ideal, she thought, but it would probably do the job if she could get a good swing at Joel's head.

She stopped, steeled her nerves, and picked up the mic stand. It was heavier than she expected, but adrenaline gave her the strength to hoist it up like a baseball bat. She spun around and ran across the stage at Joel, screaming an angry, primal shriek as she ran. The crowd's roar turned into a collective gasp as Lisa's arms flexed and the mic stand swung around toward its target. Joel stood frozen in shock as he realized what was happening.

Christine gasped and Matthew leaned forward as the events on the television screen seemed to play out in slow motion. They saw Lisa run at Joel with the mic stand over her shoulder.

Lisa swung.

The heavy steel base of the mic stand began its deadly arc.

A gunshot!

Lisa dropped to the floor. The crowd's angry shouts turned to terrified screams. People ran for the exits. Christine and Matthew both sat in shock, feeling helpless.

Mike stood in the wings with his arms outstretched, the barrel of his service revolver still smoking. Everything had happened in an instant, but Lisa's actions were clear. She had tried to murder Joel Wood on live television. Mike dropped his stance and ran onto the stage just as Officer Thompson got to Lisa.

"She's still alive," he told Mike. "I had the musicians between me and her, couldn't get a clean line. I'm glad you had a clear shot."

Mike grabbed Joel, who still hadn't moved from his spot.

"Come on, we need to get you off the stage."

Joel didn't respond to Mike's urging. He seemed to be in a trance, his eyes were glazed over, and his body was stiff. A voice boomed into Joel's wireless mic.

"You were warned."

The crowd recognized the voice instantly. The rush for the exits halted and everyone turned around to look at Joel. They waited with hushed anticipation.

"You were warned."

Christine turned and saw that Matthew was in a trance just like Joel, just like Rabbi Jacob had been the week before. She held her breath. Matthew's voice sounded identical to Joel's.

"You were warned," he said again.

Mike stared at Joel, unsure of what had just happened. Joel's arm felt hot, even through the suit fabric. The crowd held its collective breath, waiting to see what would happen next.

Joel blinked a few times, then shook his head as if trying to clear his mind. He looked at Mike, then at Lisa lying on the stage. He noticed the silence in the room, and turned to face the crowd. Thousands of anxious faces stared back at him. Everyone seemed afraid to move.

Officer Thompson was kneeling next to Lisa. He had her head in his hands. Blood was pooling under her and running out onto the stage.

"Did it happen again?" Joel asked Mike. His question echoed through his mic over the sound system.

"Come on, don't leave us," Officer Thompson said to Lisa, who was struggling to breathe. She gasped, choked, her body convulsed twice, then she fell limp and lifeless. She was gone.

They heard it before they felt it. A shuddering, explosive rumble preceded the jolt to the earth that knocked Mike and Joel off their feet. The building and everything in it shook violently. The television cameras toppled, and people standing in the aisles of the arena tumbled down the steps toward the stage. Huge theatrical lights rained from the rafters and crashed around them, showering sparks and shrapnel. Mike managed to pick himself up off the floor, and he pulled Joel to his feet.

"We need to get off this stage! Now!"

Matthew came out of his trance just before the living room began to shake.

"Lie down on the floor!" he yelled.

She got down on the floor against the sofa and Matthew got down next to her and covered her with his body as best he could. He pulled the sofa cushions over them to shield them from falling debris.

"What's happening?" Christine yelled above the noise.

"Earthquake, I think."

"We never have earthquakes. Not even little ones."

The house shook around them. Bookcases fell over and threw their contents to the floor, dishes rattled themselves out of the cupboards, and pieces of the popcorn ceiling rained down on them. Christine and Matthew held onto each other and prayed.

Thelo had just gotten to his car in the hospital's underground parking garage and was about to call Christine when the shaking began. He leaned against the BMW as it rocked, and the sound of a hundred car alarms added to the rumbling noise from the earth. A chunk of concrete broke away from the roof and fell a few feet from him with a heavy crash. Thelo opened his car door and dove inside as the madness intensified around him.

Zara clutched the handrail in the hospital corridor and lowered herself to the floor. She curled into a ball with her hands over her head, and leaned against the wall. Ceiling tiles crashed down around her, and the screams of nurses and patients filled her ears. It seemed to last forever.

Gloria Deo was chaos. The building began to collapse, and panic gripped the crowd as they attempted to escape. Mike had Joel by the hand and tried to lead him off the stage, but the shaking floor made it nearly impossible. Mike saw that the exit off the stage where he had been earlier was blocked by debris.

"How else can we get off the stage?" Mike yelled.

He heard a deafening crash and felt Joel's hand yanked from his.

Mike turned around and saw Joel's body crushed under a large spotlight that had fallen to the stage. Blood oozed from beneath the crumpled mess.

The quake stopped.

The place looked like a war zone. Much of the building had collapsed, and he knew that thousands of people were dead. Mike looked around to see where he could be the most help. Above him, a sound of creaking metal. Mike looked up, but there was no time to react. Impact. Pain. Floor.

His vision went black.

CHAPTER
TWENTY-SEVEN
One Year Later

Laura Carter sat in Christine's living room and sipped a glass of wine. Matthew and Christine sat across from her on the sofa. Laura set her glass down to free up her hands.

"You have a lovely home," Matthew interpreted as Laura signed the words.

"Thank you," Christine signed back. She knew that gesture, but she relied on Laura's lip reading skills for anything else she might want to say. She made sure to face Laura directly when she spoke. "It was a mess after the quake, but luckily the structure held up okay. The repairs were mostly cosmetic."

"You were lucky," Matthew said as Laura signed. "My parents' home was much older and already in disrepair. They were buried under it when it collapsed."

"I'm so sorry," Christine said.

Laura sighed. She nodded to the framed photo on the coffee table of Ivan and Senator Lakey. Christine had rescued it from what was left of his office at the *Post*.

"I wish I had known him," she signed. "I only knew him as Emily. He turned out to be quite handsome, didn't he?"

"He was a wonderful man," Christine said. "We all loved him very much."

"Matthew has been helping me through the guilt," she signed with a nod toward him. "I don't know what I would've done if I hadn't found him." Matthew blushed as he said the words for her.

The conversation was interrupted by a knock at the door. Christine sat her wine down and went to answer it.

Matthew reached across and took Laura's hand. He gave it a gentle squeeze.

"Things all work out for the best, somehow," he said. "If I hadn't given up the priesthood, I wouldn't be running the help center, and you wouldn't have met me when you came to us for counseling. You wouldn't have met Christine and the others that are coming here today, either. They all knew Ivan, and they can be the link for you to get to learn about your brother. You can finally have the closure you need to move on."

"Look who's here!" Christine called from the kitchen.

Mike and Zara appeared in the doorway with sacks in hand. Matthew stood up and made his way to the kitchen to greet them, and motioned for Laura to follow.

"Zara and I got some wings and some wine on the way over," Mike said.

"Wonderful," Christine replied. "Just set the wings here next to the rest of the food, and I'll open the wine. Perfect timing, by the way, we'd just poured the last of the bottle I opened earlier."

"How was your flight, Zara?" Matthew asked.

"Dreadful," she said. "I've got terrible jet lag. I'm not even sure what day it is."

"It's Monday, and it's the one-year anniversary of The Balancing," Mike said.

"Is that what it's called over here?" Zara asked. "In the UK, everyone has a different name for it."

"Same here," Mike admitted. "That's just what I'm calling it."

"'The Great Shakedown' is my favorite, I think," Zara said.

"Mike and Zara," interrupted Christine, "I'd like you both to meet Laura Carter, Ivan's sister."

Zara stared at her in astonishment. "Bloody hell. When you said we'd have a surprise guest at the reunion, I assumed it would be Thelo."

Zara shook Laura's hand in greeting. Christine got out two more glasses and poured wine for the newcomers.

Laura tapped Matthew on the shoulder to indicate that she needed him to interpret. "I believe I should thank you," Matthew said to Zara for her. "I understand that it was you who helped the hospital find me."

"I wasn't sure you would even want to be found," Zara admitted. "Ivan said you didn't exactly part on good terms."

Laura's face showed her sadness. "Our church and my belief in their teachings was the reason for that," she signed. "But that one Sunday last year, our preacher gave The Sermon. He told us that the Bible was all made up, and we were following the wrong rules. That shook me up pretty bad. My parents, too. We started to realize that all that stuff we'd been taught was just lies. The guilt of what we'd done to Emily…" she paused and swiped her hands in the air as if erasing something. "I mean, Ivan. The guilt was terrible. We started trying to find him, but we didn't know he had changed his name."

"I wish you had been able to find him," Zara said. "He loved you very much."

"Me too," she signed. "The guilt and grief have been unbearable. Both my parents were killed in the quake, and then I found out from the hospital a few weeks later that Ivan was dead. I wasn't handling it well at all. I tried to cope with it on my own for awhile. Lots of people were grieving then. I don't think I know anyone who didn't lose a loved one in the quake. Anyway, I was getting worse as time went on, not better. Then Matthew's counseling center opened up a couple of months ago, and they had a deaf interpreter, so I started going there to try to get some help. That's how I met Matthew, and then Christine."

"The center was originally going to be for people who were dealing with traumatic events in their past," Matthew explained. "We still do that, but with so many deaths in the quake a year ago, our main focus now is on grief counseling. We're planning a major expansion next year so we can help even more people."

"That's wonderful," Zara said. "But where are you getting the money? Ever since the quake, the economy is shit."

"Joel Wood's wife was good friends with Simon Forrester, the man who created the center I'm running. She had been helping him plan it out before she died, and she had donated more than a million dollars to help get it up and running. She even left a ton of money for it in her will."

"Can you even get that money?" Mike asked. "She was up to her ass in financial fraud. I'm surprised those funds would be available."

"It will take a while to probate, but my understanding is that her personal accounts were entirely separate from the ones in Joel's name that she used for the fraud, so as long as the money from the two sets of accounts didn't blend, we might luck out. Regardless, Simon has plenty of money to keep us going."

"I'm glad it all worked out," Zara said. She turned to Laura. "It's very nice to meet you."

"So, Zara," Christine said, "how's life at a real newspaper?"

"It's fab! I would have loved to stay at the *Post*, but all the shit happened before I could apply for my work visa. I had several offers from papers back home, though. My article on Joel Wood got me noticed, plus I was an eyewitness to the Big Event over here. They were practically in a bidding war to hire me in London, so staying here seemed like the lesser of my options. Besides, all my friends and family are back in London. Present company excepted, of course."

"Plus, London was still in one piece," Mike said. "Everything here was rubble."

"And we're glad you got out of that rubble," Zara said. She raised her glass to Mike.

"Thanks," Mike said. "A skull fracture and a couple of broken bones. Not bad at all, considering how many people died that day."

"And you," Zara said to Christine. "Still going strong at the *Post*, I see."

"Yes, but the new editor and I don't see eye-to-eye as much as Ivan and I did. I'll admit, though, the religion page is a bit more exciting and challenging than it used to be. Everything is in flux with regard to what people believe now."

"What do you all believe?" Zara asked.

They all looked at each other awkwardly.

"I think we witnessed an event of biblical proportions," Matthew said. "I mean, everyone is calling what happened an earthquake because that's what it felt like, and we don't know what else to call it. But quakes don't happen here, certainly not on that scale. Scientists have been looking for a fault line near the city that could produce that kind of movement, but they've come up empty."

"I'm inclined to go along with Matthew for the most part," Christine added. "But I'm having difficulty with the fact that it was all centered here. I mean, if God were going to announce Himself in a way that could change human history, why not shake the whole earth? Why just have the quake here?"

"Maybe because Lisa and Joel were here," Matthew offered. "The epicenter was right under the stage where they were standing. It happened right after Joel had his trance."

"Have you had any more messages?" Zara asked Matthew. "Have you spoken any more words from on high?"

"He talks in his sleep sometimes," Christine said. "Scared the hell out of me the first time I heard him do it, but now I know it's not related to this."

Everyone laughed.

"No, I haven't," Matthew said. "The day of the quake was the last time. We all just said, 'you have been warned,' and then everything crumbled. There's been nothing since then. I've kept in contact with the other people who spoke the words, but they haven't had any more, either."

"I'm more inclined to believe Lisa," Mike broke in.

"Really?" Zara was surprised. "Even after you watched her try to kill Joel Wood?"

"She explained it to me before she went on stage. She said that if she died, the world would end almost immediately. But then she said that if Joel Wood died, humanity would have a chance. She asked me to shoot him, but I said I wouldn't do it, obviously. I also warned her that if she tried, I'd have to stop her."

"And you did," Christine said.

"Yes. I only meant to wound her and stop her from getting to Joel, but…" He sighed. "As soon as she died, that's when the quake started."

"No shit?" Zara asked.

"Lisa was lying on the stage bleeding, then Joel said, 'you were warned,' then she died and the whole place fell apart. It was pretty obvious to me that her prediction of the end of the world was coming true and it happened right after she died, just like she said it would."

"But the world didn't end," Matthew argued.

"Because Joel died," Mike said. "I think that when Lisa died, it started us down one of those timelines that she'd seen. But when Joel died a few moments later, it shifted everything to one of the other timelines. She said that the timelines where Joel died all continued on beyond where she could see. She didn't say what would happen if they both died, though. I'm not even sure she looked at that possibility. No matter. I saw enough to make me believe that she had an understanding of things that none of us do."

"There are pockets of people who believe that, too," Zara said. "Even in the UK and Europe and elsewhere. A few of them have tried to start churches, but they haven't taken off."

"I think that a church in her name would be the last thing that Lisa would've wanted."

"I agree," Zara said. "Of course, there are still plenty of people who believe that God spoke through those preachers. They spoke The Sermon and they all spoke that 'you were warned' thing as well. Some of the preachers have their own groups of followers. They're in a holding pattern, waiting for the next message to tell them what to do now."

"And some think it was a demonic possession," Matthew said. "The Catholic Church is still holding onto that idea, especially after the quake. They're fighting a losing battle, though. Their membership is a tiny fraction of what it used to be just a year ago and their opinion doesn't hold the clout that it used to, not even the Pope's. Most people who still believe in God have stopped believing in organized religion."

Laura tapped the table with her hand to indicate that she wanted to add something. Matthew spoke for her as she signed.

"So what are we supposed to believe, then?" she wanted to know.

"If you ask me," Matthew answered, "nobody's explanation is any better or worse than anyone else's. The one thing that we all can agree on is that we can't go back to how it was before, when everyone was so sure that they had the answers and they tried to make everyone else conform to their beliefs. In the year since the quake, or whatever you want to call it, we've all come to realize that whatever we believed before wasn't the whole truth. That put everyone on the same level, and look at what happened. Enemies reconciled their differences. Wars ended. Earth has been at peace, more or less, ever since. So instead of trying to figure out what to believe, maybe we should just try to be the best people we can be. Help each other. Love each other. Not because we share a belief in what's written in a book or what was said by a spiritual leader, but because we are all human beings and we all want to live and be happy. We will probably never know for certain if there's a god, or understand how the universe works, and that's fine. As long as we can be open-minded enough to accept that, then we can all live together in peace. It's better to admit and accept that you don't know the answers than to pretend that you do."

"Hear, hear!" Mike raised his glass. "To blissful ignorance."

"How about we toast peace instead?" Matthew suggested. "A world almost without war. One year and counting."

"To peace," they agreed, and clinked their glasses.

"So Thelo's not coming, then?" Zara asked Christine.

"I sent him an invitation, but he never answered. He's shut everyone out. He quit the *Post* and took a job at the *Tribune* across town right after the quake, and I never hear from him anymore. I see his byline on the stories he's published, but that's about it."

The doorbell surprised them. Christine shot a glance at Mike, who looked back at her with wide eyes.

"You think?"

Christine went to the door while the others waited in the kitchen. Mike took a big sip of wine. He almost hoped it wasn't him.

"Holy shit," they could hear Christine exclaim from the foyer. "I didn't think you'd come!"

She appeared in the doorway with Thelo. Everyone but Mike and Laura cheered and went to greet him with hugs. Thelo thanked them all for the greetings, handed Christine the bottle of wine he'd brought, then noticed Mike standing alone next to the counter. His smile vanished.

"Mike," he said. The tension crackled between them.

"Long time, no see," Mike said, without looking up. "Or hear from. Or anything."

"I'm sorry. I'm sorry to everyone. Please, I might as well just say it. I've been a shitty friend to all of you this past year."

"It's okay," Christine said.

"No, it's not. I was angry because Ivan was dead, and I blamed everyone else for it. I blamed Lisa for getting him to believe in her ideas, and I blamed Mike for saving her instead of Ivan that day. Neither of those things was rational. I understand that now." He hung his head and took a deep breath, then let it out slowly. "I lost both my parents and a lot of friends in the quake, and I just fell apart." He bit his lip to keep focused. "I withdrew. I left the *Post* because I couldn't handle the memories there. I avoided everyone who had any connection to the past. That was wrong, I know. It's the exact opposite of what I should've done." He clinched his hands together and brought his eyes up. "I've been in therapy for a few weeks now, and I'm getting better, but I should've been here to help you all through this, too. I wasn't the only one hurting. I've been selfish, and I'm sorry."

He turned to Mike. "Especially sorry to you. I put blame on you that you didn't deserve. When I finally realized it, I was too ashamed to face you and make it right."

"You're right," Mike said. "You were selfish. I reached out to you over and over, and you shut me out. I was grieving, too. We could've helped each other through it, but you wouldn't even answer my calls."

"I know. When you finally stopped calling, I figured you had moved on. I assumed you had given up on me."

"It felt like you were the one who gave up on me."

"I know I don't deserve it, but can you forgive me?"

"Already done," Christine interrupted. "We're glad you're here."

The rest chimed in their agreement, but Thelo was still looking for a response from Mike.

"You need to understand something about that day at City Park," Mike said. "The reason that I saved Lisa instead of Ivan. You need to know what happened, so you don't hold that grudge anymore."

"Ivan insisted you get Lisa to safety first."

Mike stared at him. "Did he tell you that before he died?"

"No. But I wouldn't have expected anything less from him. Once I thought about it, it was obvious. That's just who he was." He looked into Mike's eyes. "I know it'll be awkward, especially at first, but I really enjoyed the time we were dating. If you're not seeing anyone, could we start over from the beginning?"

Mike searched Thelo's eyes and found sincerity. "Communication is the basis of any relationship. If you shut me out whenever shit gets difficult, then we're doomed from the beginning."

Thelo nodded. "I know. I've learned my lesson on that one."

Mike sighed. "You've got to earn my trust again, though. It'll take time." He opened his arms. "C'mere."

The two men hugged. When they let go of each other, Thelo turned and finally noticed Laura.

"I'm sorry," he said to her. "I don't believe we've met."

"This is Laura," Christine said. "She's Ivan's sister."

Thelo blinked twice, then shot a puzzled look at Christine. "I didn't know Ivan had a sister."

"Oh, there's a lot you didn't know about Ivan!" Zara laughed.

"We'll fill you in later," Christine said. "Meanwhile, I've got something I want to say."

She set her glass down on the counter and turned to Matthew. She took his hands in hers.

"I've known you for a long time, but I've gotten to know you much better over this past year. I've loved having you here at my home, I've enjoyed our time together, and I've been inspired watching you work at the counseling center. We all lost loved ones that day, but you somehow work through your own sorrow by giving comfort to others. You're a beautiful, kindhearted man, and I feel honored to know you."

"Hear, hear!" Zara said.

"I'm genuinely touched," Matthew said. "Thank you, Christine." He pulled her close, and they kissed.

He had his own speech prepared about Christine, but he planned to give that one later, after dinner. He had been working on what he'd say for weeks, rehearsing it in his mind, planning the perfect moment to get down on one knee and produce the little black box. He knew it would be terribly old-fashioned, but it felt right.

"I promised you all in the invitation that this would be a celebration and not a pity party," Christine announced, "but I think that we should at least have a moment of silence to acknowledge all those people we lost one year ago."

Everyone agreed and they bowed their heads to remember those who were gone.

Laura stepped away from them and went back into the living room. She picked up the photo of Ivan from the coffee table and gazed at it for a few moments, trying to imagine the sort of man he had become. Her vision blurred with tears as she set the photo down and raised her glass in a silent toast.

'To Ivan.'

CPSIA information can be obtained
at www.ICGtesting.com
Printed in the USA
LVOW08s1240080917
547977LV00001B/10/P